THE GUILTY ONES

KYLA STONE

The Guilty Ones

Copyright © 2026 by Kyla Stone All rights reserved. This book or any portion thereof may not be reproduced or used in any manner whatsoever without the express written permission of the publisher except for the use of brief quotations in a book review.

This book is a work of fiction. Any references to historical events, real people, or real places are used fictitiously. Other names, characters, places, and events are products of the author's imagination, and any resemblances to actual events or places or persons, living or dead, is entirely coincidental.

Printed in the United States of America

Cover design by Damonza

Book formatting by Vellum

First Printed in 2026

ISBN: 978-1-962251-56-3

 Formatted with Vellum

For my husband Jeremy, for all the meals and coffees and running errands and ferrying the kids around while I peck away at a keyboard, making up stories in my head. Without you, none of this would be possible. I love you.

Prologue

The incident didn't start with us. But it ended with us.

I say *us* like the mothers were a team in this, that we were all on the same side. At first, I believed that we were. Together, united, one front. We were friends, after all. Deep in these messy, exhausting, rewarding trenches of motherhood. We knew each other, relied upon each other, trusted each other.

Or at least, we thought we did.

How little we knew each other, or our own children, what they were capable of.

How little I understood what *I* was capable of.

Until that night.

The night that changed all our lives forever.

Chapter One

The phone rang, jolting me upright in bed.

I fumbled for it in the dark, knocking over a half-empty glass of water in my rush. My heart pounded, my body reacting before my brain could catch up.

The screen glowed in the dimness. Whitney Alistair.

The phone read 5:40 a.m. A deep and terrible dread coiled in my stomach. Whitney never called me this early. No one did, especially not on a Saturday morning.

I swiped to answer. "Whitney? What's wrong?"

"Dahlia." Her voice was tight, urgent. "You need to come. Something awful has happened."

The words sent a cold spike of fear through my chest.

I swung my legs over the side of the bed, rubbing at my gummy eyes with one arm. "What do you mean? What happened? Is it Mia? Is Mia okay?"

Whitney hesitated. I could hear movement in the background, muffled voices. Someone was crying. "Mia is..."

I stopped breathing. "Are the girls safe? Did something happen to Mia?"

"Just come to Rowan's," she said. "Now."

The line went dead.

For a second, I sat there, the phone still pressed to my ear, my palms clammy, my throat dry.

Then I was moving. I yanked on my jeans, pulled a sweatshirt from the hamper, and raced from my bedroom.

I flicked on the hallway light and hesitated at Mia's bedroom door. I pushed it open. Her bed was empty but for our sleeping German Shepherd, curled at the foot of the bed, the sage-green comforter rumpled, the bed unmade.

She wasn't here. She was at my friend Rowan's house down the street, at her daughter Chloe's slumber party.

Fear formed a hard knot in my stomach. I had to lay eyes on her. I had to know she was okay. That she was safe. I was merely overreacting, again.

But then why had it been Whitney, Peyton's mother, who called, rather than Rowan? And what was Whitney doing at Rowan's home before dawn?

Fumbling with the phone, I called Mia's number. No answer. No response to my frantic texts, either. Where was she? What had happened?

I needed to get there. Fast.

I took the stairs two at a time and sprinted down the hall to the living room, stumbling as I shoved my feet into sneakers with shaking hands and fumbled for my keys from the hook by the door.

The house seemed to shift around me. The old floorboards creaked. The wind rattled the loose windowpane above the sink.

I raced out the door, slammed it shut, and turned the key, then double-checked the house was locked tight against the possible terrors lurking outside the walls.

Panic clawed at my throat. Was she hurt? If so, how badly?

I ran down the pitted gravel driveway and turned north onto Wyld Wood Lane. My breath came in short, uneven bursts as the cold April morning air stung my cheeks.

The homes of Blackthorn Shores loomed like silent sentinels in the gray half-light of predawn. Their massive windows stared down at me, cold and unblinking, as if they were watching. As though they knew I didn't belong.

My pulse roared in my ears. I ran past house after house. My feet thudded against the pavement.

Everything was eerily still, quiet but for the dull roar of the wind, the waves crashing against the shoreline far below the bluff. No cleaners arriving, no cars moving, no rumbling lawn mowers, and no joggers on the sidewalks yet.

Something awful had happened. I was certain of it. Not again. Not my child. I couldn't endure another tragedy tearing my world asunder.

I wouldn't survive the loss of Mia. I couldn't. My brain whirred with all the ways something might have happened to her. A slip in the shower, a sudden heart attack, a fall down the stairs.

I sprinted past my friend Camille's house, then Whitney's. Rowan's house appeared ahead of me. My breath was ragged, my stomach twisted into knots.

There were no police cars in the driveway. Maybe that meant everything was okay. It wasn't as bad as I feared, as Whitney's stricken voice had implied.

I was exaggerating. Mia was fine. Everything was fine. I was the overprotective mother, imagining all sorts of horrors when my daughter had only scraped her knee, or come down with the flu, or had a nasty nightmare and wanted her mother again.

Something easy. Simple. Safe.

I ran through the open wrought-iron gates and up the cobblestone drive, barely registering the grand stone and cedar façade as my focus lasered on the wide front porch.

Several women stood huddled together, their heads bent, murmuring intently. As I approached, they fell silent. Their faces were pale and drawn.

A sick feeling twisted in my gut. My instincts weren't off. Something was wrong. Very wrong.

Whitney's tense gaze flicked to me and then away. Whitney Alistair, the picture of athletic prowess with her lean, yoga-toned body encased in Lululemon leggings and matching jacket, her sleek white-blonde ponytail pulled tight. Her usually tanned skin was ashen.

I halted at the bottom of the porch steps. My lungs burned. I felt faint. "What happened?"

Rowan Westinghouse stood tall and composed on the top step of her porch, her arms crossed over her chest. Even at this ungodly hour, she wore a charcoal pencil skirt and a cashmere pink sweater, with her honey-blonde hair falling in shining waves around her shoulders. Only her manicured hands trembled slightly.

"Where's Mia?" My voice came out too sharp, too raw.

Rowan didn't move from the top step. "Dahlia, keep your voice down, please. We don't want to alarm the neighbors."

I was plenty alarmed. I started up the steps. "Where is she?"

Whitney still didn't make eye contact. "She's inside. She's not hurt, Dahlia. It's not her."

Pure relief flooded my body. My legs went weak. I could have collapsed right there on the bluestone slate steps.

I forced myself to remain upright. If it wasn't Mia... "Then who—?"

Rowan's lips parted. "It's Leah."

For a moment, the words barely registered.

My stomach dropped. Leah Cho. My daughter's best friend. "Is Leah okay?"

No one responded.

"What happened?"

Rowan gave a mournful shake of her head.

Brooke August stared at me with unfocused, reddened eyes. Her glossy brunette hair tumbled down the middle of her back, a matching sweatsuit replacing her usual Instagram-ready polish. Without her heavy makeup, her bare face looked vulnerable—and scared.

"They're fine," Rowan repeated. "Our daughters are fine."

"You didn't answer my question. Is Leah okay? Was she hurt?"

Brooke made a strangled sound, pressing a hand to her mouth.

I turned to Camille. As a top defense attorney for a private law firm, she was the logical, practical one.

Camille Hayward stood slightly apart from the other women. Her sharp brown eyes scanned me with quiet intensity. She, too, had been abruptly pulled from bed, still dressed in pajamas with a cobalt blue silk headscarf covering her hair.

"The police are on their way," Camille said in a brisk voice. "They'll be here any minute."

I glared at them. It was like they were terrified of saying the words aloud, of making it real. "Just tell me."

Rowan blinked rapidly, fighting back tears. "Oh, honey, I'm so sorry, but Leah is dead."

I felt the world tilt, the ground shifting beneath me.

No.

Not Leah. "What? How?"

"The girls are inside," Camille said. "They're incredibly confused, shaken, and in shock. We're still working out what happened."

"It was an accident," Whitney said quickly. "It was a terrible accident."

I couldn't wrap my head around it. Leah was dead? How could that be? She was just a child, barely fourteen years old. The shy, timid, kind-hearted girl I saw nearly every day, often in my home, whom I'd cooked for and laughed with, who'd spent countless hours in Mia's room. How could she be gone?

My skittering thoughts kept running away from me; I could barely grab onto them. It seemed impossible. A terrible joke that I didn't understand yet. I stared in shock at the somber faces of my neighbors, my friends.

Leah's mother was missing. "Where's Vivienne? She needs to know."

Camille glanced warily at Rowan, reproach in her eyes. Brooke sniffled. Whitney pressed her lips together and wouldn't meet my gaze.

Rowan raised her chin. "We haven't called her yet. We thought it best that the police arrive first. To know how to handle it."

My heart broke for Vivienne, but it was my daughter I thought of now. My living, breathing daughter.

Mia must feel devastated. Absolutely gutted. I needed to get to her, to pull my baby into my arms and comfort her, to feel her heartbeat safe against my ribs.

"I need to see Mia."

My legs moved before I could think. I climbed the porch steps with numb feet, pushed past Rowan, and yanked open the massive front door.

Inside, the air was thick with the scent of jasmine and lavender, Rowan's signature scents. The other mothers followed close behind me.

The girls were in the high-ceilinged living room. They huddled on the sofas bracketing the floor-to-ceiling stone fireplace, their hair rumpled, faces tear-stained, several still in pajamas.

Mia sat apart from the others, slumped in a linen armchair next to a white oak built-in bookcase. She wore her favorite Hello Kitty pajamas, her white-socked feet crossed at the ankles.

The color had drained from her freckled face, her expression blank with shock, a terrible hollowness in her green eyes.

Several scratches marred her forearms. Thin, angry red lines.

Scratches that she didn't have last night when she left our house, with her sage-green overnight bag slung over her shoulder and her camera on its yellow strap around her neck.

I inhaled sharply.

Mia looked up. Her gaze met mine. No recognition in her glassy eyes. She looked straight through me, as if she'd forgotten where she was, or even who she was.

"Mia," I said. "What happened?"

Chapter Two

A lemon-scented candle burned on the mantel above the fireplace. Outside, the wind howled through the jack pines along the bluff, rattling the windows like a monster breathing at our backs.

"Mia!" I said again, louder, as I crossed the room.

My voice shook her out of her stupor. A low cry escaped her lips. She clamped her hands over her mouth, moaning softly. I went to her and embraced her, drawing her close. She circled her arms around my waist and clung to me.

I wanted to tell her it would be okay. But I already knew it wasn't true. I felt frozen in place, stricken. Shocked into stillness.

This couldn't be real. Leah couldn't be gone.

"Mom!" Chloe Westinghouse rose and stumbled across the living room into her mother's arms. Her heart-shaped face was blotchy, her big eyes, the same ice-blue as Rowan's, were glossy with tears. Petite, slender from years of ballet and dance, she was doll-like, luminously beautiful. Strands of her wavy honey-blonde hair clung to her wet cheeks.

Chloe burst into fresh sobs. "It's awful, so awful."

"What happened to Leah?" My voice echoed, too loud in the too-big room.

Peyton Alistair sat rigid on the sofa, her athletic swimmer's build hunched inward as if trying to make herself smaller. Her highlighted blonde hair was pulled into a messy ponytail. She clutched her purple Stanley like a lifeline. Swim meet stickers peeled at the edges. "She...she fell. From the bluff."

"When?" I asked. "How?"

Whitney hovered behind her daughter on the sofa, her hands on Peyton's shoulders as if to hold them both steady. Her thin lips pressed into a bloodless line. "They don't know."

"I'm asking the girls," I said.

"It must have happened after we went to sleep," Peyton said. "We did the photoshoot in our dresses, out on the bluff, but then we all went inside to eat and watch a movie. Then we went to sleep."

It was the week before the Sadie Hawkins dance at Lakeshore Prep, the prestigious private school Mia attended on scholarship, along with the other girls in the neighborhood. The girls had wanted a glamorous photoshoot in their beautiful gowns before the dance, and Mia had volunteered to be the photographer.

"Leah, ah, must have gotten up again and gone out to the bluff in the night." Peyton twisted and glanced uncertainly at her mother, who nodded in encouragement. "I didn't see anything. Nobody did. We were all in here, sleeping."

Zara Hayward fidgeted next to Peyton. She clutched a throw pillow to her chest. Her breath came too fast, in shallow little gulps, like she was trying to keep from drowning. She was lean and lanky, dressed in running gear—a garishly cheerful yellow hoodie with black leggings and sneakers.

"I can't stop seeing her," she said hoarsely, her expressive dark eyes too big in her face. "Lying there like that. I keep thinking... what if we'd stayed outside a little longer? Or one of us woke up and stopped her, or went with her. I never even heard anything."

"Me, neither," Alexis echoed.

"Me, neither," Peyton said.

Chloe lifted her head, struggling to speak through her hitching sobs. "I didn't... I didn't hear anything, either. I—I must've been sleeping—like everyone else."

She shrank back against her mother and let out a low moan. "I could've stopped her. If I'd known—if I'd just stayed awake..."

Rowan stroked Chloe's hair. "It's okay, honey. It's okay."

"Did you hear anything?" Camille asked Mia.

Everyone looked at Mia. Mia shook her head but said nothing. Her shoulders were tense. Her arms dropped away from me, and she pulled back, curling into herself in the armchair.

A pang shot through me. Mia's eyes were unfocused, fixed on some distant point. What was going through her mind? Why wouldn't she look at me? She was the only girl who hadn't said a word yet.

"Who found her?" I prayed it hadn't been Mia.

"I did." Zara rubbed her arms hard, like she was trying to scrub the horrible memory away, and pushed her long black braids over her shoulder. "I was up early to go running."

"What time?" Camille asked.

"Um... like 5:35? I set my alarm for 5:30 a.m." Zara swallowed. "When I went outside, I saw her phone in the grass on the edge of the bluff, so I walked over there and looked down. She was just... lying there, halfway down, on her side, half covered by the underbrush. Her body. She looked... she looked so strange. All broken, with her neck turned a weird way. It was—it was awful."

Beside me, Camille's face tightened. She gazed at her daughter but didn't offer comfort.

"Why was she even out there?" Alexis August asked. "I don't get it. Why would she go back outside?"

Peyton took an unsteady sip from her Stanley, then set it between her knees. "She left her phone out on the bluff, where we were taking pictures, so she must've woken up and realized she didn't have it. She probably just went back to get it and got too close to the edge, and she... she must've slipped and fallen in the dark."

A heavy silence settled over the room. Chloe let out a sob and covered her mouth with her hands. Zara and Peyton sniffled and wiped at their eyes.

Sirens wailed in the distance.

Camille glanced toward the front window overlooking the street. "Before the police get here, we need to make sure everyone is on the same page." Her authoritative tone left no room for argument. "Tell us what happened, so there aren't any discrepancies."

The girls blinked as if waking from a nightmare. Zara glanced at Chloe, then Peyton. Alexis and Chloe exchanged another look. Apprehension flickered in their eyes. Mia stared listlessly at nothing.

These were just girls, kids still. They were scared, confused, and hurting. In shock.

Alexis clenched her jaw. Her hands balled into fists. "The cops? Why?"

"The police investigate anytime someone dies," Camille said briskly. Her sharp eyes narrowed as she gazed at each girl. "Just tell them the truth, and you'll be fine."

Zara's breath hitched. "It was an accident. Right?"

"Of course it was." Rowan's voice was calm, warm, soothing. "It was an accident. Not your fault. A terrible accident."

"No one's in trouble," Whitney said.

"You don't know that." Alexis made a sound in the back of her throat and rose to her feet. She circled the sofa, retreated to the archway separating the kitchen and living area, and leaned against the wall. She wore an oversized Nine Inch Nails T-shirt over boxers. Her dyed, purple-black hair hung loose across her face. "Not for sure."

Brooke moved across the living room toward her daughter, skirting the sofas and coffee table. "Oh, honey, you must be devastated. I'm so sorry."

Alexis waved her mother away, her mouth set in a scowl. She'd always been the tough one among the girls. Her gaze locked on Camille. "What if she did it on purpose?"

Everyone stared at her in shock. Brooke's arm dropped limply to her side. She looked at her daughter, aghast. "How can you say that?"

Alexis swiped fiercely at her face with the back of her arm, as if embarrassed to cry in front of her friends, though Chloe, Peyton, and Zara were teary-eyed. Only Mia's eyes were dry. "She'd been acting weird lately, like depressed or something. Maybe she did something to herself..."

A fresh wave of shock washed over me. Not Leah. Not Mia's best friend. Though she had seemed more withdrawn lately when she'd visited my house, so had Mia.

They were eighth-grade girls. Moodiness was par for the course.

Mia had been fine. Leah had been fine. Hadn't she?

Rowan clapped her hands. "Let's not talk like that. This is sad enough. We'll wait for the police. There's no blame on any of you."

The sirens grew louder. A terrible nervous energy rippled through the room.

Peyton pulled her knees up and curled her bare feet beneath her. Her toenails were painted lavender. "What if the police think it's our fault?"

Whitney said, "Just tell the police what you told us. Everything will be fine."

I wished I shared her certainty. I glanced at Mia again. She was so still, so distant. She was in shock.

A chill ran down my spine. A thousand questions swirled in my mind. How could this have happened? Poor Leah. Poor Vivienne. My poor daughter.

The sirens closed in. Several police cars and an ambulance pulled into the driveway. Through the front bay windows, the flashing lights of the police cars bathed the street in stark red and blue.

Neighbors clustered on the sidewalk and across the street. So much for Rowan not wanting to wake them. They pointed at Rowan's house, covering their mouths in shock, dismay, and morbid curiosity.

Several officers strode up the sidewalk. A moment later, the doorbell rang.

Rowan disentangled herself from Chloe, glided to the foyer, and opened the front door. Three uniformed police officers entered, followed by a man and a woman in plainclothes. They spoke with Rowan at the door in hushed tones, then entered the living room.

"I'm Detective Judah King," the man said. "And this is my partner, Detective Sarah Callahan."

In his forties, Detective King was a mountain of a man. Dressed in a camel-colored overcoat, his broad shoulders filled the entryway, and his grizzled black beard and dark eyes carried an air of quiet authority.

The female detective was also in her forties, with her red hair cut short in a pixie style, a spray of freckles across her nose. There was a sharpness about her face, a canniness, like a fox.

Detective King spoke first. "We're so incredibly sorry for your loss. We're here to talk to you about your friend Leah and how she died, okay?"

Peyton and Zara seemed to shrink further into the sofa. Against the wall, Alexis stiffened. Chloe's eyes widened in trepidation. Whitney squeezed Peyton's shoulders. Mia didn't move, her gaze on the detectives.

To my right, movement caught my eye. I glanced across the living room, through the floor-to-ceiling windows overlooking Lake Michigan, to where a half-dozen police officers and a few EMTs milled in the backyard. Some officers wore PPE gear, including disposable suits with gloves and booties. One carried a medical bag with him. The medical examiner.

Several officers descended the bluff. Two of them carried a stretcher between them with a body bag on top of it.

My stomach lurched. Leah was still out there. On the bluff.

No, not Leah anymore, but a body.

Detective King turned toward the girls. His baritone voice was steady, measured. "About what happened last night—"

"We were all sleeping!" Peyton burst out. "We don't know what happened. She was in her sleeping bag when we went to bed, and then when we woke up, she wasn't. That's all we know."

"She must've slipped and fallen," Chloe said through her tears. "She fell, and none of us saw it."

Callahan turned to Rowan. "May we look at the basement where the girls were sleeping? It's standard procedure."

Rowan nodded numbly. "Of course, officer. Anything we can do to help. Please go ahead."

Camille's head snapped up. She'd been staring at her daughter, Zara, with a distant, dazed look on her face. "You don't have to let them look, Rowan. In fact—"

"It would just be a quick walk-through," Callahan said, "to gather Leah's things and see where she spent her time last night."

Camille opened her mouth to protest again, but Rowan waved a hand. "This was a horrible accident, nothing more. Vivienne and Daniel are our dear friends. Of course, we want to aid the police however we can. The stairs to the basement are down the hall to the left, off the living room."

Callahan and a male officer made their way to the hall and disappeared. King turned to the girls again.

Before he could ask another question, Rowan's front door burst open. A woman rushed inside, dressed in a long-sleeved nightgown with lacy frills at her wrists and collar. Her bare feet tracked grass and dirt inside Rowan's pristine foyer.

Vivienne Cho's whole body convulsed. Her jet-black hair, normally styled in a sleek bob to her chin, was in disarray around her head like a dark corona, her pupils blown with fear and panic.

Her frantic gaze swept the room, searching, desperate. "Where's Leah?" she cried. "Where's my baby?"

Chapter Three

Vivienne Cho sagged as if her body's internal structure had collapsed, and she could no longer hold herself upright. Rowan rushed forward and gripped Vivienne's arm to keep her on her feet.

"Where's Leah?" Vivienne screamed. "Take me to my baby! Please! Take me to her!"

Everyone watched in horrified silence as Detective King strode across the room and placed his hand gently upon Vivienne Cho's other arm. He leaned in and spoke gravely to her in soft, comforting tones, his head bowed.

"No, no, no!" Vivienne moaned as the detective and Rowan led her to the dining room and helped her sit down. Her face blanched. She kept shaking her head, denying the awful news that her beloved only child was dead.

She bent in on herself, clutching her stomach. Her petite frame trembled violently as Rowan rubbed soothing circles on her back. A low broken sound escaped Vivienne's throat, a keening cry of strangled grief, the sound of an animal caught in a trap.

My heart shattered into pieces. We were friends. I wanted to go to her, to hug her, to offer comfort, but I couldn't leave my child, either. I could only watch, appalled and horrified.

Only minutes before, it was I who had panicked, certain Mia was in mortal danger, that I had lost her, that something terrible had occurred.

That dreadful intuition hadn't been wrong. Only it had been my friend's daughter, not mine. Guilt silted the relief that flooded my veins. How could I rejoice while Vivienne suffered unimaginable pain?

Whitney looked away, biting her lip, as if Vivienne's suffering might be contagious. Brooke swayed on her feet, her face pale, like she might faint.

Two female officers went to Vivienne and spoke to her in soft tones. "Your husband is outside," one of them said in a kind voice. "He's asking for you."

I turned and glanced through the front windows behind me. Leah's father stood on the drive next to several police cars, speaking to another officer. His shoulders stooped, his stricken face a garish mask in the flashing lights.

In the kitchen, the police officers helped Vivienne stand, supporting her on either side, and escorted her from the house. Vivienne howled her sorrow, her suffering, her outrage, her pain so close to the surface of her skin it was nearly incandescent.

She shuffled like an old woman, her back bent, shoulders slumped like the weight of her grief had broken something elemental that could never be repaired. I understood her new reality better than anyone here, how nothing would ever be the same again.

The front door closed, followed by a stunned silence. The girls looked at the floor while the mothers looked at each other in disbelief, in horror, in pity.

Rowan and Detective King returned to the living room. Rowan swept across the room and gathered Chloe into her arms again. She sank against her mother as if her legs had forgotten how to hold her up.

A moment later, Callahan came up the basement stairs and through the arched hallway. A police officer in his twenties was beside her, holding several gowns on hangers. Their fabric shimmered under the chandelier's lights.

Callahan took a dress from the officer and held it up.

It was Mia's.

The beaded rose-gold mermaid gown I had helped her pick out just two weeks ago, the one she had tried on in the mirror at the resale shop with a hesitant smile, tracing the delicate beadwork with her fingertips.

She had thought she looked fat. I'd told her she was stunning. It wasn't an expensive designer gown, but it was nevertheless beautiful.

Now, it was no longer pristine. The hem was torn. Dirt smudged the entire front of the dress, and the fabric was snagged in several spots as if it had caught on something sharp.

Along the delicate beading on the bodice, dark against the soft blush fabric, was a stain. Small, scattered droplets dried to a dark brown.

It looked like blood.

My breath caught in my chest.

Detective King stepped forward. "Whose dress is this?"

"Mine," Mia said.

His gaze settled on Mia. On the scratches on her arms. Something dark beneath her fingernails, crusted in the creases of her skin. Dirt. From what? From where?

My pulse stuttered. Instinctively, I moved closer to Mia's side. To protect her, shield her, save her. To whisk her away from the horror and grief.

A sudden, vivid flashback hit me—the police arriving at the scene of my husband's death. The flashing lights. Voices blurred together. A police officer speaking in low, steady tones. Frantic sobbing. The sirens wailing.

Mia kneeling, her hands clenched into fists, her breathing too shallow. Marcus, limp on the kitchen floor, blood pooling across the linoleum.

I'd been screaming. Or perhaps I had only felt the scream,

trapped inside me, lodged deep in my ribs. Now, standing beside Mia, the same scream clawed up my throat.

"What's your name?" the detective asked.

"Mia," my daughter said in a small voice. "Mia Kincaid."

Detective King narrowed his eyes. "Mia, where did you get those scratches?"

Mia stiffened. "Um, we were all out on the bluff. I was kneeling on the ground, getting a low shot with my camera, and I slipped. I fell a few feet down the bluff, into the bushes. The branches scratched my arms."

"Stop right there." Camille's voice cut through the room like a scalpel. "That's enough."

Detective King raised his hands, his expression neutral. "We're simply trying to ascertain what happened."

"I know exactly what you're trying to do, detective," Camille said. "This is an unfortunate, tragic accident. Nothing more."

Detective Callahan's expression hardened. "With all due respect, a girl is dead. We'll need to speak with each of the girls to determine what happened."

Rowan straightened to her full height, commanding and authoritative, the gracious but cut-throat PTA president again. "Detectives, these children have been through a trauma. They need rest and comfort. A calming environment, not more stress."

"Which is why we need their accounts while memories are fresh," Callahan said. "Before details get confused."

"Not without our lawyers present," Whitney said.

Mia stared up at me in alarm, as if I could save her. But I couldn't. I couldn't afford a lawyer. I could barely afford Netflix after our monthly bills. My whole body went numb.

Camille shot a questioning glance at Rowan. Something unspoken passed between them, then Rowan moved swiftly to my side. She put her arm around my shoulder, bent, and whispered in my ear, "Don't worry."

I nodded stiffly. The room seemed to contract around me. It was difficult to breathe.

Camille stepped between the detectives and Mia. "I am a defense attorney with Hayward and Monroe, and I now represent Mia Kincaid. All communication should go through me. If you'd like to speak with Mia, we can agree on a time that's conducive to the Kincaid's schedule."

Callahan's eye twitched. "We'll need to speak to her as soon as possible."

"My client will make herself available for an interview at a mutually agreed-upon time, with counsel present," Camille said.

The detectives didn't look happy, but they grudgingly agreed. I'd never been more relieved to have Camille at our side.

King said, "At your earliest convenience, then."

Camille's jaw tightened, but she nodded curtly.

King took a step closer to Mia. "In the meantime, we'll need to photograph those injuries and take samples of the substance under your fingernails, Mia."

My gut clenched. "No. Absolutely not."

Callahan glowered at Camille. "We either take the samples right now, or we detain Mia and transport her to the station, where an officer will watch her in a cell until we get a search warrant, probably within the hour. Your choice."

Dizziness washed through me. It felt like everything had gone distant and fuzzy, like this wasn't really happening; it was a bad dream, unreal. Detaining Mia? A search warrant? For what?

"Go get the search warrant then," Camille snapped, "and I'll slap you with a lawsuit so fast your heads will spin."

"You're welcome to try." Callahan nodded at a nearby uniformed officer, who took out a set of handcuffs. "Cuff her and take her to the car."

Mia let out an alarmed gasp. "Mom!"

"Wait, no!" I said. I couldn't imagine the trauma to Mia, to be dragged out of Rowan's house for all the neighbors to see. For what? For a terrible accident she had no part in? That couldn't happen. I couldn't let it happen. "We consent. Don't take her anywhere. Do it here."

Camille shook her head. "Dahlia—"

But she didn't understand. It wasn't her daughter. It was mine.

My throat closed. I looked at Mia. Her face had gone pale, her eyes wide and glassy. She looked utterly terrified.

The thought of them photographing her like evidence made me physically ill. But what choice did we have?

"Fine," I said. "Just... make it quick."

King made a call, and a few minutes later, two evidence technicians arrived. They brought Mia to Rowan's den, with Camille and me present, where they swabbed her and took scrapings from beneath her nails.

The technician brought out a camera. "I need you to hold out your arms, Mia. Palms up first, then palms down."

Mia's breath hitched. She gave me an anxious, pleading glance. I nodded, my throat too tight to speak. My hand strayed to Marcus' titanium wedding ring, which I wore on a silver chain beneath my sweatshirt. As if that could hold me together.

I watched as my daughter extended her arms. The scratches appeared worse under the den's bright overhead lights, more red, angrier.

The camera clicked. Once. Twice. Three times.

Each flash was like an accusation.

"Palms down now," King said gently.

Mia turned her hands over. More clicks. More flashes. I wanted to pull her away, to cover her arms and make this all go away, but I stood rigid, forced to watch as they documented every mark on my daughter's skin.

As if she were already guilty of something terrible.

And there was nothing I could do to stop it.

Chapter Four

I stood in the doorway of Mia's bedroom. "Mia?"
No answer.
The soft glow of her bedside lamp cast a warm circle of light. She lay curled on her side, her back to me, the sage comforter pulled up to her shoulders. Her chocolate-brown hair fanned out across the pillow.

It was Saturday evening. Mia had been in bed for hours. She hadn't eaten, had barely spoken. I'd checked on her several times throughout the day, but she barely acknowledged me, exhausted from the shock and grief of that morning's tragedy.

Our dog pressed into my side, panting as I petted his black-furred head absently. Apollo was our three-year-old German Shepherd, a lovable 90-pound beast who greeted strangers with delighted enthusiasm but relentlessly protected us from birds, squirrels, and the mailman with the ferocity of a tiger. His guard dog abilities had been grossly oversold.

I stepped inside Mia's room with Apollo following at my heels. The floorboards creaked beneath my weight as I lowered myself onto the edge of her bed and gently brushed a strand of hair from her face.

Her skin felt cool to the touch. Her expression was slack, as if she were asleep, but I knew better. The tension in her jaw and the slight furrow between her brow were signs of the turmoil beneath the façade. She was awake.

"Mia?"

She didn't acknowledge me. She just lay there, curled on her side, facing the wall.

"I'm so sorry about Leah, sweetheart. I know how much she meant to you."

The heavy silence stretched between us. Just when I thought she might not respond at all, her voice emerged, muffled and distant. "I don't want to talk about it."

"Honey, I know you're hurting. This is awful. Losing Leah is devastating."

Nothing. Not even a flicker.

"I'm here if you need me. For anything."

I reached out, my hand hovering over her shoulder, then pulled back. I was useless, impotent, unable to offer comfort or ease her grief, when that's all I wanted to do for her.

I glanced around the room, at the dirty clothes spilling out of the hamper, piles of books and homework on the desk, the collection of smooth stones and beach glass lining her windowsill: fossilized Petoskey stones—Michigan's state stone—the banded red-and-white Agates, reddish-orange Jasper, smoky quartz pebbles, and the deep, dusky blue of Leland Blue slag glass.

A gallery of photographs she'd taken over the past year hung on the wall above her desk: black and white shots of Lake Michigan at dawn, a close-up of weathered driftwood, and the St. Joseph lighthouse at Tiscornia Beach silhouetted against storm clouds.

And my favorite, a candid photo of Leah laughing on the beach, her black chin-length hair whipping across her round cheeks, pure joy captured in that single fixed moment in time.

Mia had a gifted eye for composition, for finding beauty in unexpected places. She loved her Nikon camera, the yellow strap festooned with pins from our National Park visits to Zion, Arches,

Isle Royale, and Yosemite a constant around her neck or slung over her shoulder.

It had been a gift from Marcus for her twelfth birthday, a week before he died. An accountant by trade, he'd loved nature, hiking, and especially photography, and had passed on his passion to our daughter.

I frowned, confused, as I scanned the room again. The camera wasn't on her desk, or the nightstand, or on the shelf next to her dresser, where it usually was. She'd had it last night for the photo shoot, but it wasn't next to her green overnight bag or dumped on the floor in her closet, either.

"Where's your camera?" I asked.

She stiffened but didn't respond.

"Honey, your camera. Where is it?"

A long silence. Then, muffled against the pillow, she said, "I don't know."

"What do you mean?"

"It's gone," she said flatly.

"Gone? What do you mean, gone?"

"Someone took it."

"Took it? When? From Rowan's house?"

"I don't know. Last night it was in my camera case by my overnight bag. When I woke up this morning, it wasn't there anymore."

"Do you think someone might have borrowed it? Maybe one of the other girls wanted to look at the photos?"

"Maybe." But she didn't sound convinced.

"Could it have gotten left at the beach when you were taking pictures?"

"No. We never went down to the beach. We were only at top of the bluff. I put it back in the case last night, okay? I know I did."

"We'll find it, honey. I'm sure it just got mixed up with someone else's things. One of the girls probably picked it up by mistake."

She said nothing.

A buzzing sound vibrated from beneath the covers. Mia propped herself up on her elbow, tugged her phone out, and stared at it grimly. She'd changed into long-sleeved plaid pajamas, hiding the scratches on her arms, and she'd scrubbed the dirt from beneath her fingernails, too.

Her thumb flicked over the screen. Her frown deepened. She tilted the phone away from me to keep me from seeing, but I glimpsed something pink on the screen and a blurred image of something I couldn't make out. I couldn't make out the caption above the image, either. "What's that?"

"It's nothing."

I thought of Camille's daughter, Zara, how she'd helped Mia set up encrypted messaging last year, teaching her about privacy settings with the alacrity of someone who actually understood code. Zara was perpetually on her laptop or spouting some new tech jargon she'd learned. "Are people texting about what happened?"

"It's just something on Instagram. Some girl drama." Mia shoved the phone under her pillow.

I wanted to press her further, but her walls were up. Pushing now would only make her retreat further. She was a stubborn, moody teenager on her best days. I'd get nothing from her now.

I sighed. "You can tell me anything, you know. I'm here to listen."

She didn't respond. Her arm tightened around her gray stuffed sloth, Flash Slothmore, named after the *Zootopia* character she'd loved at four years old. She still slept with it every night, though she'd die before admitting that to anyone. Only Leah had known.

I sat with her for a while longer, listening to the sound of her breathing. The shadows in the room grew longer and darker as the thick silence of the house settled deep into my bones. Outside, the distant crash of waves against the bluffs echoed in a relentless rhythm.

"Do you need anything, honey? Water? Something to eat?"

"I just want to sleep."

I leaned down and kissed the top of her head. "I love you, sweetheart. So much."

She didn't answer, though she leaned slightly into the kiss before pulling away again.

I stood and made my way to the door, Apollo trailing behind me, his nails clicking on the worn hardwood, before pausing in the doorway, looking back at her still form beneath the covers.

Above Mia's bed hung the painting that Leah had made for her for Christmas: a vibrant watercolor of the pier at Tiscornia Beach, the sunset sky awash in streaks of violet, rose, and crimson, contrasting with the red-and-white lighthouse in the distance. In the foreground, clusters of blue wild lupine and purple beach peas bloomed among golden dune grasses.

Leah had loved art as much as Mia loved photography. Leah had been sweet-natured and smart, a straight-A student as well as a gifted artist. Though she'd been timid and often self-conscious about her full-bodied figure, she had also been incredibly empathetic, observant, and thoughtful. Her goofy sense of humor only emerged around people she trusted, like Mia. They would laugh together for hours about the silliest nonsense.

My chest tightened. That talented, vibrant girl was gone forever.

Another photo drew my attention, this one taped to the mirror above Mia's desk. The group of six girls—Leah, Mia, Alexis, Chloe, Peyton, and Zara—their arms slung around each other's sun-kissed shoulders as they lounged on Rowan's speedboat, grinning widely with the blue expanse of Lake Michigan glittering behind them.

They looked so young, so innocent, so happy. Beautiful and perfect.

What had gone wrong?

Chapter Five

On Monday morning, Mia insisted on going to school. She sat listlessly at the breakfast table, staring at her untouched bowl of Fruit Loops, normally her favorite cereal. Her phone was face down beside her elbow, her dark hair tugged into a messy bun, her eyes distant and unfocused. "They're doing an assembly. For Leah. I should be there."

The name lay between us, sharp-edged as a dagger. She pushed soggy cereal around with her spoon. Neither of us had slept well. Last night, she'd awakened screaming from a nightmare, and it had taken me an hour to calm her down.

"You don't have to go," I said, my voice gentle. "I can call the school. They'll understand."

She wouldn't meet my eyes. "I need to, Mom."

I wanted to argue, to keep her home where I could watch over her, where she'd be safe, but I recognized the stubborn set to her jaw that she'd inherited from Marcus.

"Honey, if you're not ready yet, that's okay."

"I'm going." She stood abruptly, abandoning her uneaten breakfast, and grabbed her backpack from the hook by the door. She wore her usual wide-leg jeans, well-worn Converse sneakers, and oversized flannel, the sleeves tugged down to hide the scratches on her arms.

Apollo whined and pressed against her leg. She didn't pet him.

"Okay, let's go then." I grabbed my keys, locked the front door, and we climbed into my 22-year-old rusty blue Honda Accord. It sure wasn't flashy, but it was reliable.

The ten-minute drive to Lakeshore Preparatory Academy in St. Joseph was silent except for the hum of tires on pavement. Mia stared out the passenger window. I tried to find the right words to comfort her, but my throat felt lined with barbed wire.

We drove through downtown St. Joseph, past the Victorian storefronts with their gingerbread trim and brick-paved streets lined with charming art galleries, tourist shops, and boutique restaurants.

Nestled in Southwest Michigan, the coastal town sat at the mouth of the St. Joseph River where it met Lake Michigan. Less than a two-hour drive from Chicago, it was a popular vacation destination in summer and fall, when throngs of tourists would visit the beaches, restaurants, souvenir stores, and ice cream shops.

Now, in early April, joggers in windbreakers passed the Silver Beach Carousel. A woman pushing a stroller laughed on her phone outside the Chocolate Cafe. The smell of roasted beans and baked sugar drifted through my cracked window.

It felt wrong. This cheerful, oblivious normalcy, while somewhere across town, Vivienne wept for her dead daughter.

When we reached Lakeshore Prep, I pulled up to the curb at the middle school drop-off zone. Mia was out of the car before I could say goodbye. I watched her disappear into the throngs of students, something inside me cracking open a little wider.

"I love you," I said into the silence.

My phone buzzed in the cupholder. It was Camille: *Police interview tomorrow at the precinct with Mia, 10 a.m. I delayed it as much as I could. Don't worry. It's standard procedure, like we discussed.*

Dread tightened like a vise around my ribcage. Yesterday afternoon, Camille came over and met with Mia and me. She'd kindly agreed to represent Mia pro bono. For now.

I could have cried with relief and gratitude. I would've hugged her to show my appreciation, but Camille wasn't the hugging sort.

In our small living room, Camille had talked Mia through what had happened Friday night through Saturday morning, detail by detail. She'd explained what would happen at the precinct, the questions the detectives were likely to ask.

As the girls had all said on Saturday morning, Mia had gone to sleep when everyone else did. She had heard nothing. Nothing out of the ordinary had happened that night. Nothing amiss—until she'd woken up to Zara's screams and learned that her best friend was dead.

My mind churning, I pulled back onto the street and drove home on autopilot. Camille claimed it was a standard witness interview, but I'd seen the way the detectives had looked at Mia, like they'd already found her guilty of something.

But Leah's death was an accident. Leah had wandered out on the bluff in the middle of the night, likely to retrieve her phone, as the girls had suggested. She'd slipped, fallen, and struck her head on one of the sharp rocks or fallen logs that littered the bluff.

Though it wasn't a sheer cliff, the bluff was still incredibly steep and treacherous, especially in the dark. Over 100 feet down in some spots, formed of layers of clay, silt, and sand, dotted with grass, bushes, and trees in some sections and bare earth in other spots where the ground had given way and great chunks had slumped down to the beach.

One wrong step was all it took. We'd all warned our kids to stay away from the edge a million times.

Yesterday, while Mia had remained in bed, too heartsick to even eat or shower, I'd watched the news and obsessively scrolled social media. The news stations described Leah's death as a terrible accident.

But I couldn't relax. What if there was something the police weren't saying yet? And what about the blood-stained dress? The scratches on Mia's arms? The missing camera?

Back home, I couldn't sit still, couldn't work, couldn't think straight. The silence pressed in on me, heavy and suffocating. I needed to move, to do something with my hands.

I was supposed to be working. I had a freelance assignment from my editor waiting for me on my laptop, on my desk in my office. Before Marcus died, back when we lived in Chicago, I worked as a journalist for the Chicago Tribune.

But after Marcus died, I couldn't do it anymore.

I'd switched to freelance writing so I could work from home to be close to Mia. I churned out articles on parenting, motherhood, and life for women in their forties: beauty treatments, fitness advice, tips and tricks for dealing with perimenopause, how to stay young forever.

I figured I didn't have long before generative AI made freelance writing gigs obsolete, but for now, we scraped by.

Today, though, I couldn't focus enough to write. Not now. Not with Leah's tragic death hanging over us. Instead, I cooked.

Apollo watched from his bed in the corner as I pulled ingredients from the refrigerator and cabinets: chicken breast, broccoli florets, Kraft shredded cheese, and two cans of cream of mushroom soup.

I was a horrible chef. Marcus had done most of the cooking during our twenty-year marriage, but my mother's baked broccoli and cheese casserole recipe, the one she'd made when neighbors were sick or grieving or in trouble—that I could do.

I chopped broccoli with more force than necessary. The knife thudded against the cutting board. The mechanical rhythm of the familiar chore soothed something in me. Shred the chicken. Grate the cheese. Mix it and slide it into the oven. Simple, concrete. Something I could control.

While the casserole baked, I changed out of my sweatpants into a pair of faded skinny jeans, an oversized U of M sweatshirt that had belonged to Marcus, a jean jacket, and my knockoff Uggs.

Michigan in April meant dressing in layers and hoping for the best. You might get sun, you might get rain, you might get a blustery snowstorm. Today, the forecast was for low fifties and partly cloudy skies, with the sun supposedly making its first appearance in three weeks.

Once the casserole was done, I transferred it into an insulated bag and clipped Apollo's leash to his collar. I checked the lock on the back door, then exited, locked the front door, and slipped the keys in my pocket.

I'd given Brooke a spare set last year in case I accidentally locked myself out. I never put a spare key anywhere outside. Not after Marcus.

Briefly, I touched the titanium wedding band beneath my shirt to steady myself. *Breathe*, I told myself. *Just breathe.*

I tugged Apollo's leash as he pranced excitedly around my legs, panting enthusiastically. He was always eager for a walk. "Come on, boy. Let's go."

The neighborhood was quiet as we walked. Tulips bloomed in planters, chickadees and robins called from the pines, and new leaves budded vibrant green from the branches of dogwoods, sycamores, and black walnut trees.

I turned off Wyld Wood Lane and headed east on Driftwood Terrace.

In the gated community of Blackthorn Shores, Wyld Wood Lane ran north-south along the bluff, where two dozen estates claimed waterfront views and beach access via private staircases. Driftwood Terrace, where Brooke and Vivienne lived, and Windward Point both ran perpendicular to Wyld Wood, running west-east before curving to meet Cliff Harbor Drive in the center.

Cliff Harbor Drive was the principal thoroughfare, where the clubhouse, the Olympic-sized pool, and the playground were located, ending at the gated entrance and guardhouse. The homes on Cliff Harbor, Driftwood Terrace, and Windward Point were as large as the ones on Wyld Wood Lane. Though they lacked water views, homeowners accessed the beach through the community stairs beyond Rowan's house, which was the northernmost lot.

Vivienne's house was a grand moss-green Craftsman with cream trim, a gingerbread-style porch, and a four-car garage for her husband Daniel's collection of vintage cars: a 1969 Acapulco Blue Ford Mustang, a 1970s gold Camaro, and a jet-black Porsche 911 from the 1980s.

I climbed the porch steps, Apollo panting at my side, and knocked with the heavy brass knocker.

Daniel Cho opened the door. He was short at 5'7", heavy set, with silver threading through his combed-over black hair. His round face looked hollowed out, eyes red-rimmed and swollen. He looked like he'd aged a decade overnight, ten years older than his early fifties.

His voice was hoarse. "Dahlia."

"I'm so sorry, Daniel." I held out the insulated bag. "I brought a casserole for you, and I'll bring another meal over on Friday. Rowan's starting a meal train, so you won't have to worry about food."

He took the bag. "Thank you. That's very kind."

Apollo whined, his tail wagging tentatively. Daniel usually loved to pet him and would throw sticks for him to chase while chatting with Vivienne and me. Now, he didn't seem to see the dog at all. The lines around his mouth, which usually crinkled with warmth and laughter, had deepened into something harder.

I peered around him. "Is Vivienne...?"

"She hasn't left her room since Saturday. The doctor prescribed Valium. She can't... she's not doing well." An orthopedic surgeon at the Orthopedics and Sports Medicine Center in St. Joe, he was accustomed to competence, to repairing shattered bones and torn ligaments, to fixing broken things.

Now, he was helpless. He could do nothing to bring his daughter back or ease his distraught wife's pain, or his own.

My chest ached for both of them. "I understand. If there's anything you need. Anything at all."

He nodded, his gaze unfocused. "Thank you, Dahlia. Vivienne and I appreciate that, truly."

I stood there for a moment after he shut the door, staring at the brass knocker. I pictured Vivienne lying upstairs behind drawn curtains, sedated against the unbearable weight of her grief. Every waking moment a nightmare, her only child gone forever.

I imagined them trapped in that house, locked in their grief. I knew what it felt like, the misery within those walls. The despair.

Apollo nudged my hand with his nose. I couldn't bear the thought of going home, of sitting alone in my quiet house with my spiraling thoughts and the ticking clock counting down to tomorrow at 10 a.m.

We kept walking. Brooke's house came next, a modern black farmhouse with huge black windows and a gleaming copper roof. Her Mercedes was absent from the driveway. I knocked anyway, but no one answered.

She should've been home. Brooke was a lifestyle influencer, her Instagram and TikTok accounts showcasing filtered images of her perfect family—vacations to Europe and the Maldives, charity galas for various causes, and glowing moments with her two kids, Alexis and her younger brother, Falcon—each caption an eye-rolling humble-brag. Her husband Jason was a hedge-fund manager with offices in Chicago. He was hardly ever home.

We kept going. I headed west back to Wyld Wood Lane and turned north instead of south toward my cottage. A few houses down, the Everett place sat dark and vacant, a FOR SALE sign tilted in the overgrown lawn.

Apparently, the family had left suddenly last spring before we'd moved in. Something terrible had happened to their daughter, though no one talked openly about it. Just another empty house, another family vanishing under a dark cloud of tragedy.

Apollo and I continued down the street. The morning had warmed, the sun breaking through the clouds in pale streaks.

At Camille's, a modern steel-and-glass house with floor-to-ceiling glass panels for walls, her son Zion was shooting hoops in the circular driveway.

He was tall, wiry, and athletic like his parents and younger sister, Zara. A junior at Lakeshore Prep and the team's starting point guard, he should have been at school.

As Apollo and I approached, he glanced up and gave me a brief wave, then took a shot. It bounced off the rim. "My mom's at work."

"I know." I hesitated at the edge of the driveway. Camille's husband Jerome often played basketball with Zion for hours in the evenings, though Jerome was at work now. He was a beloved math teacher at Lakeshore Prep. "Is Zara home?"

Zion caught the ball and held it against his hip. "She's up in her room. She's not sleeping or eating or anything."

"Yeah, Mia, too. Well, tell your mom and sister I stopped by."

"Sure thing."

I waved goodbye and continued walking. We passed Whitney's house—no Range Rover in the driveway, no lights on—and kept going.

Near the end of the road, Mrs. Atkins was kneeling in her front garden, pruning daffodils, pansies, and hyacinths with a pair of shears. She sat back on her heels, set down the shears, and shaded her eyes with one gloved hand. "Dahlia, dear. How are you holding up?"

"As well as can be expected." I managed a wan smile.

Mrs. Atkins had lived in Blackthorn Shores longer than anyone, since the 1980s, before it was transformed into a gated community, when the lots were bigger and the houses significantly smaller. Now in her late seventies, she spent most of her days rocking on her front porch, monitoring the neighborhood for infractions, real and imaginary.

"Such a terrible tragedy," she said, shaking her head. "That poor girl. And poor Vivienne. I can't imagine."

"None of us can."

"Just terrible." She clutched her cardigan closer. Her squinty hazel eyes were bright with something that might have been concern, or more likely, curiosity. "Were you there when it happened?"

"No, I—"

"I told Harry something didn't feel right that night. I said, 'Harry, something's not right.'" She leaned in, lowering her voice as if we were co-conspirators. "I couldn't sleep, you see. It was like my bones knew something terrible was about to happen. The neighborhood's not the same anymore. I told him they keep letting in those maids and housekeepers. You know all those landscapers are up to no good."

Mrs. Atkins had a reputation for frequently crying wolf to the HOA about suspicious activities, from teenagers smoking marijuana to strange vans that turned out to be the HVAC company servicing a nearby home.

"What happened to Leah was a terrible accident," I said firmly.

"I truly hope so." She picked up her shears again. "You take care of yourself and that daughter of yours, dear."

Almost without thinking, I continued down the street toward Rowan's house.

The neighborhood's grandest homes lined Wyld Wood Lane, perched high on the bluffs with sweeping views of Lake Michigan, and Rowan's house was the crown jewel of them all.

It was a massive stone-and-cedar modern lodge with soaring windows and a wraparound deck that looked out over the water.

As I approached, my steps slowed.

Brooke's Mercedes sat in the circular driveway. Whitney's fluffy Pomeranian, Percival, was tied to the front porch post. He leapt to his feet when he spotted Apollo and barked, his squat body wiggling in excitement, his rhinestone collar glinting at his furry throat.

Voices drifted through the open living room window, low and urgent. I recognized Whitney's low tenor, Brooke's shrill whine, and Rowan's calm, steady reply.

Heat flushed my face as I pulled out my phone and checked my messages. Nothing. No group text. No invitation. Just the same three messages I'd been staring at all morning: Camille's text about the interview, a notification from my cell phone provider, and a reminder about Mia's dentist appointment next week.

Last night, Rowan had texted a link to a podcast about supporting friends after a tragic loss, but there was no invitation to her house.

The realization that I'd been excluded sat cold and heavy in my stomach. They were grieving, pulling back to be with their families, holding their daughters tighter. They simply forgot to include me.

The silence still stung.

The old shame rose, choking my throat. I was twelve again, watching the popular girls whisper and laugh in the hallway while I sat alone at lunch. Thirteen and invisible in the back of the classroom while my classmates passed notes and made weekend plans.

Things were different now. I was a mature adult, not a cowering, mousy kid anymore. I owned a house in this luxurious neighborhood, a dilapidated fixer-upper, yes, but didn't that still count? I wasn't sure that it did.

We only lived in this exclusive gated community because the ramshackle cottage set on the undeveloped plot at the end of the road had been in my husband's family for three generations, and after his eccentric great-aunt died within a month of Marcus's passing, it had been willed to Mia and me.

Built long before the HOA was formed, it was the only house left standing from the original 1940s neighborhood that hadn't been bulldozed and replaced by a mansion.

The taxes remained cheap because the house was about to slide over the bluff into Lake Michigan. Not next month or even next year, but its days were numbered. I was probably the only one crazy enough, desperate enough, to bet that it wouldn't happen soon.

I shouldn't have been here with these people. These effortlessly chic, successful, beautiful women, with their glossy salon blowouts and dewy skin from monthly facials that cost more than my grocery budget, with their elegant style and natural coolness.

They all owned lavish, expensive houses. They vacationed in Aspen and Turks and Caicos, drove Range Rovers and Teslas, and discussed nannies and housekeepers like I discussed couponing. Most of them filled their days with leisurely lunches, book clubs, spa appointments, hot yoga, and charity fundraisers. Other than Camille with her high-powered career, of course.

I looked down at myself. In my dead husband's ratty old U of M sweatshirt, with my chipped nail polish, frumpy off-brand jeans, and frazzled auburn curls that I could never tame. Constantly calculating the property taxes due next month, the climbing electric bill, and how many more freelance assignments I could pick up to cover the bills.

And yet somehow, impossibly, I was included here. Welcomed. Invited into the inner sanctum. They'd made me feel like I belonged, like the gap between us didn't matter that much. Like I had real friends.

I'd had coffee with Camille and Vivienne last week, volunteered with Rowan twice for the Lakeshore Prep bake-sale fundraiser, and often jogged with Whitney and Rowan on Sunday mornings, though I hated every second of the actual exercise part.

Running was torture, but I did it to be included among them, to breathe the rarified air of their approval and acceptance, to become a small part of their glittering world. If I stayed close enough, maybe a bit of their sparkle would rub off on me.

Why, then, were they all here without me? There were so many unspoken rules to follow to fit in, and though I tried as hard as I could, I was certain I must still be breaking them somehow. And now here I was, excluded once again.

I stood rigid at the end of the cobblestone driveway, uncertain, torn. Part of me wanted to turn around, to pretend I'd never walked this far, had never spotted Brooke's car or heard their voices. But I couldn't.

I couldn't move, couldn't walk away.

Apollo whined softly, pressing against my leg. I reached down and scratched behind his ears. I was being silly, ridiculous. After all, these women had been there for me when I moved here last April in the aftermath of Marcus's death, still traumatized and shell-shocked.

We had fled Chicago, grief-stricken, hurting, desperate for a safe place to land.

I had convinced myself it was enough. That Mia and I could carve out a new life here in the safe enclave of Blackthorn Shores, a gated lakefront community nestled in the coastal town of St. Joseph, Michigan, where Marcus had grown up.

I had no family anywhere else. My mother had died of breast cancer when I was in my early twenties, and my father had abdicated his role long before that, abandoning my mother and me to start a new family in Sturgeon Bay, Wisconsin. We saw him and my two grown half-brothers once or twice a year for holidays.

They weren't my family. Marcus had been my heart, my everything, together since we'd met our freshman year at DePaul University in college algebra, which I'd nearly failed. He'd offered to tutor me, and the rest was history.

After his death, I was desperate for a place where we could belong. That we would be safe.

These women had barely known me, yet Rowan had organized meal trains, Whitney had driven Mia to school some mornings, and Brooke had shared the juiciest neighborhood gossip to distract me.

My aching heart longed for Whitney's dry humor, for Camille's steady capableness, for Brooke's boisterous laughter, for Vivienne's soft encouragement, even for Rowan's Type A volunteer-for-everything, everywhere, all at once personality, always dragging us along with her.

They wouldn't exclude me. Not now. Not when I needed them most.

I forced myself forward. I wound Apollo's leash around one of the porch's cedar beams so he and Percival could sniff each other. Their tails wagged in curious enthusiasm.

The voices inside went quiet.

A shadow moved behind the frosted glass panel beside the door.

My heart hammered against my ribs. For a moment, I considered running, turning tail and fleeing before anyone saw me, before I had to face the humiliation of the cool girls meeting in secret without me.

But I was being ridiculous. These were my friends. I wasn't in middle school anymore, and I no longer needed to fret about being excluded from the popular lunch table.

Pushing down my sense of disquiet, I raised my fist and knocked. Three sharp raps that echoed louder than I'd intended.

Footsteps approached. Rowan opened the door with a wide dazzling smile. "Dahlia! We were just talking about you."

Chapter Six

"Come in, Come in." Rowan beckoned me inside with an elegant wave of her hand. "Oh, honey, you look wrecked. You could use a break."

I managed a smile. In her presence, I felt myself straightening, smoothing my frumpy jeans, desperately wanting her approval. "That's one way to put it."

Effortlessly commanding and gracious, Rowan wore a soft taupe turtleneck, black cigarette pants, and leather loafers. She moved with the confidence of someone who'd never doubted her place in the world.

At 41, she was beautiful, with pale ice-blue eyes that could shift from warm to glacial in a heartbeat, high aristocratic cheekbones, a defined jawline, and that luminous porcelain skin she shared with her daughter Chloe.

There was steel beneath her beauty, though. Rowan was a woman who knew what she wanted and how to charm and cajole others into getting it.

While her husband Gregory worked as a hedge fund manager for Blue Star Capital, a financial firm based in St. Joseph, Rowan volunteered constantly, as the PTA president at Lakeshore Prep and the HOA president of Blackthorn Shores, as well as serving on the board of directors at the Krasl Art Center, the Humane Society, and the Boys and Girls Club in Benton Harbor.

I stepped inside. The warmth of the house enveloped me as she led me through the formal living room, past the cream sofas and oil paintings that cost more than my car, and into the gleaming all-white kitchen.

Whitney and Brooke were in the glassed-in breakfast nook off the kitchen, bathed in late-morning sunlight. Lake Michigan glittered through every pane of glass. They both smiled when they saw me.

"Hey, Dahlia." Whitney stood, one hand braced against the table's edge, doing a calf stretch. She wore athleisure wear, rose-pink leggings with a matching jacket zipped to her throat and bright white sneakers.

Her sleek white-blonde ponytail swung as she switched legs, her cobalt blue eyes tracking the movement with the same precision she brought to everything else.

A former college athlete and tennis state champion, she was obsessed with optimization: her fitness regimen, her ketogenic diet, her alkaline water intake, and her daughter's rigid academic and athletic schedule.

"For heaven's sake, Whit, sit down," Rowan said, her tone light but firm. "You're practically cleaning my floor. I have a cleaning service for that."

"I'm almost done." Whitney reached for her pearl-white Stanley and gulped water. At 43, her intense energy filled every room she entered. Her strong jawline was set in perpetual determination, her straight nose and thin lips giving her face a lean, hungry quality, as if she were always measuring, calculating, ardently pushing toward the next goal.

"Whitney," Rowan said. "For all our sakes, please."

With a sigh, Whitney sank into her chair but kept tapping her foot. "I need to keep moving. It's the only thing that distracts me."

Brooke sat next to Whitney. She flashed me a tight smile as she nursed a mimosa, two empty wine glasses on the table at her elbow. She wore a creamy cashmere sweater with high-waisted black pants, a Gucci belt, and nude Louboutins, designer brands I only knew because she'd told me.

Whitney's fingers drummed against the table. "How is Mia?"

I slid into the chair Rowan indicated. I wasn't sure how much to share. Normally, I would tell these women everything, but something held me back. That disquieting unease swirling in my gut hadn't let up. "She's upset."

Rowan reached across the table to squeeze my hand. Her touch was warm, reassuring. "Leah and Mia had such a close relationship. She must be devastated."

"She is," I said.

"Mmm," Brooke murmured into her glass.

Rowan strolled to the beverage niche with the fancy espresso machine and returned a moment later, handing me a steaming latte in an oversized mug, the foam art a perfect rosette. "Extra honey, almond milk, no Stevia, right?"

"Right. Thanks." That she remembered warmed something in my chest. Somehow, she'd instantly eased the sting of being left out. Rowan had a way of making you feel seen. Special. That warmth was Rowan's gift, and everyone wanted to be included in her orbit.

Of course, being chosen meant that you could also be unchosen.

Brooke twisted the massive diamond on her ring finger. Her words were careful, over-enunciated. "We were just talking about... everything."

I sat stiffly, the mug warm between my palms. Something felt off. The women seemed cool, distant. Whitney's foot kept tapping, quick little movements that made her knee bounce. Brooke kept glancing at her near-empty mimosa like she wanted another but didn't dare ask.

"How are you holding up?" Rowan settled into the chair opposite me with practiced grace and took a sip of her cappuccino.

"Okay, I guess," I said automatically, then corrected myself. "Awful, actually. I can't stop thinking about how Leah died. How tragic and meaningless it is. To die from a fall, from getting too close to the edge. It's terrible."

"Leah *was* behaving strangely lately, even if no one wants to admit it." Brooke's gaze flicked to Rowan as if seeking permission for something, then away. Her words came out slightly thick. "What if Alexis was right? And she got upset and did something reckless?"

Whitney's brows lifted. "Are you saying you think it was on purpose?"

A timer dinged in the kitchen. Rowan rose smoothly, moving to the oven. She pulled out a tray of cinnamon scones and transferred them to a crystal platter. "Vivienne said Leah was depressed. She hadn't come over to the house in weeks. Even Chloe noticed, and that girl is oblivious."

She set the platter on the table, adjusting it until it sat perfectly centered. "Eat up, ladies. They're keto."

I took a sip of the latte. Perfect as usual. But the creamy sweetness did nothing to lessen the growing knot in my stomach.

Whitney looked at the scones as if carbs were poison. She fingered the Cartier tennis bracelet on her wrist, a recent gift from her husband, Graham, who worked as the executive vice president of Strategy and Development at Whirlpool Corporation's headquarters in Benton Harbor. "I can't even imagine what Vivienne is going through right now."

"We should get the girls into therapy." Brooke lifted her glass, found it empty, and set it down with a forceful clink. "Alexis is a wreck. I hear her crying in the middle of the night. But she won't talk to me."

Rowan gave Brooke a weighted look. "Another mimosa, Brooke?"

Brooke flushed but nodded. "Just a splash."

It was barely eleven in the morning. A pang of sympathy struck me. Brooke tried so hard to look the part, to say the right things.

At 37, she was the youngest of the mothers, and three years younger than me. Though she was naturally beautiful, she never seemed to believe it was enough.

Her brunette waves were freshly highlighted, her heart-shaped face sharpened by microbladed brows, lash extensions, and strategic fillers, every detail calibrated for the invisible camera that followed her everywhere as a lifestyle influencer.

She was fun and spontaneous when she let her guard down, fiercely loyal to her friends, quick with a joke or a story that could turn the blandest committee meeting into a juicy tale everyone leaned in for.

But lately it seemed like she couldn't relax without a drink in her hand, her smile rarely reaching her eyes, her laugh coming too quick and too bright. The effort showed in every gesture. It had to be exhausting to feel like you had to telegraph perfection continuously, every second of every day.

Rowan refilled Brooke's glass without comment, then returned to her seat. She picked up a scone, took the smallest bite, and set it back down. "Chloe thinks it's all her fault because it was her party. She's taking it very hard. She had terrible nightmares all night."

"Mia did, too." I took a scone and nibbled it. It was delicious, but I had little appetite. I glanced out the window. Outside, yellow crime tape fluttered between two trees on the edge of the bluff.

Brooke followed my gaze and took a long gulp of her mimosa, her hand unsteady. "How long is that going to be there? I can't imagine how you must feel, seeing that reminder every day. That she... that a girl died right there. I would want to move."

Rowan's eyes narrowed almost imperceptibly. "They finished processing the area this morning. I asked the detectives to remove the crime tape, but they're taking their sweet time. I'm sure it'll be taken care of by tomorrow. And this is my home. While what happened is tragic, I could never consider moving somewhere else."

"Of course, " Brooke murmured, not meeting Rowan's probing gaze.

An awkward silence descended. Whitney's anxious foot-tapping accelerated.

"Have any of you seen Mia's camera?" I asked.

All eyes turned to me, questioning, curious. They shook their heads.

"I haven't," Rowan said, "and the police did a most thorough search of our house. Why do you ask?"

I shrugged and tried to appear nonchalant, though my heart was racing. "Mia seems to have misplaced it, I guess." Though I wasn't sure I believed that.

Rowan's phone dinged on the counter. She pushed back her chair, rose, and went to the counter, then frowned down at the screen. "It's Camille. She says to turn on the news right now. It's about Leah."

We rose hurriedly and moved to the living room. Rowan commanded the TV to switch on, her voice tight. "Turn to the local news."

Detective King filled the screen as he stood at a podium, surrounded by several detectives and officers, including Detective Callahan and the police chief. His expression was grave.

Cameras flashed in his face as he spoke. "Leah Cho's death has been ruled a homicide. We are asking anyone with information relating to this case to please contact the St. Joseph Police Department immediately."

No one moved. No one spoke.

Whitney's face went bone white. Her water bottle slipped from her hand and hit the floor with a dull thud. She didn't seem to notice. "Homicide?"

Brooke's glass trembled in her hand. "They think someone... " Her voice came out strangled. "They think someone did this?"

The room contracted around me. I couldn't get enough oxygen. For two days, I'd been waiting for the announcement that the police had determined that Leah's death was a tragic accident. Case closed. We could all grieve and move on.

Not anymore.

My chest tightened until I couldn't draw a full breath.

Brooke looked at Rowan, appalled. "They think someone killed Leah."

"Yes," I said, my voice sounding distant, strangely alien. I recalled what Zara had said about finding Leah on the bluff, her broken body. "She didn't fall. She was pushed."

"That's not possible," Whitney said shakily. "Who would do that?"

Brooke lifted her glass with both hands and drained it in one long swallow. "What does this mean for us? For our girls?"

"It means they're going to ask more questions," Rowan said. "They're going to look more closely at everyone who was there that night. Our girls have nothing to hide. They were sleeping. They saw nothing."

"Then what happened?" Brooke's voice rose with barely contained panic. "Who killed Leah?"

The silence that followed felt different from before. Thicker, heavier, weighted with apprehension and foreboding. I waited for someone to say something about the evidence the police had already collected.

No one did.

No one mentioned Mia's scratches. The torn dress. The missing camera.

"The detectives will find the culprit," Rowan said calmly. "We just have to trust them to do their jobs."

Whitney sucked in a sharp breath. "Peyton's going to hear about this. Everyone's going to hear about it. She'll be absolutely gutted."

Brooke looked at Rowan, her eyes wide with alarm. Her words were slurred. "What do we do?"

Rowan squeezed Brooke's hand. "Our job is to support our daughters. None of them had anything to do with this."

Footsteps sounded on the stairs. Chloe appeared at the bottom, barefoot and wearing a long white nightgown. Her face was blotchy, her blue eyes red-rimmed. She looked small and breakable. "Mom?"

My chest tightened. Had she heard the news already?

Rowan crossed the room to her daughter. "Sweetheart, what are you doing up? I thought you were resting."

"I saw it," Chloe said. "It's all over Instagram."

"Oh, honey—"

Chloe's face crumpled. "I keep having nightmares. Everything's dark, and I'm screaming. I can't stop screaming. I keep trying to save her, but I can't. She just keeps falling, over and over. I'm so, so sorry."

"Shh, baby, it's okay." Rowan wrapped her arms around Chloe, stroking her hair. "They're just nightmares. They can't hurt you. It's not your fault. None of this is your fault."

She glanced at me, tears spilling down her cheeks. "What if there was something I could've done?"

"Did you remember anything else?" I asked.

Chloe hesitated, pursing her rosebud mouth. She was poised, articulate, and charismatic, the kind of precocious, polite girl that adults instantly adored, though she'd always seemed sensitive and a little fragile, striving to meet Rowan's standards, though Rowan herself treated Chloe like something delicate, requiring constant protection.

Chloe shook her head mutely. "I'm letting Leah down."

"Of course, you aren't." Rowan frowned slightly as she guided her daughter toward the stairs, one arm around her shoulders. Obediently, Chloe went with her mother. "There's nothing any of you could have done. Come on. Let's get you back to bed."

Whitney bent and retrieved her dropped Stanley, then she straightened and smoothed her outfit. "I should go. I have Pilates and tennis, and I need to be there when Peyton gets home from school."

Rowan said over her shoulder. "Go be with your daughter. That's what matters most."

Brooke set her empty wineglass on the coffee table. "I should go, too. I have to pick up Falcon soon, and Alexis..." Her voice trailed off.

Brooke and Whitney gathered their things, gave me perfunctory hugs, and hurried out the door. The homicide announcement had changed everything. They weren't just leaving; they were fleeing. I heard their murmured goodbyes, the click of Percival's leash, his yapping bark.

The house went quiet. I stood in the middle of the living room, unsure if I should leave as well.

A moment later, Rowan descended the stairs. Her expression softened. "Dahlia, stay a moment?"

I nodded, relieved. "Of course."

We collected the plates, mugs, and glasses from the breakfast table. I followed Rowan to the sink, wanting to help, to be useful.

Rowan scraped the uneaten scones into the trash, set the dishware in the sink, and turned to me. "I know this must be so hard for you. Especially after everything with Marcus. Losing him so suddenly, so violently. And now this. Another tragedy touching your family."

I flinched. "It's not about me. It's about Leah. About Vivienne."

"Of course. But you've been through so much already. It's a lot to bear. We're all thinking of Vivienne and Daniel now, but no one's thinking of you."

My throat tightened. "I just keep thinking... what if the police don't believe Mia? What if they think—?"

"They won't." Rowan took my hands in hers. Her grip was firm. "Because Mia did nothing wrong, just like Chloe didn't. We all know that. Anyone who knows her knows that."

Tears pricked my eyes. "Thank you. I just... I don't know what I'd do if they took Mia from me, if I lost her."

Rowan's eyes held mine. "Camille is representing Mia. She's the best defense attorney in Berrien County."

"You're right," I managed. "I know you're right."

She squeezed my hands once more before releasing them. "You're not alone. You have us."

The words settled over me like a warm and cozy blanket. For the first time since Saturday morning, the crushing weight on my chest eased a fraction. I had friends. Real friends who would stand by me, who would help me keep my daughter safe.

But the thought niggled at the back of my mind, refusing to dissipate. Safe from what?

Chapter Seven

I pulled into the parking lot of Lakeshore Prep ten minutes early, so I parked rather than join the queue of luxury SUVs, sedans, and sports cars waiting to collect their students.

My brain buzzed. My skin felt electrified. Homicide. Someone had killed Leah. I thought of Viv and what she must be going through. I knew how violence could utterly destroy you.

I had to go see her again; I couldn't let her do this alone.

I tugged my phone from my oversized white faux-leather purse and called her. It went to voicemail, no surprise. I left a message, then sent her a quick text: *Viv, I just heard. I'm so sorry, I'm here for whatever you need.*

I stared at the phone for a moment, hoping for a response that didn't come. I'd text her again later tonight.

Before I put the phone away, a text from Camille appeared: *Detectives pushing hard to interview Mia now. I've held them off until tomorrow. Make sure Mia eats and gets sleep. See you then.*

I swallowed hard. The words blurred on the screen. She didn't say everything would be okay or offer any reassurances. That wasn't her style. Still, part of me wished she had.

A million thoughts whirred anxiously inside my head. Had someone sneaked onto the Westinghouse property that night?

Who? For what reason? And how? The community was gated and secure, although someone might have come up from the beach access stairs. Or was the killer lurking closer to home?

And what did all this mean for Mia? The scratches on her arms. The suspicious way the detectives had looked at her when they saw the blood on her dress.

It was too much. I had to focus on what I could control: picking up Mia from school, keeping her safe, and getting home and cocooning ourselves away from the madness.

I exited the car and headed toward the school. From inside their cars, I felt the stares of several mothers I recognized from the PTA meetings Rowan encouraged me to attend.

Without Rowan, Brooke, or Whitney by my side, I was pretty much invisible here among the wealthy and privileged families of St. Joe.

Which was fine with me. I didn't care. At least, I told myself I didn't.

Let them gossip. I had bigger things to worry about.

I knew better than to enter the school. Mia would be mortified, so instead, I waited outside beneath the portico.

Through the glass doors, I spotted Mia standing by the drinking fountain, her shoulders hunched, head down in a way that tore at my heart. Peyton Alistair leaned in next to her, whispering in her ear while Mia nodded, her face blank.

At least her friends were on her side, still talking to her. At least they had each other.

Peyton patted Mia's arm, then turned and headed back into the building, on her way to debate club, maybe, or swim practice. Whitney kept her daughter's schedule packed tighter than her own.

Jerome Hayward pushed through the double doors, leather satchel over one shoulder, a folder of math papers in his other hand. Tall and lean with close-cropped graying hair, he had the practiced calm of someone who'd spent twenty years teaching middle school math.

When he spotted me, he crossed over in a few long strides, his expression somber. "Dahlia. I'm so sorry. Zara's just heartbroken. I can't imagine what Mia's going through."

I'd always liked Camille's husband. Where she was bold and commanding, Jerome was steady and reserved, except at games, when he was the loudest parent in the stands, whether it was Zara's volleyball or Zion's basketball games.

"Leah and Mia are in my pre-algebra class. They always partnered up for group work. They're good kids." He cleared his throat and winced, as if realizing his mistake. "Leah was a good kid."

I nodded, not trusting my voice.

"If there's anything Camille or I can do," he added, "you let us know."

"I will, and Camille is already helping us immensely. Thank you, Jerome."

He gave a small nod and headed toward the parking lot, papers shifting in his grip.

A minute later, Mia exited the front doors. Conversations buzzed around her, along with hushed whispers and pointed glances. She strode through the crowd of students as if she were oblivious, but she wasn't. Her shoulders hunched, head bowed as if she felt their suspicion like burrs on her skin.

Indignation burned in my chest. I wanted to yell at her classmates, but that wouldn't do any good.

"Hey, you," I said when we were both back in the car. She slumped in the front seat, backpack at her feet, her phone clutched in both hands.

"Mia, I need to tell you something. About Leah. The police announced—"

"I already know, Mom. It's all over Instagram. It's all anyone is talking about."

She angled the phone away from me, but not before I glimpsed that familiar pink emblem on the screen. Captions and images scrolled past too swiftly to read. Her knuckles were white around her phone case.

"I'm so sorry you had to find out that way."

Her voice was flat. "They're saying it was murder. That she—that someone killed her."

"The police will figure out what happened," I said carefully. "They'll find the truth."

"What if they don't?" She turned to look at me, her eyes glassy, unfocused, like she'd been crying. "What if they think..." She cut herself off and stared down at her phone.

"Mia—"

"Can we just go home?"

My chest tightened. I didn't want to push her. I didn't know what to say, how to make any of this better. "You want to stop at Forté Coffee for some hazelnut lattes on the way?"

It was usually her favorite treat. She shook her head and slumped deeper into the seat.

The rest of the car ride home was silent. At the Blackthorn Shores security gate, several white vans were pulled off to the side of the road. A dozen people stood on the berm, setting up video cameras and microphones.

I drove past them and pulled up at the security gate. "Great, the media is here."

Frank Hastings, the head of security, gave me a friendly smile as he waved us through. In his late fifties, with a beer belly and salt-and-pepper beard, Frank had always treated Mia and me with the same easy warmth he gave everyone else, regardless of our tax bracket. "Vultures, more like it. Don't worry, we won't let them in."

"Thank you, Frank. I appreciate that."

He smiled at Mia, but she didn't look up from her phone. "You have a nice day now."

"You, too." I drove down maple-lined Cliff Harbor Drive, past the clubhouse and the playground, where a few nannies watched their charges climbing the jungle gym. Alexis sat on the bench, scrolling on her phone while her younger brother Falcon played on the swings.

"You want to head to the playground to hang out with Alexis for a while? I bought cinnamon rolls at Martins, so you could bring her and Falcon one."

"I'll pass."

"Just a thought."

"I'm fine, Mom."

A minute later, I turned left onto Wyld Wood Lane. At Camille's house, Zion was practicing basketball on their circular driveway.

Mia slung her backpack over her shoulder as we exited the car and approached the house.

Something wasn't right.

I couldn't name it at first. Just—wrongness. A prickle at the base of my skull.

I unlocked the front door and stuffed my keys in my purse. Inside, the house felt too quiet, too still. Mia dropped her backpack by the stairs. She glanced back at me, her features tense; she felt it, too.

"Apollo?" I called.

The dog appeared from the kitchen, his tail wagging. Apollo trotted over immediately, circling Mia and whining softly before sitting at her feet and placing one heavy paw on her shoe, his way of saying *I'm here, love me.*

For the first time since we'd left Rowan's house on Saturday morning, something in Mia's face softened. She patted his head, then headed straight for the stairs. "I've got a ton of homework."

"Wait." I grabbed her arm gently. "Stay here for a second."

"Why?"

"Just... stay here. Let me check the house."

She rolled her eyes. "Mom. Are you for real right now?"

It was so like her old self, I could have cried. "Humor me."

I moved through the house, checking everything. Living room: nothing disturbed. Kitchen: dishes still in the sink from this morning. Mia's bedroom: jeans and sweatshirts scattered across the floor, textbooks piled on her desk. My gaze lingered on the empty spot on her closet shelf where her Nikon usually sat, then moved on.

Everything looked normal.

It didn't feel normal.

I checked every window. Every door. All locked. No signs of forced entry. Nothing missing that I could see.

In my office, papers sat in a messy stack on my desk, a huge oak monstrosity I'd found at Goodwill. On my desk sat the coffee mug I still needed to wash, my laptop, the blue composition notebook, and the desk lamp.

I turned to leave, stopped, and glanced back.

The window was open. Just a few inches. A cool draft slipped through and rustled the papers on my desk.

I stared at it for a moment. Had I opened it this morning? I couldn't remember. The forecast had been cool and cloudy, though the sun had peeked out by midday. Perhaps I'd cracked it before that.

I crossed the room and pulled it shut. Locked the latch.

Then I went back downstairs.

Mia stared at me as if I were out of my mind. "Mom, it's fine. Everything's fine."

"I know."

"Nothing's going to happen here, that's what you said, right? We're safe here."

I nodded absently. It was PTSD from the stress. Had to be. That's what the grief therapist we saw after Marcus's death used to say. *Just breathe*. Be calm, be steady. Breathe through it.

"Mom?" Mia looked at me, concern on her face mingled with teenage impatience.

"I know, you're right. Old habits." I forced a smile. Slowly, my heartrate decreased. "Are you hungry? Want me to whip up our favorite grilled cheese and tomato soup combo?"

"I'm not hungry. I just want to finish my algebra and English assignments and go to bed."

"Okay." I watched her climb the stairs. Apollo padded faithfully after her. His nails clicked against the hardwood floor. A moment later, her bedroom door closed with a soft thud.

I stood there for a long moment, staring at the empty staircase, then I forced myself to move, to do something productive.

The freelance article wouldn't write itself. It was due in three days.

In my office, I opened my laptop and stared at the blinking cursor. The title mocked me from the top of the screen: "Effective Communication with Teenagers: Five Ways to Connect."

I'd written variations of this article a dozen times for different parenting magazines and websites. The advice always came easily: active listening, open-ended questions, creating safe spaces for tough conversations.

All the things I was apparently failing to do with my own daughter.

My fingers hovered over the keys. Nothing came. Maybe looking at my notes would jog some inspiration loose.

I reached for the blue composition notebook I always kept beside my laptop.

It wasn't where I'd left it.

I always set it to the right of my laptop, my pen clipped neatly to the top. Now it lay skewed at an angle, next to the desk lamp, with the pen out of its clip, lying on top of the notebook instead.

A prickle of unease ran along my scalp.

I hadn't noticed the placement when I'd checked a few minutes earlier. Had I moved it? This morning felt like a year ago. Perhaps I'd flipped it open to jot something down and forgotten.

I took notes longhand, old-school, ink on paper. Writing by hand slowed my thoughts, allowed me to make sense of them, and anchored them in my memory.

I glanced at the window over my desk. Still closed. Still locked. I needed to get hold of myself. I couldn't spiral, not now when Mia needed me most.

This was what stress did. What grief did. It made you forget small things, invent patterns that didn't exist, and made your mind spiral with paranoia, unsure which fears were real or imagined.

My therapist had warned me about hypervigilance after Marcus died, how trauma could make you see threats everywhere.

But what if some of those threats were actually real?

I slid the notebook back into its proper place and flipped it open, but I couldn't focus on any of the notes I'd written for the current article.

Instead, I tried to focus on the screen. *When your teen shuts you out, that's often when they need you most...*

The sentence felt hollow. Cliche. I deleted it and tried to write it again.

My phone buzzed on the desk. Vivienne's name lit up the screen: *I need to talk.*

I responded that I'd be right over. A second later, another text appeared: *I can't take another minute in this house. Can I come to you?*

I was already on my feet and headed down the hall toward the kitchen and the back door, texting as I walked: *Meet me on the patio.*

Chapter Eight

The patio stones were uneven beneath my feet, cracked and sloped from years of erosion. I'd meant to fix them when we first moved in. Another item added to the list of things I'd failed to do.

I stood at the edge where the patio met the grass. Just past the patchy lawn, a mere twenty feet from the foundation of my house, the bluff dropped away in a steep 100-foot plunge to the beach below. Lake Michigan stretched endlessly beyond, darkening from steel-blue to slate as the sun began its slow descent.

At 60 miles across, Lake Michigan often felt more like an ocean than a lake. On a clear day, I could occasionally make out the indistinct outline of the Chicago skyline on the opposite side of the immense lake due to the height of the skyscrapers and atmospheric refraction.

I wrapped my jean jacket tighter against the damp chill rolling off the lake and stared out at the horizon, the line blurred where water met sky. I tried not to think about Vivienne's daughter lying broken halfway down the bluff.

Behind me, footsteps crunched on gravel. I turned.

Vivienne stood at the corner of the house. Her face was pale in the fading light, dark circles marred her usually flawless complexion. Her ink-black hair hung limp and unkempt around her face.

"Vivienne. I'm so sorry."

Her features went slack. "Someone killed my baby."

"I know."

"I can't be at the house. Every corner reminds me of her. Every time I walk past her room... Daniel tries, but it's too much. I cannot be responsible for his grief and my own. I just can't do it right now."

I gestured to one of the mismatched metal patio chairs beside me, each painted a cheerful blue, purple, red, and green. Another Goodwill find. "Come, sit."

We settled into our seats. Vivienne refused my offers of tea, coffee, or water, so I simply sat beside her, waiting quietly, offering whatever comfort with my presence that I could.

She broke the silence first. "Don't say sorry. I can't stand hearing it anymore."

I clasped my hands in my lap. "Okay."

She stared out at the lake. "I'll never see her again. Never argue about stupid chores or laugh at inside jokes. She'll never roll her eyes at my lectures or sneak out past curfew. All those little moments... gone. How am I supposed to be a mother without a child?"

"I wish I had answers. I can't imagine what you're going through."

She turned to face me. A flicker of resentment in her gaze. Anger. "No one can."

I swallowed. She was right. I hadn't lost Mia, but I felt her slipping away. A dark shameful part of me was relieved it was Vivienne's daughter and not mine. Guilt gnawed at me for the traitorous thoughts, but I couldn't help it.

"I'm here for you," I offered. "Whatever you need."

An uncomfortable silence settled between us. Apollo padded over and rested his head on Vivienne's knee. She absentmindedly stroked his fur. "The detectives haven't told me much, but there's no sign of an outside intruder. Nothing on the security cameras, not the neighbors', not Rowan's, and they've checked all the Ring cameras and security footage of everyone's homes. They interviewed the community security team, too."

She paused, her gaze fixed on the darkening horizon. "I can see it in their eyes, Dahlia. They won't say it out loud, but I know what they think."

My stomach knotted. "What do they think?"

She turned to look at me, her expression raw. "They suspect it's someone she knew. They think it's one of the girls."

I went still. One of the girls. Chloe. Alexis. Peyton. Zara.

And Mia.

"How could they think that?" My voice came out thin. "They were her friends. And they're practically babies, still kids."

Vivienne gave a sharp, bitter laugh. "Younger children have killed before. I looked it up on the internet. Bad idea."

My hands went cold. I clasped them tighter in my lap.

"I keep wondering what I missed."

"You didn't miss anything. You're a wonderful mother, Viv."

She ignored me. "There was an incident just before Christmas. Leah came home with a chunk of her hair cut off, that beautiful, waist-length hair she'd been growing for years. She was terrified, not embarrassed. Terrified. She said Alexis cornered her after school in the bathroom and cut it with art scissors."

I remembered the drastic change. Leah's long locks were abruptly cropped into a bob just before winter break. I thought it looked cute on her, edgy even. The new cut fit her full, round cheeks and accented her beautiful dark eyes.

"I demanded a meeting with the principal," Vivienne continued. "Mrs. Nelson claimed she'd look into it, then a day later, she called back and said it was a misunderstanding. The girls had talked and agreed it was mutual, that Leah had asked Alexis to do it." She shook her head in disgust. "When we talked to Leah again, she said the same thing. That she'd wanted it cut, regretted it halfway through, and was upset with herself. Everyone had the same story."

"What do you think really happened?"

Viv snorted. "Someone got to her. Brooke, maybe. You know she can't show any cracks, how everything always has to be perfect, even her kids. The school wouldn't want the scandal, that's for sure. But I know my daughter. The way Leah looked when she first came home, it wasn't regret or embarrassment. It was fear."

My chest tightened. I thought of Mia's silence, her withdrawn behavior. What things had she been afraid to tell me? What secrets had she been keeping, too?

"After that, Leah changed. She stopped wanting to go to school. Stopped drawing, stopped painting. I'd find her crying in her room, but she wouldn't tell me why. She kept a diary. I'd see her writing in it late at night, but I can't find it now, and I've searched everywhere."

My pulse quickened. "A diary? Do you think Mia knows where she kept it?"

"I don't know. The police didn't find it, either. They've already taken her phone, though Detective King told me they found nothing useful on it, just the usual teenage girl stuff, Instagram and TikTok. Whatever was bothering her, she only wrote it down in that diary."

"I'll ask Mia if she knows where it is."

Vivienne's hands twisted in her lap. "I kept asking what was wrong, kept pushing, but she shut me out. I thought it was teenage moodiness, that it would pass, then a few days before the slumber party, she started acting happier. When Chloe invited her to the sleepover, and Leah wanted to go, I thought maybe things had turned around, that I'd been overreacting. I was wrong. I should have trusted my instincts and kept her home that night."

"No, Viv. It's not your fault. Someone did this to Leah. Someone is responsible. Not you."

She looked away and wiped her eyes. "It's too late. Leah's gone. Nothing matters anymore."

"Justice still matters," I said. "The detectives will find whoever did this."

"Will they?" Her voice was hollow.

"Yes," I said with more conviction than I felt. I hoped with all my heart that it wasn't one of the girls, that it wasn't someone we knew, here in this community that was supposed to be safe.

I knew better than to believe bad things never happened to good people. So did Viv.

She studied me for a long moment, her brows lowered. "Brooke told me the police documented scratches on Mia's arms."

My pulse quickened. Why would Brooke tell Vivienne when Vivienne was already devastated and heartbroken? I cleared my throat. "She said she got them from slipping into some thorn bushes during the photo shoot on the bluff," I said, trying not to sound defensive. "She fell, and the branches scratched her."

"Brooke said there was blood on her dress." Viv's voice was soft, but I caught the undercurrent of doubt, the sharpness in the words.

"From the scratches." Something niggled at me. I didn't know that for a fact, did I? Not for certain. Mia would have bled from the scratches, and the blood could have easily transferred to her dress.

It made sense. It was plausible.

Vivienne's gaze lingered on my face, searching for something I couldn't give her. Certainty. Closure. Absolution. Then her shoulders dropped, and she looked away.

"Mia loved Leah," I said.

She nodded. "If not for Mia this year, I don't know how Leah would have made it. Mia meant everything to her."

Relief flared in my chest. But something darker tainted it, something I couldn't explain or define yet. An oily sense of unease, a disquieting apprehension swirling deep in my gut.

We sat in silence, watching the sun sink lower, the sky bleeding pink, violet, and burnt orange across the water. I thought of Leah, how she loved to paint the lake, sunsets in particular, like the watercolor canvas of the lighthouse Mia had hung over her bed.

Once the sun had dipped below the horizon, Vivienne stood, brushing invisible dust from her jeans. "I should go. Daniel will wonder where I am."

I walked her around the side of the house as behind us, the last rays of sunlight transformed the entire lake into shades of copper and rose.

She paused at the edge of the driveway. "Thank you, Dahlia. For listening. For not looking at me like my grief is contagious."

"You're not alone in this. I mean that."

She nodded, her eyes glassy, and turned toward the street. I watched her shuffle away, her shoulders hunched against the evening chill, her whole being diminished somehow, until she disappeared around the corner.

I climbed the porch steps, weary and heartsick, ready to check on Mia and maybe find something mindless on TV. I should be productive and finish that damn article so I could pay the electric bill.

Inside, I checked the locks on the back door, then paused at the foot of the stairs. I touched the titanium ring beneath my shirt. Upstairs, everything was dark, silent.

I should let Mia sleep. But Vivienne's words kept circling in my brain: *I keep wondering what I missed.*

I climbed the stairs.

Mia's door was ajar, the way she'd always kept it. A part of her still scared of the dark. I inched it open.

She lay sprawled across her bed, still fully dressed in her jeans and hoodie, textbooks scattered around her like fallen leaves. Flash the sloth was tucked under one arm, her face turned toward the wall, her breathing deep and even. Her phone lay in one hand, its screen dark.

I tiptoed across the room, pulled the comforter from the foot of the bed, and spread it over her. She didn't stir. Apollo lifted his head from where he lay curled at her feet, then gave a soft woof and settled back down.

I smoothed a strand of hair from her cheek. My chest ached with the depth of my love for her. She was so young. So vulnerable.

My gaze drifted to her closet. The door was half-open, clothes spilling out in the haphazard manner only a teenager could achieve. In the corner, nearly hidden behind a pile of dirty clothes, I spotted the edge of her overnight bag. The sage-green duffle she'd taken to Rowan's house.

I thought of the press conference on TV. What Viv had said: *They think it's one of the girls.* How she kept wondering what she'd missed. What had I missed?

Before I could second-guess myself, I knelt and pulled the bag free. The zipper was half-open. Inside was a wadded T-shirt that smelled faintly of lavender detergent. Several tampons. A tangled phone charger. Her toiletry bag.

At the bottom, stuffed into the corner, were her pink fuzzy sloth slippers. The ones Marcus had bought her on our Costa Rica vacation two years ago.

I dragged them out.

They were damp. Not soaked, but distinctly wet. Moisture darkened the fuzzy fabric. Sand crusted the soles and clung to the sides in gritty streaks. A few grains scattered onto my palm as I turned them over.

My mouth went dry. Mia had been outside, not just on top of the bluff, for these weren't muddy from dirt or clay. This was beach sand.

Mia had told me they never went down to the beach. They'd gone to bed before midnight. She'd stayed in her sleeping bag all night.

But these slippers told a different story.

The interview at the precinct with the detectives was tomorrow morning, less than twelve hours from now. How could I possibly prepare myself and Mia for something like this?

I looked down at the slippers in my lap, then at Mia sleeping on the bed, her face peaceful in the dim moonlight filtering through the curtains. Perhaps I should toss them in the washing machine, scrub away the crusted sand, the lake water, the potential evidence.

I forced myself to slide the slippers back into the bag. For now.

Icy dread seeped into my veins. The traitorous thoughts kept swirling inside my head, unbidden. Mia had lied about the slippers. But why? And what else could she be lying about?

Chapter Nine

The interview room at the precinct felt like a freezer, the chill sinking deep into my bones, despite my Detroit Lions sweatshirt. The walls were painted an institutional gray, and the air reeked of coffee and sweat.

Mia sat beside me in a metal chair, her shoulders curved inward as if trying to make herself disappear. Her fingers twisted and untwisted in her lap. Dark shadows smudged her bloodshot eyes, evidence of the sleepless nights that plagued us both.

On her other side sat Camille Hayward, exuding a calm steadiness I didn't share. Anxiety curdled in my stomach. Even though Camille had gone over every detail with us earlier, I didn't feel any more prepared.

Still, if I wanted anyone by our side in this mess, it was Camille. At 45, she was striking and stylish, her warm brown skin glowing, her natural hair worn in a short coiled fro she often accessorized with colorful headscarves.

She wore bold colors and statement earrings like armor, owning any room she entered. Camille didn't waste time on fake pleasantries or pretending to like people, and her tolerance for nonsense was about two seconds long on a good day.

I admired her confidence, her boldness, her brutal honesty. She was impossible to intimidate, and we needed that brashness right now.

The door to the interrogation room opened. Detectives Judah King and Sarah Callahan entered, their expressions friendly, open, and sympathetic.

It was their eyes, though, that I feared, that they would turn their sharp suspicious gazes on my daughter.

"Good afternoon, Mia, Ms. Kincaid, and Ms. Hayward." Detective King pulled out a metal chair across from us. Callahan settled beside him as Detective King reached across the table and turned the little black recorder on. An ominous red light blinked on.

He leaned back, his posture deliberately casual. "Mia, you're here voluntarily. You can leave anytime. Your mom and your lawyer are here, and you don't have to answer anything you're not comfortable with. We're just trying to understand what happened to your friend. Okay?"

Mia nodded, barely perceptible. "I understand."

To the camera, he said, "This is Detective Judah King and Detective Sarah Callahan with the St. Joseph Police Department. It is 10:03 a.m., on Tuesday, April twelfth. We're in Interview Room Two with minor witness Mia Kincaid, her mother, Dahlia Kincaid, and their attorney, Camille Hayward. This interview is being recorded."

"Let the record reflect that Mia is here voluntarily as a witness, not a suspect." Camille's hand tightened on Mia's forearm. "Mia will answer questions she feels comfortable answering. If this becomes adversarial or coercive, we will terminate this conversation and leave."

King said, "Understood."

Camille said to Mia. "Answer only what you know. If you don't know, say you don't know. Look at me if you need a break."

Mia nodded again.

My heart raced, my palms clammy. I wanted to gather her up,

tuck her under my arm like when she was little, and run with her out of this grim, soulless place.

"I'm right here," I said under my breath, just for Mia.

King pulled a pen from his pocket and flipped open his leather notebook. "Okay, Mia. We just have a few questions we'd like to go over with you."

Callahan clasped her hands on the table and leaned forward. "We know this is a difficult time for you, and we're sorry for the loss of your friend, Leah. We really appreciate your help."

Mia's jaw tightened. "Okay."

"We've talked with the other girls as well, and now we'd like to hear from you, in your own words, what happened that night," King said.

Uneasiness slithered through me. What had the other girls said? Did their stories match Mia's? What would happen if they didn't?

"Can you tell us what happened when you arrived at Chloe's house?" King asked.

Mia took a shaky breath. "We got there around 5 p.m. We got ready in Chloe's bathroom, did our hair and makeup, put our dresses on, and went out to the bluff. I took a bunch of pictures of all the girls. Then we went back inside and ate the chicken tacos that Mrs. Westinghouse ordered from Azul Tequila. We watched the newest Hunger Games movie, talked about school and the dance, and went to bed around 11:30 p.m."

"Did you go down to the beach for photos?" King asked.

"No, we stayed on top of the bluff. It was more dramatic high up with the lake in the background."

"So, you never went down to the beach?"

Mia shook her head. "No."

I went still, thinking of Mia's sandy slippers in her closet.

"Mia," King said mildly, "did you and Leah have any disagreements Friday night? Even a small one? It's okay if you did. Friends argue. That's normal."

"We... we were fine," Mia said. "Everyone was just laughing and goofing off. Taking pictures. No one was fighting." She blinked and looked down at the table.

I glanced at Camille. She maintained her composed façade, her expression unreadable. Her gold hoop earrings glinted under the harsh lights. She looked unflappable, while my heart hammered in my chest, each beat echoing loudly in my ears.

"Did you or the other girls drink any alcohol or smoke some pot or anything else?" Callahan asked.

"Not that I know of."

"Have you ever sleepwalked or are you on any sleep medication like Ambien?" Callahan asked.

"Don't answer that, Mia," Camille said. "Detective, you told us this was a witness interview. If you consider Mia a suspect, we're done here."

Callahan smiled, showing too many teeth. "We're simply trying to determine if there was any impaired behavior that may have affected memory or altered normal behavior with anyone at the sleepover."

Mia jumped in. "No, we didn't do anything like that."

Camille gave the detectives a sharp look. "You have your answer. Now move on."

"What time did you go to bed?" King asked, though Mia had already answered that question.

"Around 11:30 p.m., I think. Around then. We were tired. It was a busy week."

"And you stayed in your sleeping bag all night?" Callahan asked.

"Yes," Mia said. "I was tired. I didn't get up."

"And you didn't see Leah again after you went to sleep?" King asked.

"No. She was in her sleeping bag when I fell asleep. That's all I know."

"Alexis mentioned waking up around 12:30 in the morning to get a drink of water," Callahan said. "She says your sleeping bag was empty."

"Alexis is wrong," Mia said quickly. "She must've... gotten confused."

"She was quite specific," Callahan said. "She remembers being annoyed that she had only slept for an hour, and she claims Leah's sleeping bag looked empty, too."

Mia looked affronted. "Alexis was the one not in her sleeping bag, not me!"

"I thought you were sleeping the whole time?" Callahan asked.

"I—I woke up once, I guess, to adjust my pillow. I saw her bag was empty then."

Camille cut in, "We don't know what Alexis saw or didn't see in a dark basement with other girls moving around."

"That's what we're trying to clarify." King spread his hands in a conciliatory gesture. "We're not accusing anyone. We're just seeing some patterns we'd like your help to understand, Mia."

"Move along," Camille said.

"There are also some things we heard from the neighbors," Callahan said. "Specifically, Mrs. Atkins, who lives next door to the Westinghouse home."

Camille cleared her throat. "If you have a statement, we'll review it later. But you know as well as I do you can't treat neighbors' gossip like fact."

"Mrs. Atkins called the non-emergency line Saturday," Callahan continued as if Camille hadn't spoken. "She reported that she heard voices out by the bluff around 12:15 a.m., early Saturday morning. Female voices, talking loudly. Whose voices, Mia?"

The room chilled. Mia's gaze snapped up, wide and startled, meeting Callahan's for the first time. Raw panic flared for a moment before she forced her gaze back down to the table. "I don't know who that was."

"Mrs. Atkins is seventy-nine years old," Camille said. "I will need to see her auditory records before I accept the reliability of her hearing from two hundred feet away. Next question, detectives."

"Let's talk about your camera," Callahan said, changing tactics. "A Nikon D780, correct?"

"Yes," Mia said. "My dad gave it to me for my thirteenth birthday. It was his before."

"Sounds like it's special to you."

Mia nodded.

The missing Nikon had been a constant ache in my chest since Saturday. His last birthday gift to her. The way he'd placed it in her hands with exaggerated ceremony. How she'd thrown her arms around his neck, nearly knocking them both over, laughing with delight.

Mia wouldn't misplace it. I knew that with all my heart.

Callahan said, "You took your Nikon to the Westinghouse property on Friday night, correct?"

"Yes," Mia said.

"And you used it for the photo shoot by the bluff. And then took it inside, right?"

"Yes."

"Where is it now?"

"I don't know. It wasn't in its case in the morning."

"When was the last time you saw it?"

"When I came in from the photo shoot. I put it in the case, next to my overnight bag, beside the patio doors. Maybe someone took it out by accident, and it got left somewhere."

I could picture Rowan's spacious walk-out basement. It was the size of another house, with an open floor plan that included a game room with ping-pong, air hockey, and a pool table, a movie room with a giant screen, a full-sized kitchen, and a second family room.

Plenty of space for something like a camera to disappear without anyone noticing.

"The problem is," Callahan said, "we did a thorough search of the basement with the homeowners' consent. We didn't find your camera. Not in the basement. Not near the bluff. Nowhere."

A buzzing started in my ears.

"It's a camera," Camille interjected. "Portable. Handheld. It could've been moved. It could've been stolen. One of the other girls could have taken it."

"Perhaps," Callahan agreed evenly. "We've talked to the other girls and looked through their phones. Mia, your camera also has photos from the night Leah died, which we haven't seen yet. That makes it pretty important to our investigation." She let that sit for a moment. "Mia, if that camera turns up, what will we find on it?"

Mia's voice was barely a whisper. "Pictures from the photo shoot."

"Just the photo shoot? Nothing from later that night?"

"I don't know. I don't remember."

"You don't remember if you took more photos at midnight or later, or at any other time before the camera went missing?"

Mia looked at Camille helplessly.

"Don't answer," Camille said. "Detectives, unless you have that camera and can show us what's on it, this is pure speculation. I'm going to say this again: she's here voluntarily. You start throwing out hypotheticals you can't substantiate, we're out."

King's eyes flicked to Callahan. Callahan straightened and uncrossed her arms. The air in the room shifted, sharpened. "We can substantiate something. The dress."

I saw it again in my mind's eye, on the hanger the police officer had held up in Rowan's living room on Saturday morning: the rose-gold fabric torn along the hem, the muddy smears, the dark stains blooming down the front like dead flower petals.

Mia tensed. The air thrummed between us.

Camille's eyes narrowed. King seemed to sense her impending protest and attempted to head her off. "It was visible evidence at a crime scene. The homeowner consented to our collection of evidence from her property. We secured the scene first, and then we notified parents after collecting evidence."

"I'll be reviewing the exact circumstances of that seizure. If I find any Fourth Amendment violations, the judge will suppress that evidence, if it comes to that."

"You're welcome to try, Counselor. But the dress was in plain view at an active crime scene. The homeowner gave the police permission to go downstairs. Any judge will uphold that seizure."

"The girls had a reasonable expectation of privacy. Each child's parent needed to give consent to search that area. My daughter was present, and I know I didn't give consent."

"We'll leave that up to the judge to decide," King said mildly.

Camille's lips pressed into a thin line of disapproval, but she let it go.

"Mia," Callahan said. "How did your dress get those tears in it?"

"During the photo shoot, I was taking photos of Peyton, trying to get a low shot, with her dress billowing in the wind. I slipped. I fell a few feet down the bluff before I caught a branch. My dress tore. It got dirt on it."

"Did Peyton witness this?"

"I dunno. I don't think so. She was turned away from me. The other girls were busy talking."

"And the scratches on your arms?"

Mia's fingers dug into the sleeves of her sweatshirt. The fabric pulled tight across her knuckles. "Thornbushes, from when I slipped."

"We spoke with the other girls. Not one of them remembers you slipping. Not one remembers you climbing anywhere near thorny bushes." Callahan paused. "They said you were careful with your camera, that you wouldn't risk dropping it."

Mia's voice wavered. "They... maybe they didn't notice. I told you, they were distracted, talking, and laughing."

Callahan glanced down at her notes. "The blood on the dress. Whose blood is it?"

Camille leaned in, her hand on Mia's forearm. "You don't need to answer that."

Something moved across Mia's face. A hitch at the corner of her mouth, then it was gone. "It was mine. From the bushes. My arms were bleeding, so I wiped them on the dress without thinking. It was the golden hour, so I didn't have time to go back in the house for a Band-Aid, or the light would be gone."

"Didn't it upset you that your dress for the dance got ruined?" Callahan asked.

Mia shrugged. "Not really."

She didn't look at me. She'd known we had no money for a replacement, that I'd spent a significant chunk of our meager savings to ensure she had a gown to wear that wouldn't get her mocked by her swanky friends. Bougie, she called them. She would've been upset that she'd ruined it.

"There's no possibility that the blood could be Leah's?"

Mia's gaze darted away.

"Detectives," Camille warned.

Callahan opened the manila folder and slid a glossy eight-by-ten photo across the table toward Camille. "We had the dress tested. We're still waiting on DNA, but they did a basic ABO blood typing at the lab."

"Hold on," Camille cut in, tapping the photo with her pen but not looking down at it yet. "Let's not represent preliminary lab work as conclusive science."

"It's blood typing," Callahan said. "The stains on the front of the dress came back A-positive. Leah's blood type."

She turned her eyes to Mia, sharp and bright. "Do you know your blood type, Mia?"

Mia shook her head.

The buzzing in my ears grew louder. Mia's blood type was B-negative. It couldn't be Mia's blood on that dress. She'd lied to the police—again. Camille shot me a warning look to keep my mouth shut. I clenched my jaw and wiped my clammy hands on my thighs.

"It's incredibly premature to suggest whose blood is on that dress," Camille said, her voice edge with steel. "You have a common blood type and a garment that passed through non-secured locations. Chain of custody will be an issue if you try to rely on that."

"It's valid," King said. "We followed procedure."

Mia's breathing had gone shallow. I could see the rapid flutter at the base of her throat. Her gaze remained fixed on the table, as if the scratched metal was suddenly fascinating.

"Mia," King said. "Are you positive it's your blood on that dress? Is there any way Leah's blood might have gotten on your dress Friday night?"

Mia shook her head hard.

He leaned forward, forearms on the table, his voice dipping even softer. "Your friend says your sleeping bag was empty at 12:30 a.m. A neighbor heard girls' voices by the bluff around 12:15 a.m. There's A-positive blood on your dress, the same type as Leah's. Your camera, with photos from that night, is missing. How do you explain all of that?"

I could taste metal at the back of my mouth. I clenched my teeth so hard that my jaw ached. Mia had lied. She'd lied to the police. I couldn't wrap my head around it.

Trepidation curled in my gut like a snake eating its tail. Why would she lie? Unless she was hiding something. But what? And why?

Mia's lower lip trembled. "I was in my sleeping bag," she whispered. "All night."

King continued, "You look like you're carrying something heavy. And I get that. This is a lot. You lost a friend. People are asking you questions you don't know how to answer without making things worse. Secrets don't get lighter, though. They get heavier."

I watched Mia's face as conflicting emotions flared across her features. Doubt. Fear. Hesitation. Regret. She was fourteen. She still slept with the door cracked open, still got nervous when thunderstorms rolled in, still cried at sad animal commercials. How had we gotten here?

Camille put her hand on Mia's arm. "You don't have to answer questions that make you uncomfortable. In fact, let's stop this right now."

"If we stop," Callahan said, "we'll have to work with what we've got. When the lab reports come back, if they don't match what you told us..." She made a small, almost delicate gesture with her hand. A little explosion.

Camille gave a dismissive grunt. "Detective, while that might scare someone representing themselves pro se, I am hardly that. If you've decided my client is a suspect, continuing this interview will hardly be productive."

King kept his focus on Mia. "Is there anything you want to change about your statement that you stayed in your sleeping bag all night?"

Silence. Mia's eyes glistened. She blinked hard, refusing to let the tears fall. "No. I wasn't... I didn't... "

"Mia," Camille said, and there was real warning there now.

Mia's head dipped lower.

Apprehension filled me. I twisted Marcus's ring on the chain beneath my shirt, the repetitive motion the only thing keeping me anchored to my chair, to this cold hostile room.

"I didn't want anything bad to happen—" She sucked in a breath and shook her head hard, as if she could dislodge whatever memories haunted her. She pressed her hands to her face, her sleeves covering her fingers. A small half-sob escaped her throat.

I couldn't stand it anymore. The words tore out of me. "Tell the truth, honey. Whatever it is, we can handle it."

Camille shot me a reproachful look as she rose to her feet. "I think we're done here for the moment. I need to consult with my client right now."

"We went out again," Mia blurted. "To the bluff."

Chapter Ten

The interview room went in and out of focus. It was difficult to breathe. I couldn't take my eyes off my daughter.

"Careful," Camille said to Mia, looking flustered for the first time. This was not what we'd gone over in our pre-interview meeting. "If you're going to change anything about your earlier statement, we need to take a break now—"

"No," Mia said with more force than anything she'd said all morning. "No breaks. If I stop, I won't say it. I just need to say it."

A vein pulsed in Camille's temple. "Mia—"

Mia looked at me, desperation in her eyes. "I want to, Mom."

I looked between them, uncertain whether to agree with Camille or defend Mia. Camille was the expert, but Mia wanted to unburden herself, and I only wanted to support her, however I could. The truth mattered. For Leah, for her grieving family, for all of us.

Tremulously, I nodded. Camille scowled in irritation but waved a hand for the interview to continue.

"When did you go back out to the bluff?" King asked, his voice low and gentle, coaxing.

"After everyone went to bed." Her words tumbled out now, tripping over each other in their rush to get out. "For another photoshoot. A midnight photoshoot. Chloe said the moon was bright and that it would look better. She wanted... she wanted different vibes. Just us."

Callahan leaned in. Her eyes were glinting and laser-focused on Mia. "Who's 'us'?"

"Me, Chloe, and Leah," Mia said. "The three of us."

"What time was this?" King asked.

"After midnight. Everyone else was asleep. Chloe came over to my sleeping bag and kicked it, like, gently. She said, 'Wake up, Kincaid, we're doing Round Two.' She said the moon was perfect."

"And Leah?" King asked. "How did she end up going with you?"

"She was awake," Mia said. "Or half-awake. Chloe said we needed her. She had us get dressed again in the downstairs bathroom. Then we snuck out."

"How?"

"Through the patio doors, in the basement."

The image unfolded unbidden in my mind: three girls tiptoeing through a sleeping house, their whispered giggles, their phone screens illuminating the dark. Moonlight pouring silver over the backyard with the bluff looming, the lake like a black mouth.

"You took your camera?" King asked.

"Yes."

"Did Zara or Alexis or anyone else wake up?" Callahan asked.

"I don't think so," Mia said. "No one said anything. We were quiet."

"Then what happened?" King asked. "Take your time."

Mia gulped for air. Her hands shook. "I took pictures of Chloe posing, then Leah, and then Leah took a few pictures of me. Leah said she was dizzy. She... she would get like that. With heights. Chloe wanted, like, edgy shots. She told Leah to stand closer to the edge, to lean back a little, like she wasn't scared. Leah kept saying she hated heights. It happened sometimes when she was nervous. She got these stupid nosebleeds."

"How bad was the bleeding?" King asked.

"It was dripping," Mia said. "Down her lip. Onto her chin. And onto my dress. I was holding her arm. She grabbed me when she got dizzy. It—" She gestured helplessly. "It got on me. That's why..."

"That's why Leah's blood is on your dress," King finished for her.

"Yeah."

"The match proves nothing." Camille scribbled on a notepad. "Leah got nosebleeds. You can confirm this with her parents and friends."

Camille was right. Leah had the occasional bloody nose, especially when the air was cold and dry, or when she was nervous or stressed. I'd helped her a few times when it happened at my house.

I studied the detectives, trying to ascertain whether they believed her. It was plausible. Mia was telling the truth. They had to believe her.

"Leah said she was fine," Mia said. "She just needed a tissue. She kept pinching her nose. We weren't, like, fighting or anything."

"And then?" Callahan prompted when she didn't continue.

"And then we went inside, all of us, together. We shut the door. We wiped the blood off. I changed into my pajamas, they went to the bathroom, and we went back to the basement. I got into my sleeping bag. That's it. I didn't see Leah again. I thought she was in her sleeping bag, asleep like everyone else."

I exhaled. Something released inside me. It made sense. It made horrible sense. The blood on the dress, the second photo shoot, the neighbor hearing voices, and even the scratches on Mia's arms. It fit if you smoothed the edges and didn't look too hard at the gaps.

Except for the missing camera. And the sandy slippers, which only I knew about. Those pricked like burrs beneath my skin.

"You're saying," Callahan said, careful, like she was handling something volatile, "that all three of you—Chloe, Leah, and you—went back inside together after Leah's nosebleed. That you saw Leah walk back into the house."

"Yes. She was right there, behind me."

"You're certain of that," Callahan pressed. "She wasn't left outside. She didn't go somewhere alone."

"She was with us," Mia insisted. "Ask Chloe. She'll tell you."

"We're interviewing you right now, not Chloe," Callahan said, her voice cool.

Mia glanced at me, her face flushing. "Leah must have gone out later, alone. When we were all asleep. I didn't see anything. I didn't do anything!"

"Mia," King said. "You've done the hard part. Just help us understand what happened at the bluff. You say you didn't push Leah. Okay. Then did anyone touch her? Did she slip? Did she climb over the edge? Did you see or hear anyone else outside during that time?"

Tears spilled down Mia's cheeks. Her breath came in shallow gasps. "I didn't see anything! I told you, I didn't do anything!"

"That's enough," Camille said, sharper now. "My client is clearly overwhelmed. Detectives, we're done here."

King held up a hand. "Ms. Hayward, if we could just..."

Camille stood. "This interview is over."

Callahan leaned forward. "In about seventy-two hours, we're going to have DNA results back. Fast-tracked due to the publicity and the sensitive nature of this case. DNA from the blood on your dress. From the skin cells under Leah's nails. From anything she touched. If your story doesn't match what the science shows, it will be a lot worse than telling us the truth now."

Camille snorted. "Save the dramatics for a jury. When the DNA comes back, you'll have nothing. To recap, Detectives, you may lose the dress in a motion to suppress, there's a viable explanation for the blood of the victim on the dress, and your eyewitness is so old she could have worked in a factory during the Second World War, making ball bearings for B-17s. Hardly a slam dunk case."

She turned to Mia now. "Stand up. We're leaving."

As she stood, Mia's desperate gaze landed on me. For a moment, there was nothing else in the room. Just my daughter's teary eyes and the questions she didn't have words for. *Can you believe me? Can you still love me if you don't?*

My throat closed. Despite Camille's bravado, anxiety curdled in my gut. I didn't share a shred of her confidence. Seventy-two hours, Callahan had said. Three days.

Camille's hand pressed into the small of my back, guiding me toward the door. Mia moved woodenly beside me.

As we exited the interrogation room, the world came rushing back. Officers watched us with suspicious gazes. The precinct buzzed with activity: murmured conversations, an officer laughing too loudly at something in a cubicle, the distant bark of a dispatcher's orders.

Mia clung to my arm as Camille strode down the hallway, her gaze fixed straight ahead. She looked capable, formidable. Once again, I was incredibly grateful she was on our side.

A knot twisted in my stomach. Did she believe Mia? Or was she already doubting her decision to take on our case?

"Mom," Mia whispered. "I'm sorry I lied."

I squeezed her hand. "We'll talk later."

Camille halted a few steps ahead, glancing back at us before scanning the hallway. Satisfied that no one was within earshot, she lowered her voice. "There will be reporters outside. Someone tipped them off that Mia was at the station. They'll assume she's a suspect, even without an arrest. We need to discuss our next steps, but here's what happens next. Go home, stay off social media. Dahlia, consider keeping Mia home from school. Don't talk to anyone about this case. If the police call, you call me. If a neighbor asks a single question, you say 'no comment'. 'No comment' is the only thing you say from now on. Both of you. Understood?"

Dread settled like a stone in my stomach. "If they think Mia did it, what are they waiting for?"

"Mia is only fourteen," Camille said. "This case could draw national attention, and the police are treading carefully. Arresting a grieving eighth grader without solid, indisputable evidence could very easily backfire on them, the mayor, and the D.A. And in an election year, too. They're building their case methodically. But make no mistake, they are building it."

"What does that mean for us?"

"It means," Camille said, "that we need to build a vigorous defense. Gather our own evidence, line up character witnesses, anything that can help."

"The blood, her fingernails..."

"We concede nothing without the actual DNA results or context. They're attempting to intimidate us into revealing information. We don't give them anything more. We make them work for it. Leah and Mia were together, and transfer happens in a dozen ways."

Her phone buzzed. She glanced at it and swore under her breath. "They're moving fast. An article in the Detroit Free Press just released. The story is gaining traction, which is attention we don't need."

"How bad is this?" I asked.

Camille's eyes met mine. Something like sympathy flickered for a moment, then vanished. "It's bad enough. Keep your head. Protect your kid. And Dahlia?"

"Yes?"

"Find that camera before the authorities do."

Mia's grip on my hand tightened. Her nails dug into my skin.

I nodded numbly. "Thank you, Camille. For everything."

"Don't thank me yet." A commotion in the foyer drew our attention. The muffled sounds of voices grew louder, more insistent. Camille's expression hardened. "The media. We have to get through them."

I peered toward the glass doors at the front of the precinct. The exit doors waited, panes of glass reflecting our warped shadows. The sky had transformed into a drab, dreary gray.

Beyond the doors, a cluster of reporters pressed against the barriers, camera lights flashing. Rain slicked the sidewalks. Umbrellas bobbed like dark mushrooms in the crowd.

Mia's face paled. "I—I can't. I don't want to go out there."

"Just keep your head down and stay close to me." Camille adjusted her coat, her gaze steely. "I'll lead the way. Do not engage with them. No comments, no reactions. Understood?"

We both nodded. Taking a deep breath, we pushed forward. The moment we stepped outside, the icy rain hit us. The scent of wet pavement and exhaust filled my lungs.

Raindrops spat against my face as I blinked against the blinding flash of cameras. Two dozen reporters swarmed us, their mics thrust forward, lenses clicking, voices overlapping.

Questions bombarded us from all sides:

"Did your daughter push Leah Cho to her death, Mrs. Kincaid?"

"Mia, do you have anything to say to the victim's family?"

A reporter thrust a microphone an inch from my face. "Mrs. Kincaid! Is your daughter a murderer?"

Alarmed, Mia reeled toward me. I folded her behind my body, my arms a makeshift barricade. My entire body thrummed with anger and humiliation.

I couldn't summon the words to respond. I knew how this worked. They would twist whatever I said anyway.

"No comment!" Camille cut a path through the crush of jostling reporters. "Back up!"

A reporter with spiky blond hair stepped directly into our path, his eyes lit with rabid glee. "Mrs. Kincaid, did your daughter murder her best friend? How does it feel to be the mother of a monster? What kind of mother are you, anyway?"

I couldn't hide the tremble in my voice. "Get out of our way!"

He smirked. "Mia, did you kill your best friend?"

Outrage surged through my veins. I wanted to punch him in his smirking face. Before I could respond, Camille forced her way between us. "This is harassment. Back off or I'll taser you."

We finally reached the car. Mia scrambled inside, and I followed. My hands shook so hard I fumbled with the seatbelt twice before it clicked. Camille shut the driver's side door, acting as a shield from the mob.

I locked the doors. The reporters pressed against the windows, their faces distorted through the streaming rain. I accelerated hard, scattering the crowd as I screeched out of the precinct parking lot. The man with the spiky hair jumped back and glared at me, shouting expletives as we passed.

In the rearview mirror, the clumps of jostling reporters grew smaller as we drove down M63. The tires hissed against the wet asphalt, and rain splattered the windshield, the streetlights like smears of amber in the downpour.

The town slid past: brick storefronts, a flag snapping on the pole outside the courthouse, a couple wearing ponchos darting into the Copper Pot diner. Normal life marched on.

My hands gripped the wheel so tightly my knuckles turned white. I blinked rapidly as tears of anger and frustration welled up.

"I can't believe those animals," I muttered, more to myself than to Mia. "How dare they ambush us like that?"

A soft whimper came from the passenger seat. I glanced over. Mia was curled in on herself, the sleeves of her sweatshirt drawn over her hands as her shoulders shook with silent sobs.

I remembered her chubby toddler hands cupped around a lightning bug, the careful way she'd opened them to let it go.

Without thinking, I pulled into the parking lot of a hardware store. The neon sign flickered weakly. I turned off the engine, reached over, and pulled her into my arms.

"I would never try to hurt her."

"I know, honey. I know."

Still, I couldn't stop the thought that speared through my mind: someone had killed Leah Cho.

The prime suspect was my daughter.

Chapter Eleven

"It's okay," I said, even though nothing felt okay. "I'm here. I've got you."

Mia clung to me desperately. "I'm so sorry," she choked out between sobs. "I didn't mean for any of this to happen."

I smoothed her damp hair. "We'll find a way through this."

She pulled back. "You don't understand. Everyone thinks I did it. Even you might think so."

"Mia, look at me." I waited until her eyes met mine. "I love you more than anything in this world, and I don't believe you killed Leah, not for a second."

She wiped at her cheeks angrily. "I should've been there for her. I should've been better..."

"No, don't blame yourself."

The rain drummed on the roof of the car. I wasn't sure if I should say anything else, or if she simply wanted my presence, my comforting touch.

I tried not to think about the damp slippers stuffed at the bottom of her overnight bag, the crusted sand, the way they'd felt cold and heavy in my hands.

We went inside. All of us. Together.

That's what Mia had told the detectives. That's what she'd sworn.

My throat tightened. Maybe I should have mentioned the slippers, should have told King and Callahan, or asked Mia right there in the interrogation room, with Camille present, with everything on the record.

But I hadn't.

I'd kept my mouth shut and let my daughter lie.

The questions the reporter had screamed at me echoed in my skull. *What kind of mother are you, anyway?*

Did keeping quiet make me a better mother? Or a terrible person?

I replayed Mia's story in my mind, testing each piece against what I knew. If they'd all gone inside and no one had gone to the beach that night, then why were Mia's slippers damp with beach sand?

The bluff consisted of clay, dirt, and rocks. The beach was a hundred feet down a steep slope, accessible only by wooden stairs or a perilous scramble down slick clay, through scrubby underbrush and thornbushes.

Why would Mia go down to the beach?

When would she have gone?

I glanced at her out of the corner of my eye. She sat motionless, staring out at the rain, her profile small and shadowed.

"I need to ask you something. Be honest with me, no matter what it is."

"I am being honest."

"Last night, I went through your overnight bag."

Her eyebrows pinched. "You what?"

"You told me you didn't go down to the beach that night." I kept my tone clinical, detached. I didn't want to make her more upset or defensive. "You said everyone stayed at the top of the bluff."

"Yeah. It'd be too hard to go down all those stairs and back up again in our dresses."

"I found your slippers stuffed at the bottom of your bag, damp and full of sand."

Whatever color had come back to her face faded again. Even her lips went pale. "What?"

"When did you go down to the beach, Mia?"

The denial was instant, reflexive. "I didn't."

"Then how did your slippers get wet and sandy?"

"I don't know. I didn't end up wearing them. I slept in my socks, so I never took them out of my overnight bag. Ask the girls."

I watched her closely, hardly daring to breathe. "Where was the bag?"

"By the patio doors, beside my camera case. Anyone could have borrowed them." She wrapped her arms around herself, fingers digging into her elbows. Her sleeves slid up her arms, revealing the scratches. "I didn't go to the beach that night. I know how bad it looks, but I swear, Mom, I didn't."

My heartbeat thudded in my ears. She was telling the truth, or she had grown into an excellent liar, which frightened me more than I wanted to admit. I used to know with absolute certainty whether she was keeping something from me. Now, I wasn't certain at all.

"Okay." Still, something bothered me, like I wasn't getting the complete picture yet, but pushing her harder would only make her withdraw further from me than she already had. "Okay, honey."

Mia exhaled shakily. Some of the tension leaked from her shoulders. Her tears had subsided. "Can we just go home?"

"Of course." I started the car again, pulling back onto the slick road. The wipers beat a steady rhythm against the windshield. Rain sheeted down in waves, turning the world beyond the glass into a smeared watercolor.

I swallowed and focused on the road through the windshield. The heater blasted warm air that smelled faintly of mildew.

Seventy-two hours. Three days until the DNA results came back.

Three days to find out if my daughter was telling the truth. To decide what I was going to do with the evidence I was hiding. Should I wash the sandy slippers? Throw them out? What was on the camera? How was I supposed to find it?

Apprehension, doubt, and worry pressed like heavy stones on my chest.

We slowed as we approached the Blackthorn Shores security gates. Security lights cast harsh white pools across the wet pavement. A cluster of reporters stood right behind the private property line, their umbrellas tilted against the wind, cameras at the ready.

The reporters surged forward, shouting questions I couldn't hear through the glass. Frank waved us through quickly, stepping between our car and the mob.

I nodded my thanks and drove past the security gates, then headed west on Cliff Harbor Drive. Inside the gates, the neighborhood felt different from before, like we were being watched from every direction.

The Cromwell's front door opened and two small faces peered out. Mrs. Cromwell appeared behind her twins, saw our car, and pulled them inside. The door slammed shut.

"Great," I muttered. "The rumor mill is in overdrive."

Mia sank lower in her seat. "They're all gonna hate me. Everyone at school. Everyone here."

"Let them think what they want." The words came out sharper than I had intended. I softened my voice. "We know the truth. That's what matters."

But even as I spoke the words, doubt gnawed at me.

Did we know the truth?

At the community playground, the swings sat empty and forlorn. The rain lightened to a soft sprinkle.

I kept my eyes forward. Almost home. Almost safe.

We passed Whitney's house, then Camille's. As we approached our house, I spotted Alexis at the foot of our driveway, in front of our mailbox.

The hood of her sweatshirt was cinched over her head,

obscuring her face. She watched us approach, then lifted her phone and aimed it at our windshield.

The sleeve of Alexis's sweatshirt slipped down as she raised her phone, revealing a bruise on her wrist. Deep purple. Circular. As if someone had grabbed her arm hard.

I blinked, looked again. It was still there.

Alexis lowered the phone and waved. The bruise disappeared beneath her sleeve. The smile that spread across her face was slow, deliberate. Something cold in it.

"Do you see that?" Mia asked, her voice ragged. "She's taking pictures. Of us."

"Yeah, I see her."

"She knows those reporters are out there. She's going to send them the photos. Or worse, post them on..." Her voice trailed off.

"Post them where?"

"Never mind."

My stomach sank. "Alexis is your friend. Why would she do that?"

"Ugh, Mom. Whatever gets her more likes, okay? She pretends she hates her mom, but they're the same like that. That's all she cares about."

I forced my foot to stay steady on the gas pedal, to refrain from slamming on the brakes, rolling down the window, and demanding Alexis delete the pictures she'd just taken.

It wouldn't matter. The damage was already done.

What I really wanted to do was to ask her a few pointed questions about that suspicious bruising. Had the police seen it? They must have. "Did you know Alexis has a bruised wrist?"

"I dunno, Mom. What does it matter? Just let it go, okay?"

Alexis stalked down the street toward Driftwood Terrace and her house. I bit my lip. What if that bruise was from Leah? What if Leah had grabbed Alexis as she fell? Was Brooke's daughter the one who pushed Leah? And why did it look like Alexis had been walking down our driveway when we'd turned the corner?

Questions swirled in my mind. But I wouldn't get them

answered right now, so I forced myself to let Alexis go, like Mia wanted. As she disappeared around the corner, I pulled into our gravel driveway.

The cottage sat dark and silent. Beyond the bluff, the lake had disappeared in the spitting rain, the horizon blurred, as if the edge of the cliff was the edge of the world itself.

From our cottage, I couldn't see Rowan's house. But I could imagine it blazing with light, every window glowing. I could picture it perfectly: the mothers clustered around Rowan's marble island, wine glasses in hand, voices low and urgent as they discussed the latest rumors surrounding the case.

I killed the engine. The tick of the cooling motor broke the silence. "Once the police find out what really happened, this will go away."

"What if they don't?"

"They will." I hoped I sounded certain, for Mia's sake.

She stared straight ahead. "I'm tired. I just want to go inside."

I reached over to squeeze her hand before we stepped out into the rain, then we hurried to the front door. Our shoes splashed through shallow puddles on the uneven driveway.

I fumbled in my purse for my keys. Then I saw it.

I seized Mia's arm. "Wait."

The front door was ajar.

Chapter Twelve

I stared at our little house. That feeling struck me again—a sense of violation, of wrongness. The feeling of not being alone in a place where you believed you were very much alone.

Mia had gone rigid. "Did you forget to lock the door?"

"No, of course not." I rubbed my exhausted, heavy-lidded eyes with the back of my arm. How much had I slept last night? Two hours? Three? Even less the night before. "At least, I don't think so."

We were both thinking of Marcus, of that terrible night that had scarred us both.

The front door had been ajar then, just like now.

The memory surged through my brain, relentless and unbidden. The cake box in my hand. Mia in her canary-yellow dress with the white flowers laughing at some dad joke Marcus had told as we walked up the path to our home. A celebration for straight A's.

The key had never touched the lock. The front door was cracked open. Cold air spilled out.

Marcus's shoulder brushed mine as he stepped ahead. His voice came out low and rough. "Stay back."

But we hadn't. Of course, we hadn't.

We slipped in behind him, our shoes squeaking on the hardwood. The house was too quiet. The TV was off, no cartoon noise, just the hum of the fridge. Our dog was at the groomer's. No one was supposed to be there.

The hallway seemed to stretch on forever. Every shadow looked like a crouched creature waiting to spring at us.

"Hello?" Marcus called. No answer.

We moved deeper into the house. The cake box grew heavy in my hands, its cardboard edges biting into my fingers.

Then I saw it. A blur of movement at the end of the bedroom hallway. A large dark figure bolted sideways into the kitchen. Headed for the back slider.

Marcus charged. "Stop! Hey!"

My body moved before my brain could catch up. I grabbed Mia's arm and yanked her with me, shoving her down behind the kitchen island. Her yellow dress fanned out on the cold linoleum.

"Don't move!" My heart hammered in my throat. Adrenaline surged through me, making me slow, clumsy, stupid.

I fumbled for my phone but couldn't find the right pocket. My fingers felt thick, unwieldy. The cake box slid from my other hand. It hit the floor with a wet thud.

I peeked around the corner of the island. Marcus and the intruder were locked in a vicious battle. A chair skidded, then fell onto its side. Someone grunted. Shoes scraped across the floor.

The gun appeared. Black metal in the intruder's hand, materializing out of nowhere.

A thin, broken sound tore from my throat. "Marcus—!"

A single shot rang out. A crack that split the world.

Marcus's body jerked.

Time went wrong, thick and slow.

He collapsed straight down, like his strings had been cut.

The dark figure sprinted through the kitchen, into the foyer, and out the front door.

I dropped the phone. It squawked, "911, what's your emergency?" I crawled to my husband on my hands and knees. Something cold and sticky soaked my palms. Melted ice cream cake. And blood.

His shirt blooming red. I pressed my hands to the wound, hard then harder. I felt the hot, slick gush under my fingers.

"Stay with me," I begged. "Stay, just stay." The words useless and frantic. "Don't leave me!"

He tried to breathe. The sound came out wet and rattling. His eyes searched my face, then slid past me. "Mia..."

"She's okay, Marcus. She's okay. You saved us, baby. It's okay, stay with me. Stay with me!"

Sirens wailed somewhere far away. Faint at first, then growing louder. They were still too far, still utterly useless.

"Help is coming, Marcus. Hold on," I said, my throat shredded. "I love you, I love you, I love you."

Marcus's fingers twitched against my wrist. They loosened. His hand went slack. His eyes unfocused. They stared straight through me.

The sirens screamed closer. Pointless now. Too late. Always too late.

In horror and disbelief, I turned toward Mia.

She was standing trembling beside the island. Her yellow dress too bright, garish. Her face white, her eyes too big, too empty. At her feet, cake leaked from the torn box, melting pink ice cream spreading in a slow puddle that mixed with the red. Strawberry and iron, the scent of urine, of bodily fluids. The metallic taste of blood in my throat—

"Mom?"

Mia's voice cut through the haze of memory. The kitchen dissolved, the blood, the ice cream cake. I was back on the uneven stone walkway in the rain, soaked through and shivering, facing my open front door.

The police had caught the man who'd killed my husband two days later. He'd been a heroin addict, in and out of prison several times, with a rap sheet as long as my arm for burglary, armed robbery, and aggravated assault.

A random act of violence. Wrong place, wrong time. Bad luck. The criminal got 20 years. We got a life sentence of grief, heartache, and loss.

That wouldn't happen again. Not here. Not in this safe, elite enclave.

That's why I chose this place. I told myself we were safe here. The words rang hollow inside my head.

My hand strayed to my phone in my jacket pocket. Calling the police sounded like a terrible idea. They were already suspicious. I didn't want to give them access to our house, our things, or our lives, unless we were forced to.

Certainly not before I figured out what to do with those damn slippers.

From inside the house, Apollo barked loudly. My knees went weak with relief. There probably wasn't a sadistic killer lurking inside with Apollo enthusiastically slobbering all over him.

Then again, Apollo was about as likely to lick a burglar as he would Mia or me.

I turned to Mia. "Wait on the porch with Apollo. Let me check it out."

I managed to open the door enough for the German Shepherd to barrel out and pounce on Mia. I extracted the Mace from my purse and held it in one hand, my phone in the other hand, 911 at the ready.

Anxiety thrummed through my veins. I checked the house. In the bathroom, I yanked the shower curtain back in one exaggerated sweep. The linen closet held stacks of towels and haphazardly folded bedsheets. The kitchen held day-old dishes in the sink.

I went back downstairs, into my office.

My blue composition notebook was gone. The one where I kept handwritten notes for my freelance assignments, to-do lists, and snippets of ideas. The same one that had been moved the other day. It had been right here on my desk this morning, sitting next to my laptop.

Now, it was missing.

Dread sank its claws deep into my chest. A rush of nausea rolled through me so hard I had to brace a hand on the desk. Cold sweat broke out along my spine.

Someone had stood here. At my desk. In this room, where I wrote, drank coffee, and surfed the internet. Someone who knew when we left for school, when we got home, when the house sat empty with Apollo snoring on the couch.

I scanned the room for anything else out of place.

The coffee mug I'd left on the coaster had been moved to the windowsill. A framed photo of Marcus, Mia, and me at Navy Pier was face down on the shelf where it had been upright this morning. The table lamp had been shifted to the other side of the desk. My desk chair was pulled out too far.

The smallest things. A stranger's signature, written in negatives.

Like they wanted me to know.

I had locked everything. I knew I had. After the opened window, I'd triple-checked the deadbolt before we left for the precinct.

I'd changed the locks the day the house closed.

Brooke was the only person with a spare key. I'd given it to her over fall break last October when Mia and I went to Grand Rapids for the day and needed someone to let Apollo out. Rowan, Viv, and Camille had all gone on quick getaways. Only Brooke had remained home.

Once she had it, I figured she might as well keep it in case Mia or I accidentally locked ourselves out. I never left a spare under a planter or anywhere else. I wasn't taking chances after last time.

Either she had come in here, or someone she trusted enough with the key had entered my home. Like her daughter.

I didn't think Brooke would enter my house without permission, but what about Alexis? She had been standing beside our mailbox when we'd arrived home. Had she just walked down our driveway after letting herself inside?

My skin prickled all over.

The house no longer felt safe. It was all we had. We had nowhere else to go. We couldn't even afford a cheap motel at this point. My bank account was woefully empty, even more so since I'd had to delay the deadline for my latest freelance assignment. If I didn't work, we didn't eat.

I would call a locksmith today to change the locks again. I wasn't sure of the cost, but I'd put it on my credit card and pray my limit wasn't maxed out. And then I'd talk to Brooke to get my spare key returned. I didn't know what else to do.

Through the window above the desk, I could see the street, wet and gray, where someone must have watched us pull away this morning, then watched us drive back after the precinct, waiting for their chance to slip inside.

I longed to call the police. But if I notified the cops that someone had broken in, had only taken a single notebook and moved some objects around, they'd think I was crazy. That I was unhinged, losing my damn marbles. That I was unraveling.

Even worse, they already considered Mia a suspect. If I invited them in now, they'd tear through everything—our rooms, our devices, our lives—and still conclude Mia was guilty. I thought of the slippers again and shivered.

I stared at the empty spot on my desk, feeling the eyes of whoever had been here as if they were still watching me through the glass.

Chapter Thirteen

I didn't sleep that night. I lay there in the dark, eyes open, mind chewing on itself until dawn bled through the blinds. Every time I shut my eyes, I saw Leah's face. Then Mia's. Then the interrogation room, the careful way the detectives watched Mia.

When the clock hit 5 a.m., I rolled out of bed, bright and early Wednesday morning. I cleaned because I couldn't stand doing nothing. I wiped the counters. Re-wiped them. Scrubbed the sink, bathtub, and toilet in the bathroom upstairs.

I organized the same drawer I'd organized yesterday. Rubber bands, takeout menus, ancient Chapstick. I threw things away until the trash can overflowed. Apollo shadowed me, watching everything I did intently.

Mia wanted to go to school, but she looked so wan and exhausted that I insisted she stay home for one more day to rest. Besides, Camille had advised that she remain at home for a few days.

I wanted to wrap her in bubble wrap so nothing could hurt her ever again. Instead, I let her sleep upstairs while I made a cup of coffee that I was too wired to drink.

I checked the locks. Twice. Front door deadbolt. Side door latch. Back slider lock.

My brain wouldn't stop churning. Someone had been *inside* my house. Someone was watching us. But who? And why?

I called every locksmith in town yesterday. The earliest anyone could come was Friday morning. Two more days. I texted Brooke about the spare key and was waiting to hear back.

Around 9 a.m. on Wednesday, I caught movement on the street outside my window. A dark sedan I didn't recognize parked three houses down. Detective King stood on the Henderson's front porch, notebook in hand. Callahan climbed the steps to the Cromwell place.

They were canvassing. Going door to door. Talking to everyone. They were building a case, piece by piece, witness by witness, tracking closer and closer to us. To Mia.

Alarm flared through every cell in my body. What were the neighbors saying? What had they seen? What had they heard? What rumors were they spreading about us?

I forced myself away from the window and returned to scrubbing the same counter for the third time. Twenty minutes later, the doorbell rang. My heart slammed into my throat. Apollo barked and raced for the front door.

I checked the peephole.

Not the detectives. Instead, Rowan Westinghouse stood on my porch, dressed in a navy cashmere V-neck, cream linen pants, and ballet flats, her hair swept in shiny loose curls around her shoulders. A bouquet of roses was cradled in her arms in shades of pink, cream, and coral, their stems wrapped in burlap tied with twine.

Chloe stood beside her mother, hands tucked into the pockets of an oversized cardigan, her face pale and drawn. Dark circles shadowed her eyes. She looked physically ill.

I opened the door partway. "Rowan, Chloe. Hi."

"Hello, Dahlia." Rowan's voice was warm, concerned. "We won't stay long. We wanted to check on you. And Mia." She held out the roses. "From my garden. I know how much you love them."

I did. I'd admired them at her Fourth of July party last

summer, the way they spilled over the arbor in riotous colors. I'd always loved the fragile beauty of flowers, though I could never water them enough to keep them alive and thriving.

I took the bouquet. A thorn pricked my finger through the burlap. "Thank you."

Chloe looked past me into the house, her gaze searching. "Is Mia here?"

"She's upstairs, sleeping. She didn't feel up to school today. I'm so sorry, but I don't want to wake her."

"That's okay, Ms. Kincaid." Something flickered across Chloe's face. Relief? Disappointment? It was gone before I could read it. "I couldn't go back to school, either. Not yet. Everyone else went back, though."

Rowan squeezed Chloe's shoulder. "It's different for you, sweetheart. It happened at our house."

Chloe's eyes welled. She blinked rapidly, trying to hold back the tears. Apollo pressed his snout into her hands, and she petted his head between his ears.

"May we come in?" Rowan asked. "Just for a moment. I wanted to talk to you about an idea."

I hesitated. Normally, I would've happily invited her in. Today, my paranoia made me suspicious of everyone, but Rowan more than anyone had always been kind to me. She'd welcomed me into the neighborhood, invited Mia to Chloe's parties, and ensured both Mia and I felt like we belonged.

I stepped aside. "Of course."

Apollo stayed glued to my leg as I led them to the living room. I retrieved a glass vase from beneath the sink in the kitchen, filled it with water, and returned to the cramped living room. I undid the burlap and set the roses inside the vase, careful of the thorns. A few still pricked me. I wiped the droplet of blood on the burlap.

Rowan settled on the worn couch, her posture perfect. Chloe curled into the corner, knees pulled up, her glossy honey-blonde hair spilling down her back.

Rowan's gaze swept the small living room, the cramped

kitchen. "This is darling. It reminds me of the cottage we rented in Door County years ago. I admire how you've embraced the vintage aesthetic. Very authentic, and so *you*, Dahlia."

"It's not much, but it's ours." I glanced around the room, at the scuffed baseboards, the mismatched throw pillows, the water stain on the ceiling I kept meaning to paint over.

For a second, I saw the shabbiness through her eyes. Embarrassment curdled my stomach. I tried so hard not to care. But I did, too much.

Rowan's smile seemed nothing but genuine. When I looked at her face, I saw only kindness. I was being ridiculous. She'd brought flowers. She was here to help. I was exhausted, jumpy, and seeing shadows everywhere. "I'll make us some coffee."

"Don't trouble yourself," Rowan said. "We really can't stay that long."

Obediently, I sank into the armchair across from them. Apollo lay at my feet. His eyes tracked Rowan's every movement as I settled my hands in my lap and forced a smile I didn't feel. "What's up?"

"I was thinking that we should hold a memorial service for Leah. Something uplifting, to celebrate her life. Not the official funeral or anything like that, but something small, to show the Cho family our community support."

Viv would probably loathe the additional attention, especially the false sympathy of near-strangers, but I didn't have the heart to say that. Besides, I didn't want to project my own feelings onto her. "That's a lovely idea."

"I'm so glad you agree. I was thinking we could do it soon, this Sunday evening perhaps, at the clubhouse. I know it might be difficult, given everything, but I think it would mean a lot to Vivienne. To all of us."

Sunday. Four days away.

"Of course we'll be there," I said. "I'm happy to help, just tell me what you need."

Rowan's smile was gentle. "Excellent. We'll keep it small,

simple. Immediate families, the girls, and a few teachers. Nothing public. The media has been... relentless."

I thought of the reporters outside the precinct. The cameras. The shouted accusations. "I know."

Chloe spoke up, her voice thin. "Everyone's been so awful online. People are saying terrible things. About all of us."

"Try not to read it, honey," Rowan said.

"I can't help it." Chloe's hands twisted in her lap. Her eyes were reddened. She looked genuinely wrecked. "They're saying it was one of us. That we... that we did something awful to our friend..."

Rowan reached over and squeezed her daughter's knee. "The police will figure out what happened. Until then, we support each other."

"Right." The word felt hollow. I thought of the missing camera, the sandy slippers, the scratches on my daughter's arms.

"Yesterday must have been exhausting for both of you."

I kept my expression neutral. "We're managing."

"It must be so hard for Mia, losing her best friend like that. What with the police questioning all the girls so intensely."

"It was rough," I said, careful to keep it vague. I wasn't ready to reveal how harrowing it had been, the cold sterility of the room, the walls closing in as if we were already locked in a kind of prison. The terror of the detectives' sharp eyes homing in on my daughter as her story changed, as she'd lied.

"They're just covering their bases. I'm sure Mia has nothing to worry about."

Her certainty steadied me. I swallowed and nodded. "We're trying to find some sort of new normal through this."

A car door slammed outside, muffled through the front windows. I flinched, half expecting a heavy knock from the detectives with badges. But no one came.

Rowan's gaze remained on my face. Her lipstick had bled into the lines around her mouth. Up close, she looked tired for the first time since I'd met her. "That's why I wanted to come by in person.

Whatever you need. If you need someone to talk to, or if Mia needs anything at all, let me know."

I almost told her about the break-in last night, the missing notebook, my things shuffled around, but something, some small niggling hesitation, stopped me.

"I keep thinking I should know what to do," I admitted. "Like there's a manual I missed out on. How to Parent Through a Murder Investigation."

Her mouth twitched. "If there is, I certainly never got a copy. Sounds like an article you need to write."

I snorted. "I pass."

We shared strained smiles.

A creak sounded at the top of the stairs. "Mom?" Mia's voice floated down from upstairs. Her footsteps descended, and a moment later, she appeared in the archway in her old Lilo and Stitch sweatpants and a matching, oversized sweatshirt. Her hair was pulled into a messy braid that had slipped over one shoulder.

"Oh," she said when she saw Rowan and Chloe in the living room.

I gestured toward the roses on the coffee table. "We have company."

"I have a headache. I ah, needed more water. I didn't mean to interrupt."

"There's nothing to apologize for." Rowan stood and smoothed her slacks. "Dahlia and I were just chatting. Chloe wanted to see how you're doing."

Chloe had risen from the couch. For a moment, the two girls just looked at each other, then Chloe offered a small uncertain smile. "Hey."

"Hey." Mia stood in the archway, holding the doorframe. "I was just... thinking about yesterday. The questions with the police."

Rowan's expression softened. "I'm so sorry you had to go through that."

"They asked about the photo shoot." She stepped farther into the room and kept her eyes on Chloe. "About who was where, and what time we went to bed."

"What did you tell them?" Rowan asked.

Mia's gaze slid to Chloe, just for a second. "I—I lied at first, because I was so scared. But they knew about Leah's blood on my dress, so I told them how we went back out and took some photos on the bluff around midnight. Me, you, and Leah. After everyone else was asleep. How Leah had that nosebleed, that's how the blood got on my dress."

For the briefest moment, Chloe went still, as if the memory had caught her off guard. Then she nodded, her voice quiet. "Yeah, the midnight shoot thing."

Mia didn't look at me. "I told them that after we were done, we went back inside. That we went straight to our sleeping bags, like before 1 a.m. All three of us, together."

Chloe scrunched up her face. "I didn't want to say anything because I thought it would get you into trouble. But Mia's right, nothing happened. We came back in and went to sleep. That's the truth."

I let out the breath I'd been holding as relief flooded through me. Their stories matched. That was good. That had to be good.

Rowan offered a sympathetic smile. "You girls have been through something terrible. It makes sense that you'd want to protect yourselves. The important thing is that you support each other."

Even though Mia had lied at first, so had Chloe. They'd feared getting into trouble, but they were telling the truth now.

My hands curled into fists in my lap. My throat tightened. "As long as you tell the truth."

I said it more sharply than I'd meant to. Mia flinched. "We are."

"Are you sleeping okay? I keep having these nightmares." Chloe twisted a strand of hair around her finger. "Like, I'll wake up, and I'm on the bluff, and someone is falling, and I can't help them. I keep trying, and I keep hearing her scream as she falls. Dr.

Monroe says it's my brain trying to process the trauma. That even though I was asleep when it happened, part of me knows something terrible occurred."

I felt a pang of sympathy. Chloe looked so young, so lost. Just a kid trying to make sense of something incomprehensible.

"Yeah," Mia said quietly. "I'm not sleeping much, either."

"It's so awful, isn't it? Not being able to turn your brain off."

Mia looked at the floor. "I just want this to be over."

Chloe stepped closer, reaching out to touch Mia's arm. "Me, too. But we'll get through it. Together."

Mia nodded.

My heart ached. I wanted to reach for her, pull her close, promise her it would be okay. But I couldn't, not with Rowan and Chloe watching. It would embarrass her too much.

Chloe shifted her weight, glancing toward the stairs. "Can I use your bathroom real quick? I've been holding it since we left our house."

"Sure," I said. "You remember where it is. Upstairs, first door on the left."

"Thanks." She moved past us toward the stairs. Apollo trotted curiously after her.

Rowan cleared her throat. "We should let you rest, Mia. Dahlia, I'll email you the mock-up I drafted for the memorial program, if you could look it over for editing errors. If you and Mia could go through your photos of Leah and send them to me, Chloe's going to make a slideshow."

I stood, too. "Of course."

"It would be lovely to have candid shots. The girls at the beach, at birthdays. Leah deserves to be remembered the way she was. So vibrant and sweet."

Mia nodded. "I can do that."

A moment later, Chloe reappeared at the top of the stairs, tucking a strand of hair behind her ear as she descended.

"We were just discussing the slideshow," Rowan said.

Chloe said, "I can come back later this week. To help you pick out the best pictures."

Rowan placed her hand between Chloe's shoulder blades and steered her daughter toward the front door. "We'll figure out a time, but only if you're up for it, Mia."

"Sure," Mia said. "Yeah, I'd like that."

At the door, Rowan paused. "Don't forget, we're meeting at noon to finalize the details for the memorial."

I raised my brows. "Um, I didn't get that text."

Rowan looked aghast. "Oh, I'm so sorry. You must've been left off the text string accidentally. Normally, I'd never let that happen, you know that. I'm just not myself this week. I did the same thing the other day, for which I apologize profusely. Brooke is hosting. Say you'll come."

I forced a smile. "Of course, I'll come."

Rowan beamed at me. "Excellent."

Chloe gave Mia a pensive wave, then followed her mother out. I watched them walk down the front path. Rowan paused to say something to a police officer at the curb. Chloe toed at a crack in the concrete. Her head down, shoulders tense, like Mia.

Mia lingered in the entryway, arms wrapped around herself, her eyes distant, fixed somewhere just past my shoulder like her mind was a million miles away.

"How's your head?" I went back into the kitchen, opened the cabinet next to the sink, and handed her some Advil. Apollo weaved in between our legs in a sinewy figure eight.

She gave me a thin smile. "Getting better. Thanks."

"I bet you're starving. How about turkey sandwiches on sourdough with extra tomatoes and a side of Baked Lays for the crunch factor?"

"Sure." She leaned against the counter, phone in hand, frowning at something online. That pink emblem again. It looked like an Instagram account. She saw me looking and swiftly pocketed the phone.

"What was that?"

"Nothing."

The image of the slippers pushed in, damp and gritty with sand. My tongue felt thick. The question was right there, pressing against the back of my teeth. *Why do you keep lying to me?*

I pictured her face if I asked her again. The flash of hurt, or worse, something I didn't know how to name. How fast she would shut down, shut me out. I wasn't sure which answer I feared more, yet another lie or a terrible truth.

Instead, I collected the supplies from the fridge and the cabinets. I lined everything up in a neat row: bread, mayo, turkey, tomatoes, lettuce, chips. An assembly line of normal.

I picked up a slice of turkey, laid it on the bread, then another. "Hey. Vivienne mentioned Leah's diary was missing. Do you know if she kept it anywhere specific?"

There was a small pause. "Her diary?"

"Mm-hm."

Mia's mouth pinched. "I mean, she moved it around. She was always paranoid someone would read it."

Paranoid enough to hide it. "Do you know where?"

Her gaze slid past me, toward the window. The detectives were still outside, going from house to house. "I'm not supposed to say."

I kept my tone gentle. "Viv's tearing the house apart. If that diary holds a clue to who hurt Leah, then the least we can do is help her find it."

"Leah didn't want anyone to know, okay? She made me promise. She said if her mom ever found it, she'd die. She made me swear I wouldn't tell."

I put my hand on her shoulder. Her body went rigid under my palm. "I know. And you kept that promise when she was alive. You were a good friend. But whoever did this to Leah is still out there. Leah would want us to find the truth. She'd want you to be safe."

Mia's face contorted. She was conflicted, torn between her promise to her dead friend and her desire to see her friend's killer brought to justice.

"Whatever is in that diary can't embarrass Leah anymore, okay?

The little things don't matter anymore. Telling us where the diary is could help the police believe you're cooperating, that you're telling the truth."

Finally, Mia nodded, as if the movement physically hurt. "Leah, she... the last time I saw it, she'd taped it to the back of one of her canvases."

"Taped it?"

"Like, duct-taped it flat. You can't see it unless you take the canvas off the wall and check the other side. It's the one with the scarlet flowers in the dunes, downstairs in the movie room, on the back wall."

"Okay, that's good. Very good." That was something. Mia and I were finally on the same page for a moment. "Thank you."

She pulled away from me, her shoulders sagging, her gaze fixed on the floor as if she couldn't bear to look at me. "I wasn't supposed to tell."

"You did the right thing, honey." I hoped with all my heart that the diary pointed to someone else, to anyone but Mia. Guilt wormed its way inside me, but I brushed it aside. Mia was my priority.

The roses Rowan had brought sat on the coffee table in my living room, bright and cheerful. I thought of Rowan's hand over mine, the grounded certainty in her voice.

I set my phone on the island, then picked it up again. My thumb hovered for a second over Vivienne's name before I opened our thread and told Viv where Mia thought the diary might be located, then I hit send.

Chapter Fourteen

At noon, I stepped into Brooke's sleek, modern black farmhouse. The door had been left open. Brooke had texted me an hour earlier: *Just come on in.* No response to my text regarding the spare key, though.

The entryway was decorated in neutral shades of charcoal and cream. Black-framed windows lined the far wall, facing several acres of woods where the HOA had constructed walking paths for the community's enjoyment.

The house was huge, ten thousand square feet at least. Twice the size of Rowan's and somehow half as impressive, though it made my tiny cottage look like a dilapidated shed in comparison.

Brooke had money. Everyone knew that. Her husband Jason managed hedge funds and made upwards of seven figures a year, Whitney had informed me once. But they'd bought late, after all the lakefront lots were gone. Whitney had said it like an insult.

"Dahlia!" Rowan's voice carried from deeper inside. "We're in the great room."

Everyone had arrived ahead of me, like I'd been added as an afterthought. Again.

I checked my phone one last time. No response from Vivienne

yet about the diary location. A frisson of concern passed through me. I would check on her after this meeting.

I followed the sound of voices through a hallway lined with family portraits: professional, posed, everyone's perfect teeth showing. Except for Falcon, who was nine or ten. He wasn't smiling in any of the family photos. He looked blankly off camera, if he showed up in the photos at all.

In one spot, a pale rectangle marked the wall, edges faint but sharper than the rest, as if a larger frame had recently been removed. A large portrait of Brooke and Jason at their wedding in the Maldives used to hang here. It wasn't there anymore.

The state of Brooke's marriage was none of my business. I hurried down the hall and entered the great room, a huge open-concept space that was all sharp angles. White marble countertops. Matte black fixtures. An expensive chandelier made of geometric brushed brass shapes. It felt modern and expensive.

Brooke stood near the kitchen island, holding a wine glass half-full of dark liquid.

Rowan sat on the corner of the linen sectional, the seat with the best view of the room. She patted the cushion beside her. "Dahlia, sit. We were just getting started."

Whitney perched on the other end of the sectional, her back straight, ankles crossed. Her white Stanley stood on a marble coaster. Her right foot tapped the white oak hardwood flooring.

Camille stood by the floor-to-ceiling windows in a bold African-print blazer over a sapphire-toned blouse. Her gold chandelier earrings caught the light as she turned from the window, her arms folded and her lips pursed as if she'd rather be anywhere else.

She gave me a grim nod. "I'm just here on my lunch break. I've got court at 2 p.m."

I sat between Rowan and Whitney. "Thanks for having us," I told Brooke.

She waved it off, almost sloshing her drink. "Of course." The words blurred at the edges. "How are you doing, Dahlia?"

"One day at a time," I said.

"I was just saying how Chloe keeps having nightmares," Rowan said. "She won't talk about them, but I hear her crying through the walls at two, three in the morning. It's like she's afraid to go to sleep."

Brooke took a long drink. "Alexis wakes up screaming. Which wakes Falcon up, and then he's impossible to get down again. His schedule is absolutely ruined." She pressed her fingers to her temple, as if the thought physically hurt. "He doesn't do well without a rigid schedule. It's been hell."

Camille stared out the window at a cardinal pecking at the birdfeeder in Brooke's backyard. "Zara wants to move away. She says she can't stand the sight of the bluff anymore. She won't go down to the beach, either."

Whitney sighed. "Peyton's been going to school, but as soon as she gets home, she disappears. Three days now. I checked the nanny cam yesterday—" She caught herself, glanced at me, then kept going. "She was in the same spot on her bed for four hours. Just staring at the TV. That's not like my Peyton. She's always doing something, either homework, practicing the piano, exercising or training. She's usually so driven."

"You have a nanny cam?" I asked.

"Doesn't everyone?" Whitney looked genuinely surprised. "How else do you know what your kids are really doing?"

I thought of Mia's closed door. Her furtiveness with her phone. The way she flinched when I walked into a room.

I didn't need a camera to see she was in pain. It was the only thing I saw.

"The point is," Rowan said, "they're all traumatized. Which is why we need to help them through this. Get them back to normal."

"Normal," Brooke repeated. She let out a bitter laugh. "What's normal now?"

"Structure," Whitney said immediately. "Routine. Peyton has state championships in two weeks. I told her that's her focus. College scouts will be there. This isn't the time to fall apart."

I stared at her. "A girl died."

Whitney's voice sharpened. "I know that. But Peyton's future is on the line. Scholarships. Recruitment. You can't just decide to go to Stanford on a sports scholarship in senior year. You start now. She can't let this derail her."

"Derail her?" I echoed. "She's in eighth grade."

Whitney smoothed her plum-colored leggings with the palm of her hand and sighed. "You know what I mean."

I didn't, but I didn't argue with her. With Whitney, it was better to choose your battles.

Brooke reached for the half-empty bottle tucked behind the stand mixer. It was a Caymus Special Selection, the label still visible. She refilled her glass. "The worst part is not knowing who did it. If they're still out there."

"They're not," Rowan said. "Security's been tripled. There are cameras everywhere, and police crawling all over the place. Whoever it was, they're long gone."

"What if it wasn't an outsider?" I asked.

Silence dropped over the room. Camille turned away from the window and shot me a warning look. Whitney's smile held, but something in her eyes went flat. "What are you suggesting?"

"I'm not suggesting anything." My voice sounded thin to my own ears. I swallowed and tried again. "I'm just saying, the police are focused on the girls who were there. Not gardeners. Not contractors."

Brooke grimaced. "You really think one of our daughters did something this terrible?"

"I think the police do." I rubbed my damp palms against my jeans. The room felt stifling.

Whitney's foot tapped faster against the floor. "The police are wrong. They're grasping at straws. Looking for someone to blame because they can't find who really did this."

"Who do you think did it?" I asked.

"A stranger," Brooke said immediately. "Someone who doesn't belong here."

"Like who?" Camille asked.

"The construction workers," Brooke offered. "There's that crew redoing the Martin's new infinity pool, only two houses down from Rowan's. They're here every day. You don't think they're watching our beautiful daughters? Walking around in their crop tops and shorts?"

"They have background checks," Camille interrupted. "The HOA requires it."

"Maybe one of them lied," Whitney said. "Maybe someone slipped through."

"It's April, no one's in crop tops," I said, but no one heard me. Or they chose not to. I hated the way they were looking at me with consternation, like I was the problem, the outlier. Something they didn't understand and weren't sure they wanted to.

I listened to them circle the same theories—the construction workers, the lawn service, someone's socially awkward nanny. Some faceless intruder who'd managed to sneak in from the public beach access. Anything to avoid looking at what was right in front of us.

My gaze drifted across the great room to the opposite window where Camille stood tense, typing something on her phone. A ring light stood on a collapsible tripod, its circular LED face tilted toward a white oak side table. A camera and a lapel mic lay coiled next to a pop filter, and behind it, a carefully arranged vignette: a lavender candle, a stack of design books with the spines facing out, a small potted succulent.

It looked like Brooke had been filming just before we arrived. Her "authentic life" content was shot, lit, and staged with precision.

I glanced at Brooke, at her anxious darting eyes, the tremor in her hands, the single droplet of wine that stained her ivory turtleneck. She was still clinging to false perfection while everything was falling apart around us.

"The detectives will figure it out," Rowan said, bringing me back to the conversation. "Once the forensics come back. Once the autopsy is finished. It takes time. And speaking of time, the memorial is in four days. We need to talk about photos for the slideshow. Dahlia, do you have anything from that night? The girls were dressed up so beautifully. Leah was practically luminescent. I'm sure Mia took some lovely photographs."

My throat closed. I forced myself to meet her eyes. "We still haven't found it."

Brooke's brows rose in surprise. She and Whitney exchanged a weighted glance. "Really?"

"It's still missing?" Whitney asked. "The police didn't find it?"

"Someone definitely stole it that night." I didn't say it must be one of their daughters. But I watched them closely.

"Someone must have misplaced it accidentally," Whitney said airily. "Or maybe Mia forgot what she did with it. I asked Peyton, but she has no idea."

"Alexis hasn't seen it, either," Brooke said.

Camille frowned down at her phone.

No one said anything. I felt their attention on me like heat. Sweat broke out on the back of my neck.

"I'm sure it'll turn up," Whitney said.

"I'm sure," I echoed faintly. I didn't share their optimism.

"What is it, Dahlia?" Rowan prodded. "There's something else bothering you. I can see it."

"Come on, Dahlia. Don't hold out on us," Brooke said, pushy as usual.

The words caught in my throat. I hadn't planned to say anything else. I didn't want to. But the silence stretched. Their expectant faces—all of them, watching me, waiting for the rest—pulled it out of me.

"There was a break-in." I kept my attention on Brooke, watching for any twitch, any sign of recognition, guilt, or realization. If it was Alexis who'd entered my house, did Brooke know? Did she suspect her own daughter? "Someone was in my house on Tuesday morning. While Mia and I were at the precinct."

All four of them spoke at once.

"What? What happened?"

"Why didn't you tell us?"

"That's terrible!"

Whitney rose abruptly and began pacing behind the sectional. "I can't believe it. Here? Really?"

"The front door was open when we got home. Whoever it was, they went into my office. They moved things. The lamp on my desk, a family photograph."

A faint ringing started in my ears. Saying it out loud made it feel less like a bad dream and more like a real thing that had happened to us.

"What did they take?" Camille asked.

I hesitated. "Just the notebook on my desk."

Brooke's brows pulled together. "That's all?"

"I know it sounds weird, but it was like they wanted me to know they'd been there. Inside my house. Like they were messing with us, trying to make us afraid."

Whitney cocked her head. "Are you sure you didn't just leave the door open? Forgot where you put your notebook last?"

I wanted to tell her I had felt the violation, deep in my bones. "I'm sure."

"Did you call the police?" Rowan asked.

"I thought maybe it was some kind of..." I searched for a word that didn't sound insane. "Misunderstanding. I wanted to ask if any of you had been over to my house and forgot to tell me."

They all looked offended at once. It was almost funny. Only I was beyond laughing.

"I haven't been anywhere near your house," Whitney said.

"Me, neither," Camille said.

Rowan shook her head. "Only when you've been home."

All eyes went to Brooke.

"You have a key, don't you?" I already knew the answer. "From fall break last year."

Brooke blinked. "Oh. Right. Yes. From when you went to Grand Rapids with Mia. I forgot I even had it."

I watched her intently. "Do you still have it?"

She shifted her weight, glass tight in her hand. Her face was smooth, blank. "I think so."

"You think so?"

"I'm not sure where it ended up," Brooke said. "It might be in my junk drawer. I'm sure I put it back on your hook when I returned Apollo."

"You didn't." I could picture the empty spot on the key rack clearly, along with the spare key with the green and yellow Isle Royale keychain, another of Marcus's purchases from our hiking trip to the island four years ago. "I never got it back."

Brooke let out a shaky laugh. "Then I must still have it. I'm sorry. Things have been... I can barely remember what day it is." She set the wine glass down a little too hard. "I'll look for it after we're done here."

"Could you check now?" The question slipped out before I could modulate my tone. I heard the edge in it and winced. "I'm sorry. I just, I'd feel better having it back."

Brooke's gaze darted to Rowan. "Actually, I think I gave it to Rowan."

Rowan smiled. "I think you're mistaken."

"No, I remember, I gave it to you before Thanksgiving, because Jason and I went to visit his parents in Aspen."

"Don't you have a copy of everyone's keys?" Whitney rolled her eyes. "It's like you collect them."

Rowan smiled. "A few. But in this case, I don't. Brooke, you gave it to Whitney, remember? Around Christmas, wasn't it?"

After a moment, Brooke's eyes lit up with recognition. "Oh, right. I gave it to Whit. I mean, I had Alexis bring it over to Whitney's house right before Christmas break, when we went to Tahiti. In case someone needed to get into your house while I was gone. For Apollo."

I went still. "Alexis?"

Whitney played with her diamond tennis bracelet. "I completely forgot. Alexis gave it to Peyton. I told her to put it on the hook by our back door with the rest of our keys. I'll bring it by tonight. I haven't used it. We don't even notice it anymore."

Alexis had handled the spare key at some point. Alexis had been standing outside my house right before we discovered the opened door.

But Alexis wasn't the only one with an opportunity. The key had passed from Brooke to Alexis to Peyton to Whitney. Two of the girls knew its location and whose house it belonged to. Any of them could've used the key yesterday morning.

Plus, it was Brooke who'd told Vivienne about Mia's scratches and the blood on her dress. For what purpose? To insinuate that Mia was guilty to a grieving mother? Simply to gossip behind my back?

Brooke loved a salacious scandal, as long as it didn't involve herself. It hurt to think of her speaking of Mia like that, though.

I looked from one face to the next. Brooke, sweating into her wine glass. Whitney, her heel tapping an anxious rhythm into the rug. Camille with her jaw tight, eyes unreadable. Rowan calm and composed, as if she were moderating a PTA meeting.

I didn't detect any signs of guilt. That didn't mean there weren't any. I filed the information away to consider later and forced my voice to remain steady. "Thanks, Whit. I didn't think anyone had done anything. I just wanted to know where it was."

"Of course," Rowan said smoothly. "I'm sure you'll feel better once you have your key back safely, but we should get back to the reason we're here. The memorial." She picked up a notepad from the counter. Her handwriting already filled the top few lines in tight, slanted script. "Flowers. Music. Venue's obviously the clubhouse. Pastor Ramsey confirmed the date works with Daniel."

"I'll handle the program," Whitney said. "Order of service, speakers, printed handouts. I know a printer who can turn it around fast."

The doorbell chimed.

We all flinched.

"Were we expecting anyone?" Rowan asked.

"No." Brooke frowned. She set her wine glass on the counter and glided from the great room down the hallway to the foyer. Muffled voices. A woman's voice, strained and sharp. Brooke's response, accommodating, then pleading.

The others looked at each other. No one spoke. Whitney had gone still; even she seemed to forget to move.

Then rapid footsteps sounded and Vivienne appeared in the doorway. She still wore her pajamas. Her eyes were swollen, her black hair uncombed. But it was the expression on her face that made my blood run cold.

It was pure rage.

"Vivienne?" Camille stepped forward. "What's wrong?"

Vivienne's sharp gaze swept over us. "I found Leah's diary."

My heart stopped.

Viv said, "And your daughters are all in it."

Chapter Fifteen

Vivienne stood in the archway, her whole body vibrating with hostility. She gripped something in one hand. A bulging manila envelope, the edges crumpled.

"Vivienne, sweetheart." Rowan rose from the sectional, her voice hostess-smooth though it was Brooke's house. "Why don't you come sit down? Let me get you some water—"

"I don't want water! I want answers."

Camille tucked her phone into the pocket of her black slacks. Her posture shifted, her shoulders back, eyes sharp. "What's this about a diary?"

"Leah kept one. She kept it hidden. Secret." Vivienne's hands shook as she pulled papers from the envelope. "I tore that house apart looking for answers. The police looked, too, but they didn't find anything in her room." Her gaze flicked to me briefly. "Turns out she hid it behind a painting in the basement. I found it this morning. I made photocopies for you."

She marched to the coffee table in the center of the room and dropped the stack. The photocopied pages fanned out across the marble. Several slid onto the sisal rug.

I leaned forward, my heart in my throat. Handwritten entries in different-colored ink, though the photocopies were in black and white. Dates. Names. Words underlined and circled. Leah's familiar doodling and drawings of flowers edged the diary entries —bleeding hearts, black-eyed Susans, forget-me-nots, Indian paintbrush, and wild roses.

Rowan moved fast. She came around the coffee table, placing herself between Vivienne and the rest of us. Brooke returned to the island and gripped her wine glass like it could protect her from something. Whitney sat frozen for once, her eyes locked on the pages.

I picked one up. "'December 12,'" I read. "'After school. Alexis cornered me by the lockers outside the art room. No one else was around. She grabbed my wrist so hard I thought it would snap. She shoved me into the locker. I couldn't breathe.'"

Brooke made a strangled sound in the back of her throat.

I read it again, certain I'd misunderstood, but the words stayed the same. I kept reading, a sick feeling hollowing my gut.

"'Then she dragged me to the bathroom and pulled out the art scissors. She cut my hair. The one thing I was proud of. A huge chunk right above my ear. Just cut it. She held my head and cut off the rest. She said, "You're so ugly it won't even matter." Mom found the bruises. I told her I fell. She wanted to go to the school. I begged her not to. She did anyway. Nothing happened. Alexis's mom came in with her husband for a private meeting with the principal. The principal said there wasn't enough proof. That I agreed to let her do it and then changed my mind when I didn't like it, for attention. They pressured me to change my story. Alexis said she could make me out to be the psycho one if I told everyone. That Peyton, Chloe, and Zara would have her back. Mia, too.'"

Brooke shook her head, hard. "That is not true."

I stared at Brooke in shock. When I'd spoken with Vivienne, I hadn't realized it had been this bad. My mind flashed to the bruising on Alexis's wrist. Her presence outside my house right after the break-in. Her access to my spare key. And now this— she'd physically harmed Leah.

My mouth went dry. "You knew your daughter was a bully. All this time."

"It wasn't like that. She didn't mean it. It was just girls being girls. It got a bit out of hand."

Vivienne's eyes met mine. "Leah cried herself to sleep for a week."

Whitney stood abruptly. "This is completely out of line, Vivienne. You can't just barge in here and—"

"And what?" Vivienne demanded. "Tell the truth? Is that what you're afraid of?"

"We handled it," Brooke said. Her words blurred at the edges. "We talked to her. The school said that there was no proof. What were we supposed to do? Ruin her whole life over one stupid mistake?"

Whitney seized on that. "Exactly. We can't just take Leah's word as gospel. She was clearly troubled. She misinterpreted things. Twisted them."

"We are all grieving," Rowan cut in, her voice soft, empathetic. She moved closer to Vivienne. "Accusations won't help anyone. Perhaps we should speak privately, Viv."

Vivienne let out a bitter laugh. "So you can spin this? So you can protect your daughters like you always do?"

Brooke flinched. "That's not fair. Teen girls are dramatic. They fight and make up. It's messy. You can't blame us for every little thing they do."

"Cutting someone's hair off isn't a little thing," Vivienne snapped.

Whitney crossed her arms, chin lifting. "Do we even know if this diary is authentic? Anyone could have written this after the fact."

Vivienne's eyes sparked with outrage. "You think I forged my dead daughter's diary? Peyton's all over this diary, Whitney."

She snatched a page from the pile and thrust it toward us. "January 24. 'Peyton whispered it in the locker room when no one else could hear. You should suicide yourself. No one would miss you.

You're so ugly and fat, I can't stand having to look at you every day.'"

Whitney blanched. Her hand went to her throat. "No. That's... Peyton would never say that."

"Your daughter is a monster," Vivienne said flatly.

"How dare you insinuate such a thing!"

"How dare I? Your daughters tormented mine for months. They smiled in her face and destroyed her behind her back."

Rowan picked up a page, glanced at it, and set it down. Her jaw ticked. "This is a child's diary. We don't know what was going on in Leah's head when she wrote any of this."

With a trembling hand, I grabbed the page Rowan had just discarded. "February 17. Swim team incident."

Rowan shot me a warning look. I ignored it.

"'Someone took my suit and hung it from the ceiling. They poured red dye or animal blood on the crotch to make it look like I'd started my period. When I got upset, Chloe said it was a joke. Peyton said I was being extra. Alexis recorded the whole thing. Zara just laughed. Mia looked away.'"

The words lodged in my throat. I couldn't breathe. *Mia looked away.* My daughter— quiet, sensitive Mia—had watched her best friend be publicly humiliated and said nothing.

When had that been? February, right after Valentine's Day. I tried to remember. Had she seemed different? Acted guilty or ashamed? I couldn't recall. I'd been working on a deadline. I'd missed everything.

"Leah had problems before any of this," Whitney said. "Everyone knew she struggled. She lied about things, Vivienne. She always wanted attention. Peyton told me all about her hysterics."

"She was scared," Vivienne shot back. "Because your daughters were tormenting her."

"Girls go too far trying to be funny," Whitney said. "It doesn't mean anything serious."

Their voices layered over each other, building a wall of rationalization. I watched them close ranks. Whitney shifted closer to

Rowan's shoulder. Brooke straightened despite the alcohol. Even Camille took a half-step from the window.

"Stop!" I said. "Just stop it!"

The room stilled. There wasn't enough oxygen in the room.

"We failed them. All of them. We were so busy that we didn't see what was happening."

Brooke's voice rose. "That's not fair."

Tears tracked down Vivienne's face. "You all knew something was wrong. And you did nothing."

The unified front wavered. Brooke's gaze dropped, like she couldn't bear to see Vivienne's incandescent grief a moment longer. Whitney's foot resumed its anxious tapping. Rowan's mouth flattened, in frustration or perhaps remorse.

"These are serious allegations," Camille said. "We're not taking this lightly, Vivienne. Please don't think that."

Vivienne turned to Camille. "Your daughter was there, too, Camille."

Camille stiffened. Something flickered in her eyes, not quite guilt, not quite fear. She took a breath. "I understand you're upset."

"Upset? You don't know the meaning of upset." Vivienne sneered. "Your daughter was complicit. And so was Mia."

The words slammed into me. Shame flooded my face. Pure, scalding shame. Because Vivienne was right, I'd been so focused on protecting Mia, on believing in her innocence, that I'd never asked harder questions.

"She watched. She didn't stop them." Vivienne's eyes found mine. The fury had burned out, leaving only grief. "I thought you were different, Dahlia."

"Viv—"

"You're just like them. You'd rather believe your daughter is innocent than face what she did. Or what she watched and did nothing to stop."

"That's not true."

"Isn't it?"

The realization settled like lead in my chest. I thought of Mia's silences. Her withdrawn behavior. Her refusal to meet my eyes. Not just grief. Could it be guilt? For what? For not stopping the bullying? Participating in it? Or something far worse?

What if the girl living in my house was someone I didn't know at all?

I wanted to say something, to defend my daughter the way the other mothers had defended theirs, while also acknowledging Vivienne's pain and any part my child may have played in it.

But no words came. I was in shock, blindsided. Horrified and appalled and sickened. I didn't know what to do or what to say. I said the only woefully inadequate thing I could think of. "I'm so sorry."

Vivienne watched me, then nodded slowly to herself. As if I'd confirmed every terrible suspicion she'd held about me.

"They're not bullies," Brooke said, her voice shaking, gesturing wildly as if she were desperate for any scrap of evidence to defend her daughter from guilt she knew she deserved. "They're just teenage girls. They screw up. They'll grow out of it. You can't brand them for life because one girl couldn't handle it..."

She stopped. Too late.

Vivienne's voice went hard and quiet. "Because one girl couldn't handle it? Leah couldn't handle it? And now she's dead? Is that what you just said to me?"

Brooke's mouth worked, but no sound came out. Her face had gone bright red, whether in anger or shame, I couldn't tell.

"Have you gone to the police with this information?" Camille asked.

"Of course." Vivienne spun and stalked back to the foyer. At the front door, she paused, looking back at each of us with loathing, like we were her mortal enemies. "My daughter is dead. And one of yours killed her."

The door slammed shut behind her.

Chapter Sixteen

I stared at the photocopied pages scattered across Brooke's coffee table and rug. Dates. Names. Splotches of ink like bruises.

No one moved. No one spoke.

The dark ink. Leah's careful handwriting. Mia's name, over and over.

My eyes focused on a page with a name circled several times in dark ink: Taylor Everett. The Everetts had lived in the now empty house several lots down from mine. A tragedy had occurred, and they'd moved away. That's all I knew.

Whitney paced toward the bay window. Her movements were sharp and anxious, all elbows and angles. Her gaze shot to Rowan. "What do we do?"

"Whitney, sweetheart," Rowan said. "For Heaven's sake, sit down. All that nervous energy isn't helping anyone."

Whitney paced faster. "She's gone to the police with that thing, that pack of lies—" She cut herself off as her gaze slid to me. Her jaw snapped shut.

"No one can find out about this," Brooke said. Her voice rose an octave. She could barely contain her alarm. "We have to stop it. How do we stop it?"

"Let's not panic," Rowan said. "This is one perspective. That's all." She didn't say Leah was lying. She didn't have to.

My throat tightened. One perspective. As if Leah's handwritten words, her documented terror, were just an opinion to be debated. I reached for the diary pages. I wanted to read the rest, to see if there were more clues hidden within it.

"I'll take those." Abruptly, Brooke stood, wobbled across the room, and started gathering them up, clutching them haphazardly against her chest. She snatched the last pages from my hand. "Give those to me."

"I'd like to read them," I said.

"I can't have copies of this garbage floating around." Brooke crumpled the photocopies in her hand and stumbled to a glass curio cabinet against the wall. She jerked open a drawer and stuffed them inside. "Can you imagine if the press got hold of this? Or another influencer? They'd use it to destroy my whole brand."

She didn't want the details about Alexis getting out. Out of all the girls, Leah's damning words had painted Alexis in the worst light.

It didn't matter where she tried to hide the pages; the police already had the diary. It was getting out, every ugly detail, no matter what she did.

"But I want to read it," I said again.

"What for?" Brooke narrowed her eyes at me. "I'm putting it through the shredder as soon as I can."

"Reading the diary will only serve to upset us further," Rowan said. "It's not helpful."

I pressed my lips together, resigned. Brooke wasn't giving me those pages. The detectives would figure out whether anything in it was relevant to the case.

"The detectives will blame the girls," Whitney said. "This is not good."

Rowan shook her head. "Let's not work ourselves up unnecessarily. The girls were all friends. They've known each other for years.

They loved each other in their way. And Leah was... sensitive. We're all upset, Vivienne most of all. It's understandable. Of course, she's going to react. But that doesn't mean the police will just take it as gospel."

"Won't they?" Whitney finally sank into an oversized armchair, but her leg bounced so hard the cushion moved. "How could they not?"

"We'll talk to the girls." Brooke stared at us with her wide, darting eyes. Her chest heaved. She looked on the verge of a panic attack. "We need to minimize the fallout."

There it was. The pivot to self-protection mode. My throat went dry. Was Brooke only worried about her influencer status, or was there a darker element at play? What else was she trying to hide?

Brooke must have seen something on my face because she added, "Not because we have anything to hide. But you know how these things go, people hear what they want to hear. They love any excuse to tear someone apart. They'll judge and condemn the girls, and not just the girls, but us, too. We're the mothers. We're always the ones to blame."

I thought of that damn reporter's words. *What kind of mother are you?*

Camille uncrossed her arms and rose to her feet. "I can't be involved in this conversation. Not ethically."

Rowan inclined her head. "Of course. We understand."

"I represent Mia," Camille continued, looking at a spot between us instead of at any one of us directly. "And by extension, I'm concerned about exposure for all of the girls, but I can't be part of a joint strategy session."

"You make it sound like a PR crisis," I muttered.

Camille didn't take the bait. "The police have the diary now. They may subpoena the girls' phones, start poring through their social media. Be prepared."

Brooke looked taken aback. "But that's so invasive."

Camille shrugged. "I suggest you contact your lawyers."

"I'll call Mr. Avery today," Whitney said. "We have to protect our girls."

At the doorway, Camille adjusted the strap of her bag on her shoulder without meeting my gaze. "I'll call you later, Dahlia. We'll go over everything. In detail."

I wanted to reach for her, to ask her to stay. I had a million questions regarding Mia's case, but she was already halfway out the door. She was protecting herself. Protecting Zara, as any good mother would do.

Then she was gone. The door clicked behind her.

"This is bad. This is really bad." Brooke returned to the corner of the sectional and slumped into her seat. She grasped her wine glass from the end table and cradled it in both hands like it was the only thing keeping her from sliding onto the floor. Her lipstick smeared the rim.

"I'll lose tens of thousands of followers," she said, her face tight with panic. "Once this gets out, it'll ruin everything. Everyone will know. Our friends. Jason's boss, the school..."

"We'll handle it," Rowan said. "Girls letting off some steam online is a far cry from pushing a girl over a cliff. They weren't physically violent, ever." Her sympathetic gaze flicked to Brooke. "Except for Alexis."

Brooke looked like she was about to faint. "It was one time."

"How did Vivienne even find that damn diary?" Whitney asked suddenly. "Viv said the police looked through Leah's room and didn't find anything. Nothing on her phone, either."

Rowan lowered herself back onto the loveseat, smoothing her pants of wrinkles. "Someone must have told her where to look."

Heat surged under my skin, prickling along my arms and the back of my neck. As one, the others shifted, a collective recalibration, as if they were turning toward a noise I'd made without realizing it. The room felt smaller, airless.

"I texted her," I heard myself say, already wishing I'd kept my damn mouth shut. "About the diary. Viv asked me to see if Mia knew where Leah hid it."

Whitney's head tilted, as if confused. She rubbed her thumb along the diamonds in her tennis bracelet. "You told her?"

"Why the hell would you do that?" Brooke's eyes had an angry glint to them, the first spark breaking through her worry. "That was a stupid thing to do."

My heart pounded too fast. It vibrated inside my ribs. "She's Leah's mother. She deserved to know."

"Of course she did," Rowan said after a pause. "No one's blaming you."

Brooke's taut expression suggested otherwise. I felt myself shrinking from their disapproval. Shame heated my cheeks, even though I didn't have anything to be ashamed of.

The clock on Brooke's mantel ticked. My breath sounded too loud in my ears. Too fast, too shallow. The air had changed. The molecules were rearranging themselves. Blame in Whitney's face, anger in Brooke's scowl.

"I should get home," Whitney said abruptly. She rechecked her phone as if some emergency had materialized in the last thirty seconds. "Peyton has swim practice from four to six, then piano, and her personal trainer comes by after dinner."

I thought of the circled name in the diary. "Who's Taylor Everett?"

Whitney froze mid-step. Her hand tightened on her phone. "What?"

"The name is in the diary. Circled multiple times."

Whitney waved a hand dismissively. "A girl from the neighborhood. She got high on something and went swimming at a pool party. Nearly drowned. It was terrible. The family moved across the country within weeks of the accident."

Rowan and Brooke exchanged a weighted glance. Another look between Rowan and Whitney, and between Rowan and Brooke. Tiny, invisible messages I wasn't a part of. My stomach lurched.

"It was such a shame," Rowan said. "They were a lovely family. But that has nothing to do with Leah."

Before I could say anything else, the rumble of a car engine sounded outside. Brooke's head snapped toward the window. Her body went rigid. "Oh, that'll be Jason. I didn't realize he'd be stopping by for lunch."

A moment later, the garage side door opened. Jason stepped in, phone already in hand, thumbs moving. In his early fifties, several years older than Brooke, he was lean and rangy, his linen shirt rumpled at the elbows, his square, black-framed glasses slightly skewed. He was handsome in a disheveled professor sort of way.

Brooke slid her wine glass behind the lamp on the end table and stood, smoothing her already glossy hair. Her smile appeared, bright and practiced. She went to Jason and kissed his stubbled cheek. "Hey, babe. You didn't tell me you'd be home for lunch. I would've made avocado toast or a smoothie for you."

He didn't look up. "Just looking for my hunter green tie. The Hermès one. I've got the Dearborn meeting at 2:00 p.m."

"It's at the cleaners, remember? I told you this morning." Her voice was light and cheerful. "I can grab the navy striped one from your closet."

"Never mind, I'll find something." He finally glanced up, seeming to register the room for the first time. His gaze swept over the other mothers, landed briefly on me, then returned to his wife. "Oh hey, ladies. Everything okay?"

Rowan's smile matched Brooke's. "We're fine, Jason. Nice to see you."

He kissed the air near his wife's cheek, automatic, perfunctory. Brooke flushed. "Don't have too much fun, ladies."

He headed down the hall. His footsteps receded toward the primary bedroom.

Brooke turned back to us, the brightness still fixed on her face. She laughed lightly, rolling her eyes. "Sorry about that. Always something."

Whitney was already halfway out the door. "I'll text the group chat."

"Wait. I'll walk you out, Whit." Brooke followed Whitney, a slight drag to her steps.

Whitney didn't say goodbye. Brooke offered a vague wave over her shoulder. The front door opened. The afternoon light sliced across the hall rug, then vanished as the door shut.

"Come on. I think we've overstayed our welcome." Rowan's hand found the small of my back with a practiced lightness as she guided me toward the door.

In the foyer, she turned to face me. "I know this is hard for all of us."

Hard was one word for it. The floor beneath me felt unstable. Words were slippery. My daughter's face appeared behind my eyes and then Leah's, overlaid like a double exposure.

"The police will want to talk to all of the girls again about what's in that damn diary." Rowan watched my reaction. "Just remember, our daughters were friends with Leah."

"They were cruel to her," I said before I could stop myself.

Rowan's smile appeared. The kind that could sharpen if you weren't careful. "Mia was right there, too, wasn't she? Every time."

The word was like glass in my throat. "Yes."

"I'm not judging. I understand. Truly, I do. I'm appalled, too, at Chloe for standing by and remaining quiet. Laughing isn't the same as actual bullying, but it's still impolite. I'm just saying, this is a valuable lesson for our girls to learn now." Rowan's eyes softened. "We all have something to protect."

She meant my daughter. Mia with the blood-stained dress, the scratches, the missing camera. Who'd possibly lied about staying inside all night. The weight of it pressed against my ribs until I couldn't draw a full breath.

She reached for my hand and gave it a quick squeeze. Her fingers were cool. "Think carefully about what you say to anyone. For Mia's sake."

I nodded. She opened the door for me. Brooke and Whitney were still at the end of the driveway, standing close, heads bent, murmuring intently. They went quiet as I approached.

Disquiet prickled at the base of my spine. They'd gone outside so they could talk without me.

Stiffly, I walked past them without saying anything, then turned west toward home. My legs felt like they belonged to someone else. Boneless, unreliable, as if they couldn't hold me upright.

The sun was out. The April air should have felt fresh, but it tasted metallic in my mouth. Wrong. Everything felt wrong.

My hands were shaking. I shoved them into my jacket pockets and kept walking, head down. Rowan's words replayed in my head. "Mia was right there, too."

My chest ached. Since moving here, I'd hovered at the edges of their circle, the not-quite insider. I'd spent months trying to fit into their world—attending their parties, volunteering for fundraisers, laughing at their jokes, grateful for every scrap of inclusion. I'd been so desperate for us to belong that I'd missed every warning sign.

If I wanted the truth, I'd have to find it myself. I'd done this before. I'd tracked down sources, pieced together evidence, and exposed uncomfortable truths. I'd been a journalist for fifteen years before Marcus died. I'd let grief turn me soft and needy.

No more.

The cottage came into view around the curve in the road. The maple in our front yard dappled the lawn with sunlight like spilled coins.

From here, I could see the Everett house. Empty windows looked back at me, dark behind the glass. Another young girl, another tragedy connected to this neighborhood, to these families.

A twitch of movement behind a curtain on the second floor of the Henderson house snagged my eye. Fabric swished and went still. No silhouette. No face. Just the afterimage of someone having been there, watching.

I checked the mailbox and headed up the driveway. Apollo's barking floated faintly through the closed windows. He always knew when I was approaching the house.

Mia's silhouette filled the front window. She was waiting for me, one hand flat on the glass.

My heart felt like someone had stomped on it. The diary had proved Mia wasn't innocent. Not the way I'd wanted her to be. But complicity had degrees. Lines, borders.

How complicit was my daughter? How many times had she gone along, laughed, stood silent, participated? Could I bear the truth, whatever it was? Part of me wanted to turn around, get in the car, and drive until none of this was real anymore.

But I couldn't. Mia needed me. Even if what she'd done was unforgivable, she was still my daughter.

First, I needed to get the truth from Mia.

I took a breath and stepped onto the porch. The front door swung open. Apollo burst out, nails scrabbling on the front porch. Mia caught his collar with one hand, holding him back. Her anxious gaze scanned my face, searching for answers. "What happened?"

I didn't have to tell her. Her face went pale. She knew. Of course, she knew. The diary was out there now. There was no more hiding.

I stepped into the doorway. Apollo pressed himself against my knees, whining eagerly. The house smelled like his fur, last night's pizza, and the lemon cleaner I used on the countertops.

Mia's hand was still on the doorknob.

Mine closed over hers. "We need to talk."

Chapter Seventeen

"We're going to the beach," I said to Mia. "Get your jacket."

Mia hesitated. She wore pink sweatpants and an oversized Taylor Swift sweatshirt, her hair pulled into a damp knot at the nape of her neck.

"Now?" she asked.

"Now."

Her eyes flicked past me, to the kitchen, the living room, anywhere but at my face, as if searching for an escape hatch. There wasn't one. Not this time.

Apollo whined eagerly. He paced in tight, anxious circles by the door while I pulled on my sneakers. When I opened the hall closet to grab his leash, he trotted over, his whole tail end wagging in anticipation.

"At least let me change."

"You're fine," I said. "Shoes, Mia. That's it."

She raised her chin at my tone, but she knew better than to argue. She disappeared into the mudroom and came back, slipping her bare feet into her white knockoff Vans.

I locked the patio door behind us and pocketed the keys. We walked along the road to the community beach access north of Rowan's house.

Mrs. Atkins was in her usual rocking chair, her cardigan wrapped around her shoulders. She stared at us, nodding when we passed. I nodded back.

We strode past the leaning oak at the corner of Wyld Wood Lane and Windward Point to the community gazebo and the wooden staircase leading down to the beach. All 179 steps.

Apollo scrambled down the stairs, his leash taut. The air smelled like wet earth, pine needles, and fresh water. The steep bluff was choked with bushes, weeds, and a few scrubby trees.

We descended the last stairs. The beach spread out before us, a hundred feet deep, stretching as far as the lighthouse to the south and further than we could see to the north. Ahead of us, Lake Michigan dazzled a rich cobalt blue. Blue water under a blue sky. The horizon line was hazy.

We discarded our shoes by the stairs, our feet sinking into the sand. The waves rolled in, low and steady. The wind off the water was cold, needling through my jacket as I unhooked Apollo's leash and let him run.

He exploded into a joyous sprint along the wet strip by the waterline, his legs flinging arcs of sand everywhere.

The beach was almost empty. A man in a dark parka walked a golden retriever near the bluff. Farther down, a couple stood shoulder to shoulder, looking out at the water. No one was close enough to hear anything unless we started shouting.

I didn't know how to start the conversation gently, so I just came out with it. "Vivienne showed us Leah's diary."

Mia's mouth pressed flat. "Oh."

Every bitter detail from the diary looped in my head. "She read from it. Your name is in there. A lot."

The color drained from Mia's face. She knew what was coming.

The waves hissed and sighed. A gull wheeled overhead. We trudged along the firmer sand where the waves had just receded while Apollo darted in and out of the waves, water beading his flanks, sand clinging to his fur.

"Leah wrote about being bullied. Why didn't you tell me what was happening?"

Mia kicked at a stray piece of driftwood and didn't answer. We kept walking. I waited, giving her space.

Along the coastline, broken staircases and massive oak trees tipped like toothpicks littered the bluff, as the lake gradually ate the bottom of the bluff out from under itself and groundwater loosened great gaping chunks from the topside. Some properties boasted seawalls to keep the erosion at bay, but mother nature was relentless.

Finally, I stopped walking. "Look at me."

She kept her gaze pinned somewhere near my shoulder. I stepped in front of her, forcing her to either crash into me or stop. She stopped.

"Look at me," I repeated.

Slowly, she did. Her eyes were glassy.

"Explain it to me. Because right now, what I see in that diary is my daughter participating in bullying her best friend. I need you to explain that to me."

She dragged the back of her sleeve over her face, leaving a damp streak. "It wasn't—it didn't feel like that. Leah would make jokes, too. It was... how we talked. It was stupid, but it wasn't that bad. Not at first." She swallowed.

"But you saw it was hurting her."

Her shoulders curled inward, like she wanted to fold herself inside out. "After Christmas, it got worse. Alexis and Peyton, especially. They'd push it farther. Leah stopped laughing."

"You still laughed."

"I was scared." She said it fast. "Okay? I was scared they'd turn on me if I didn't. You don't get it, Mom. They... they pick. One person. And then it's just... constant. Every outfit, every answer in class, every post. If I didn't go along, they'd choose me next."

"Better her than you, right?"

Mia recoiled. "That's not—I didn't think—"

"But that's what happened." I kept my voice even. "You watched. You participated."

Her tears spilled faster now. She swiped at them, angry with herself. "I know, okay? I hate myself for it. I think about it all the time. Every time you say her name, I feel like I'm going to throw up."

"Then why didn't you say something earlier?" I asked. "When I asked you what happened that night. When we sat at that table, and you told me she was fine."

"Because you'd look at me like this," she said in a strangled voice.

That landed hard. I took a breath, forced myself to stay calm, to listen.

A few dozen feet in front of us, Apollo lunged at a length of driftwood bobbing in the shallows, barking when the wave tugged it away. I whistled him back, needing the distraction. He loped over, sand plastered to his legs, water dripping from his chest.

Mia tugged her phone out of her hoodie pocket and held it close to her face. She put it away swiftly, but not before I caught a telltale glimpse. "What is that you keep looking at?"

"Nothing."

"Mia."

Her gaze darted toward the water, the sky, the curve of the pier in the distance. Anywhere but my face.

"I need you to show me that app or website or chat or whatever it is you keep looking at."

"Mom, can we not do this right now?"

"No," I said. "We are absolutely going to do this right now. Whatever you're not telling me could be the difference between you ending up in prison or finding the real killer. You don't get to keep that to yourself because it's uncomfortable."

She bit down on her lower lip. Her shoulders sagged.

"Tell me. Now."

"There's this account," she said finally. "On Instagram."

"What account?"

She hesitated, then retrieved the phone again. "LakeshoreTea. It's like an anonymous gossip thing. People send stuff in, and whoever runs it posts it. Screenshots. Photos. Polls. DMs between people. Edited photos. AI videos. Rumors about teachers. About students. It gets mean."

I held out my hand. "Show me."

Reluctantly, she set the phone in my palm.

The screen glowed. The account's profile picture was a cartoon teacup, bright pink, with a tiny cartoon school drawn inside the teacup instead of tea. Handle: LakeshoreTea.

I scrolled as rows of posts flicked past my thumb. Text, images, and videos, many focused on Mia: Mia's yearbook photo, but with glowing red eyes and corpse-like skin. AI-generated videos of her laughing at Leah's funeral, which hadn't even happened yet. Faked screenshots of texts reportedly from Mia confessing to the murder. Another AI-generated image of Mia pushing Leah off a cliff with Mia's hands photoshopped, covered in blood.

Then the comments:

She wanted to be the main character SO bad she literally unalived her bff.

Ultimate pick me behavior is killing your best friend for attention.

Bet she thought the guys would feel sorry for her.

No literally she's a psychopath.

Her eyes are dead inside if you look close.

FR she needs to be in jail like 4ever.

I cursed under my breath. Outrage burned beneath my skin. I wanted to throw the phone into the lake, to confront these girls who would so callously destroy my child with their poisonous words. An ugly part of me wanted to make them hurt as much as they'd hurt Mia. "Oh, honey. I'm so sorry."

"They're trying to make me look guilty." Her voice dropped. "That's what they do. Everyone believes it, too. They know it's fake, but it looks real, so they start to actually believe it."

I took a deep breath, trying to process what I was seeing, the awful things Mia had endured in silence. It was hard to believe kids could be so hateful so young. But then, maybe it wasn't. The entire world was bristling with hatred. "When did this start?"

"Since Leah died. I guess I got what I deserved."

"No one deserves to be treated like this. Ever. Not for any reason."

She gave a resigned shrug.

"Why didn't you tell me?"

She looked away. "I didn't want to bother you. You were so happy about this move. I didn't want to ruin it."

Guilt stabbed between my ribs. I fought back tears. "I want you to be happy. You're my priority, always."

She still didn't look at me. "Okay."

I pulled her into a hug. "I'm so sorry they're doing this to you."

She let me hold her for a moment, her body tense, then pulled away. "They were worse to Leah. Before she died, most of the posts were about her. Other girls, too, though. Last year, I heard it was all about Taylor."

I scrolled back. Mia was right. The posts about Leah were sadistic in a different way. AI-generated images showed her yearbook photo with her head placed on a pig's body, captioned "When the pig filter is an upgrade."

The comments were worse:

She ate the whole buffet, and it shows.

Genuinely a jump scare when she walks into class.

POV: you have to sit next to Leah in class. Followed by a vomiting emoji.

Another showed her Korean features distorted, eyes exaggerated into slits, skin yellowed, along with a photo of her eating food, captioned: "watch the whale feed." Body-morphing edits made her appear grotesquely overweight. There were sexually explicit images with her face superimposed on naked bodies in crude, degrading positions. The comments underneath were relentless:

Her face card is PERMANENTLY declined

Genuinely a health hazard.

Do us all a favor and just kill yourself.

Every hateful post was designed to strip away her humanity, to make her something less than human. Something acceptable to mock, degrade, and destroy.

My hand went cold around the phone. Tears stung my eyes. My heart ached beneath the anger that sizzled red-hot just beneath the surface. "Oh, Mia. I had no idea."

She kicked at a piece of driftwood. "Yeah, well."

"I wish you had told me sooner."

"It wouldn't have changed anything."

"Of course it would," I insisted. "We could have talked to the school, the police."

"Mom, no," she cut me off. "They'd find a way to twist it, make me look even more pathetic. Same with Leah. It was pointless."

"You're not pathetic," I said firmly. "Leah was being harassed. Now you are. And it's not pointless to report it. This is cyberbullying."

She gave a hollow laugh. "Yeah, just like Leah's bullying stopped after she reported Alexis cutting her hair. Just like that, huh? It got worse, Mom. Not better."

I watched her, my heart heavy. Much as I hated to admit it, she wasn't wrong about that. But if the school hadn't put a stop to it, I would've pulled her out. I would have moved across the country if that's what it took to keep her safe, to protect her. I knew Viv and Daniel would've done the same for Leah.

"You mentioned the name Taylor. Do you mean Taylor Everett? The girl who used to live in this neighborhood?"

"It happened the year before we moved here. I heard the rumors, though. This account started targeting her, posting AI-pictures and videos of her, but fat, or with warts all over her face, or her naked in a vat of blood, her on her knees... you know." Mia picked at a loose thread on her sleeve. "I guess there was some investigation last year after she, ah... she almost drowned in a pool accident and was brain-damaged or something."

I felt sick. "Who the hell runs this account?"

She shrugged. "No one knows. It's anonymous."

I tucked the phone into my jacket pocket.

"Hey, that's mine."

"You'll get it back. Right now, I need it more than you do."

Panic edged her words. "For what? To stalk my friends?"

I had Mia's phone. I had names. And I was going to find out which one of those girls had Leah's blood on their hands. "To figure out the truth."

We stood there in the thinning light, wind pulling at our clothes. Apollo trotted back and shook himself, spraying water all over us, then he leaned his flank against my leg, his sides heaving from his run. The waves kept rolling in.

"Mom," Mia said. "I know it sounds bad. I know I look bad. I didn't go down to the beach. I told you about the diary so Leah's mom could find it, even though I knew it probably had bad stuff about me in there, too. That counts for something, right? I didn't... I didn't want her to die."

I believed her, and I didn't, simultaneously. The worst part was that both could be true: she had never laid a hand on Leah and yet had helped push Leah somewhere she couldn't climb back from.

I stepped close enough to smell the faint coconut shampoo scent clinging to her damp hair. "My job is to protect you. Even from your friends. Even from yourself."

She let out a shaky breath. "You're mad at me."

"I'm furious with you. For what you did. For what you didn't do. For what you still might be hiding."

"But you still—"

"I still love you. That doesn't change. It also doesn't mean there aren't consequences."

She nodded once, as if she'd braced for that. She stared out at the lake. "What if it's someone I know. What if it's... one of us?"

"Then we'll face it," I said.

She didn't pull away when I reached for her hand. Her fingers were cold and damp. I tightened my grip on the leash, on her hand,

and kept walking. The wind pushed at our backs, up toward the streetlights and houses and the tidy lies waiting there.

Chapter Eighteen

I sat at my desk after dinner, the house finally quiet. Mia was upstairs, supposedly doing homework with her door cracked, the newest Sabrina Carpenter song playing on her iPad.

Apollo snored pleasantly on the rug beside my chair, legs twitching as if he were chasing something that only he could see. I envied him.

My browser was open to Instagram. Mia's phone lay in front of me, screen dark, face down. I flipped it over, unlocked it with the code I'd watched her use a hundred times, and opened the app.

I started where I'd left off, with LakeshoreTea.

I went to Mia's DMs. Most of her messages were what I'd expect from a teenage girl. Homework questions. Funny, mildly inappropriate memes. Comments about the hottest guys at Lakeshore Prep. Snaps of outfits posted on her own Instagram account. A long-running group chat with some classmates full of slang and inside jokes that felt like eavesdropping on another language.

I navigated to the "Recently Deleted" folder, expecting to find the usual—bad selfies, failed attempts at aesthetic posts. Instead, I saw a thread of gray boxes where messages should have been, each marked "Message unsent."

All from the same username: @alexis.august.

I exhaled slowly and clicked.

Most of the messages were gone. The visible fragments were one-sided—Mia's responses, still present, hanging in the air with no corresponding texts. The conversation looked like a phone call recorded with only one person's voice.

i didnt say anything i swear
alexis pls
pls i promise
i literally cant do this rn
alexis pls just stop

One message remained, dated the morning after Leah died, unsent but partially cached by a glitch or a lag in the system. A digital ghost.

I leaned in closer.

From: @alexis.august: *if u snitch ur literally dead idc*

A threat. Against my daughter.

My stomach churned. With anger, with horror, with sympathy for Mia.

I sat back, heartbeat loud in my ears. Alexis August. Once Brooke's highly curated golden child, who now defiantly wore Doc Martins and black hoodies, scarlet lipstick, and charcoal cat-eye eyeliner, with a perpetual scowl on her face.

I recalled how she'd stood next to our mailbox on Tuesday morning, watching us as she held up her phone. That mocking wave as her sweatshirt sleeve slid down her wrist to reveal the mottled bruising.

Bruises like fingerprints. A hand encircling her wrist. As if someone had seized her arm to keep from falling.

Alexis had a capacity for violence. Leah's diary had described the bathroom incident in humiliating detail. Alexis with scissors in her hand, advancing on a cowering Leah. Hair falling to the tile in clumps. Leah trapped against a tiled wall, sobbing and helpless.

Mia had claimed Alexis wasn't in her sleeping bag that night.

Then where was she? Outside on the bluff, pushing Leah over the edge?

I checked the time. Past 8 p.m. The kind of hour when respectable mothers were settling into their wine and Netflix, not expecting unannounced visitors.

I didn't care.

If Alexis was threatening my daughter, I wanted to see her face. I wanted to watch her reaction when I asked her where she'd been when Leah died. I wanted to press until something cracked.

But I needed a reason to show up. An errand, a prop.

Brooke no longer had my key, or so she claimed. I made a mental note to get my house key from Whitney as soon as possible. Tomorrow, in fact.

I needed something else. I recalled Brooke at the Easter party a few weeks ago, wearing a mint-green dress sprinkled with white polka dots, her perfect teeth bared in a laugh as she handed me leftover lemon cream pie in a cake stand with a cut-crystal dome.

"Just drop it by whenever," she'd said. "I can't keep dessert in the house, or Alexis will stuff it in her face all in one night."

That would work.

I shut down the app, powered off Mia's phone, and slid it into my pocket. Apollo lifted his head as I pushed back from the desk.

"Want to go for a walk?" I asked him.

His ears perked. He scrambled to his paws and nosed at my thigh impatiently.

"That's what I thought."

I slipped into my jean jacket, then grabbed the cake stand from the pantry where I'd shoved it two weeks ago, wrapped a dishtowel around it to protect the crystal, and tucked it into a reusable grocery bag from Meijer.

Upstairs, the light under Mia's door still burned bright.

"I'm taking Apollo out," I called up.

"Okay." Her voice was flat, cautious. We were both nursing bruises from our conversation on the beach earlier.

I should go up to her. Sit on the edge of her bed. Ask again, quietly, if there was anything she hadn't told me. Hug her and tell her I loved her, the way Marcus would have.

And I would, as soon as I returned.

"Come on, boy." Apollo and I stepped out into the night.

I adjusted the bag with the cake stand as I walked, heading east on Driftwood Terrace. Apollo trotted ahead, sniffing everything. The cool night air carried the distant crash of waves against the bluffs. Porch lights glimmered up and down the street, like little amber islands in the dark.

We passed Vivienne's craftsman home. The curtains were drawn, their porch light dark. No lights in the windows except a glow from a single second-story window. A few minutes later, Brooke's house came into view.

Noise drifted. Muffled voices, punctuated by something sharp. The sounds were coming from Brooke's black farmhouse.

I slowed.

One of the HOA walking paths through the wooded acreage behind the community's property lines was located next to Brooke's house, separated by a line of tall arborvitae trees.

From the gravel walking path, the back patio was partially visible. Brooke had complained often about the lack of privacy.

Before I could think better of it, I swiftly moved off the sidewalk onto the pathway, heading as near to the backyard as I could without drawing attention to myself. Apollo followed close behind me.

Angling myself behind the prickly branches, I cautiously peeked between the trees. Fifty feet away, Brooke and Alexis were standing outside on their 2000-square-foot bluestone patio. Light cast a halo through the sliding glass doors.

Brooke stood a foot from Alexis, angrily shaking her finger in her daughter's face. Alexis was barefoot, in ripped jeans and a cropped Nirvana T-shirt, her hair a wild purple-black mess. Even at this distance, the tension was visible in her shoulders, her chin down, eyes averted defensively.

Brooke's voice rose, slurred and vicious. "You think I don't know what you've been doing? Sneaking around. Taking things that don't belong to you."

I went still, though I was hidden behind the screen of tall arborvitae trees. I should move on, leave them to their privacy. But the acid in Brooke's tone pinned me in place.

Alexis's voice came out thin, pleading. "Mom, I didn't do anything."

"Don't lie to me." Brooke's hand shot out, gripping Alexis's wrist. The girl flinched. "My pills, Alexis. You think I wouldn't notice? You think I'm too drunk to count?"

"I didn't take your stupid pills!"

"Liar." The word came out wet, the consonants blurred. "You steal from me. You embarrass me. You ruin everything you touch."

I pressed against the needle-like foliage, the woody conifer scent strong in my nostrils, heart hammering. Pills. What pills? Brooke was clearly drinking heavily, but pills, too? Or was she accusing Alexis of something else entirely?

Guilt pricked at me. I shouldn't be hearing this. But I couldn't unhear it now. Apollo sniffed around the base of the nearest arborvitae. I pulled the leash, keeping him close to me, praying he wouldn't choose this moment to bark at a squirrel or a falling leaf.

"Let me go!" Alexis tried to pull away. Brooke yanked her back. Alexis inhaled sharply. "Mom, please. Stop it! You're hurting me." Alexis's voice cracked, stripped of its usual bravado. She sounded so young, so scared.

Brooke's hand flashed up, not quite a strike, but close. A practiced threat, as if she'd done it before. Alexis recoiled like she'd been hit.

Brooke swayed on her feet. "You think I'm stupid? We're in this mess because of you. You steal, you lie, you embarrass this family. If this gets out, what do you think will happen?"

"Mom," Alexis pleaded.

"I need you to tell me you understand, Alexis, or I swear, I'll ground you until you're 25, and worse. You think I'm a terrible mother now? Just you wait."

"Fine! Okay, okay!"

From inside the house, a young male voice yelled something. Brooke and Alexis stiffened.

"Now look what you did." Brooke swore under her breath as she shoved Alexis toward the door, then herded her daughter inside with a hand between her shoulder blades. The gesture looked affectionate from a distance.

Now I knew better.

I swallowed, my mouth dry, and backed away cautiously. Brooke had a drinking problem. We all knew that, though she was a master at hiding it from the rest of the world, especially her rabid Instagram followers.

This was far worse than I had imagined. Behind Brooke's carefully curated Instagram persona, the perfect house, the perfect family, and the perfect life, something much darker was lurking.

Apollo whined.

"Yeah," I said under my breath. "I know, buddy."

My phone buzzed in my pocket. I pulled it out and saw a text from Rowan: *Thinking of you. Don't believe what you read. We know who Mia really is.*

There were now so many posts and articles. The comments calling Mia a monster, threads dissecting her Instagram photos, think pieces analyzing her "dead eyes" in the school yearbook. I couldn't keep track anymore.

I sent a quick text thanking Rowan and pocketed the phone, my mind churning. I had painted Alexis as a violent bully in my mind, but here she was, a frightened, hurting kid, harmed by her own mother.

What didn't Brooke want Alexis to talk about? The abuse itself? The pills? What accident was she talking about?

Hurt people hurt people.

Was this the terrible secret Alexis didn't want exposed? That she'd threatened both Leah and Mia over? That her mom was a closet drunk. That the image of their perfect family had devastating cracks. Or something else entirely, something related to Leah's death?

I felt sick. I wanted to hug Alexis, not investigate her.

Just because she was a victim didn't mean she wasn't also a perpetrator.

There was the circular bruise on Alexis's wrist, bruising Leah may have caused as she fell, grabbing wildly at the person who'd pushed her. Alexis at our mailbox right after our house was violated, and my notebook was stolen. Alexis, the bully, who threatened Mia and assaulted Leah months before she died.

The pieces of the puzzle were slowly falling into place.

I had to stay focused, to keep my head clear.

I needed answers. It was time to talk to Brooke.

Chapter Nineteen

The black modern farmhouse loomed ahead, porch lights blazing too bright for 8:50 p.m. The whole place glowed like a showroom.

The bag with the cake stand nestled inside it banged softly against my knee as I climbed the steps. It had weight. Enough to knock someone out if I swung hard enough. I rang the doorbell. For once, Apollo sat obediently beside me, his tongue lolling.

The sound echoed. For a second, I saw Alexis again—her frightened face, Brooke's fingers digging into the soft skin of her upper arm.

The door swung wide. Jason August filled the frame.

He wore dark joggers and a white T-shirt that looked ironed, probably by Brooke. His hair was mussed, deliberately. He was holding his phone at shoulder height, the screen's glow reflected in his glasses.

He frowned, not at me, but at whatever was on the screen. Then he seemed to register that there was a person in front of him. A neighbor. An intrusion.

"Hey," he said. "Dahlia, right?"

He didn't indicate that he knew I'd been in his house earlier today. "Sorry to bother you so late."

He smiled then. Boyish, handsome. And he knew it, too. He and Brooke both liked pretty things. "What's up?"

I lifted the cake stand carefully. My voice was steadier than my hands. "I borrowed this for the Easter thing a few weeks ago. I figured I'd bring it by."

"Oh. Right. Thanks." His forehead pinched. He took the stand from me as if it might bite him. He stepped back, as if about to retreat without inviting me in. "Uh, Brooke?"

"It goes in the cabinet over the fridge." Brooke's voice came from somewhere down the hall. When she appeared, he handed the stand to her.

"Well, I'll leave you ladies to it." He gave me a wave and a grin before he disappeared deeper into the house. "Good to see you again!"

Brooke rolled her eyes at his back, then turned her attention to me. Her hair was loose around her face. She had a wine flush along her chest, just visible at the edge of her silk camisole. Her feet were bare, her toenails the color of dried blood.

She placed the cake stand on the narrow entry table. "Sorry. He'd lose his own head if it weren't attached to his neck." She glanced at Apollo, then stepped forward and pulled the front door mostly closed behind her until it rested against her hip. The muted sound of the television drifted out.

"I won't keep you." My throat felt tight, head buzzing. "I wanted to talk for a minute."

Her eyes sharpened, scanning my face. In the harsh porch light, the lines around her eyes and mouth were more pronounced. "So, talk."

"I'm worried about Alexis."

Brooke stiffened. "What?"

I kept my voice low, even. "I've seen some bruises on her arms. I just wanted to make sure she's okay. That you're okay."

"What are you talking about?"

"I just know things can get... overwhelming. With kids." I

flicked my gaze past her, toward the sound of the TV. "With everything you have going on."

"Overwhelming," she repeated, like it was a foreign word. Her jaw worked. Her face reddened. "You saw a bruise and thought what, exactly? That I'm beating my daughter?"

The neighbor's porch light across the street clicked on. A car rolled down the street, engine low, music a muted pulse.

"No, that's not what I meant."

"Sure, it is." Her face shifted, emotions passing across her features in rapid succession—fear, calculation, embarrassment, fury. Then something hardened. "Falcon has special needs. As you well know. He can be violent during meltdowns. You have no idea what it's like living with that."

"I know it's hard," I allowed. "But those marks on her arm—"

"He choked her, last week." Brooke barreled on, voice low and fast, as if, if she kept talking, she could outrun me. "He gets into these states, and he's so much stronger than he looks. He throws things. He hits. He bites. He went after me with a fork the other day, and where was Jason? At work, again. At the gym. On his phone. Telling me to just stay calm."

A thud sounded from somewhere inside, followed by a burst of high-pitched laughter.

"Alexis—"

"My daughter is fine." The lie sat between us, heavy. Her pupils were blown wide. "You come over here all concerned and judgmental, and you act like you're some kind of authority. Like you're the perfect parent."

For a heartbeat, my anger softened into something like pity. Exhaustion radiated off her like heat from asphalt. The hollows under her eyes looked carved into her flesh.

None of that made what I'd seen okay.

"I saw you," I said, louder, firmer.

She blanched.

"I saw what you did." I took a breath, steeled myself. "Earlier tonight, I was out back with Apollo. I could see your patio. I saw you grab her, Brooke."

Her eyes flared. A flush crawled up her throat. "You were spying on us?"

"I was walking my dog." I held up the leash as evidence. Apollo panted agreeably. "You were out on the patio. You were yelling at Alexis. You told her to keep her mouth shut."

Her words slurred slightly. "You have no idea what you saw."

"Then tell me. Help me to understand. I'm not the enemy here."

"You sure sound like the enemy to me."

"I'm not." I took a breath. "Brooke, listen. If you need help, there are resources. I could give you numbers. I could help."

"Resources. What are you gonna do, give me a pamphlet?"

"If you want to talk to someone—"

"I have a therapist. Two, actually. I have a pediatric neurologist on call, an IEP team, a behaviorist, and an occupational therapist, all for my son's special needs. And you know what? None of them show up at my door late at night to make me feel terrible about myself. Is that what you want, Dahlia?"

"I'm not trying to make you feel bad. I'm trying to make sure your daughter is safe."

"I don't need your advice. Or your pity."

"I'm not offering pity. Just support."

Her mouth twisted, teeth flashing. "You think you're better than me, don't you?"

I blinked, taken aback. "No, I just—"

"I see it in your eyes," she snarled. "Judging me, my children. Well, newsflash, Dahlia—we're not all perfect."

"I'm not judging."

"Save it for someone who cares."

"Let me help you."

She recoiled. "I don't need help. Certainly not from you."

"Brooke, please. I'm just trying to be a friend."

She laughed hollowly. "Friend? We were never friends."

Her words stung more than I cared to admit. I took a step back, aghast. "You don't mean that."

"Don't I? You're Rowan's little pet project, that's all. She loves to adopt lost birds with broken wings, or haven't you noticed?"

I flinched. The insult landed, and she knew it. Brooke's sharp gaze raked over my face, cataloguing the damage. She almost smiled. "Hit a nerve?"

"I'm not your enemy," I said again, quieter now. "And I'm not Alexis's. Alexis has a right to be safe in her own home. And you are obligated to keep her safe."

"I said she's fine." Each word was bitten off, final.

Something crashed inside, loud and metallic. A child's shriek followed an instant later, high and piercing and wordless. Falcon.

Brooke winced like someone had fired a gun next to her ear. Her hand moved behind her instinctively, catching the door as if trying to keep the whole house from bursting open.

Falcon's wordless wail tore down the hall, ragged with distress. "No! No no no—"

"Let me help," I said. "I can stay with Alexis. Or with Falcon. Whatever I can do. I want to help."

"Stay away from my family. I'm warning you, Dahlia."

"Brooke—"

Another wail echoed from inside again, shrill, hitting a frequency that made my teeth ache. Something hit a wall with a hollow bang.

Apollo tensed, a low whine of apprehension in his throat.

"Falcon, honey, it's okay," Brooke called over her shoulder. She spun to face me, fury in her face. "Leave us alone. Or I'll call the cops and have you arrested for harassment and trespassing. Don't think I won't. And Alexis will back up her family, every word. So will Rowan and Whitney and everyone else, everyone but you. Get off my property."

Brooke slammed the door in my face.

The house swallowed Falcon's cries.

Apollo whined again. He pressed his shoulder to my leg, restless. His panting breath fogged the cool night air.

Across the street, a second-story curtain lifted an inch. Someone was watching. Someone was always watching.

I stood rooted under the porch light. I pressed my palm against the door. For half a second, I imagined shoving it open anyway, walking down that hallway, scooping Alexis up if she were the one crying. Standing between her and whatever rage lived in this house.

When I pushed, the door didn't give. It was locked.

I let my hand drop.

The law wouldn't care about bruises I couldn't photograph. About something I'd glimpsed in the dark, from a distance. Brooke's excuses about Falcon's meltdowns would sound reasonable if written up in a report. A wealthy, beautiful, loving mother struggling with a neurodivergent child. Doing spectacular considering the circumstances.

Plus, the August family had the resources to bury me in court if they thought I was doing anything to tarnish their spotless reputation.

I backed away from the door. The porch light hummed overhead. The night pressed in at the corners of the yard, thick and watchful.

I closed my eyes, feeling physically sick. The Brooke I'd just witnessed wasn't the friend who'd shown up on my birthday with homemade cookies, who made me laugh until I cried at book club, who texted the perfect meme at exactly the right moment.

Was that Brooke even real? I wanted to believe she was. But then, so was the one who grabbed Alexis behind closed doors.

Brooke was straining under the burden of living a double life. One glossy, perfect, alluring. The other, not so much.

I thought of Brooke snatching the photocopied diary pages from my hands before I could keep reading, then stuffing them into a drawer and slamming it shut. How she'd told Viv about the scratches on Mia's arms and Leah's blood on Mia's dress, as if she'd been planting suspicions in Vivienne's mind, even then. Painting Mia as the villain, rather than her own daughter.

The August family had secrets. Mother and daughter, together. How far would they go to protect those secrets if someone threatened them?

Tomorrow, Alexis would walk Falcon to the bus stop like she did most mornings. I'd try to get her alone then. If she wasn't there, I'd make a plan B, find another way.

I just needed a crack in the armor. A moment without Brooke's watchful eye.

I would find her in that moment.

"If the mothers won't tell the truth," I said to Apollo, my voice carried away by the wind, "the daughters will."

Chapter Twenty

Thursday morning dawned bright and deceptively cheerful. I winced against the band of pressure behind my eyes. I'd slept in fits and starts. My eyes were gritty. None of that mattered.

Mia was at home getting ready for school. Despite the swirling rumors and Camille's advice, she was desperate to go, and I didn't have the heart to keep her home if a routine was what she wanted.

Maybe it was what she needed. It seemed like a better option than leaving her home, miserable in her room all day.

I took Apollo for his morning walk. I was on a mission, walking fast. Apollo trotted beside me, eager and alert. His leash pulled taut as we crossed the grass, headed for the community playground.

It was 7:30 a.m. School didn't start until 8:30 a.m. Alexis often brought Falcon to the playground before the bus arrived to take him to a private elementary school that specialized in students with special needs.

This was my chance to get her alone. Possibly my only chance. I'd rehearsed a dozen openings on the walk over.

The playground sat at the far end of the community park, a rectangle of sand bordered by manicured grass and mature oak trees. Only one swing was occupied.

Alexis stood behind it, pushing Falcon in slow even arcs with one hand, checking something on her phone in the other. She wore ripped black jeans, scuffed Doc Martens, and a faded Metallica T-shirt under a leather jacket.

"Hey, Alexis," I called.

She glanced up, instantly wary. Her hazel eyes were outlined with black eyeliner in a cat-eye shape. There was something brittle in the way she held herself, shoulders tensed like she was bracing for a hit that might come from any direction.

"Mind if we join you?"

She rolled her eyes. "I don't own the park. It's a free country. For now, anyway."

She slipped her phone into her pocket, but not before I saw the familiar pink emblem on the screen. The LakeshoreTea account.

My gut tightened. I stepped closer. "Hi, Falcon."

Falcon's legs pumped with perfect rhythm. The Paw Patrol sweatshirt he wore clung to his narrow frame. His dirty blond curls fell into his brown eyes, the same color as Brooke's. He leaned back into the swing, face expressionless as his gaze slid past me and landed on Apollo.

"Dog," he said, voice monotone.

"This is Apollo," I said. "Remember him? He loves playing fetch."

He didn't respond, but his focus sharpened. The swing slowed as Falcon's feet dragged through the sand.

"Want to throw the ball for him?" I reached into my pocket and pulled out a tennis ball.

Falcon nodded.

"Gently," Alexis said. Her voice softened when she spoke to him. "Remember what we talked about. No hitting, no kicking."

"No hitting. No kicking." He slid off the swing and came toward us. His steps were careful and measured.

I unclipped Apollo's leash. "Go on. Let's see that throw."

Falcon took the ball from my hand. He lobbed it toward the

stand of oak trees at the edge of the park. Apollo bounded after it, tail wagging, crashing through last year's leaves.

"That should keep him busy for a few minutes," I said.

Alexis watched Falcon jog after Apollo. She stepped away from the swing, putting a few extra feet between us, and dragged one sleeve over her nose. A fresh bruise peeked out of the sleeve of her jacket. "What do you want?"

Fresh anger flared through me at the sight of the bruise. I had to look away for a second and remember why I was here, remember Leah's handwriting in her diary. The scissors.

"Just to talk," I said. "If that's okay."

"It's not." Alexis glared at me. She was solidly built, broad-shouldered and heavy-set, her face dusted with acne she tried to hide under foundation. Her expressive brown eyes shifted between guarded and defiant.

She was loud, blunt, and tough, but underneath the swagger and combat boots, I'd caught flashes of raw insecurity: the way she flinched at Brooke's comments about her skin or weight, the defensive hunch of her shoulders, the sarcasm she wielded like a weapon.

"I'll only take a few minutes," I said. "Please."

She rolled her eyes. "You're going to do it anyway, so whatever. Start your interrogation, then."

I ignored the jab. "How are you doing?"

Her eyebrows shot up. "Seriously? You came all the way here to ask me about my feelings?"

"Yes."

"I'm thrilled. Obviously." She swept a hand around the empty playground. "Hanging at the park with my defective brother while my mom curates her perfect life on Instagram. Living the dream."

"You know he's not—"

"I know who he is," she snapped. "I live with him. He's my brother."

Across the grass, Falcon threw the ball again, a little farther this time. Apollo barreled after it like it was the best game in the world.

Falcon's face stayed serious, intent. He adjusted his stance before each throw.

I tried a softer approach. "I know things have been hard since Leah died."

"Understatement of the century," she muttered.

"We all miss her."

"Do we? Seems like everyone just wants to blame someone and move on."

She wasn't entirely wrong. "Did you break into my house?"

Her eyes narrowed. "What are you even talking about?"

"Someone broke into my house on Tuesday and moved our things around. Then someone broke in again and stole my notebook. Was it you?"

She gaped at me. "No way."

"You were standing in front of our mailbox right after it happened. Like you'd just left our house."

"Nope. It wasn't me. I was just walking."

"In the rain?"

She glowered at me, but she met my gaze without blinking. "I'm not the Wicked Witch of the West. I'm not gonna melt. Duh. I can walk in my own neighborhood."

I studied her for a minute, looking for a tell, but I didn't see anything. That didn't mean she wasn't lying through her teeth, though. I decided to switch tactics for now. "I'm here about the slumber party."

Her mouth flattened. "I already told the cops everything."

"I know what you told them." I stepped closer. "I don't think it was everything."

"Wow, thanks for the vote of confidence."

"I need the truth. About all of it. About what really happened."

"I don't know anything."

"A girl is dead, Alexis. I need to understand what really happened."

"Like I said, I already told the police everything."

"I don't think you did."

"I was asleep when it happened, okay? I didn't touch Leah. I didn't go near her."

"You hurt Leah, though. Before she died."

Color rose in her cheeks. Spots of heat against her pale skin.

"Vivienne showed us what Leah wrote. In her diary. About what you did to her."

Alexis went rigid. "That's ancient history."

"It's not."

Alexis turned away from me and reached for the backpack resting against the swing set. "You don't know what you're talking about. This conversation is scintillating and all, but I've got things to do."

I steeled myself. I needed to shift tactics. I didn't want to, I had to. It was the only way to get Alexis to talk. "I saw what your mother did to you last night."

Alexis froze.

The swings creaked faintly in the breeze. The aluminum slide glared in the sun.

"I saw her grab your wrist. Hard. I heard what she said to you."

Fear flickered in her eyes, followed by a flash of humiliation. Then the shutters came down. She angled her body away from me, her chin up, defiant. "You should mind your own damn business."

"Abuse is serious."

Her jaw clenched. "You don't know anything."

I nodded at her sleeve. "I know a bruise when I see one."

"You hide in bushes with binoculars like a creeper, or is that just for fun?"

"I was walking my dog. Your patio is perpendicular to the walking path. I saw everything."

"You don't know what you saw."

"I saw her hurt you. I heard her threaten you. I can see the bruises."

Her breath quickened. She stared down at her Doc Martins, refusing to meet my eyes.

"I know you're scared of her. I know she controls you. And I know you haven't told the truth about Friday night. I'm going to tell the detectives what I saw."

Her cheeks reddened. "You can't."

"If you don't talk to me, I'm going to the police about the abuse."

Sheer panic flared in her eyes. "You can't—she'll kill me—"

"Then help me. Tell me what really happened that night, and I'll keep what I saw between us. For now."

There was a long pause as Alexis weighed her options. Part of me wanted to hug her, another part wanted to shake her until her teeth rattled and the truth fell out.

Finally, she looked up at me. "If I tell you, you can't tell my mom. Ever."

"If it's the truth, and it helps clear Mia, I'll do everything I can to protect you."

Alexis studied my face, as if trying to decide whether to trust me. She had no choice, and she knew it.

The urge to back off tugged at me. This girl had been hurt. But she had hurt others, too. Leah was dead. My daughter was a suspect. Sympathy couldn't override that.

I let a beat stretch between us. The chains on the empty swings rattled in the breeze. A crow called from somewhere beyond the oaks. "Why did you really cut Leah's hair?"

"The hair thing was months ago," she said. "Like, forever. It doesn't matter now."

"It mattered to Leah," I said. "She wrote about it. It traumatized her."

Alexis's jaw worked. She took a step back until her spine brushed the swing's chain. Metal clinked softly.

"She saw."

"Saw what?"

"Stuff she shouldn't have." Her laugh was humorless. "Welcome to the Brooke August Experience."

"You're talking about your mom."

"No, I'm talking about Santa Claus."

"Leah saw your mom hurt you," I said to clarify. "At your house."

Alexis gave a sharp nod. "She was there for the Christmas party. My mom was drunk. Falcon was having another tantrum, about to go off in front of everybody, and I didn't catch it fast enough. She got pissed. We were in the kitchen, she grabbed my arm and shook me, told me I was ruining everything, God forbid someone see Falcon throw his goldfish crackers at the wall."

I had attended the Christmas party, but I hadn't seen this incident. I pictured it. The immaculate kitchen. The Christmas lights twinkling, candles on the mantle, the towering Christmas tree. Brooke's smile, slipping like a mask, turning feral. "Leah walked in on it."

"Yeah. A Front row seat. My mom didn't know she was there. But I saw Leah hanging in the doorway, doing that innocent doe-eyed Bambi thing of hers."

"Did she threaten to tell?"

"Leah didn't say anything at first. But then a few days later, at school, she asked if I was okay. If I needed help. If she should tell someone."

"And you panicked."

"I might've freaked out, okay?" Alexis' mouth twisted. "If anyone found out—CPS, the school, my dad—everything would blow up. My whole life would get ripped apart. Falcon would end up in some facility. I'd probably get stuck in some boarding school half-way across the country. My dad sure doesn't want to pay attention to us."

"You hurt her to keep her quiet."

"I cornered her in the bathroom during art. Told her to keep her big mouth shut. She said she was just trying to help, that she was worried about me. I grabbed the scissors I'd brought from the art room, and I just... I wanted to scare her. Make her understand how serious I was."

I felt sick. "You assaulted her."

"I needed her to know she couldn't just say and do whatever she wanted. And she didn't, after that, did she? So, it worked." The words came out flat. She was trying so hard to be tough, impenetrable.

"Is that why you sent threatening messages to Mia, too?" I asked.

Her pupils dilated. A flush crawled up her neck. "I don't know what you're talking about," she said too fast. Deflecting again.

"Alexis. I've seen the LakeshoreTea account. You had it open on your phone just a minute ago."

She swallowed and shifted her gaze to Falcon. He had lost the ball in the leaves and was circling, muttering to himself, hands patting the ground. Apollo danced around him.

"You told her to keep her mouth shut. Or she'd end up like Leah. Ring a bell?"

"I wasn't going to actually do anything. It was just—" She made a frustrated noise. "You don't get it."

"Then explain it to me."

She watched Falcon again. He was making Apollo sit before each throw. Apollo faked compliance, then lunged for the ball early. Falcon corrected him, voice low, patient.

Alexis sighed. "Mia was poking around in my stuff. In my toiletries bag. At the slumber party."

I stilled. Alexis was being honest, finally. "What did she find?"

"Just a vape and a couple of pre-rolls. For later. For after I got out of that Stepford sleepover." She flicked her gaze to me. "I wasn't going to smoke there."

"But Mia saw it. And you would've gotten into trouble."

"My mom. She goes nuclear about everything..." Her voice trailed off. "That's why I was walking in the rain the other day. Things just get really intense sometimes, and I need a break, okay? That's all."

"I get it," I said, and I did. It made sense why she happened to be outside our house in the rain, walking off the tension, escaping the stress of her home life. "You were afraid your weed use would get back to your mom."

She shrugged, attempting nonchalance. "I reminded Mia that if she opened her mouth, there would be consequences. That's all. To make sure she didn't say anything. But that was before the police said that Leah was... that she'd been..."

Before the homicide announcement. The space between the words pulsed.

Across the field, Apollo yelped triumphantly as he found the ball again. Falcon clapped his hands in approval.

"And the LakeshoreTea account, is that yours?"

Her eyes flicked away. "Nope. No one knows who runs it."

"But you took photos of us with your phone that day in the rain."

"It's an anonymous email account. People can send in photos, and whoever runs it posts them. I didn't send them in, though."

"But you were planning to?"

She shrugged. "I dunno why I did that, okay? I was maybe going to, but then I decided not to."

A lie? Or a deflection out of guilt? I checked my phone. 7:55 a.m. I only had a few minutes before Alexis had to take her brother to the bus. Time to focus before I lost her. "Tell me about Friday night. Did you take Mia's camera?"

"Nope. I never saw it again after the photo shoot."

"What about her slippers? The pink ones with the sloths?"

Alexis frowned. "Why would I take her stupid slippers?"

"They were wet. Sandy. Like someone wore them down to the beach."

"Wasn't me." She sounded genuinely confused. "I brought my own shoes. Black Converse. Chloe was pissed I didn't wear heels with my dress. I've told her a million times that I don't do heels. And I definitely don't do furry animal slippers."

I studied her face. Her eyes were steady, no flinch or blink. Alexis wasn't lying about this. I could feel it. I believed her about this, anyway. "Did you see anyone else with the slippers?"

"I don't know. I don't think so. And none of us went down to the beach, anyway."

That corroborated Mia's story, too. "Mia said you were out of your sleeping bag in the middle of the night."

She exhaled, long and slow. The fight left her shoulders in increments. "I couldn't sleep. I checked my phone when I slid out of the bag. It was around 12:30 a.m. Something like that. I remember because I thought, if my mom checks my location now and sees I'm outside, she's going to lose it. But she was probably asleep. Or drunk. So, I slipped outside for a while."

"Did you leave through the basement French doors?"

She shook her head. "I saw that a few of the sleeping bags were empty, and I didn't feel like talking to anyone, so I went upstairs and left through the side door beside the garage, off the kitchen."

"Whose sleeping bags were empty?"

"Mia's, for sure. I thought maybe Chloe, and maybe Leah, but it was dark. I wasn't sure."

"Where did you go?"

"The community gazebo." She jerked her chin toward the line of trees at the far side of the park, as if mapping the direction. The gazebo was located near the community stairs, close to Rowan's house, but out of sight. "I sat there. Vaped. Listened to music on my phone."

"Did you see or hear anyone else?"

"No."

"How long were you outside?"

Her mouth pressed flat again. "Twenty minutes? Half an hour? I wasn't timing every second."

"Anything else happen? Did you see anything?"

"I heard something." Her eyes went somewhere else. "I was on my way back. A scream."

The air itself seemed to shift around us. Even the swings seemed to go still.

"A scream?"

"Short. Cut off. Like someone got surprised. I thought maybe it was an animal at first."

"But you don't think it was an animal now."

She shook her head.

"What time was that?"

"I checked after." She shut her eyes for a second. "It was like 12:40, maybe 12:45. Something like that."

"So, you heard the scream around 12:40 a.m.," I said.

"Yeah."

"What did you do?"

"I stayed outside for a while. I stood there like an idiot. Smoked another joint to settle my nerves."

"When did you go back in?"

Her brows drew together. "I remember checking again. It was 1:05 a.m., 1:10 maybe. Around there."

"Who was awake when you got back?"

"Peyton was shifting around in her sleeping bag. I think she was asleep, but restless. Mia's bag was occupied. I could see the lump. And Chloe, I think, but it was dark."

"And Leah?"

"Her bag was facing the wall away from me. I assumed, but I didn't look."

"Who else?"

Alexis stiffened.

There was more. I could see it. "Alexis."

Alexis glanced at her phone. "Falcon! Three minutes to the bus. We've got to go!"

She slung her little brother's backpack over her shoulder and turned away from me.

I was about to lose her. And once she'd had time to think it over, to clam up, for Brooke to get her hooks into her again, I wouldn't get another chance. I took a step closer. "Just tell me."

Alexis crossed the grass to Falcon and Apollo. She grabbed Falcon's hand and made him drop the slobbery tennis ball. Over her shoulder, she said, "Zara. It was Zara."

Alexis and Falcon trudged toward the bus stop on the corner. Alexis didn't look back.

My mind raced. Zara Hayward. Camille's daughter.

My phone vibrated in my pocket. Three times in quick succession.

I pulled it out. Message requests from my Facebook account. The previews made my stomach lurch.

Your daughter is a killer. When she goes to prison, inmates will—

You are a monster. We know where you live. Someone should push YOU off that cliff and see how you—

Your daughter deserves everything coming to her. So do you.

I hit delete without opening any of them. My hand shook so badly I had to try twice. Another notification appeared immediately. I silenced the phone and shoved it back in my pocket. I couldn't think about what the rest of the world thought.

Zara. I needed to focus on Zara.

Chapter Twenty-One

My mind looped through Alexis's words as I walked Apollo up and down the neighborhood.

After Alexis boarded the school bus with her brother, I'd taken Mia to school. Then I returned home, braving the media gauntlet each time, and settled at my desk to work all day.

I finally finished the communication with teens assignment and turned it in. The irony was not lost on me.

It was after 3 p.m. by the time I leashed Apollo and headed out the door. The crisp air carried the heady scent of blooming flowers. Crocuses, daffodils, and early tulips pushed through the mulch in every front yard.

Guilt tugged at me. I'd threatened an abused kid. Used her bruises as leverage. The memory tasted bitter in my mouth.

But it had worked. And now I knew.

Someone had screamed at 12:40 a.m. that night. Was that scream from Leah, when she was pushed? Zara's sleeping bag had been empty at 12:30 a.m. What did that mean?

Zara, who'd found the body. Zara, the quiet one everyone overlooked. Zara, who'd been missing when Leah was killed.

Alexis wasn't off the hook, either. Not yet. No one could alibi her; she'd been alone at the gazebo. She still had a motive to shut Leah up for good, to protect herself and her secrets.

Mrs. Atkins stood at the curb when Apollo and I approached. One hand rested on her rolling trash bin, the other lifted in a practiced little wave. She wore a prim twinset with pearls, her gray hair shellacked into tight curls.

I slowed. Apollo's leash went taut.

My first instinct was to cross to the other side and keep moving. Instead, I stopped at the edge of her driveway. Politeness opened doors. Lately, I needed every door.

Plus, I remembered the detectives mentioning Mrs. Atkins's testimony in Mia's interview.

Apollo leaned against my leg. "How are you doing? Everything okay?"

"Well," she said, drawing the word out, "I suppose I'm as 'okay' as anyone can be with... all this." She flapped the hand not on the trash bin, taking in the whole street, the bluff, the lake, the houses. "You move into a place like this, you don't expect crime-scene tape and detectives knocking on doors at all hours. It's not what this neighborhood used to be, I'll tell you that much."

She waited, watching me intently.

"They were pretty thorough. They mentioned canvassing the whole neighborhood."

She pursed her lips, pleased. "They certainly did. In and out of every house. Taking notes. Some people didn't have much to say, of course."

"But you did?" I kept my tone light, curious, not desperate. She'd smell desperation.

She straightened a little, smoothed her cardigan with one liver-spotted hand. "Well. When something like this happens practically in your backyard, you pay attention. Some of us do, anyway. It's a tragedy what happened to that Cho girl. Her poor parents."

"It is a tragedy." I hesitated, then gave her what she wanted. "The detectives told me they were grateful for how observant the neighbors here are. Some people were especially helpful."

"Well, I certainly try." Color rose in her cheeks. She tilted her chin, like she was deciding whether I deserved the story. She glanced up and down the street, although no one else was outside. When she looked back at me, her voice dropped. "Between you and me, I didn't tell them everything at first. You never know how things will be twisted."

Of course, she hadn't. She'd rationed it out, one teaspoon at a time.

"I get that." I shifted Apollo's leash, as if I might move on. "I just keep thinking if someone saw or heard anything that night, it might help me make sense of it."

Mrs. Atkins inhaled sharply. "Funny you should say that. The night that poor Cho girl died, most people around here were asleep."

"But you weren't?"

She paused, savoring it. "No," she said at last. "I wasn't. I went for a glass of water. My kitchen looks straight out over the bluff. Sometimes I step out for a bit of fresh air, to hear the waves. Calm the nerves. I remember looking at the clock. 12:30 a.m. exactly. It stuck with me."

"12:30 a.m.," I repeated. "And?"

"I saw something down there, on the beach. The moon was out, reflected on the water. There was a figure. On the sand."

I waited. She wanted me to ask. "What did they look like?"

She pinched her lips, savoring it. "Tall and slim. With a hoodie pulled up. Walking toward Rowan's beach access. They had their phone on, that's how I could see them."

"Did you see a face?"

She shook her silvered head. "No. Too far away. But the way they moved. There's a look about some kids, the sporty ones. Long stride, that spring. You can tell."

"What are you saying?"

Her eyes flickered. "Well, that Hayward girl is tall for her age. And you know, they're out at all hours. That family..." She smoothed the front of her cardigan again. "New money. Everything's very showy. And their mother is always working. Children need eyes on them."

My jaw clenched. "Camille is a highly respected attorney helping my daughter. And Jerome is a dedicated teacher."

Mrs. Atkins's smile didn't move. "Of course. I'm only saying what I observed. One hears shouting over there sometimes. Music. It's a different energy. And that girl, she has a look about her."

I stroked Apollo's spine to stop my hands from shaking. "Let's go back. You saw someone at 12:30 a.m., tall, in a hoodie. Color?"

"Bright yellow." She smiled. "That's how I could see it so clearly. Like a fluorescent marker."

Zara had a yellow hoodie. With the Lakeshore Eagles emblem emblazoned on the front. She wore it constantly. I filed that information away. Mrs. Atkins's property bordered Rowan's acreage, though her house was significantly smaller. "Did you see them turn up at Rowan's?"

"I saw them angle toward it and then disappear against the bluff."

"Did you tell the police?"

She leaned in close, as if divulging a secret. "I only told them I saw someone, not that I thought I knew who it was. I don't get involved in criminal matters. I'm telling you because we share a street, and I like you. You deserve to know what's going on around you."

"If you're certain enough to tell me this, you should tell the police."

"Oh, no. I wouldn't want to get myself involved in such unseemly matters. I have standing. Reputation matters." She shuddered delicately. "I just thought you'd want to know."

I nodded, as if this were a normal, neighborly exchange. "Thank you for telling me."

"Of course, dear. We look out for each other up here."

"You're right."

She mistook my tone for agreement and clicked the trash bin lid closed. "Keep your doors locked. You can never be too careful."

"Have a good day, Mrs. Atkins."

Apollo nudged my knee. I tugged his leash and walked on.

Mrs. Atkins was a bigot. But she'd given me a time, a direction, and a silhouette. Zara fit the description. Zara, whom Alexis had already confirmed was out of her sleeping bag around the same time period.

Camille might get upset at me for speaking with her daughter. Hell, she might fire Mia as a client if I pissed her off too much. But I desperately needed to know what Zara knew. I had to take the risk and pray that Camille would stick with us. She wanted the truth, too.

I glanced at my watch. 3:20. Zara would be home already. Mia had Yearbook after school. I had time.

Chapter Twenty-Two

Camille's steel-and-glass house sat on its lot like it had been placed there by a machine. It didn't exactly blend in with the community's more traditional grand houses. I'd always thought it looked like a glass watchtower.

A cherry-red BMW M3 gleamed in the driveway. It was Jerome's car, but Zara stood next to it with a hose, water misting in the sun. Her sleeves were pushed up. Like I did, the Haywards believed in chores for their kids, even though they could afford the help.

She looked up and saw me. The hose slipped from her hand.

"Zara."

She flinched and edged toward the garage. I moved faster.

"My mom isn't home," she said, her voice tight, defensive. "I can't talk. I have homework."

"While you're detailing your dad's car? This is about Leah."

Her gaze slid past me. Across the street, the Handlers were walking their golden doodle. They slowed to look. Mrs. Handler wore oversized sunglasses and a pinched mouth.

"See something interesting?" I asked, unable to stop myself. I was losing patience with everything and everyone.

Mrs. Handler sniffed. Mr. Handler tugged his cap.

I wanted to tell them to mind their own business, but I swallowed it down and smiled hard instead. They faltered but kept walking, faster now.

Zara sighed. "Fine. Five minutes. Come to the backyard. No one will see us there."

She was more worried about being seen with me than actually talking to me. Good. I could use that.

We walked down the side of the house to the back. The backyard featured a sunken slate patio, a zero-entry pool, and a high-end outdoor kitchen.

Zara hung the hose and leaned against the counter like she needed something solid at her back. She tossed her braids over her shoulder and met my gaze.

I'd always liked Camille's daughter. She had a magnetic presence, with her wide generous mouth always quick to grin, her expressive brown eyes crackling with intelligence and mischief, and her strong, confident demeanor reminiscent of her mother.

She was brilliant, a computer whiz who coded circles around most of the adults I knew, and she was also warm and engaging, drawing others in with that infectious energy.

Now, she looked wary, cautious. "My mom isn't home," she repeated. "I really have to do homework. I have a volleyball game at six."

"Mrs. Atkins saw someone on the beach that night around 12:30 a.m. Tall, slim. Bright yellow hoodie. She thinks it was you."

Zara's mouth opened in surprise. "What?"

"Alexis told me you were out of your sleeping bag that night."

Her expression darkened. "Alexis told you that?"

"What were you doing on the beach at one in the morning?"

"Nothing."

"Zara. What do you think will happen if Mrs. Atkins goes to the police, and you lied about being in bed all night?"

She wouldn't look at me.

"She saw you in your yellow volleyball hoodie. The one you wear all the time on the weekends."

Zara stiffened.

"I'm trying to help Mia, that's all. The police... I think they suspect her. I just want to find the truth."

Her shoulders slumped. "I was... I was meeting someone."

"Who?"

She sighed. "Leah."

My stomach dropped. Leah was meeting Zara in the middle of the night? Why hadn't anyone mentioned this before? I kept my face neutral, but my mind was already racing through the implications. "Why would you need to meet on the beach when you were both at the sleepover together?"

"Leah asked for my help. On a project."

"What kind of project?"

She fidgeted, looking anywhere but at me.

"Zara, please. Before Mrs. Atkins goes to the police."

"She came to me for help."

I went still. "What do you mean?"

"She wanted me to use my tech skills to help her figure out who runs the account."

"The account?" I asked, even though I already knew.

"An Instagram account. LakeshoreTea. They eviscerate people. Especially the girls. She was trying to figure out who was behind it."

"Why?"

"Because they were targeting her. But also, because of Taylor. The girl who had that awful accident."

"Taylor Everett," I said.

Zara winced. "Yeah, her."

The vacant house. The family that disappeared. Whatever had happened to Taylor had been bad enough to drive them away entirely. And now Leah was dead, too. Another girl tangled up with LakeshoreTea.

"What happened to her?"

Zara chewed her bottom lip. "LakeshoreTea targeted her. But then, there was an accident at a pool party here. She took some pills, I guess, sleeping pills or something. There were lots of rumors. It's hard to know what's real, what's not. But she was acting super weird, I remember that."

I raised my brows. "You were there?"

"Yeah, it was at Peyton's house. The Alistairs, at their pool. The annual summer pool party that Mrs. Alistair always throws."

When I'd asked Whitney about Taylor Everett at Brooke's house, she'd said nothing about it happening at her own pool. At her party. She'd made it sound like it had nothing to do with her, just a neighborhood tragedy she'd observed from the sidelines, not something that occured in her backyard while she was hosting.

"What happened at the pool party?"

"She, like, fell in the pool when no one was paying attention, and almost drowned."

"That's awful."

"I went to see her once in the hospital. It was intense. She had brain damage from it. Really bad. She couldn't talk or walk anymore. The family was devastated. Her parents and little brother moved away, a week or two after it happened."

Anger flared hot in my chest. Whitney had lied by omission. They all had. Protecting themselves, their reputations, their shiny perfect lives. While a girl lay brain-damaged in a hospital bed.

"After that, LakeshoreTea stopped for a while. But then at the beginning of this year, it started up again like nothing had ever happened."

"Who runs the account?"

"We weren't sure. We suspected Alexis or Peyton, or even Chloe, maybe. Based on posting times, captions, and who benefited. Nothing solid. Whoever runs it is careful. They use VPNs, fake emails, maybe even a burner phone. We needed the source, the phone itself, to clone it."

"So, what, you guys had a plan at the slumber party?"

"Sort of." Her mouth twisted, in pride or shame, I wasn't sure. "Leah would take the phones at the party, while they were distracted. All three, if she could snag them. Then she was gonna meet me on the beach at 1 a.m. I'd go back to my house via the beach so no one would see me, then clone each phone. Fifteen minutes each, twenty if security was decent. Then I'd bring it back the same way, and she'd put it back in Peyton's bag, or next to Alexis and Chloe when they were sleeping. No biggie, as long as no one saw."

"And if Leah got caught by one of the girls, it would all be on her, and not you." The words came out harsher than I'd intended. But I was tired of these girls protecting themselves at each other's expense. Tired of the calculated risks that left someone else holding the bag.

Zara dropped her gaze. "Look. I did some things I'm not exactly proud of. Not everything, but enough. I helped spread the rumors. I laughed at some bad stuff I regret now. Leah knew what I'd done. She said if I wanted to do better, to be a good person, I should do something that mattered."

"Where were you that night? Exactly."

"I got to our meeting spot on the beach early, around 12:15 a.m. I sat on the bleached log near the seawall at the bottom of the Westinghouse property. Close enough to hear if someone came out on the bluff."

"Did you hear anything?"

"Girls' voices. At least three. Mad, like they were arguing, but keeping it down. I couldn't catch the words. The wind off the lake made it hard to hear clearly."

"Leah, Chloe, and Mia," I said. My daughter's name felt like rubbing a burn.

Zara shrugged. "Maybe."

"Did you hear anything else?"

She glanced around nervously. "Ah... a scream."

I went still. "What time?"

"Around 12:45, I think? Maybe a couple of minutes earlier. I was chilling on my phone."

A cloud passed over the sun. I shivered, though it wasn't cold. So far, the details matched Alexis's story.

Two witnesses. The same time, the same scream. That meant something. That scream was Leah. It had to be. Which meant someone had pushed her between 12:40 a.m. and 12:45 a.m., not later. The timeline was tightening.

"Then what?"

"The wind picked up, and I couldn't hear much anymore. I kept waiting for Leah to come down. She never did. I told myself Leah changed her mind, that she didn't take the phones. I was afraid Leah got caught and ratted me out." Her voice dropped. "I was scared. I didn't want them to turn on me, too. Peyton's done stuff like this before. Hurt other girls. I didn't want to be next."

"What do you mean about Peyton?"

Zara pressed her lips together and shook her head. "Just stuff. Rumors."

She wasn't going to tell me. Not now. I moved on. "What happened after Leah didn't show?"

"I stayed on the beach. In case someone was still up there. I messed with my phone for quite a while, kinda lost track of time. Then I heard something."

The hairs on my neck raised. "What?"

"On the bluff. A scrape. A thud. Heavy rustling in the bushes."

"An animal?"

She shook her head. "Something big. Something careful. It sounded like someone climbing down from the top."

"A person."

"Yeah."

"Did you see who?"

"It was too dark. They were up higher on the bluff. I was more worried about not being seen than seeing them."

"What time?"

"Around 3:30 a.m. My phone had three percent battery left, the same as the time. I remember thinking that."

3:30 a.m. Nearly three hours after the scream. Leah was already dead by then. So, who had been climbing the bluff? And why? Were they checking to see if she was really gone? Moving evidence? Something worse? My throat tightened. "What did you do?"

"When the noises finally stopped, I left. I... I didn't want to climb the stairs where I'd just heard the noise. I was kinda freaked out. So, I just stayed out there, thinking, worried. My brain does this thing where it won't turn off. I finally decided to go back inside when it was almost light out. At the top of the bluff, I saw a glint in the grass. It was Leah's phone. When I went over to check, that's when I saw her." She rubbed her nose, sniffing. "She was there all that time, when I was on the beach, and I had no clue."

"I'm sorry, Zara." I meant it. Though she was tall and looked a few years older than her age, she was still just a kid. "The next morning, were any phones missing?"

"Alexis still had hers. Same pink case, the cracked corner. Peyton had her new iPhone with the purple case. And Chloe had hers. If Leah took any of the phones, she'd put them back. Or she never took them at all."

I weighed what Zara had given me and what she hadn't. Her fear felt real. Her guilt had sharp edges. But she was still holding something back.

"Why didn't you go to the detectives?"

She let out a humorless laugh. "I'm a Black girl who can hack. I don't have an alibi. The only person who could confirm my story is dead. And those girls, if they think I'm snitching? They'll join ranks against me. Mrs. Atkins already thinks I'm guilty of moving her stupid garbage cans because of how I look. How would that work out for me?"

The fear in her voice was real. Raw. I recognized her fear of being judged before you opened your mouth, to have people decide who you were based on what they saw. Zara wasn't wrong. The system wouldn't give her the benefit of the doubt. Neither would this neighborhood.

But I had to think about my daughter first. "The detectives suspect Mia. Would you stay quiet while they cuffed her?"

She swore under her breath. "I wasn't going to stay quiet forever. I just..."

"You were scared."

"I'm still scared. If my mom finds out, I'm grounded for life. If the school finds out, I'm expelled. No one hears the part where I stopped being a part of the bullying, the part where I'm trying."

"A girl is dead, Zara."

She flinched. "I know."

"You can still choose to be brave. You need to tell the detectives what you heard and when. And all the stuff with Lakeshore Tea."

She closed her eyes. "Mom's going to kill me for lying to her, to the police. It's obstruction of justice. It's a crime."

I let the quiet do its work. The pool pump hummed. A gull squawked overhead. Waves slapped the sand below the bluff.

"I need one night," she said. "I need to tell her myself."

"You can have until morning," I said. "Or I walk into the station and hand them what I know. It will be better coming from you."

Was I doing the right thing? Giving her time felt like mercy. But it also felt like a risk. What if she clammed up? What if Camille shut her down? What if she was dangerous and I just gave her twelve hours to cover her tracks?

Zara had the information. It was Zara who needed to act. If she didn't tell Camille by tomorrow morning, I would.

Zara sighed, her mouth set. "I'm not a bad person."

"Then do the right thing."

She nodded. It didn't make either of us feel better.

I turned, walked back around the side of the house, and headed toward home. Apollo trotted after me, his tags jingling.

By the time I reached my car in my driveway, my hands were shaking with adrenaline. I had a timeline now. Voices at 12:15. A scream at 12:40 a.m. Someone on the bluff at 3:30 a.m., climbing down and back up. Leah was already dead by then, pushed at 12:40 a.m. by someone.

I checked my phone. 3:47 p.m. Mia's afterschool Yearbook class ended at four.

I opened the back door of my car, and Apollo jumped inside. He loved car rides. I started the engine and drove toward the school, my mind already racing ahead to what came next.

Chapter Twenty-Three

I gripped the steering wheel as I drove toward Lakeshore Prep to pick up Mia. Apollo was curled in the backseat, snoring pleasantly.

I longed to call Detective King. To tell him everything. But I'd promised Zara she had until morning. And at Mia's interrogation Tuesday morning, the detectives had said DNA results would take seventy-two hours. That meant the earliest was Friday afternoon, maybe evening.

I had a small window. Not much, but enough to let Zara come forward first, to hand King something concrete instead of breadcrumbs that would just lead back to Mia.

The carpool line crawled along at a snail's pace. I drummed my fingers on the steering wheel, glancing at a cluster of middle school mothers chatting on the sidewalk. Their conversations hushed as I passed, eyes shifting toward me with a mix of curiosity and thinly veiled hostility.

I tried to ignore them. It didn't work.

My phone vibrated on the passenger seat. Another unknown number. Likely a reporter or another prank call. I let it go to voicemail, glimpsing the notification count: fifteen new messages.

Threats, harassment, journalists circling. I left the phone where it was.

A minute later, Mia emerged from the school entrance, her backpack slung over one shoulder, head bowed, one of Marcus's old baseball caps pressed low over her face. She moved quickly, weaving through the throngs of students with practiced invisibility.

I grabbed my phone and moved it as she slid into the passenger seat and pulled the door shut.

"Hi, sweetheart."

Mia stared straight ahead.

I pulled away from the curb, the murmurs and stares of the other parents fading behind us. The silence in the car was heavy. Apollo uncurled himself and shoved his torso between the front seats. He nosed Mia's face until she gave in and scratched him between the ears.

"How was school?"

She let out a bitter laugh. "Fantastic."

"That bad?"

Mia's jaw tightened. "At lunch, I sat at the usual table. Peyton and Alexis got up and moved. Then the girls at the next table moved. Then the table behind them. Like I was radioactive." She swallowed. "I ate in the bathroom."

My heart ached. "I'm so sorry."

I checked the rearview mirror. A silver sedan had pulled out of the school parking lot and followed behind me, close to my bumper.

"Everyone stares at me like I did it. If I was a pariah before, I'm a piece of trash now."

"That's not true."

"That's how they act." She slouched lower in her seat. "Leah would've stood up to them. She was braver than me."

I twisted around, checking over my shoulder. The silver sedan was still there. Two car lengths back, matching every turn I made. Anxiety roiled through me.

"Mom? What are you looking at?" Mia followed my gaze and tensed. "Is that car following us?"

"It's fine." My knuckles whitened on the steering wheel. I sped up and took a sharp right as the stoplight turned yellow. The sedan pulled out right behind me. He was too close, right on my bumper. My heartrate accelerated.

I scanned ahead for a turn, anywhere to lose him. The intersection loomed. A yellow light. I calculated the distance, the speed, the risk, but there were two cars already stopped ahead, blocking the turn lane. The light flipped red.

I hit the brakes. Trapped.

The silver sedan pulled alongside us.

The passenger window rolled down. A man with a camera leaned out, the lens enormous. The shutter clicked rapid-fire *click-click-click-click*, the sound like insect legs on glass.

"Don't look at them," I said sharply.

Mia turned her face toward the window, pulling her hood up. The camera followed, relentless. The man shouted something I couldn't make out over the blood roaring in my ears.

The light changed. I accelerated hard, weaving through traffic. The sedan kept pace. My heart hammered against my ribs. Apollo whined from the back seat, sensing my growing panic.

Finally, we reached the gates of Blackthorn Shores. The familiar cluster of reporters and camera crews clogged the street outside the entrance. White vans with satellite dishes. Photographers with telephoto lenses. At least a few dozen of them. More than yesterday.

"Oh, Jeez," Mia breathed.

The silver sedan pulled up behind us, boxing us in. Through the rearview mirror, I saw the passenger door open. The man with the camera climbed out, still shooting.

I had no choice but to slow as we approached the gate. Frank stood at the entrance, trying in vain to keep the reporters back. They surged forward the moment they recognized my car.

Bodies pressed against the windows. Fists pounded on the

hood. Cameras flashed, blinding in the late afternoon sun. Faces distorted through the glass, their mouths moving, shouting, demanding.

"Ms. Kincaid! Did your daughter kill Leah Cho?"

"Mia! Mia, look here! Just one photo!"

Mia made a choked sound. She curled into herself, pulling her knees to her chest. Apollo leapt onto the seat and barked loudly at them.

"Don't look," I said again. "Just don't look."

A man slapped his palm against Mia's window. She flinched violently. Apollo growled. Anger and alarm thrummed in my chest. I wanted to punch him in his smug face for scaring my daughter.

"Get back!" Frank shouted, stepping between the car and the mob. "You're on private property!"

"It's a public street!" a cameraman yelled back.

Frank pulled out his radio, calling for backup. A second security guard arrived. Together, they physically pushed the reporters back, creating just enough space for me to edge the car forward.

The reporters surged forward one last time, someone pounding on the trunk, and then we were through. The gate closed behind us with a mechanical clang that sounded like a prison door.

My hands were shaking. I pulled into the community clubhouse parking lot, unable to drive home yet.

My breathing was ragged, my vision blurred. I couldn't cry, not in front of Mia, who was silently weeping beside me. "I'm so sorry, baby."

She didn't answer, just pulled her hood tighter and stared at her lap.

Anxiety thrummed in my veins. Instinctively, I touched my throat, found the ring beneath my shirt, and held it like a talisman. *Breathe. Just breathe.*

I glanced at Mia. "You're wearing Dad's hat."

Her hand flew to the brim, defensive. "So?"

"You only wear it when you're really upset. Or when you miss him." I kept my voice gentle. "Which is it?"

"Both, I guess." Mia pulled the cap off, turning it over in her hands, tracing the faded logo of Arches National Park with her thumb. "Do you think I'm a bad friend? Because right now I'm thinking about myself, and not her. And she's the one who's dead."

"Oh, honey."

"I should've done better." The words burst out. "I should've been a better friend."

I leaned over the console and pulled her into my arms. She buried her face against my shoulder. "You were a good friend. The best friend she had."

"I wasn't, though." Mia's voice was muffled. "I let her down. I failed her."

I held her tighter. "Leah knew you loved her."

Mia pulled away. Her expression shifted, something dark behind her eyes. Dread. Guilt. Apprehension. She turned the hat over again in her hands.

A mix of frustration and helplessness welled up inside me. I squeezed her shoulder. This time, she didn't pull away.

Apollo whined, his tail thumping the seats. "We should get back. Apollo wants his afternoon snack. I bet you're hungry, too. How about I make us some cheesy nachos, and then I'll help you with that English essay on Romeo and Juliet you've been working on?"

Mia nodded. We drove the rest of the way home in silence. We'd barely gotten out of the car when I saw it.

The front door wasn't latched. It rested against the frame, not flush.

I stopped so fast that Mia bumped into me. Apollo's head came up, ears forward. A low sound rumbled in his chest. I tightened the leash.

"Did you leave that open? Maybe this morning before you left?" My voice sounded wrong in my ears.

Mia shook her head.

"Stay outside the house," I said. "If I yell go, you call 911 and go to Camille's house."

Mia nodded, swallowing.

"Apollo, come." I pushed the door with the side of my foot. It swung without protest. The dog moved forward when I moved, silent, his tail level. He sniffed the rug by the sink, the air near the island, then pulled me toward the living room.

There was no mess. No drawers yanked out, no couch cushions flipped over. The house should have looked the same. It didn't.

Behind me, Mia gasped.

My gaze followed hers to the coffee table. Leah's painting, the Tiscornia Beach watercolor that had hung above Mia's bed, lay propped against the wood.

Someone had slashed it. Deep gashes carved through the sunset sky and wildflowers, the lighthouse and pier. Across the top, scarlet spray paint screamed a single word: "GUILTY."

Anger and fear churned in my gut. Someone had done this. Someone had invaded our privacy, our home, our sanctuary. Someone hated us this much.

Mia gave a short, wounded whimper. She moved past me, reaching for the canvas, then withdrew her hand like she'd touched a hot stove.

"Don't," I said quickly. "Don't touch anything."

"Why would...who would do this?" She stopped herself and looked at me, eyes glassy. "This was Leah's. She made it for me. It was hers."

"I know." My hand went to my back pocket. I tugged out my phone.

Apollo circled the room once, his nose down, tail wagging, not in alarm but curiosity. Did that mean that he recognized whoever had been here? Likely, he did. Not that he'd alert us to a stranger, either. All humans were friends to Apollo.

Mia swiped at her cheeks with the back of her hand. "We have to call someone. Mom, we have to. This is...this is awful."

"I know." I unlocked my phone. I pictured uniformed officers in our living room, their gloves snapping on. The headlines: *Psycho mother claims break-in without evidence. Daughter a suspect in classmate's death.*

Was it the wrong choice to call 911? To bring the police into the sanctity of our home, the cops with their eyes on Mia as their prime suspect? I didn't know.

But our home had been violated again. Panic bit at my throat. I looked at my daughter's stricken, terrified face. I made the call.

Chapter Twenty-Four

The squad car lights bled blue and red through the front windows, strobing against the slashed canvas. The word GUILTY appeared as though it was pulsing blood.

Apollo padded to the door before the knock came, his tail wagging. I opened it to two uniformed officers in their late twenties, both in jackets with nametags reading RUIZ and HARRIS.

They examined the canvas as I explained that the door had been unlatched when we returned, even though I had locked it, that Apollo had been calm inside, that the house had looked normal until we found this.

Mia hovered in the hallway, eyes too big in her pale face, her arms wrapped around herself. I reached for her hand and found it colder than mine.

Ten minutes later, Detective King arrived with another unmarked car. The squad lights had been cut, but I could still feel the neighborhood watching from dark windows.

King wore a camel overcoat, the collar turned up, a dark suit underneath, smelling faintly of coffee. His eyes swept the room.

I led him through the kitchen. He crouched, studying the jamb, the latch plate. He ran a gloved finger along the painted wood.

"No splintering," he said. "No pry marks."

"I told you, it wasn't forced. I think whoever did this had access to my spare key."

Before I could say more, Whitney and Peyton appeared in the opened doorway. They hovered on the threshold, their cheeks flushed from the chill.

"Everyone okay in here?" Whitney called out. "We have dinner plans at the Bistro on the Boulevard with the new Whirlpool CFO, but I wanted to make sure you were okay first. We saw the cruisers as we were driving by."

Whitney wore a fitted cream sheath dress with a gold belt and matching heels. Peyton wore a navy cocktail dress with cap sleeves, her purple Stanley in one hand as usual.

Through the living room window, I caught sight of Whitney's husband Graham waiting in the idling Mercedes at the curb. His blond head was bent, his clean-shaven jaw clenched as he scrolled through his phone. He didn't look up.

"We're okay, thanks," I said.

Whitney glanced between King and me, her eyes wide. Her gaze dropped to the painting, and she gasped. "Oh Dahlia, that's awful."

"Yep," I managed.

"Okay," King said to Ruiz. "I'll take it from here."

The uniformed officers filed out.

Peyton's gaze was glued to the slashed painting. "Wow. Was that one of Leah's?"

"Yes." I watched Peyton. I hadn't been this close to her since the Saturday morning of Leah's death. Peyton Alistair was tall and lean, all sharp angles, with her square jaw and prominent features mirroring her mother's, her high ponytail pulled tight. Her blue eyes were sharp, calculating.

She was the leader of the group, the one who set the pace and expected everyone to keep up. Driven, motivated, constantly in motion, always busy with practices, meets, lessons, races, and competitions, living at a sprint to meet Whitney's impossible standards.

But I recognized a darker, simmering energy in the clench of her jaw, the way her knuckles went white around her Stanley. She was strung too tight, wound like a rubber band ready to snap.

"Who would do such a thing?" Whitney asked, drawing my attention away from Peyton. Appalled, she pressed a hand to her sternum. The diamond bracelet on her wrist glinted. "With everything you're already dealing with, and now someone breaking into your home, vandalizing Leah's painting." Her voice dropped in sympathy. "It's almost like someone wants you to know they can get to you whenever they want. How awful."

I could only nod numbly. They'd entered our house. Gone to Mia's bedroom. Someone who knew our routines. Someone most likely with a key. I thought of Alexis once again, outside our house, videoing us with her phone.

"You have my spare key, Whitney. I'd really like it back, now."

King's attention shifted to Whitney. "You have a spare key?"

Color rose in her cheeks as she fumbled in her Prada bag. "I've been meaning to give it back since, well, with everything happening. You understand."

She held the key with the Isle Royale key chain out to me like an offering.

I took it and slipped it into my pocket. "Thanks."

She gave a high-pitched, nervous laugh. "I hope you don't think I had anything to do with this."

"Any copies of that spare?" King asked her.

"No. Just this one. Brooke had it before I did. Though the girls have used it before to walk Apollo when Dahlia and Mia are out of town. It's been through... well, let's just say a lot of people." She laughed again, glancing back at her daughter. "I can't vouch for what anyone did with it before it got back to me, of course. But I didn't make copies. Peyton?"

Peyton's eyes flicked to her mother, then to King, then back to the painting as King dusted for prints and then slipped the canvas into an evidence bag. She shook her head, her face a careful mask. "Not me."

King turned back to me. "Anything like this happen before? Threats? Messages? Vandalism?"

Whitney's eyes were on me. Peyton's, too.

I recalled the notebook stolen from my desk. Items rearranged. That feeling of violation, of invasion, that had haunted me for days. "Well, yes, actually—"

"Oh, Dahlia, don't you remember?" Whitney said. "Didn't you say that someone broke in? On Tuesday?"

The detective's gaze lifted to mine, questioning. His eyes narrowed. "Someone entered your house before?"

I rubbed my face, rattled. And more than a little irritated. Whitney had somehow made me look deceptive, even though I was about to tell the detective myself. Had it been intentional, or was I reading into things? "On Tuesday, after Mia's interview. I'd locked the door. I came home, and it was open."

"Anything taken?"

"A notebook I use for my freelance articles. Things were moved around."

He raised his brows as he jotted something down, probably that he thought I was crazy. Who only steals a worthless notebook? I bit my tongue.

Whitney flashed him a winning smile. "I hope you find the hooligans who did this quickly. This is a safe neighborhood. Or at least, it used to be."

"We'll see what we can do," King said.

Whitney lingered in the doorway. "Call me if you need anything, Dahlia. I can stay. Or take Mia for the night, if you want. She could come to dinner with us. It'll give you a break."

The offer sounded generous. Reasonable. Like something a good neighbor, a good friend, would say. Peyton's smile matched her mother's.

Beside me, Mia stiffened. I thought of Zara's voice: *Peyton's done stuff like this before. Hurt other girls.*

Right or wrong, the thought of Mia in anyone's house but mine made my skin crawl.

"Thank you. We'll be okay."

Hurt flickered across her face. She suppressed it quickly. "All right. I'm just down the street if you need me."

"I know," I said.

She strode from my house with Peyton right behind her, silent as a shadow. She glanced back once, her gaze catching mine. There was something there I couldn't read. Then her eyes shifted, and it was gone.

The door clicked shut behind them. A moment later, their Mercedes pulled away from the curb.

"Please find who did this," I said. "Before they do something worse. I'm getting the locks changed tomorrow morning, but that won't stop someone who truly wants to get inside."

"Ms. Kincaid, I promise we will investigate." He looked past me to the dishes in the sink, the knife left on the cutting board, pausing on the family photo on the fridge. All of us, grinning and happy. "We'll need Mia to come to the station tomorrow morning at 9 a.m. There are some inconsistencies we need to address."

Ice water trickled down my spine. My throat closed. "I'll text Mia's lawyer."

At the door, he looked back at me, the painting held carefully in one hand. "Oh, and Ms. Kincaid, I suggest you also get some security cameras immediately."

The door closed behind him. I locked the deadbolt. I listened to the hum of the refrigerator. The distant rush of a car somewhere on the main road. The old ticking clock.

Mia sank onto the couch. I sat beside her and pulled her into my arms. She was stiff for a moment, then she sagged against me, boneless with exhaustion.

Apollo settled at our feet with a soft grunt.

Mia snuggled into me. "I'm scared, Mom."

"It'll be okay," I lied. "I promise."

"Are we safe?"

"You're safe," I lied again.

I would sit up all night keeping watch until those locks were changed. Tomorrow morning, we'd be back in front of those detectives, Mia lined up in their sights.

What did they want from her now? What did they know that we didn't?

The key Whitney had given me lay cool and heavy in my pocket. I curled my fingers around it and stared at the space on the coffee table. Though the police had removed the painting, the word GUILTY was burned in my retinas.

Chapter Twenty-Five

The second interview room was colder than the first. The same steel table anchored to the floor, the same hard chairs, and the same detectives, staring us down.

King started the recorder, then went through the formalities, advising Mia of her rights and confirming her verbal consent to be interviewed.

King glanced at Callahan. She gave the smallest nod. Neither of them mentioned the break-in last night, the slashed painting, the accusation in dripping red letters that had haunted my sleepless night: GUILTY.

"Mia," King said, looking at my daughter. "We've been reviewing the evidence from the night Leah died. Crime scene analysis. Forensic reports. Witness statements. Some new information has come to light, and we need your help understanding it."

Mia's hands twisted under the table. I kept my own hands flat and still on my thighs. Camille sat stiffly at my other side.

Camille had warned us they'd have more. That this wasn't just "a follow-up."

The first interview had felt exploratory, almost clinical. Fact-gathering. Now the air vibrated with something else. Direction. Anticipation. Suspicion.

They had something, something that implicated Mia.

"The preliminary autopsy findings." King looked down at the file, then up again, directly at Mia. "We know that Leah didn't die right away."

My spine went rigid. Sound thinned around the edges, as if the room was wrapped in cotton.

Mia's head came up. "What... what do you mean?"

"Leah sustained a severe head injury when she fell from the bluff. But the medical examiner determined that she hemorrhaged for several hours, probably two to three, before she died."

Mia folded forward, as if the information had physical weight and it was pushing her down. "For... for hours?"

"Evidence at the scene supports that timeline," King said. His voice was almost gentle. "Blood patterns, the extent of the hemorrhaging. She did not die immediately upon impact."

Callahan said, "She regained consciousness for a period. We can't give you an exact duration. But it's clear she was moving."

My mind flashed to Zara's testimony. The sounds she'd heard at 3:30 a.m. Scraping, rustling in the bushes, something heavy moving. It wasn't another person, as we'd thought. Those sounds must have been Leah, injured and disoriented, trying to crawl back up. Trying to save herself while everyone slept a few hundred feet away.

Camille's face had gone ashen. "Moving how? Where?"

Callahan said, "The crime scene technicians found drag marks, blood smears. Disrupted leaf litter. Compressed vegetation. Patterns consistent with someone attempting to crawl up the bluff."

I felt like I might float away. Zara had been on the beach at 3:30 a.m. Three hours after Alexis heard the scream at 12:40 a.m. Leah had been out there for three hours. I imagined her waking in the dark, pain exploding in her head, covered in blood. Alone. Bewildered. Frightened.

Had she called out for help? Had her voice been too weak, the wind too loud? How many times had she tried to stand, to crawl, before collapsing again?

A wave of nausea roiled through me. The taste of metal rose in the back of my throat.

"Could she have survived, if someone had found her earlier?" I asked.

King hesitated. "She was bleeding heavily from the blow to her head. Brain swelling would have begun immediately. It was a catastrophic injury. However, if emergency medical services had reached her within the first hour, she probably would have survived. We can't say with absolute certainty, but her chances would have been significantly improved."

Beside me, Mia made a sound. Not a sob. Something lower, primitive, torn from her throat. The hair on my arms stood up.

"I didn't know," Mia said in a choked voice. Her lips were gray. "I didn't know... if I'd known... if I'd known she was out there..."

I rubbed her back, the only comfort I could give. "You couldn't have known, honey."

Camille cut in. "Detective, my client was a fourteen-year-old at a sleepover. Unless you're suggesting she had a duty to provide medical care she didn't know was needed, I'm going to object to this line of questioning as designed to elicit guilt rather than information."

"Fair enough," King said mildly. "The evidence indicates Leah was alive for a period of time after you last saw her. That's important for understanding what happened. That's why we're talking about it."

Mia nodded jerkily, wiping her nose on the back of her hand. She was trembling, pale from shock.

King said, "The medical examiner collected biological samples, including scrapings from under Leah's fingernails. Those were submitted for DNA analysis. Given the circumstances, the lab expedited some of the testing."

I knew what was coming before they said it. Maybe some part

of me had been braced for this from the moment I first saw Mia's arms.

Callahan slid a photograph out from the file and turned it around. I forced myself to look. A close-up of Leah's hand, fingers curled slightly, nails caked with dirt and rust-colored blood.

"The DNA profile developed from the epithelial cells under Leah's fingernails is a match to Mia's."

Cold went through me down to the bone. Sound seemed tinny and far away. Next to me, Mia shivered uncontrollably.

"Transfer happens in all kinds of ways," Camille said. "They were friends. Leah bled on her. Your DNA proves nothing."

Undeterred, Callahan flipped to a second page. "We've also documented superficial linear abrasions on both of your forearms, Mia. The ME noted that they're consistent with forceful physical contact between two people. For example, someone clawing or grabbing at another person."

Mia's voice was thin and high. "I told you about that. The first time. I slipped when I was taking pictures. On the bluff. Into some thorny bushes. That's all."

King nodded. "Okay. Then why do you think your skin cells are beneath Leah's fingernails?"

"When she... when she had the nosebleed. When she got dizzy. That must be how it happened."

"Let's go over that again."

Mia's frantic gaze darted to Camille. Camille's expression was neutral, professional, but I caught the quick movement of her throat as she swallowed. The reveal that Leah hadn't died immediately had rattled her, too.

Mia took a shaky breath. "It was during the midnight photoshoot. When we went out, after everyone else was sleeping. Me, Chloe, and Leah. We went to the bluff to take pictures. It was... sometime after midnight. I don't know exactly."

"And what happened out there?"

"Chloe wanted Leah to stand near the edge," Mia said. "I got scared and told her not to go so close. Then her nose started bleeding. Like, a lot. She got really pale and said she felt dizzy. She grabbed my arms to steady herself. That's when she...when her nails—" Mia glanced at her own forearms, as if expecting to see fresh blood there. "Maybe she scratched me then a little, I don't know."

"She grabbed your arms," Callahan repeated, skepticism in her voice. "Deep enough that your skin cells were embedded under her nails."

Mia's pupils were too wide. "Yes."

Camille interjected, "That's the medical examiner's interpretation, not fact. My client has explained the circumstances of the DNA transfer to the point that your DNA evidence seems useless. While I appreciate your help with the defense of my client, Mia has said all she's going to on the subject. Move on."

I could tell the detectives didn't believe her story. I wasn't sure that I did, either. I wanted to believe her. I needed to. The blood on the dress she'd explained away. But the scratches, only sort of. But not the missing camera, or the sandy slippers. Little lies that kept adding up.

"No argument on the bluff?" Callahan pressed. "No shoving, no grabbing?"

"No," Mia said. "I was trying to help her."

"Did you hear anything later?" King asked. "A scream? Leah calling for help? Did anyone leave the house after lights-out that you know of?"

"I told you everything. We took pictures. Her nose bled. We went in. I went to sleep."

King exchanged a weighted glance with Callahan. Something passed between them that I couldn't read. My stomach churned.

King flipped another page in the folder and pushed a glossy photograph at us. The blue cover of Leah's diary, every inch covered in drawings and sketches in colored ink. "We've also reviewed Leah's phone, computer, and her diary. Her mother gave it to us earlier this week."

Mia's shoulders hunched. Her breathing went shallow.

"There are multiple entries documenting extensive bullying. Did you participate?"

"No, of course not! Leah was my friend."

"You let it happen, though," Callahan said.

Mia's voice was a frayed thread. "I didn't do any of it!"

"But you didn't stop it."

"I...I'm sorry."

Callahan leaned forward. "Did Leah tell you she was keeping records of what her bullies were doing?"

"No. I mean, I guess. I know she wrote about stuff in the diary."

"Plus, you'd witnessed it."

Mia winced. "Yes."

Callahan asked, "Were you worried that whatever Leah said might implicate you? That your silence made you complicit?"

Mia's hands twisted in her lap. "No! I... I'm the one who told my mom where Leah hid the diary! I didn't help her, I know, but I didn't hurt her. I wasn't like the others."

"But if Leah exposed the bullying," Callahan continued, "your name would be in that story, too."

Camille cut in sharply. "Detective, you're testifying again. Ask a question or move on."

Mia shook her head hard. "That's not why... If I tried to protect Leah, they'd turn on me, too, okay? I wasn't upset about the diary. I already knew about it."

King nodded. "Okay, Mia, did Leah seem angry with you? In the days before she died?"

Mia's voice was barely audible. "No. I don't think so."

"Was anyone angry with Leah? Upset enough to hurt her?"

"I—I don't know."

"Leah documented months of harassment. Did she tell you she was planning to report it?"

"I don't know."

"Did she confront the other girls at the slumber party? Tell them she was going to report their behavior? Were they angry with her? Anyone in particular?"

Mia fidgeted, clearly agitated. "No! I don't know. I don't remember."

Camille cleared her throat. "My client has more than thoroughly answered your questions on this topic. Move along."

King said, "We conducted multiple searches of the bluff area and the Westinghouse home. We have not found your camera."

"I don't know where it is," Mia said.

"Is it possible," King said slowly, "that you went back out to the bluff to look for it? After everyone was asleep?"

"No." The denial was instant, reflexive. "I told you. I didn't go back out there."

"Mia," Callahan said. Her name, just that, but the way she said it made my skin crawl. "We have Leah's blood on your dress. We have your DNA under her fingernails. We have scratches on your arms in a pattern the medical examiner says is consistent with defensive wounds. We have a missing camera last seen in your possession, and we have your sleeping bag empty around 12:30 a.m."

As she listed each item, she tapped a fingertip lightly on the folder, as if stacking bricks to create an impenetrable wall. A case against my child. "Taken together, that paints a different picture than the one you've given us."

Camille gave a hard smile. "The missing camera proves less than nothing. If you're so sure you have a case, charge Mia right now."

I recoiled. Mia gaped at Camille in horror. She was shaking harder now, tiny tremors running through her shoulders, her neck, her hands.

The air in the room crackled as if electrified. For half a beat, no one moved. King watched Mia intently. Callahan sat back. A subtle shift in her body language sent a jolt of terror through me. She'd decided Mia was guilty. I could see it in her face, her posture, and those sharp eyes.

"No?" Camille said. "I didn't think so. We're done here."

Chairs scraped as everyone stood. My legs felt unsteady. Callahan walked us to the door. Her gaze flicked to me, intent and assessing.

Camille turned to the detectives. "If you are contemplating any change in my client's status—"

"The prosecutor will review the evidence," King said. "But this is an active investigation. It's moving quickly."

"In other words," Callahan said with the slightest smirk, "don't leave town."

Chapter Twenty-Six

The new keys the locksmith pressed into my palm looked wrong in my hand. Too clean. Too bright. The locksmith had arrived just as we returned from the precinct, shell-shocked and devastated.

I shut the door behind him. And locked it.

Apollo bounded in from the kitchen, then stopped short. His tail went up, stiff. He paced a tight circle near the base of the stairs, his nose working. He whined in the back of his throat, a high, anxious sound. He looked back at me, ears pricked, then up toward the second floor. His whole body was tense.

"What's wrong, buddy?"

He paced restlessly, circling me, then Mia, then back to me. He whined again.

Mia stood in the foyer, dazed. Her eyes were unfocused, like she was still in that interrogation room we'd left only thirty minutes ago, still trapped beneath the glaring fluorescent lights, staring at the glossy photos of Leah's broken nails.

Apollo trotted to her and urgently shoved his nose into her hand. She didn't react. He tried again, nudging her thigh, his tail wagging harder, not playful but almost frantic.

He'd picked up on the tension in the room. As if he could

sense Mia's palpable distress and was trying as best he could to offer comfort.

"They said she was alive." Mia's words were toneless. A recitation. "They said she was alive for hours."

She stared past me, past the stairs, at the far wall. Her pupils were huge, eating the green of her irises. Her skin had taken on a gray pallor.

The strain of everything overwhelmed me. My chest was tight, a headache beating dully against the front of my skull. The sorrow reared up and threatened to pull me under and suffocate me.

For Mia, it was even worse. I could see it in her face, how she was drowning right in front of me, and I didn't know how to save her.

"Mia." I tightened my grip on the keys, the metal biting into my palm. "Come sit down. Let's talk."

"If I'd just gone back out..." The sentence frayed. She blinked once, twice, her face contorting. Then she bolted. She staggered up the stairs and into the bathroom.

My body moved before my brain. I followed the sound of her feet. Apollo scrambled after us, whining anxiously.

As I reached the top of the stairs, the bathroom door slammed. The lock snicked.

I hurried down the hall and placed my hand on the door. "Mia, open up. Please."

Nothing.

I couldn't leave her like this. She was devastated. She needed me. "Mia. Open it, or I'm calling the locksmith back to remove it from the hinges. I mean it."

A moment later, there was the click of the lock turning. I pushed the door open.

Mia was on the tile floor, her back against the old cast iron tub, her knees up, arms wrapped tightly around them. Her whole body shook. The light overhead bleached her face, made her look colorless, half alive, half ghost.

"I didn't know. I didn't know she was still alive..." Her voice dissolved. She folded forward, forehead dropping to her knees. A raw, keening wail tore out of her.

Apollo stiffened in the doorway, his ears laid back. He whined in alarm, then lay down in the doorway with his snout resting on his paws, as if to protect us from whatever horrors lay outside the bathroom door. He didn't know the horror had already reached us.

I stepped over him into the cramped bathroom. The yellowed ceramic tile was cold beneath my feet. I knelt beside Mia. "Hey, honey. Hey."

I reached for her. She flinched, then collapsed into me all at once, like something inside had given way. "I didn't know. I swear, I didn't know she was—they said she was breathing, Mom. Crawling, trying to get help. Still alive. They said—"

I held her tighter. She was too light. Too hot. "Listen to me. You didn't know. You couldn't have known."

"If I'd gone back... if I'd—if I'd checked, if I'd just—I left her there, Mom. I left her!"

"You didn't know she was down there. You didn't see her fall. You told them that. You told me."

Mia sagged against me. Her tears soaked the front of my T-shirt. Her breath came too fast, shallow and ragged.

I rocked her in my arms, like when she was three and convinced the monsters in the closet would open the door and eat her face. Back when Marcus and I could vanquish anything with a nightlight and a story.

Now the monsters were real. They were pretty girls with white teeth.

I held her because it was all I could do. I held her and listened to her weep. Her head was against my breastbone, great sobs wracking her body. I kissed the top of her head and stroked her back. Eventually, her sobs dwindled to hiccups.

She raised her head, swiped at her swollen, tear-dampened face with the back of her arm, and twisted to face me. "Am I going to jail?"

"You're not." I forced my voice to remain calm. "I won't let that happen."

It was a lie, and we both knew it. I couldn't protect her from this, just like I couldn't protect Marcus from a horrific act of random violence. The truth was, the world was pure chaos. We couldn't control any of it.

"Let's get you off the floor and upstairs. I'll bring you lunch in bed. How about tomato soup and grilled cheese, your favorite?"

"Okay." Her voice was hoarse, stricken.

I swallowed the knot in my throat. I got my feet under me and hauled her up. She was lighter, thinner than I remembered. She moved like she was underwater. Apollo stood, circling our legs in tight anxious loops.

We made it to her room. The curtains were mostly closed, but a small seam of sunlight poured through the crack. I crossed to the window and yanked the panels shut, covering the collection of sea glass and beach stones. The room dimmed.

"Lie down, honey. You need to rest."

Mia crawled onto the bed without protest. She didn't reach for her phone. Didn't ask for it. She curled onto her side, knees tucked up, clutching Flash the sloth to her chest. Marcus's red cap sat on the nightstand.

I sat on the edge of the mattress and tucked the blanket around her. "Try to sleep. Your brain needs a break."

Her eyes slid closed. Opened. Closed again. Her breathing evened a little. It wasn't rest, not really. More like her body shutting down to conserve power.

I watched her face, searching for something. A tell. A crack that would let me see the things she was still hiding from me.

All I saw was a kid who'd just learned that her best friend had spent hours dying alone in the dark.

I stood. My knees popped. I stepped to the door and eased it mostly shut. The hallway was too bright. The house hummed with its usual sounds: the fridge, the furnace, the faint ticking of the hallway clock.

I went downstairs on autopilot, barely conscious of even moving. Apollo followed. I made coffee because it was something to do. Like Mia, I had little appetite. I took a mug I didn't want and carried it out to the patio.

The lake threw the sun back at me in a thousand hard glints. The sky was a flat pitiless blue.

I stepped to the edge of the cracked, sloping patio and looked toward the bluff.

Another section had gone sometime in the night. Fresh earth gaped halfway down the slope, a raw wound against the darker, older soil. Crumbled chunks of sod clung to the edge of the bluff like torn scabs. A few roots jutted into the air, exposed.

Yesterday, that piece of ground had been part of my yard.

Today, it wasn't.

The bluff was eroding, coming for us inch by inch. Gravity and water and time, doing what they always did, stripping away the illusion of permanence. Of safety.

I set the mug on the metal table. I wrapped my arms around myself and thought of Marcus, his contagious laughter, his easy smile. I longed for his steady presence, his reassuring words. Marcus would have known what to say to our daughter. How to reach her, even now.

He would have believed in Mia without question. Without the gnawing doubt that was eating away at me from the inside.

The truth was a knife with two edges: I believed my daughter hadn't killed Leah. I also knew she wasn't telling me everything. It was the space between those secrets, those sharp shards, that could truly hurt us.

That was where the danger lay.

My restless mind kept returning to the precinct, the interview, the evidence. What everything meant, or could mean, for Mia's case. The police wanted to arrest her. I had to give them another, better suspect before they did.

DNA under Leah's fingernails. A match to Mia.

Scratches on Mia's arms. From Leah, accidentally, according to Mia. Another secret she'd kept from me, and from the police.

The scream Alexis and Zara heard at 12:40 a.m.

The sounds Zara heard at 3:30 a.m. Leah, still alive in the dark.

Zara and Leah's plan to expose the LakeshoreTea account.

Alexis's testimony that she'd seen Mia's sleeping bag empty at 12:30 a.m.

The sandy slippers hidden in Mia's closet.

The missing camera.

Who had had the opportunity to harm Leah? Alexis at the gazebo. Zara on the beach. Mia, out of her sleeping bag at 12:30 a.m. Chloe at the midnight photoshoot, who'd lied about being there, just like Mia had. Peyton's whereabouts were more unclear. No one had seen her leave, but that didn't mean she hadn't.

The ground under my feet felt less solid. I curled my toes against the concrete lip of the patio.

Motive was messier. Alexis had abuse to hide, and Leah's knowledge threatened her family. That was reason enough. Alexis had a history of violence. I wanted to believe Alexis wasn't a killer, but that didn't mean she was innocent.

But why would she act now? Leah had known about Brooke's abuse for months.

Chloe was one of the last people to see Leah alive, along with Mia, but what reason would she have to hurt Leah?

Peyton was pretty, popular, and athletic. *She's hurt girls before*, Zara had said. What did that mean?

Zara had already lied to the police once. She'd agreed to help Leah expose her friends, but what if Zara had changed her mind? What if she'd outed Leah first?

Whoever ran that LakeshoreTea account had everything to lose if Leah exposed them.

And then there were the break-ins. Whoever stole my notebook and slashed the painting had access to my house. The key had passed through too many hands: Brooke, Alexis, Whitney, Peyton. Anyone who'd been in their houses could've copied it, would've seen the key with the familiar Isle Royale keychain and known whose home it belonged to.

My frenzied thoughts hit a wall. I pressed my fingers to my temples.

Even if Zara came forward now, it wouldn't help. It might make things worse. Mia was out of her sleeping bag minutes before the scream Zara had mentioned. And the later sounds Zara had heard at 3:30 a.m. had been Leah herself, not some unknown killer lurking on the bluff.

I needed something else.

Leah's diary burned in my mind.

How I missed Vivienne. Her warm smile, her kind eyes, her soft laugh. The way she'd put her hand over mine, always encouraging.

Now my daughter's DNA was under her dead daughter's fingernails.

I dug my phone out of my back pocket. The screen flared too bright. My text to Vivienne from last night stared back at me. *Call me. Please.*

No response.

Can I come over? I typed.

I hit send before I could regret it. The message thread showed the little gray *delivered* label underneath. For a second, nothing. Then the three dots appeared. Blinked. Disappeared. They didn't come back.

It was time to go see her. I just hoped she'd accept my apology.

The patio door slid open behind me. "Mom?"

Mia stood in the doorway, one hand on the frame. A crease ran along her cheek. Her eyes were swollen, her lids puffy.

Apollo slid between us, pushing his head under her hand. She scratched absently behind his ears, not really seeing him.

"I was planning to visit Viv."

She perked up. "I want to go."

Part of me wanted to bundle her back to bed. Pull the blankets over both of us and pretend the outside world didn't exist. Leaving her alone here felt worse.

"If you're sure."

"I'm sure."

"First, I'm getting some food in you. Let's make that grilled cheese and tomato soup I promised, okay? Then we'll go."

She gave a tremulous nod.

Thirty minutes later, we'd both eaten. Mia had only managed half of her sandwich, but it was something. Everything had tasted like cardboard, but I'd forced it down.

Once we finished, I retrieved the new keys from the counter. Old habit made me walk the circuit, checking every new lock, the deadbolts I knew I'd already locked. Still, I checked.

I felt the press of Mia at my shoulder. The weight of the keys in my fist. "Let's go."

Chapter Twenty-Seven

Vivienne's door opened six inches, the chain on. My chest tightened as I inhaled the familiar scent of sizzling beef bulgogi, a Cho household favorite meal.

Daniel stood in the crack. He wore a gray T-shirt and sweatpants, his feet bare. His eyes were red and swollen. Several days of beard growth stubbled his face. He looked tired, the kind of tired you couldn't scrub off. "Dahlia."

"We wanted to check on you and Viv, to see if there's anything we can help with."

Daniel blinked at us. "You didn't have to."

He looked down at Mia. Took in her hunched shoulders, zip-up sweatshirt, and the gray rims under her eyes. She stared at the welcome mat.

The chain slid back with a small metallic scrape, and the door opened wider. "Viv?" Daniel called. "Dahlia and Mia are here."

Something clinked in the kitchen. The house was wrong. Too quiet. No strains of music from Leah's playlist drifting down from upstairs. No rapid-fire Korean from Viv on the phone.

Mia's hand slid into mine. Her palm was damp with nervous sweat.

Vivienne entered the foyer from the kitchen. She wore the jade pendant at her throat, Leah's Mother's Day gift to her. She'd told me the jade was for protection. For health and good fortune.

Her hair was up in a clip. Her face was bare without makeup, a collapsed, stricken version of itself.

She saw me first. For half a beat, her expression softened.

Then she saw Mia. Everything in her went rigid.

Mia's fingers crushed mine.

My tongue felt too big. Words slid sideways. "Viv."

Vivianne's eyes didn't leave Mia. "How could you come here?"

Mia's shoulders folded in. "Mrs. Cho, I..."

Viv's nostrils flared. She looked up at the ceiling, blinked twice fast, as if shoving tears back by force. When she dropped her gaze, her eyes were dry. Cold. "I can't look at her."

"Viv," I said again. "Mia wanted to apologize. To explain."

"I'm not interested in her apology."

"It's not like that—"

"The police told us where they found Mia's DNA," she said. "Do you know that, Dahlia? Under my daughter's fingernails."

Mia made a raw sound in her throat.

"Don't." Vivienne lifted a hand, her palm out. She turned to Daniel, who hovered behind her. "I can't do this."

Mia's chin dropped. "I loved her. I loved Leah. I would never try to hurt her."

Viv's face pinched as if the word itself hurt. "Don't say her name."

Daniel took his wife's elbow. He stood near her, attentive, protective, his face creased in concern. "Viv," he said gently. "Maybe this isn't the best conversation to have right now."

"I can't do this." She stepped back. "Please leave."

Mia flinched like she'd been struck.

"I'm so sorry," I said to Viv and Daniel. The words felt like stones in my throat. "I didn't mean to make either of you upset."

"I know." His red-rimmed eyes darted to Mia again. He looked like he might be about to say something. Instead, he shut the door in our faces.

I stared at the painted wood six inches from my nose. The spring wreath hung there, its fake leaves brittle. A spiderweb ran from the brass knocker to the trim in a thin silver string. A bird chirped somewhere, too brightly.

Beside me, Mia's breath hitched. I squeezed her hand. I kept my voice light, though I wanted to curl up into a ball and weep. "We'll try again, some other time."

We trudged down the front path like we were leaving a funeral. Mia shuffled half a step ahead with her hands jammed in her pockets. "It's not your fault."

She didn't answer.

We walked in somber silence. Mr. Handler was kicking a soccer ball around in the front yard with his five-year-old son. He averted his gaze and ignored us as we passed.

At our driveway, I stopped. I couldn't go inside yet. My chest still ached from Vivienne's house. "Let's walk the beach. You need air. So do I. Apollo, too."

Ten minutes later, we had Apollo leashed and walked to the beach access, then descended the stairs to the sand. The wind off the water had more teeth down here. The gray sky pressed low over choppy slate water as gulls argued overhead.

Mia walked beside me, chin tucked down. The wind had pulled strands of hair free. They whipped her cheeks.

Ten minutes later, someone called my name.

I turned. Rowan and Chloe came down from the public access stairs. Rowan wore black leggings and a long cardigan, sunglasses perched on top of her highlighted hair. Chloe wore ripped jeans and a cropped sweatshirt.

Their expressions were careful, like they were approaching an injured animal.

"We were hoping we'd find you down here," Rowan called.

Mia's spine straightened. Her gaze went back to the water.

"Hey." My voice came out more guarded than friendly.

Apollo circled Rowan, nose to her calves. She reached down, patted him once, eyes still on Mia. "I'm so glad we ran into you. I was going to text, but you know, we didn't want to overwhelm you."

Chloe shifted from foot to foot. She stepped closer. She glanced at me, then back at Mia. "Can we talk for a sec? Just us?"

"I'll keep your mom company," Rowan told Mia, brightly. "Go ahead."

Mia followed Chloe up toward the drier sand. Chloe slowed so they walked side by side, their heads tilted toward each other.

Rowan moved in beside me, facing the water, her arms folded, her hands under her elbows. "Don't worry about collecting the photos for the memorial on Sunday. You've got plenty on your plate. We're covering it."

"I'm happy to do it."

"Chloe's going to speak. She loved Leah so much. She wants to celebrate her. Share good stories. Sleepovers. Beach days. Normal girl stuff. She's been so... haunted. She needs closure. We all do. It'll be good for the community."

Images from the Instagram account flashed through my mind. The cruel words from Leah's journal. How could anyone find closure with Leah's killer still out there? With our daughters all bearing at least some culpability? But I didn't say anything. I wasn't sure how to form the words.

Up the beach, Chloe and Mia stood facing each other, their heads down. Chloe's hand hovered near Mia's arm, not quite touching her. Their mouths moved, the wind shredding their words.

"You said you were looking for us," I said.

"Yes." Rowan shifted. Sand squeaked under her sandals. "Chloe's been struggling. Her nightmares are getting worse. Her therapist is calling them night terrors. She's waking up crying, screaming. It's like they're real to her when she's trapped in one."

"What happens in her night terrors?" I asked.

Rowan's skin was ashen, dark circles makeup couldn't conceal shadowing her eyes. "She keeps seeing Leah falling, and she can't save her, over and over. Last night, Mia was in her nightmare, too. They were both trying to reach Leah, but they couldn't."

"That sounds awful. I hope the therapy helps her soon."

"I'm sure it will." Rowan forced a smile that didn't reach her eyes. She stepped closer and lowered her voice, though the beach was empty. "But how are you? Brooke told us she saw a police cruiser passing by when she was at the playground with Falcon yesterday, and she heard from Whitney that it went to your house."

"Brooke hears all the gossip, I guess."

She rolled her eyes. "You know Brooke. She made it sound like SWAT."

"Someone broke in sometime on Thursday while we were out. They vandalized a painting of Mia's that Leah had painted for her."

Rowan's hand fluttered at her collarbone. She looked appalled. "Dahlia. Why didn't you call me?"

Because I didn't know which side you were on. I didn't say the words aloud. "It's been a lot. We've changed the locks."

"You should get security cameras. Honestly. I hate saying that about our neighborhood, but here we are. And after Leah, after what happened at your place. I'm genuinely worried for you two."

"The detective suggested the same thing."

"If you want Gregory to recommend anything, just text. Or I'll send links. Honestly, he'd be happy to come over and help you install them."

Rowan's husband worked so much that hardly anyone ever saw him. I doubted he had time to help me with anything. "That's a generous offer, but I think I'll tackle this project myself."

"I admire that about you, Dahlia. I don't think I could tackle anything on my own."

"Sure, you could. You're stronger than you think. You realize something has to be done, and you find a way to do it."

A wave surged higher than the last and broke at our feet. I sidestepped the water and glanced at our daughters, still with their heads down, speaking in low urgent voices.

"We're coming on Sunday," I said to change the subject. "What can I bring for food?"

She brightened. "Could you do your brownies? The sea salt ones? They're amazing."

They were out of a box, just add eggs and butter, but I matched her smile. "I'll make a double batch."

Rowan waved at the girls. "Chloe! We're going to head back. Say goodbye, okay?"

Chloe and Mia jogged back toward us, brushing sand off their jeans. "Thank you for talking to me," Chloe said to Mia. "It really helps."

Mia managed a tentative smile. "Yeah."

"See you Sunday," Rowan said. "Text if you need anything before then."

They headed for the stairs. As soon as they hit the first step, Chloe's hand went to her phone. I watched them disappear up the stairs.

Was Rowan genuinely interested in our well-being, or did she have an ulterior motive in mind when she and Chloe followed us down to the beach?

I hated how paranoid I felt, as if I couldn't trust any of my friends, not Rowan, Whitney, Brooke, or even Camille. Everyone seemed to be hiding something, concealing their true motives.

We climbed the stairs back up from the beach. My calves burned. Apollo pulled ahead, eagerly sniffing every single step. It felt like someone was watching us, even now. I shivered and glanced up toward the top of the bluff, but there was nothing but trees, bushes, and grass.

At home, I unlocked the front door with the new key. Mia headed upstairs to take a shower, and I went into the laundry room to finish the load of linens I'd started that morning.

The dryer hummed, then beeped. I opened the door. Warm air puffed out. Inside, a tangle of towels, sheets, and—

Mia's sloth slippers.

I pulled them out. The soft pink fleece was clean and dry. The embroidered cartoon sloth faces stared up at me.

My stomach dropped. The damp, sandy slippers I'd found in her overnight bag. The ones that suggested she'd gone to the beach that night, despite her claim that she hadn't.

"Mia!" My voice came out sharp. "Come down here, now!"

Footsteps on the stairs. A moment later, Mia appeared in the doorway, still in her sweatshirt and jeans. Her face went white when she saw what I was holding.

"These had sand in them. From Friday night."

Her jaw tightened. "They were dirty. I washed them."

"You could have destroyed potential evidence."

"It's not evidence!" Her voice pitched higher. "I told you, anyone could've used those slippers. They were by the patio door. It wasn't me! I told you that."

I stared at her. "When did you put these in the laundry?"

"This morning, right after you put the load in. Before we left."

Before the second interview with the police.

"Why?"

"Because! Because I'm scared, okay? Because everything I do, everything I say, those detectives twist it. They make it sound like I'm guilty. But those slippers—" She sucked in a breath. "They made me look like I'm lying when I'm not. You thought so, too."

I set the slippers on top of the dryer and stared at them, warm, clean, and innocuous. She wasn't wrong. I couldn't tell if I was relieved or appalled, or both.

Apollo sat between us, looking from me to Mia and back again with concern. He hated it when we argued.

"Go take your shower," I said.

Mia lurked in the doorway, her expression hesitant, uncertain. "Mom, are you mad at me?"

I sighed. "I don't know."

After she left, I stood alone in the laundry room, staring at those slippers. I didn't know what I was doing anymore. I didn't know who to trust. Not the mothers. Not the police. Not even my own daughter.

Chapter Twenty-Eight

I sat at the kitchen table and watched the clock tick to 5:36 a.m. My eyes burned. My head ached. One week ago, in the early hours of Saturday morning, Leah had been pushed, had suffered, had died not two thousand feet from where I now sat.

The house pressed in around me. Too quiet. Mia's door at the top of the stairs had been shut since we got back from the beach last night, since I confronted her about the washed slippers.

I looked out the window at the predawn street. The trash bins lined the curbs like obedient soldiers under the weak halo of the streetlights. Collection day. Blackthorn Shores paid extra for Saturday pickup so no one's trash ever overflowed.

An electric current snapped through me. People tossed incriminating evidence in their garbage all the time. This was my slim window of opportunity, while the neighborhood slept.

I had to do something before they arrested my daughter.

If Mia was telling the truth, something out there could exonerate her. If she wasn't, something out there might prove that, too.

My oversized faux leather purse hung on the back of the chair. Before I could think better of it, I grabbed the purse and crossed to the hook where Apollo's leash hung.

Apollo trotted over, his tail wagging in anticipation. "Need to go out, buddy?"

I opened the front door quietly so as not to wake Mia, then we slipped out into the predawn dark. I locked the door behind us.

The air had a wet chill that seeped under my clothes. A streetlight hummed overhead. Insects whirred in the grass.

Apollo tugged at his leash. I turned off Wyld Wood Lane and headed southeast on Driftwood Terrace.

Vivienne Cho's grand sage-green Craftsman sat silently ahead. My stomach knotted. I stopped on the sidewalk. My hand tightened around Apollo's leash.

I couldn't do this one. There was a line even my desperation couldn't cross.

Apollo whined softly, tugging toward home. "Not this one, buddy."

The next stop was Brooke August.

My heart hammered as I crouched by the black bin. The lid was gritty under my hand. I glanced over my shoulder at the dark windows facing me, then lifted.

The smell hit me first. Sour wine, rotting food, fermented sweetness. I kept my jaw clenched, breathing shallowly through my nose. Empty wine bottles rolled against each other inside, along with greasy pizza boxes, takeout containers with congealed orange sauce, and wadded tissues speckled with mascara smears.

Nothing that said murder. Nothing that said Mia.

I closed the lid. The plastic *thunk* echoed too loud in the sleeping street. I held my breath, waiting for a light to flick on.

Nothing happened.

Apollo and I continued on Driftwood Terrace until it intersected with Cliff Harbor Drive, then turned west and headed up the road back toward Wyld Wood Lane, making a circle. At the top of Cliff Harbor Drive, I decided to hit Camille's on the way back to my house after Whitney's.

I approached Whitney's house on high alert. The white house gleamed even in the predawn dark, its porcelain floors visible through the windows, the multi-tiered deck overlooking the pool stretching behind it.

I flipped back the blue recycling lid. Sephora bags with black-and-white stripes, Lululemon packaging, and tissue paper folded into neat squares greeted me.

I moved to the black bin and slipped my hand into a doggie bag. The lid made a scraping sound as I eased it up. My pulse spiked. I glanced at the second-floor windows. Still dark, luckily.

I inventoried the trash: bagged kitchen waste, a broken candle, and paper towels soaked with something reddish. Ketchup, maybe. Then I saw it. Half-buried along the side, a plastic orange cylinder bright against dark coffee grounds.

A prescription bottle.

I reached inside, pinched it by the cap, and lifted it into the glow of my phone's flashlight, keeping the light shielded low against my leg.

LORAZEPAM 3 MG

Patient: AUGUST, BROOKE

Prescriber: DR. SARAH CHEN

I sucked in my breath. Why was Brooke's medication in Whitney's trash? Lorazepam was a benzo, a downer, a sedative used for insomnia, anxiety, and panic attacks. Otherwise known as sleeping pills.

Before I could overthink it, I slid the bottle into the doggie bag and knotted it tightly. It was in the trash, so it wasn't stealing. I tucked it into my purse.

A dog barked somewhere down the street. My heart jackhammered. I jerked upright, scanning the dark yards.

In front of me, one of the two double-car garage doors rattled to life.

I froze. Yellow light flooded the driveway. The mechanical hum grew louder as the door lifted to expose the gleaming black Mercedes parked inside the garage. Whitney's husband Graham was about to leave for his executive job at Whirlpool.

Apollo's collar jangled. He started for the car. I yanked his leash, dragging him as close to me as I could, and ducked behind the recycling bin. I crouched low, my pulse hammering in my ears.

The engine started with a purr. Headlights swept across the pavement mere inches from my feet.

Eager to make a new friend, Apollo strained at his collar and stuck his big head past the recycling bin.

"Apollo!" I whispered. "Come on, get back!"

To my horror, I realized my elbow and half my leg stuck out past the bins.

The Mercedes backed out.

It was too late to move. I froze.

Through the gap between the bins, I could see Graham's shiny blond head behind the wheel. He was dressed in a charcoal suit and was already talking on his Bluetooth device, his hand making a chopping gesture at the air as if to emphasize a point. Business at 5:58 a.m.

My breath caught in my throat. If I could see him, Graham could see me. And Apollo. If he glanced at his trash and recycling bins or his mailbox, I was toast.

The car rolled past me. He never glanced toward the bins. Never looked left or right. Whitney always complained he couldn't be bothered to pay attention to anything unless it was business, tennis, or sex, in that order.

The taillights flared red at the end of the driveway. The Mercedes turned and headed down the street as the garage door descended with a mechanical whine.

I remained crouched for two full minutes. My right leg cramped. Finally, I stood on unsteady legs and shook it out. "Thanks for nothing, Apollo."

Apollo happily licked my hand. His tail wagged with enthusiasm, ready for the next game.

I pulled the dog toward the next house, continuing north to Rowan's. The big house loomed dark, its wraparound deck empty. The bins sat centered exactly at the edge of the driveway.

I lifted the recycling lid. Yogurt containers rinsed clean,

kombucha bottles, and a collapsed Amazon box. In the trash, coffee grounds, vegetable peels, and a cracked mug. Everything ordinary, typical, expected.

I closed the lid and doubled back on Wyld Wood Lane, passing Whitney's again until I reached Camille's. The indigo sky was starting to lighten. Whitney and Peyton often went jogging together at 6:30 a.m. for some God-forsaken reason, so I was running out of time.

In front of Camille's house, I paused. If Camille found out what I was doing, she might drop us.

I did it anyway. I was too committed now.

Apollo nosed at the grass while I lifted the recycling lid. Juice boxes. Cereal boxes. A graveyard of LaCroix cans. I moved to the black bin. The lid stuck, then gave with a damp sucking sound.

Something bulky wrapped in newspaper sat on the top. I slid my bagged hand down and eased the bundle up. The newspaper crackled. A thin smear of red streaked the outer layer.

I peeled the paper back. A spray paint can. The metal was cold and tacky, its rim crusted with dried pigment, the exact angry scarlet shade that had spelled GUILTY across Leah's painting.

The world narrowed to the cylinder in my hand.

A light flicked on inside the house, on the second floor. My heart stopped. Quickly, I glanced at the time on my phone. 5:57 a.m. Garbage pick-up was in less than five minutes. If I called the police now, the contents of Camille's trash would probably be in a landfill by the time they arrived.

Besides, if I called the cops on Camille's daughter, she would absolutely fire Mia, and we desperately needed her right now.

I had to be careful how I went about this. And I had no time to figure out a better solution.

Before I could change my mind, I shoved the spray paint into a fresh doggie bag, double-layered, fumbling the knots. I shoved it into my purse, backed away from the bin, and hurried down the street with Apollo.

My shoulder blades itched with anxiety. I half-expected a shout behind me. A door opening. Someone demanding to know what I was doing.

The light stayed on, but no one came out.

Every window I passed felt like an eye watching me. The weight of the purse dragged at my shoulder. It grew heavier by the minute.

The sky had softened to a bruised gray by the time we reached my cottage. Birdsong started up in hesitant notes.

I fumbled with the new keys, my hands shaking so badly I dropped them. The metal clatter on the concrete was too loud. I snatched them up, unlocked the door, and pulled Apollo inside.

I locked the deadbolt behind me and leaned against the door, breathing hard.

The clock on the stove read 6:04 a.m. Upstairs, Mia's door remained closed.

I went to the coat closet next to the stairs and shoved the purse behind the winter coats, wedging it between an outgrown backpack and a garment bag. Out of sight, for now. I needed to figure out how to present it without incriminating myself first.

I made it. I hadn't been caught.

But I had evidence, which I'd just stolen, then hidden, that implicated Zara Hayward. And I had no idea what to do with it.

Chapter Twenty-Nine

The next several hours were a blur. After Mia woke up, we had breakfast. We didn't talk about the slippers, nor did I mention my early morning trash run. I pushed the spray paint and the pills out of my mind until I could focus on them later.

After we ate, we ran some errands. I took Mia to Best Buy with me, the cart rattling over cracked concrete as we walked under the blue awning. We moved through the security aisle, past boxes promising smart protection, wireless coverage, and night vision.

I chose the cheapest system with four cameras, praying I had enough on the credit card to cover it. The guy at the check-out counter wouldn't meet our eyes.

At Martins grocery store, I pushed the cart, going through the shopping list. Brownie mix. Eggs. Butter. Disposable pans.

Mia cocked one eyebrow at me. "Memorial brownies?"

"Rowan requested them."

"They're from a box."

"She doesn't need to know that." I met her eyes. "Our secret?"

The corner of her mouth lifted. "Our secret."

Everything felt distant, like I was watching it through glass. We endured the reporters outside the Blackthorn Shores gates, Mia shrinking into her seat like she wanted to disappear.

To make matters worse, several protesters had joined the media, standing around holding signs that read "Justice for Leah" and "No Child Killers in Our Town."

At home, Mia carried in the grocery bags, then paused at the door. "Want help with the cameras?"

I looked at her, really looked at her. She was exhausted, stressed, despondent, but trying, making an effort. After the interrogation on Friday, followed by the disaster at Viv and Daniel's house, Mia seemed diminished. Of course, she was. I just wished I knew how to help her.

I forced a smile. "I've got it. But thank you, honey. Why don't you relax? Read a book or draw something. And stay off social media."

She nodded and headed upstairs. Before she disappeared, she glanced back. "You're terrible at anything involving a drill, just so you know."

I managed to wink at her. "Have some faith in your mom."

She rolled her eyes at me.

It felt almost normal. Almost.

I set the cameras on the kitchen island, lining them up like equipment before a mission, examining the instructions, spreading out screws and mounting brackets.

Something I could control. Something I could do.

Outside, I hauled the aluminum ladder from the garage and set it against the siding by the front door. One leg caught on the uneven strip of concrete where winter had heaved the slab.

I wore Marcus's U of M sweatshirt, the navy one with the cracked maize M on the chest, the cuffs frayed. I needed something of his near me right now.

The first step flexed under my weight. My hands shook from lack of sleep and adrenaline. The April air bit through the sweatshirt, my fingers stiff around the cordless drill.

The instructions might as well have been in another language. Diagram A to Diagram B, arrows pointing at screws that did not exist. The bracket refused to line up with the predrilled holes on the camera's base. I flipped it. Rotated it. Still no dice.

"Marcus would have had this done in ten minutes," I muttered.

The ladder wobbled when I shifted my weight to reach the eave. I tightened my core, leaned in, and pressed my shoulder against the siding to create a counterbalance.

The drill whirred when I squeezed the trigger. It slipped off the screw head twice, jerking, the bit skittering across white paint. I let out a frustrated curse.

Grief was not abstract. It pressed into my sternum like a blade. Marcus should have been the one up here, one foot braced, forearm steady, teaching Mia how to do this with some corny dad joke.

Instead, it was up to me alone. I measured my breathing against the distant crash of waves from the lake. The sky was overcast; gray light flattened everything.

I rechecked the screws and adjusted my grip. I forced the bracket to line up, but I couldn't focus on what was right in front of me. I kept thinking about my conversation with Whitney last night. What Alexis had told me, and Zara, what I'd discovered this morning in the trash.

Zara had been in our house during sleepovers, group projects, movie nights. She could easily have stolen the key from Whitney's house, or just asked Peyton to borrow it, or hell, maybe she'd made a copy back when Brooke still had it.

The spray paint meant Zara was guilty of entering my home, taking Leah's painting from Mia's bedroom, and slashing it with a knife, then painting GUILTY in dripping scarlet letters.

She wanted to scare us. Or she wanted to frame Mia. Or she wanted to shut me up before I uncovered something worse.

But for what reason?

It only made sense if she had pushed Leah herself.

But did it? Zara had seemed genuinely remorseful. She'd claimed she wanted to help Leah expose whoever ran the cyberbullying account. She'd confirmed the scream Alexis had mentioned, then revealed the sounds she'd heard at 3:30 a.m.

Unless she was lying, deflecting. Manipulating.

Or someone else had put the spray paint can in their trash. But if so, who? And why? It wasn't like anyone expected their trash to be rummaged through by a frantic, half-crazed mother before the crack of dawn.

Zara still made the most sense.

Mrs. Atkins had seen Zara on the beach at 12:30 a.m. in her bright yellow hoodie. She would've had ten minutes to reach the top of the stairs and head over to Rowan's bluff. She'd been at the right place, at the right time.

I had difficulty envisioning bright, vivacious Zara shoving Leah over a cliff. She'd always been so outgoing, kind, and sweet-natured.

But perhaps Leah had turned on her, outed their plan to Alexis and Peyton, and blamed Zara. That would've made Zara incredibly upset. I'd seen in her eyes how desperate she was to be accepted, included, to belong. Her fear of being rejected by the group.

The drill bit finally caught. The vibration ran up my forearm. The mechanical buzz cut through the quiet neighborhood as the bracket finally clicked into place under the eave, and the camera housing settled with a snap.

My stomach clenched. How was I going to tell Camille? How was she going to respond if she thought I was threatening her daughter's freedom? Not well, I knew that much.

And yet, we desperately needed her help.

Apprehension settled in my gut. I needed to talk to Camille. We needed to take this evidence to the police.

Then there were the lorazepam pills. Sleeping pills. Sedatives, prescribed for anxiety. Discarded in Whitney's trash can, but prescribed to Brooke. I wasn't sure what to do about those. What they meant, if they meant anything at all.

Brooke had accused Alexis of stealing her pills that night on their patio. Zara had mentioned something about Taylor Everett taking sleeping pills at Whitney's pool party, which led to the near drowning that left her brain damaged.

Could Alexis be stealing her mother's prescription pills to sell them? Taylor had lived in our neighborhood. If that was the case, Alexis could have sold them to Taylor, and to Peyton, too, for that matter. Maybe Whitney knew nothing about the pills, and it was her daughter who'd bought them and carelessly tossed the bottle in her family's trash.

Of course, I was speculating. Maybe the lorazepam had nothing to do with Leah's death. Simply another of the August family secrets that Brooke was desperate to hide from the world.

Another secret I needed to uncover.

I positioned the drill again and drilled the second, third, and fourth screws into the brackets until the casing held firm against the house. I descended the ladder, wiped my palms on my jeans, and reached for my phone on the railing.

No new notifications except junk mail and spam. I opened messages anyway, then scrolled up to Rowan's last text thread. Nothing new. I checked other conversations. Nothing from Vivienne, of course, which hurt the most. Nothing from Brooke or Whitney, or from Camille, whom I'd texted three times today. Last night, she'd said we would discuss strategy, how to control the narrative and get ahead of the rumor mill. As if that were possible.

Their silence felt louder than any accusation.

I was about to put my phone away and get back to work when a push notification slid across the top of my screen. Detroit Free Press BREAKING NEWS: LOCAL TEEN NAMED SUSPECT IN LAKESHORE DEATH.

Dread and anxiety tangled in my gut. Aghast, I read the rest: *Witness Reports "Violent Fight" Before Fatal Fall.*

Then two photos, side-by-side. On the left, Mia's school photo, the one we had argued over because she hated her hair parted on the side. Her awkward smile, chin tilted. On the right, Leah in mid-laugh, eyes crinkled, hair caught in motion. Alive.

The text below was clinical, efficient, brutal: *Sources close to the investigation confirm DNA evidence and witness testimony place fourteen-year-old Mia Kincaid at the scene. A witness reported a physical altercation between Kincaid and victim Leah Cho hours before Cho's fatal fall from the Blackthorn Shores bluff.*

It hit me like a gut-punch. Mia had said nothing about a fight. Not even an argument or disagreement. She claimed Leah grabbed her arm when she got dizzy from the nosebleed. That explained the scratches. An accident. A panicked grip.

And who reported this new information? What witness? Which girl?

Panicked heat rose from my chest into my throat. How could I protect her when she was still, even now, lying to me? Any of the girls could still be lying. I couldn't know the truth, not for certain.

It felt like fighting blind. Like the edge of the bluff shifting beneath my feet, unsteady, about to crumble. I imagined social media blowing up with this new salacious tidbit. Mia's harassment would intensify now. And this was the least of our worries.

The sky had gone darker, with thickening clouds stacked over the lake. The air carried that metallic smell that comes right before a storm, the kind that worked under your skin.

Footsteps crunched on the driveway gravel. I looked up.

Camille strode up the street toward my house, her phone in one hand, a manila folder in the other. She wore a silk fuchsia blouse, dark jeans, and low-heeled boots.

Her mouth was a tight line, her lips pressed together. She paused in front of the porch as her gaze locked onto mine. "We need to talk."

Chapter Thirty

I faced Camille at the top step of my porch. "I've been texting you. Come inside, and I'll make some coffee—"

"Dahlia." Her tone was sharp, clipped. Her courtroom voice.

"Is everything okay?"

She halted with one heel braced on the bottom step. "Brooke's Ring camera caught you. This morning. Going through her trash. Whitney's, too."

My heart dropped to my stomach.

"You were trespassing on private property. You contaminated potential evidence." She held up her phone. "I have the footage. Time-stamped. Clear as day."

"I wasn't stealing—"

"You took items from Whitney's trash. And mine!" She lowered the phone. "What the hell were you thinking?"

My mouth went dry. Clearly, I wasn't. "I was looking for evidence. Something that could help Mia."

Her voice vibrated with barely repressed anger. "You talked to Alexis. And Zara, my daughter. You questioned minors without their parents present. You pressured them for statements. That's witness tampering, Dahlia. Do you understand what you've done to your daughter's case?"

"I was trying to help her."

"You've made everything worse. The DA can use your interference to discredit every witness statement. Every piece of evidence. They could argue the entire circle has been contaminated by a desperate mother coaching testimony."

Heat crawled up my neck. "I didn't coach anyone."

"It doesn't matter what you did. It matters how it looks." She shifted the folder under her arm. "The other mothers know. Rowan. Whitney. Brooke. They are all aware that you have been interfering. They are not happy, Dahlia. They are, in fact, united in their assessment that you have become a problem."

Fear hooked in my throat. "A problem."

"They're concerned. Concerned you are not acting rationally. Concerned that you are desperate." She paused. "And that makes you dangerous."

I felt the word like sharp little shivers under my skin. "Dangerous? I asked questions—"

"You trespassed. You stole. You harassed their daughters. Whitney's considering a restraining order."

My vision blurred. I fought back tears of frustration. "I am trying to defend Mia. Since no one else appears to be!"

"You're not her lawyer. I am."

"I'm not trying to play lawyer," I said. "I'm trying to be a mother."

"And I am trying to be both." The words slipped out of her. Emotion flared in her face, a flash of something human. Apprehension. Worry. "Which is exactly why I am here."

"Zara heard something that night," I said. "At 3:30 a.m. She has information about the Instagram account."

Camille's face closed. "Leave Zara out of this."

"She's a witness. She could help."

"Zara is done talking."

"The red spray paint can was in your trash, Camille. Yours. That means Zara broke into my house, defaced Leah's painting, threatened Mia and me—"

"Enough!" Camille's face contorted. "Just stop. Stop it. There will be no more conversations between you and my daughter, or Mia and my daughter. That's non-negotiable."

"You're protecting her from what? The truth?"

Her shoulders dropped a fraction. The mask didn't fall, it never would with her, but it shifted. She looked sad, defeated. "I am not your enemy, Dahlia. I am Zara's mother. I am also..." She stopped herself. "I am trying to help you."

Desperation tinged my voice. "It doesn't sound like help."

"It is." She lowered her voice enough that I had to lean closer. She held my gaze. "Take my advice. These women will protect their children at any cost. You need to understand what that means."

"They're afraid," I said. "They're hiding something."

"They're mothers," she said, as if that was an answer.

In a way, it was.

Camille pulled a paper from the folder. "I'm withdrawing as Mia's attorney."

The ground shifted beneath my feet. Nausea churned in my stomach. I thought I might vomit. "What?"

She held the form out. "There's a conflict of interest. My daughter is a potential witness. I believed it was manageable until you started contaminating the witness pool. This is my notice of withdrawal. I'm filing it on Monday morning."

I didn't take it. "You can't do this now. Not to Mia. Be mad at me, but don't make Mia suffer."

"Dahlia, please. Let's not make things harder than they already are. I'm giving you names of attorneys who can step in. You'll need to call them soon if you want someone at the station with Mia when they bring her in again."

She thrust the paper at me. I took it with numb hands.

"Please, Camille." My voice came out high, panicked. "This is when we need you most. I can't. I won't be able to..." I couldn't bear to say the words aloud. I could barely afford groceries, let alone an experienced, high-cost criminal defense attorney to defend my daughter against murder charges.

"Then the state will appoint one for you," she said crisply. She looked somewhere over my shoulder, avoiding eye contact. Pretending Mia was just another client, that we hadn't shared coffee dozens of times.

"The system will eat Mia alive."

"That is no longer my concern."

The paper in my hand crinkled. I couldn't keep the sarcasm from lacing my voice. "And what is your concern, then?"

"My concern is my child."

I wanted to ask her whose version she believed at night when she closed her eyes, when the house went quiet, and she could hear her own thoughts. Had she stood at the foot of Zara's bed and watched her ribcage rise and fall as I did with Mia. Had she felt that absolute clawing terror that you were losing the flesh of your flesh, that there was nothing you could do to protect them?

Perhaps she had, which was why she was doing this to me, to us.

"I am sorry about Leah," Camille said. "I am sorry for Vivienne. And I am sorry for you. Truly, Dahlia. I hope someday you believe me."

Before I could respond, she was moving. Down the steps, down the gravel drive, to the street. Then she was gone. And with her, our last ally.

I looked at the paper in my hand. Three names, neatly printed. With fancy firms whose retainers probably cost more than I made in a year. Beside one, in Camille's slanting script: *Try her first.*

I let out a bitter laugh. Like I could afford any of them. I set the paper flat on the console table next to the photo of Mia at seven with her cheeks stuffed with marshmallows, laughing and wriggling in Marcus's arms.

I put my hand flat against the glass and felt its coolness leech into my skin. I rubbed my thumb over the ridge of the frame.

I thought of Vivienne, the devastation etching her face. I thought of Rowan, Whitney, and Brooke, of the gleam of their countertops and the tidy way they'd closed ranks, united against a perceived enemy.

They would protect their children at any cost.

They weren't the only ones.

Chapter Thirty-One

I boiled the pasta too long.

The timer had gone off three minutes earlier, but I stood there, fingers pressed to the edge of the counter, staring at the list of attorneys and their rates that might as well have been ransom notes. Hundreds of dollars an hour. Eye-watering retainer fees, more than the cost of a new car.

The pot hissed and rattled on the burner. I turned off the gas.

The only sound was the low roar of waves against the shoreline at the bottom of the bluff, muffled through the double-paned glass windows. The waves had always soothed me before. Not tonight.

I drained the pasta, then stirred the hot Marinara sauce, the scent of garlic and tomatoes filling my nostrils. My mind wandered to the headline I'd seen before Camille blew up our lives.

The fight between Leah and Mia. A detail Mia had never mentioned.

I needed to ask. I had to ask. I had been waiting all afternoon for the right moment, as if such a thing existed anymore. The silence between us had turned into something with mass, something alive, something dangerous.

Footsteps creaked on the stairs. I set the spoon down, wiped my hands on a dish towel, and watched the kitchen doorway.

Mia appeared. Her hair was in a knot that had mostly escaped, strands dark against her too-pale face. She hovered at the threshold, as if checking for danger, then crossed to the table.

"I made pasta."

"Thanks." She dropped into her chair. Apollo trotted in from the living room and slunk under the table, where Mia would secretly feed him, and we'd all pretend nothing was going on.

I plated the food. Spoonfuls of pasta. Ladles of sauce. Grated Parmesan snowing down over both plates. A small salad neither of us wanted.

"You have schoolwork?"

She shrugged. "They emailed some stuff. I'll look at it later."

She twirled pasta, lifted it, let it slide back down her fork. She hadn't taken more than two bites.

I took a sip of water. My throat felt tight, as if I had swallowed a stone. "I, ah, need to let you know. We don't have Camille anymore."

Her gaze snapped up at Camille's name. Her face went white. "We don't? Mom, I'm freaking out right now."

"I know, and I'm sorry."

"What happened?"

"It doesn't matter, don't worry about it." I hated the look on her face, the panic, the betrayal. "I'll figure something out, okay? I promise."

We ate for another few minutes, both of us listless, moving food around on our plates.

"I saw another article today." I kept my eyes on the spaghetti, on a stray basil leaf stuck to one of the noodles. "About Leah. About what happened."

Her fork stilled. "Okay."

"It mentioned a fight." I made my tone neutral, exploratory. "Between you and Leah. That night."

"They're lying."

"They said a witness confirmed it."

"They're making stuff up, Mom. That's what they do. They twist everything." Her eyes were fixed on the table, not me. Her hand had gone white-knuckled around her fork.

"I just need to hear it from you. Did you and Leah fight? On the bluff?"

Her lips thinned. She moved a piece of salad around her plate with the fork tine, not eating it. "It was just... it was nothing, okay? I don't want to talk about it."

"I think we need to, honey. I can't help you if I don't know everything. I must understand what really happened."

"I already told you what happened." The words came out sharp and pointed. "You don't believe me."

"Mia." I forced my hands to stay flat on the table, to keep my fingers from curling into fists. "If there was a fight, if someone saw something, we need to know what they're saying. To protect you."

"It doesn't even matter!" She shoved her chair back. Apollo yelped under the table. "It's everywhere. On Instagram and TikTok. On the news. On X. Everyone has already decided. What happened. What I am. That I'm violent. I'm a psycho. I plotted to murder my best friend at a slumber party. I'm unstable. I should be locked up for life. I should be beheaded, strangled, shot in the heart. It doesn't matter what I say. They don't care what I have to say."

"I care." My own voice had an edge now. I was weary, exhausted, frustrated, and scared. "I need you to tell me the truth."

She stared at me, breathing faster. A flush rose from her throat to her cheeks. "I already did! I don't want to talk about it anymore."

"Mia, listen—"

"No!" Her voice rose. "I said everything already. Why doesn't anyone believe me!"

She stood too quickly. Her fork clattered onto the plate. Sauce splattered the table.

We looked at each other over plates of half-eaten pasta, over the roses Rowan had brought over a few days earlier, already drooping in their vase. The silence had gone brittle. One more wrong word and it would shatter.

Mia spun and marched from the kitchen, up the stairs, to her room, where her door slammed shut. Beneath the table, Apollo whined and sniffed at my feet, seeking reassurance.

I sat for a few seconds, pulses of anger and fear beating under my skin like a second heart. Then I forced myself to move. I cleared her plate first and scraped it into the trash. I rinsed plates, loaded the dishwasher, and wiped the table.

My body ran through the motions while anxiety curdled in my stomach.

We needed a lawyer, a strategy, the truth—and none of them were coming. I checked my phone on reflex. No messages. No Viv, No Camille, No Rowan. It hurt more than I wanted to admit.

Outside the kitchen window, the sun sank toward Lake Michigan in a blaze of copper, rose, and crimson, staining the water below in streaks of molten gold. Ribbons of clouds drifted along the horizon, their edges lit from within as if they'd been set afire.

I dried my hands and stood in the middle of the kitchen, listening. I could feel her upstairs, sealed off, her walls up. Press harder, and she retreated.

I couldn't keep interrogating her. Not tonight. I had to stop pushing before I lost her completely.

Right now, I just wanted to be with my daughter.

I stepped to the bottom of the stairs and looked up. "Mia?"

No answer. A faint creak as she moved, or sat, or lay down. Impossible to tell.

"The sunset looks nice," I called, pitching my voice lighter than I felt. "Do you want to walk on the beach for a little? Just to get out of the house?"

The silence stretched. I let it. The clock in the hall ticked. From somewhere down the block, a dog barked twice, then stopped.

"I guess." Muffled, from behind her door. "Whatever."

Relief made me weak in the knees. I took the stairs two at a time, Apollo right behind me. Her door was half open. She must have opened it after slamming it shut a half-hour ago.

I knocked on the jamb anyway as I stepped in. Mia's room was dim, the curtains drawn. A mess, as usual. Mia lay on her stomach on the bed, scrolling through her phone. She glanced up as I entered.

Something caught at the edge of my vision.

The curtains ruffled in the breeze. A cool draft blew into the room, raising goosebumps on my skin. Mia had left the window open again.

I crossed her room, sidestepping a pair of dirty sweatpants piled on the floor, and reached the window.

I pushed the ruffled sage curtain back, about to close the window, and stopped.

My gaze dropped to the windowsill. Her beach stone and sea glass collection lined the sill. She kept them in careful order, everything organized by color and shape like a tiny museum. Nothing random. Nothing out of place.

Except something was out of place.

The usual treasures were there, catching the last weak light. The sea glass glowed softly in translucent blues and greens. Polished agates, granite, limestone, sandstone, and Petoskey stones lay in their usual rows, sorted by size and color.

In the midst of them sat a rock that did not belong.

It was fist sized. Grayish brown, the color of old concrete. The surface was rough, not polished by waves, its edges still sharp. It squatted among the gleaming glass and smooth pebbles like something ugly, grotesque.

I stepped closer.

"Mom?" Mia said from behind me. Her voice sounded like it was coming from a great distance. Ice water flooded my chest. I forgot how to breathe.

Dark spots mottled one side of it. Not uniform, not part of the stone. Irregular splatters and crescents dried into the porous surface. Rust-colored. Brownish red. Matte.

Like paint. Dried paint.

Only it wasn't paint.

It was blood.

Chapter Thirty-Two

I stared at the bloodied rock in shock.

Among the pretty sea glass and smooth stones, the rock looked even uglier. There were hairs stuck in the dried blood. Several glossy black hairs, chin-length. No one else had hair like that. Only one person, one girl. Leah Cho.

Horror filled me. I couldn't bring myself to touch it. Couldn't bear the thought of feeling its weight, the texture of dried blood beneath my fingertips.

How long had it been sitting in her bedroom, bleeding quietly into the air, while I made dinner and interrogated teenage girls and dug through my friends' trash cans?

Images unspooled in my mind: the bluff at night, the black outline of rock against water, the dull thud of something heavy connecting with a human skull. Leah's head wound, in the coroner's description. An impact with something hard. Blunt force trauma.

Was this rock the object Leah's skull had struck that night when she fell?

My skin prickled with sweat even though the window was cracked. My pulse whooshed too loudly in my ears. Why did Mia have this? Why was it here, among her things? What did this mean?

I half-turned toward Mia on the bed. The rock sat on the sill, low in my peripheral vision, an obscene centerpiece.

Did she know what I had found? Could she see the terrible knowledge in my eyes?

"What is this?"

The question hung in the air between us, loaded with unspoken accusations. I stared at my daughter, searching her face for something—guilt, fear, recognition, shame—anything that might tell me what I needed to know.

Mia sat up on her bed. Her brow furrowed with concern. "What's going on?"

"This rock." I pointed to the windowsill. "Where did it come from?"

Mia's gaze followed my gesture. Her eyes widened with alarm as they registered what had changed in the landscape she knew as well as I did. Her body went very still. "I don't know what that is. I didn't put that there."

"Mia. Please don't lie to me. Not now. Not about this."

" I didn't... that's not... what is it?"

Mia looked from me to the rock and back again, her lips parting but no sound emerging.

I fought to keep my voice steady. Speaking the words aloud tasted like ashes on my tongue. "I need you to tell me the truth. Did you... Is there something you still aren't telling me?"

"No!" The word burst from her with such force that Apollo startled. "No, Mom, I promise I didn't try to hurt her. I would never."

"Then why is this here? How did it get here?"

"I don't know!" Mia's eyes filled with tears. Her knees were pulled up to her chest, arms wrapped around her legs. Apollo leapt onto the bed and curled up next to her. She dug her fingers into his fur and clung to him. "That rock... that's what killed Leah?"

I crossed the room and squatted in front of her. "I don't know for certain, not until the police test the blood on it. I think so. When she fell, her head must have hit this rock somewhere on the bluff."

Mia shrank back, horrified. She looked so young, so vulnerable. All I wanted to do was pull her into my arms and hold her, rock her all night long like when she was a baby, and I could keep her safe.

"I don't know how it got there. I didn't put it there. I—I've never seen it before." A tiny hitch in her throat. The slightest hesitation. Her gaze darted to the rock and then away.

Everything seemed distant, unreal. My thoughts skittered through my head, slippery and hard to grasp. My eyes stung.

Was I seeing things? Or was she lying to my face? Or was I projecting? Reading guilt into grief? She was traumatized and terrified. Of course, she'd hesitate. Of course, she'd stare at the thing that might send her to prison.

I fought to steady my breathing, to slow my racing heart. I desperately wanted to believe her, to cling to this other possibility, this other killer, this ghost. "You think someone did this? Took the rock from the bluff and put it here in your room, among your things?"

"I didn't! Why would I crawl down there after and... and take the rock that she hit her head on and bring it back with me? And put it in my room, like a... like a trophy?" She looked at me with desperation. "Someone stole my camera. They came into our house and slashed Leah's painting. Whoever really killed her did this stuff. They hate me. They want me to go to jail forever, not them."

Guilt speared me. How could I have doubted, for even a second? What the hell was wrong with me? How could a mother doubt her own daughter? What kind of mother was I?

I took a breath. I had to think clearly.

This was Mia. This was my daughter.

No, I would not believe this of my child. I could not. I must not.

Because I couldn't lose Mia, too. Not after Marcus.

"Could the rock have been here before tonight? Yesterday? Over the weekend?"

Mia shrugged helplessly. "I haven't collected anything on the beach since... since it happened. I haven't looked closely at anything. I dunno. Maybe."

I felt the presence of the rock behind me. Pulsing with a dark sinister energy. "Think, Mia."

Her voice rose in panic. "I don't know!"

The locks had been changed on Friday morning. Yesterday. So, the rock had been placed before then, by someone who used the spare key. Or someone had put it here whom we had invited inside ourselves.

This was intentional.

The slashed painting with GUILTY painted across it. The stolen notebook. The break-in when nothing was taken, just moved, just wrong.

My breath came faster.

The rock wasn't evidence Mia kept. It was evidence that someone planted. Evidence timed perfectly. Sitting here for hours, for days possibly, waiting to be discovered by police with a search warrant.

Or by Mia, so she'd touch it, move it, contaminate it further. To leave her prints in the grooves where blood had dried.

Or by me, so I'd think exactly what I had. That my daughter was guilty.

This was a plan.

Someone wanted my daughter in prison.

What if the rock had fingerprints on it? What if it had Mia's prints on it? The thought sliced through my mind like a blade. "You're sure you never touched this?"

"I never touched it. I promise, Mom."

I sucked in a deep breath and forced my frazzled thoughts to clarify. "Okay."

"Should we call the police?" Mia asked.

"I'm not sure."

"What if the police come here and look in my room? That's what whoever did this wants to happen, isn't it? The police will think I went down the bluff and took it, for some kind of sick trophy or whatever." Mia looked like she wanted to throw up.

What would happen if I called Detective King right now and invited him in? Attempted to explain the bloodied rock among my daughter's things. It would go about as well as the slashed painting incident had. I hadn't heard an update from the police. I doubted reporting it had done anything but make them more suspicious of us.

It wasn't ours. We didn't do it. It just appeared tonight. She's innocent, Officer, I swear. She just looks guilty as hell.

I didn't have faith that the police would realize someone must be trying to frame Mia. Because she was right. Why would she place it on the windowsill like a prize? Unless she was a sociopath? Or stupid.

But perhaps the police wouldn't care. They were already building a case against her. They already had her DNA, the scratches, the blood on her dress. This would be the final straw.

"Should we hide it?" Mia asked. "Or, like, get rid of it?"

"No." Although that was my first instinct. To destroy evidence would make us culpable. It was a dangerous step in a direction I did not want to go, taking us to a place we could never return from. I thought of the sandy slippers that Mia had washed. "I'll think of something."

Mia started to cry.

"Oh, honey." I sat on the edge of the bed, opened my arms, and pulled Mia to me. She crumpled against my chest. I held her there on the bed, leaning against the peeling headboard I'd meant to paint sage-green but hadn't yet. Her body curled over my thighs as I stroked her tear-damp hair back from her face.

Apollo gazed at us with concern, his snout on his paws. His tail thumped on the comforter. He raised his head and nudged my hand with his wet nose, but I barely felt it.

What was I going to do? The bloodied rock might have

evidence that pointed to the real killer. Or the real killer might have tainted it, implicating Mia even further.

My options were limited, the choices narrowing like we were trapped in a tunnel with a train racing toward us at the other end.

"Do you believe me?" Mia whispered, her breath warm against my neck. "Say you believe me."

I stroked her hair, feeling each silky strand between my fingers. "I believe you."

Chapter Thirty-Three

That night, I didn't sleep. The house was too quiet. That grotesque rock sat on the windowsill, ever present in my mind, slick with rust-dark blood among Mia's beautiful sea glass.

At 2:11 a.m., I went downstairs.

The floor was chilly beneath my feet. The refrigerator hummed steadily. I flipped the oven to 350 and pulled the mixing bowls from the cabinet, the ritual my hands knew when my brain went static.

Now, in the darkness of the middle of the night, I baked. Butter and eggs from the fridge. Boxes of double fudge brownie mix along with an extra bag of chocolate chips from the back of the pantry.

I set a mixing bowl on the counter and poured in the ingredients. While I worked, I made a mental list inside my head of the people who could have accessed our home in the last week.

Before the locks had been changed, Rowan had been here. And Chloe. Wednesday morning, with those roses. Chloe disappeared upstairs to use the bathroom. How long had she been up there? Three minutes? Five? Long enough.

Had I heard the floorboards squeak in Mia's bedroom? I couldn't remember.

And last night, Whitney and Peyton were standing in my living room while the police photographed the slashed painting. I'd been watching the officers, watching King. Had one of them slipped upstairs? Could I swear they hadn't?

If they'd used the spare key, which was the most likely scenario, it could have been Brooke or Alexis, or Zara and Chloe. Or any of the mothers, for that matter.

I thought of Zara with the scarlet spray paint can in her trash. My skin prickled. Had Camille's daughter done all of this? If she vandalized Leah's painting, it made the most sense that she also planted the bloody rock. Which made her the killer. Didn't it?

My phone sat face up on the counter. I wanted so badly to call Detective King to report the planted evidence, but I couldn't. I already knew how it would go and who would be blamed. I couldn't risk it.

I scraped the batter into a parchment-lined pan, smoothed it with the spatula, and scattered dark chocolate chips across the top so it would be rich and gooey.

As I slid the brownies into the oven, my phone buzzed on the counter. I grabbed it, desperate for something, anything. A text from Viv, or Rowan, maybe, even though it was the middle of the night. Anything solid to hold onto.

Instead, X notifications flooded the lock screen. Facebook. Instagram. Reddit. Dozens of them. I shouldn't have opened it. I knew better. But my thumb moved anyway.

The case was trending everywhere, and there were hundreds, thousands of comments:

These rich suburban moms always think their kids are special. Wake up—your daughter's a murderer.

She raised a killer. Lock them both up.

That lady needs to be investigated, too. Covering for her kid. Disgusting.

The mother knew. She had to know. It's always the mother's fault.

My chest tightened. My breath came fast and shallow. My

thumb hovered over the reply button. I could tell them Mia wasn't like that, that I wasn't like that. But who would believe me?

The comments kept multiplying, refreshing faster than I could read. I locked the screen, dropped the phone onto the counter like it had burned me. My vision blurred.

It's always the mother's fault.

Were they right?

I *had* pushed Mia toward those girls. I *had* wanted to belong so badly I'd ignored every warning sign. Now Leah was dead. And my daughter was in serious trouble.

I forced myself to focus. To think. To act. *Just breathe.*

The rock waited for me. That was what was important. That's what I had to focus on, not random strangers who'd already condemned Mia and me.

While the brownies baked, I collected a Zip-top freezer bag from the drawer along with paper towels and a pair of dishwashing gloves from a box under the sink, not perfect but better than using my bare hands.

I checked the doors one last time. Then I went upstairs to look in on my daughter. Apollo lay curled in a furry ball at the foot of her bed. He raised his head when I entered, then chuffed and settled back to sleep.

Mia had kicked the comforter downward, one leg out, the other tucked beneath a pillow. A strand of hair stuck to her mouth. The glow from her charger made a blue square on the wall. She clutched the stuffed sloth in both arms. She was fourteen and also four, soft and unguarded.

I fixed the blanket. She stirred and settled.

I stayed until my own breathing matched hers. My chest ached. This child came from me. She was my flesh, my beating heart. She was everything.

I watched her, my hand pressed against my chest, Marcus's ring warm beneath my fingers. He'd have known what to do. He'd have had answers. I let the ring drop back beneath my shirt. I had work to do.

Moving to the windowsill, I used the gloves to carefully lift the rock and place it within the freezer bag. I stepped back, careful where I set my feet. The windowsill was bare now except for the beach stones and sea glass. The gap where the rock had been like a missing tooth.

Back in the kitchen, I opened the cleaning cabinet, filled with bleach, vinegar, and old sponges crammed into a plastic caddy. I could hide the rock behind the tall bottle of ammonia or the roll of extra trash liners wedged at the very back.

A police search would find it within minutes.

I closed the cabinet. No, not here. Not anywhere they'd look.

When the timer dinged, I removed the brownies from the oven and set them to cool on the cooktop. The kitchen filled with their rich, decadent scent. It turned my stomach. I had no appetite, only a grim resolve.

I thought of the other mothers and how quickly they closed ranks to protect their daughters. How I'd judged them for it, felt superior in my pursuit of truth.

Now here I stood, evidence held in my hand.

The hypocrisy burned in my throat like acid.

I was becoming exactly what I condemned in the other mothers. The realization sat heavy in my chest. I hated it. Despised myself.

Did I have a choice?

I couldn't go to the police, not knowing someone was actively plotting against us. What did it matter if we had truth on our side if no one believed us?

I was Mia's mother. I would do this to protect my child.

I couldn't leave it here to be discovered. I couldn't destroy it, either. It might be the only thing that could prove someone else had harmed Leah. How could I ever face Vivienne and Daniel, or Mia, or myself, for that matter, if I did that?

I couldn't get rid of evidence. That's what criminals did. That's what monsters did.

My hands moved before I'd fully formed the plan. I pulled on my jean jacket, grabbed a flashlight and Apollo's leash. The dog came bounding down the stairs, his tail wagging hopefully.

"Come on, boy. We're going for a walk."

The chilly night air bit my face as we slipped out the back door. The neighborhood slept around us, houses dark and silent, as I locked the door and headed down Wyld Wood Lane toward Cliff Harbor Drive. The streetlamps cast their orange glow across empty sidewalks.

I'd walked these streets hundreds of times since we'd moved here, Apollo pulling me along on his explorations. I knew every path, every shortcut, every nook and cranny, including the massive oak at the edge of the community playground, the one with the hollow halfway up its trunk that I'd noticed days ago when Falcon had played fetch with Apollo.

The playground loomed ahead. The swings hung motionless in the still air. I clicked off my flashlight as we approached, letting my eyes adjust to the darkness. The oak stood at the far edge, its branches spread wide. The streetlamp glow was enough light to pick out the trunk, the hollow a darker shadow against the gnarled bark.

I reached into my jacket pocket, feeling the weight of the double-bagged rock. Even through the plastic, it seemed to pulse with accusation.

This was temporary. Just until I understood what it meant, what it proved. Just until I could be certain that turning it over wouldn't destroy Mia.

Leah deserved justice. I fully intended to get it for her.

The hollow gaped dark and deep, exactly as I remembered. I wedged the bag inside, pushing it back as far as my arm could reach, then covered the opening with a clump of dried leaves.

This wouldn't hold forever. The next storm might dislodge it. Some kid exploring might find it. But it bought me time. Time to think, to understand, to figure out who had really killed Leah Cho.

Apollo and I walked home through the sleeping streets. In the east, the sky became a pale smear as darker shapes began to separate into familiar objects: the trees, the blocky houses, the ghostly lake beyond.

The Everett house sat dark as I passed. The For Sale sign was gone. A white pickup truck sat in the driveway. Contractors, probably. Someone had finally bought it. A family starting fresh. Perhaps they'd never know what happened here, what drove the last family out in the middle of the night.

Blackthorn Shores was good at that, erasing the inconvenient, replanting over the rot.

I glanced at my phone. The memorial was scheduled for 5 p.m. tonight.

The memorial would draw them all into one place. I didn't have leverage yet, but I had the object they thought would bury us. And while the mothers had warned me to stay away from their daughters, at the service, they would be distracted.

That was my chance, possibly my best and only chance, to finally get answers.

I would look each girl in the eye and watch for the flinch, the tell.

Starting with Zara Hayward.

Chapter Thirty-Four

The Blackthorn Shores Clubhouse gleamed in the late afternoon sun. I paused at the entrance, gripping Mia's hand. I had already dropped off the brownies at the clubhouse kitchen earlier in the morning.

Now, my pulse quickened. Marcus's funeral flashed across my mind. The grief and heartbreak. The devastation.

I squeezed Mia's fingers. "You ready?"

She nodded, her jaw set, her father's stubbornness in her chin.

Inside the clubhouse, wildflowers erupted from every surface: wild pink roses bursting from vases, white trillium woven into wreaths, sprays of columbine, purple coneflower, and wild lupine scattered across white linen. Leah's favorites.

The moment we stepped inside, the conversation snagged. Heads tipped our way. The room shifted toward us like a tide, then pretended not to. I swallowed the urge to flee.

Beside me, Mia went rigid. I straightened my knee-length black dress, shifted my oversized purse on my shoulder, and lifted my chin. "We can do this. We're Kincaids."

We moved to the memorial table. Framed photos traced Leah's life. Stuffed animals formed a half-moon around notes and cards.

Nearby, Jerome Hayward stood with Daniel Cho. Their heads

were close, their voices low. Jerome's hand touched Daniel's shoulder briefly, then fell away. Daniel's face was slack with grief, his orthopedic surgeon's hands hanging useless at his sides.

They stood apart from the rest of the mourners, Jerome remaining at Daniel's side to offer support and comfort. They were good men. Marcus would have liked them.

Mia touched one of the photos. "None of these people cared about her. They couldn't be bothered when she was alive, but now they loved her?"

I squeezed her shoulder. "She was loved. You loved her."

Mia nodded like she didn't believe me.

"You remember the plan?" I'd recruited Mia to help me get Zara alone. In a few minutes, she would text Zara and ask her to meet in the clubhouse kitchen. I would be there instead.

Mia nodded. She stayed at the table, small and alone among flowers and apologies.

Over by the dessert spread, Chloe, Peyton, Alexis, and Zara clustered in a tight circle. With a start, I realized that Sunday was supposed to be the night of the Sadie Hawkins dance. Instead of glittering evening gowns, nervous excitement, and first dances with boys, these girls were mourning, dressed in black, their mascara smeared.

Or at least, they all did an excellent job of pretending. The heat of their gazes scorched my back as I crossed the room, searching the crowd for Vivienne.

A hand clamped my arm. It was Whitney. Her hair was shellacked into a French twist, her charcoal dress poured over her like paint, her diamond tennis bracelet glinting at her wrist.

Her fingers bit into my skin. "You have some nerve showing your face here. Digging through our trash. Accusing Brooke of abuse. Pointing the finger at Camille's daughter for the murder that your child committed. Who do you think you are?"

I yanked my arm free. "I could ask you the same. Why was Peyton's name all over Leah's diary? What did *your* daughter do?"

"Are you going to accuse all our children, one by one? Desperation doesn't suit you, Dahlia."

"Did Peyton bully Leah to death?"

Her eyes narrowed. "You should stop before it's too late."

I kept my spine straight. I couldn't let her see my anxiety, my dread, my rising terror. "Too late for what, Whitney? If Peyton is so innocent, why are you so worried?"

She didn't answer. Her gaze flicked over my shoulder. Peyton stood across the room, watching us.

Whitney's posture shifted as a couple waved at her. Her icy smile instantly warmed. Without a backward glance, she sauntered away to greet several of the swim team moms.

Near the memorial table, a high keening sound cut through the murmur of voices. Brooke's son Falcon stood rigid beside a flower arrangement, his hands clamped over his ears, rocking back and forth. The string quartet's violins faltered, hitting a discordant note.

Brooke materialized beside him, her smile fixed for the watching crowd, a wineglass in one hand. Her other hand gripped his shoulder. Her voice was harsh, clipped. "Falcon. Not here!"

He didn't stop rocking. His cries grew louder.

Before Brooke could tighten her grip, Alexis appeared. She crouched beside her brother, her movements careful and deliberate. She didn't touch him, just stayed close, her voice low and steady. "Hey, Falcon. It's too loud in here, isn't it? Let's go outside. You and me."

His rocking slowed. His hands stayed over his ears. His breathing evened slightly.

"Come on," Alexis said. "We'll get you somewhere quiet. Away from all this noise."

Falcon nodded, a small jerky movement. Alexis rose and held out her hand. He took it. She guided him toward the side door near the kitchen. Her touch was gentle, her pace unhurried.

Brooke stood frozen, wineglass suspended mid-air, that fixed smile still plastered across her face. The watching crowd turned away, satisfied that the disruption had been handled.

I thought of Mia at that age, how gently Marcus had guided her through meltdowns. Alexis had learned tenderness somewhere, perhaps despite her mother, not because of her.

The dichotomy between her tenderness toward Falcon and her cruelty toward Leah was striking. My heart went out to her, but she was still a suspect. I couldn't let anything cloud my judgment.

I spotted Vivienne near the center of the room, standing within a circle of people offering condolences. Her grief was a black void around her. Every few seconds, her gaze slipped to the photo pyramid, all those smiling reminders of everything she'd lost.

Our eyes met across the room. Hers held no forgiveness, only exhausted grief. I looked away first.

Next to Vivienne, Rowan extricated herself from a knot of housewives around the punch bowl. She paused, looking around as if searching for someone. Her gaze landed on her husband, Gregory, who moved among the clusters of mourners with practiced ease, his tall frame cutting a sharp silhouette in his black suit.

He shook hands, leaned in with warm murmurs of condolence, and clapped another man on the shoulder. He looked every bit the somber host. He never looked her way.

Rowan pressed her lips together and spun, heading in the opposite direction, toward the clubhouse kitchen. I followed, an excuse to escape the press of the crowd. Plus, I wanted to be in the kitchen anyway.

The steel counters gleamed under the cool fluorescent lights. The music and talk outside muffled to a hum. I braced my palms on the counter and drew a long breath.

"Dahlia!" Rowan said warmly. "I'm glad you came. Thanks for the delicious brownies."

I didn't have it in me to pretend. "I'm surprised you're even speaking to me."

She smoothed her floor-length black dress, the warmth never

leaving her expression. Her hair was pulled back in a glossy chignon. She looked stunning as usual. "Now isn't the time or place to air grievances. Let's keep it together for Vivienne and Daniel's sake, shall we?" Rowan said, her voice soft, but there was iron underneath. "You seem unsettled. Take a few moments to gather yourself before you head back out there."

I nodded numbly. My grief wasn't only for Leah. I hated that I still wanted her approval while simultaneously questioning whether she'd framed my child. I hated that I could no longer trust my closest friends. Would I ever regain those friendships, or were they gone forever?

"Yeah," I managed. "Good idea."

"Rowan! Oh, there you are." Brooke appeared, cheeks flushed, eyes too bright. Her wineglass was empty. Her expression darkened when she spotted me. "They're ready for speeches. They want you to start." Her eyes narrowed. "Everything good in here, Rowan?"

"Thank you for your concern, Brooke." Rowan gave me a sympathetic smile. "We'll talk later."

Rowan floated out of the kitchen. Brooke scowled at me before flouncing after her.

My phone buzzed. I tugged it from my purse. A message from Mia: *Z coming to u.*

A moment later, the kitchen door opened. Zara slipped in. She spotted me and froze.

"I need to talk to you," I said. "About Leah."

From the main room, Rowan's voice rose and fell, poised and perfect, shaping a story about a girl her daughter's friends had mocked and bullied.

Zara glanced nervously over her shoulder like a rabbit prepared to flee. "I'm not supposed to talk to you."

I gestured toward the adjacent bathroom that connected the kitchen to the pool area. "Please. Just a minute."

Zara hesitated, then sighed. She followed me into the bathroom, and I shut the door behind us.

The pool house bathroom glittered with excess, with marble

floors so polished they mirrored us in dark glass, black-and-white tile laid like a chessboard, and gold fixtures that threw fractured rainbows across the walls.

I got right to it. "I know about the spray paint."

Zara pressed her back to the quartzite counter. She looked at me blankly.

"I found it in your trash yesterday morning."

She gaped at me. "Uh, I literally don't know what you're talking about, Ms. Kincaid."

If I hadn't known better, I'd have said she was genuinely baffled. "I know it was you who broke into my home. You took Leah's painting from Mia's room, slashed it, and painted GUILTY over it."

She shook her head, hard. Her braids swished around her narrow shoulders. "No! That wasn't me. I'd never do that to you or Mia. I was on Leah's side!"

"It was in your trash bin. The same color was used on the slashed painting. You want to tell me that's a coincidence?"

"Someone must have put it there. I didn't use spray paint. It wasn't me. I wouldn't—" Her face cleared, as if something had clicked in her mind. "Wait. What the actual—"

I leaned forward. "What?"

Her hands clenched into fists. She looked like she wanted to punch someone. "Are you kidding me? She dumped it in my trash to cover herself. So nothing would trace back to her. That backstabbing—"

"Who, Zara?"

Zara met my gaze. "Thursday before swim practice, I saw red stuff under Peyton's nails. I teased her about it. She told me to mind my own business. Then she left practice early. She didn't say why."

I sucked in a breath. "Peyton."

"Yeah, that witch just framed me."

"I believe you." I did. I believed every word. Zara was clearly upset.

"I can't believe she'd do that to me." Her eyes narrowed. She chewed on her bottom lip, like she was considering something.

"What is it?"

"I, uh, left some stuff out before."

"Tell me."

"I'm sorry, I should've said something earlier. I don't even know why I was protecting her. Peyton sure doesn't deserve it."

I slid my purse off my shoulder and set it on the counter. The mirrors multiplied us, two figures caught in a glittering box.

"You told me before that you heard sounds at 3:30 a.m." I didn't mention that the noises Zara heard was from Leah, still alive, struggling to climb the bluff. She would find out soon enough when the information was released to the media.

"I lied about not seeing who it was. I was too scared to say anything before. I thought if I just said I heard someone, that would be enough. But it's not. Mia could literally get arrested. I... I can't just stand by and do nothing. Not again."

I went very still. My mind spun. Someone else had actually been on the bluff?

Zara's shoulders tensed. She grasped the edge of the counter to steady herself. "If they find out I told you... you know what they do. LakeshoreTea. The girl last year, the one who got brain damage. I can't end up like her. I can't live like that, with a target on my back. What Leah went through? I can't do that."

"You're doing the right thing. I promise, you are. We'll figure out how to handle it."

She nodded. Her breath hitched. "I didn't go back up to Chloe's house. I just stayed on the beach. I was freaking out about why Leah missed our meeting. Like, imagining all kinds of terrible things. I kept thinking Peyton found out, or Alexis, and what they'd do to me. So, I decided to just stay and watch the sunrise. There's that big piece of driftwood by the seawall to sit on."

"What time was this?"

"Just before dawn. So, like, 5:15 a.m.?"

"Okay. What happened?"

"I heard this scratching sound. I got scared and hid behind that big oak at the base of the bluff. Someone came down the stairs holding a plastic bag with something in it. She buried it just past the seawall, covered it with leaves and twigs, then went back up."

The taste of adrenaline went metallic on my tongue. "What was in the bag?"

"It was small. Dark. Weirdly shaped. It had this brightly colored strap. Hard to see from where I was hiding, but I'm pretty sure it was a camera."

My breath stilled in my chest. The mirrors caught us from every angle—her eyes huge and hollow, my posture angled toward her, breathless with hope. "Mia's camera."

She nodded. "I waited until I couldn't hear her footsteps anymore. I should've dug the camera up, I know that now, but I didn't. I went back up. Then I saw something shiny in the grass where we took pictures the night before, so I walked over. It was getting lighter out. It was Leah's phone. I looked down and..." Her face crumpled. "That's when I saw her. Leah, lying there."

I handed her a paper towel. Our fingers brushed. Hers were ice cold. She wiped at her eyes, then tore the towel into neat strips.

"Zara," I said. "Who was on the beach?"

"I didn't know at first. When she came up the stairs, she passed right by me. I couldn't see her face, but..."

I could barely breathe. "Who?"

Zara's eyes shone with tears under the lights. The moment stretched, taut as a wire, our reflections echoing on all sides.

"I recognized the purple Stanley."

The air left my lungs.

"Peyton," she said. "It was Peyton."

Chapter Thirty-Five

The distant murmur of eulogy speeches filtered through the bathroom door. I stared at Zara's reflections in the sparkling mirrors, searching carefully for any sign of deception. I saw none. "Are you certain it was Peyton?"

Her eyes met mine in the mirror. "It was definitely her. The purple Stanley with all the stickers from her swim meets. She literally never goes anywhere without that thing. It was definitely her."

My vision tunneled. Peyton. Whitney's perfect, polished daughter, the one who stood in my living room with that spare key, who watched the police photograph Leah's painting on Thursday night. The same painting she'd slashed and defaced. Who probably planted the bloody rock in Mia's room, too.

And she'd buried the camera. The one piece of evidence that might save Mia.

There could be time-stamped photos that might show exactly what happened on that bluff. And Peyton had taken it, hidden it, let Mia take the blame while it lay buried a hundred feet from where Leah died.

Adrenaline surged through my veins. My tongue felt thick and alien in my mouth. I could barely form proper sentences. "When you came up the stairs, did you see Peyton anywhere?"

"When I screamed. They all came running out of the patio doors. Peyton, too, with that Stanley in her hand."

My pulse roared in my ears. I had to get to that beach. Now. Before Whitney figured out what Zara had told me. Before Peyton dug it back up.

"This is huge, Zara. This could help clear Mia's name."

"I can't tell the police," she said, distraught. "If the other girls find out I snitched..." She shook her head violently. "They'd, like, destroy me. You don't understand what they're like."

Part of me wanted to shake her. A girl had died, and her fear of social rejection shouldn't matter more than justice. But I recalled being fourteen, how the world narrowed to the opinions of peers, how exclusion felt like death.

Hell, sometimes it felt that way now.

"What if I tell the police without involving you?"

Hope flickered across her ashen face. "How?"

"I'll dig up the camera myself." I touched her arm. "Thank you for telling me. That took courage."

She gave a bitter laugh. "No, it didn't. Courage would've been standing up for Leah when she was alive. Courage would be going to the police myself."

"You're being brave now. That's what matters."

Zara tore more small shreds of paper towel. The pieces floated to the floor like confetti. "Do you think Peyton... do you think she actually did this? That she pushed Leah?"

I thought of Mia, alone and afraid, blamed for something she didn't do. My fear hardened into resolve. "I have to find the truth, no matter who it hurts."

Zara nodded numbly.

The bathroom door suddenly rattled. The handle turned.

My pulse jumped. Instinctively, I moved to shield Zara from the door. Luckily, I had locked it.

"Zara? Are you in there?" Camille's voice filtered through the door, sharp with impatience. "Your father noticed you were missing. He's been looking for you."

Zara's eyes widened in panic. "One sec, Mom!"

"Hurry up. The other girls are speaking. It's almost your turn."

She quickly wiped her face, trying to erase the evidence of tears smudging her eyeliner.

"Zara, what are you doing? Is someone in there with you? I thought I heard voices."

Zara's eyes met mine, panicked. "No one, Mom. I swear, it's just me."

"Go," I mouthed.

Zara unlocked the door, opened it just enough to slip through, and slid out to join her mother. The door closed behind her.

I exhaled and wiped my damp palms on my dress. That had been close, too close. I remained in the bathroom for a moment, collecting myself, steadying my nerves.

I stared at my reflection in the gilt-framed mirror. The woman looking back at me had eyes I didn't recognize. Flat, calculating. Hard.

The memorial speeches continued outside. Brooke was speaking now, dramatically, through copious tears.

I had to find that buried bag before someone else did. But I had to be careful. Peyton had hidden it for a reason. Did Whitney know about it? Did she know what her daughter was capable of?

I picked up my purse and slid it over my shoulder. I stepped out of the bathroom, made my way through the immaculate industrial kitchen, and back to the memorial service.

Near the hallway, Graham Alistair leaned against the wall, head down, phone glowing in his hands. His thumb scrolled mechanically. Whitney's handsome husband was present but also absent.

I moved past him and scanned the room for Mia. It was time to go. Now.

Chloe stood at the microphone, giving a teary, heartfelt eulogy. Her voice quavered with emotion that seemed genuine. She dabbed at her eyes with a damp tissue.

"Leah was one of my closest friends," Chloe said. "I remember this one afternoon last fall, we were supposed to study for a big science test, but instead we ended up at the beach for hours, just talking. She told me about her dream of becoming an art teacher someday."

A murmur of sympathy rippled through the crowd. Heads nodded. A few people wiped at their eyes.

"She had this incredible way of seeing beauty in everything. Even on her hardest days, she'd find something to draw, something to paint, like her sunsets and flowers. She made the world brighter just by noticing it."

Chloe's gaze swept across the crowd, pausing on faces here and there as she spoke. I found myself nodding along, caught in the current of Chloe's words. They felt true. They sounded like Leah.

Across the room, Mia stood transfixed. Her face had gone pale, her hands limp at her sides. But it was her posture that sent alarm skittering down my spine. Her shoulders drawn up, rigid, like she was bracing for impact.

"I wish I could've helped her," Chloe said, her voice breaking. "I keep having these terrible nightmares about that night. Night terrors, really. I wake up screaming, and my mom has to calm me down. But then my therapist helped me understand—they aren't nightmares at all."

The room went dead silent. Even the waitstaff froze mid-step. Someone's fork clattered against a plate, the sound obscenely loud.

Mia's throat worked. Her fingers twitched at her sides.

Chloe's gaze landed on Mia. Her pale blue eyes gleamed with something that didn't fit the tears on her cheeks, the tremble in her voice. "They're memories. And they're real. My mind had blocked them out because of the trauma. But they're coming back. In pieces at first, but now—"

We needed to leave.

We needed to leave right now.

I moved through the crowd toward Mia, weaving between bodies, trying not to draw attention. The plush carpet muffled my footsteps. It felt like wading through water, every step too slow, the distance between us stretching impossibly.

Mia's eyes found mine across the room, wide and terrified. Her mouth formed a single word: *No.*

I couldn't reach her in time.

"I remember," Chloe said. "I remember everything."

Whitney's hand flew to her mouth. Rowan stood frozen, her face carefully blank. Brooke gripped her champagne flute, and Camille pulled Zara closer, her arm a protective bar across her daughter's chest. Peyton shifted beside Alexis, her jaw tight.

Vivienne stood at the front, her spine rigid, her hands folded in front of her stomach. As Chloe spoke, Vivienne's head tilted as if straining to catch every syllable. Daniel leaned toward her, his hand finding hers.

All eyes were on Chloe.

It was like watching a slow-motion car crash. I knew what was coming, knew it in the sick churn of my stomach, the cold prickle across my skin. I could only watch, utterly helpless.

Chloe's voice rang out, clear and damning: "I saw Mia push Leah."

Chapter Thirty-Six

The community clubhouse erupted into chaos. Whispers slithered through the crowd like smoke. I lunged through the sea of bodies, my pulse thundering in my ears, and grabbed Mia's wrist.

People stepped back as we passed, brows raised, mouths open in shock. Their eyes narrowed with an unspoken accusation that burned like acid against my skin.

I wanted to turn and scream at them all, to defend my daughter, but urgency propelled me onward.

"Mom." Mia's fingers dug into my forearm. "Everyone's staring."

"Just keep walking," I said under my breath. "Head up. Don't run."

Mia's face had gone chalk-white, her gaze unfocused. "Mom!"

I pulled her closer. "Not here."

Across the room, I caught a glimpse of Whitney and Peyton locked in an apparent argument. Whitney's hand on Peyton's upper arm, Peyton shaking her head.

Next to them, Vivienne and Daniel slipped out a side door. Daniel's hand on her back, guiding her away from the chaos.

Only minutes remained before Whitney, Brooke, or Rowan called the police and offered my daughter up on a silver platter.

We reached the heavy oak doors. I shoved them open.

Mia stumbled, blinking against the sudden brightness. Her breath came in shallow bursts. "Are they gonna arrest me? Am I going to prison forever?"

The answer clogged in my throat. I wanted to reassure her, to promise everything would be fine. I couldn't. "They have an eyewitness now. They might arrest you." I squeezed her hand. "I'll get another lawyer. I'll do whatever it takes."

We hurried past pristine lawns and perfectly trimmed hedges. The neighborhood felt hostile and alien.

Mia's phone buzzed in the pocket of her dress. She tugged it out as I half-dragged her along the sidewalk, her face illuminated by the screen's glow.

"Mom." She turned the phone toward me. "It's from Zara."

I read quickly: *W and P being weird. Heard them mention beach. W just left in a hurry.*

My pulse hammered. The beach. The camera.

If Whitney was headed there, she'd retrieve whatever Peyton had buried. The evidence that might potentially save Mia would disappear forever.

My mind raced through impossible calculations: I couldn't take Mia to the beach. I didn't want her present if Whitney appeared and things turned confrontational. I couldn't leave her at home alone. Not after Chloe's public accusation. Not with the police likely minutes away. They might arrest her while I was gone.

I couldn't trust any of the other mothers.

Except Vivienne.

Viv wasn't involved. Out of everyone, she alone wasn't part of any cover-up, I knew that much. Whatever else had broken between us, she wanted the truth about what happened to her daughter as much as I did, if not more.

I paused on the sidewalk and gripped Mia's shoulders. "Go to Vivienne's house. Right now."

Mia's eyes widened. "Mom, she won't let me in, not after what the detective said about my DNA—"

"She'll let you in." I had to believe that. Vivienne had loved Mia once. She'd been the closest thing to a second mother Mia had known. "If she's not there yet, use the spare key under the planter. You know where it is. Wait inside for Viv. Lock the door behind you. Tell her I'm getting evidence that can prove what really happened to Leah."

"What if she kicks me out?"

"She won't." She had to accept Mia. Because every other door in Blackthorn Shores had slammed shut on us. Vivienne was a mother who'd lost her child. If there was a chance the truth was something other than what she'd been told, she would open that door.

I was already turning back toward the street.

"Don't leave me!" Mia grabbed my sleeve, frantic. "Mom, please. About that night—"

"Ten minutes! I promise." I untangled myself from her grasp. Guilt scorched through me, hot and acidic, for leaving her. I hated myself even as I moved.

If evidence on that beach could save Mia, I had no choice.

I left Mia standing on the sidewalk and sprinted toward the community beach access stairs. Every maternal instinct screamed at me to go back, to hold her, to listen. I ignored it.

The late afternoon sun hung low, a heavy bank of clouds approaching over the horizon. The wind had picked up. The waves roared in the distance.

My dress flapped around my knees as I ran. I reached the wooden stairs and kicked off my heels, leaving them at the top. They'd only slow me down.

The rough wood bit into my bare feet as I descended all 179 stairs, each step jarring my knees, my ankles, my spine. Splinters embedded themselves in my soles. I didn't stop. My purse slapped against my side. The roar of the waves swelled louder.

At the bottom, I paused, chest heaving as my gaze swept the

shoreline. The beach stretched empty save for a few seagulls skittering across the wet sand. No sign of Whitney or Peyton. Had I beaten them here? Or missed them altogether?

Zara had said she'd hidden behind an oak at the base of the bluff and watched Peyton dig near the seawall. I cut toward the trees, pressed my back to the largest oak, and peered out. From here, the seawall jutted right, a scar of concrete below Rowan's house perched far above.

I moved fast along the waterline, the sand cold and damp beneath my bare feet. Wind whipped my hair across my mouth. Grit salted my tongue. Then I saw it. Three driftwood sticks formed a rough triangle, too deliberate to be chance. The sand inside lay smooth, tamped down.

I dropped to my knees. Sand caked my dress. The fabric clung to my thighs.

My fingers plunged into the sand. Grains rasped my skin, jammed beneath my nails. I dug deeper, faster, wrist-deep, then to my forearms. My knuckles scraped something slick.

I clawed the edges free and dragged up a torn Meijer's bag, heavy and wet. Sand poured from its seams. Through the rip in the plastic, I felt the hard rectangle of a camera body.

I yanked it out of the plastic bag.

A Nikon SLR, the casing scratched and sand-crusted, the display fogged with condensation. The canary-yellow strap was still attached, dotted with souvenir buttons from our family road trips. Yellowstone. Yosemite. Arches. Isle Royale.

Mia's camera.

For a moment, I couldn't breathe. I clutched it to my chest with both hands. Tears blurred my vision. This was the most precious gift Marcus ever gave her, the last piece of him she'd carried everywhere, tucked against her ribs like a talisman. I'd thought it was gone forever. Destroyed, thrown in the lake, evidence buried.

But here it was, solid and real in my trembling hands.

The camera that might save my daughter. That might prove the truth.

I held it for one more heartbeat, feeling the weight of everything it represented to Mia, to me. Then I shoved it into my oversized purse, stood, and brushed over the disturbed patch of sand with my foot, erasing the hole.

A muffled sound came from behind me—footsteps, sand shifting. My pulse jolted. I whirled around.

A figure stood several yards away. In the slanting light, shadows stretched long across the sand. "What the hell do you think you're doing?"

Chapter Thirty-Seven

Whitney Alistair's blonde hair had torn free of her French twist. She held her heels in one hand, the diamond bracelet flashing on her wrist as she glared at me. "I said, what do you think you're doing?"

"Walking," I said. "Clearing my head."

"On the beach? In this weather?" Her gaze swept over me, lingering on the purse tucked under my arm. "A bit chilly for you, isn't it?"

The wind knifed through my dress. The waves churned against the sand, slate water punched white with foam. "I could ask the same of you."

"You're on Rowan's private beach. Where you're clearly not welcome."

I gestured at the waves shredding the shore. "The high-water mark is public access. Basic riparian law."

"You're well past the high-water mark, and you know it. You're trespassing."

The camera pressed like a hot coal against my hip. "Fine. I'll leave."

Whitney stood between me and the stairs. I took a step toward her. She blocked my way.

"They're going to arrest Mia," Whitney said with that icy smile on her face, gloating.

"My daughter didn't do anything. And we both know it."

"Chloe saw what happened."

"Chloe is lying." I stepped into her space. The sand shifted beneath my feet. "Just like she lied about being Leah's best friend. She's covering for someone."

Whitney sneered. "Your daughter is the liar."

"Peyton broke into my house," I said. "She took Leah's painting from Mia's room, slashed it, and spray-painted GUILTY across it." I watched her face. "Peyton's the one who's guilty."

Her tan went ashy under the perfect makeup. "That's ridiculous."

"Is it? Because I know your daughter buried something here the morning Leah died. Right here."

Her gaze cut past me to the disturbed circle of sand. Whitney's hand went to her throat. The diamond-encrusted bracelet trembled against her skin.

The sky pressed low and heavy. The air tasted metallic. A storm was coming.

"Or did you already know that?" I asked.

She smiled, small and mean. "Wake up, Dahlia. Your daughter is a killer. Leah was leaving Mia behind. Jealousy is the oldest motive in the book."

My mouth went dry. I couldn't show her any weakness. I raised my chin. "Mia is innocent. And I'll prove it."

Something calculating and dangerous flashed in her eyes. Her shoulders squared, her mouth twisting. "None of us ever liked you. We only pretended for Rowan's sake. You're a project to her, a distraction so she doesn't have to think about her miserable marriage. She keeps you around so she can feel superior."

Even now, the spiteful words burrowed under my skin. They hurt, in every raw and bruised place. I let the feeling burn through and out. "Oh, go to hell, Whitney."

"You don't belong here. You never did."

I took another step toward her. Five feet apart now. "Get out of my way."

Her gaze hooked on my purse. For one heartbeat, she hesitated. The country-club smile vanished, something feral in its place. She let her heels drop to the sand.

Whitney lunged at me.

It was quick, the strike of a cobra. Her fingers grasped my purse strap and yanked. The leather bit into my shoulder. We grappled. My heart slammed into my throat.

Sand slid under my feet, and my knee went sideways. She was stronger than she looked, all lean tennis muscle and adrenaline. The bag thudded between us.

"Let go!" she demanded through gritted teeth.

I staggered back, wrenching my purse from her grasp. We lurched to the edge of the wet sand. Waves crashed over my feet and ankles. She went for the purse again with one hand. With the other, she swiped at my face with her nails.

I dodged. One nail scraped my cheek. I brought my elbow up, a sharp ugly jab into her stomach. With a grunt of pain, she stumbled. Her bracelet snagged the clasp of the purse. I wrenched hard, then shoved her.

Whitney went backward, skidding. Her feet lost purchase. She went down hard on her butt. Her dress slid up her thighs, her Louboutin heels scattered beside her. Her diamond bracelet had fallen off; it glinted in the sand. She sat there, looking stunned, more from the insult of falling than the impact.

From somewhere up on the bluff, a siren threaded into the wind, distant but unmistakable.

My blood turned to ice water. Before I could react, my phone vibrated in my purse. Keeping one eye on Whitney, I slid the phone free. The screen glowed pale in the gloom. It was Camille: *Just FYI. Police at your house with search warrant. Do with that what you will.*

Gratitude flooded through every cell in my body. Camille hadn't completely cut me off. She'd chosen to warn me.

My only thought was for Mia. I had to get to Mia.

Whitney scrambled awkwardly to her feet, plucking her bracelet from the sand even as she reached for me, for the camera. I cut past her, felt the brush of her fingers on my arm, then nothing. I ran. The stairs reared up ahead, a ribbed gray spine up the bluff.

"You bitch!" she shouted after me.

I sprinted up the stairs. The camera banged against my hip with each stride. I hit the first flight two at a time, legs pumping. The wind tried to push me backward. I leaned into it, thigh muscles shaking, heart like a fist in my mouth.

Halfway up, my foot skidded. I caught myself with a jolt that rattled my teeth. Another splinter drove into the sole of my left foot. I barely felt it.

My daughter needed me.

I ran faster.

Chapter Thirty-Eight

Police lights slashed through the darkness, bathing the street in pulses of crimson and cobalt. I sprinted through backyards along the bluff, staying low behind the trees, praying no motion lights would catch me, then headed east parallel to Driftwood Terrace.

I stood at Vivienne's door, chest heaving, my dress smudged with sand and dirt.

Vivienne opened the door and ushered me inside. Her home beckoned me in with its warm cream walls, fluffy throw rugs, and rustic wood beams overhead.

Leah's artwork covered every surface, her watercolors tacked to the fridge, charcoal sketches pinned above the overflowing bookshelves, a half-finished canvas of a field of daffodils propped against the stone fireplace.

"Mom!" Mia was up and in my arms before the door latched shut. I held her tight. Vivienne shuffled past me and sat at the dining room table. Mia and I followed hesitantly.

Daniel hovered near Viv, as if he wanted to protect her from something, maybe from Mia, maybe from me. Concern lined his face. His suit from the memorial was rumpled.

"Are you sure you're okay with this?" he murmured.

She gave a tremulous nod.

"Thank you," I said to Vivienne. The words caught in my throat. "For letting her in. For..." I couldn't finish. For not turning her away, for showing grace I didn't deserve.

Vivienne didn't answer. Her phone rang. She stared at it sitting on the table by her elbow like it was something foreign she'd never seen before. Daniel cleared his throat. "It's your mother, Viv. I'll give her an update, don't worry."

He touched Vivienne's shoulder in support. She reached up and squeezed his hand. Then he took the phone and disappeared down the hallway, speaking quietly as his footsteps faded toward the back of the house.

They had always been warm and affectionate with each other. I was relieved that Viv still had Daniel to give her the support and comfort that I couldn't.

Viv broke the uncomfortable silence first, her voice flat. "Camille said they're going to arrest Mia."

I felt like I might faint. My arms tightened around my daughter.

At least, I'd had the foresight to move the bloodied rock. At least the police wouldn't find it in Mia's room tonight. There was that.

"Did you find something?" Mia whispered.

I reached into my purse, tugged out the Nikon D780, and set it on the table.

Mia stared at the yellow strap, the souvenir buttons. "My camera."

My gaze was on Viv, begging her to understand, to give us a chance. "Peyton buried it on the beach the morning Leah died."

"Mom, I don't think—"

"We're out of time, Mia." I looked at Vivienne. "Can we use your laptop?"

"Of course." Vivienne was already up and moving toward her office. A minute later, we huddled around the kitchen table as Vivienne connected the camera to her laptop via USB.

The screen came to life. I navigated to the folders for the night of the slumber party.

Sweet, smiling faces filled the screen. Girls with their long lean arms wrapped around each other, girls with dazzling white smiles and perfectly coiffed hair, girls in floaty, frilly dresses, so beautiful they made my chest ache. Chloe and Zara, Peyton, Alexis, Leah. A few of Mia, probably taken by Chloe or Leah.

"Talk me through these," I said.

Mia seemed to shrink into herself. "These are from the beginning of the night... here's everyone getting ready at Chloe's... these are from later, when we did the photoshoots in our dresses before dinner, then the midnight photoshoot..."

I scrolled forward. Chloe's blonde hair glistening in the moonlight, her dress a red smear. Leah balanced on the lip of the bluff with her face turned away, staring somberly out across the water. Beautiful, dark, shimmery photos.

I clicked the next image.

The screen flickered. The files were corrupted. They wouldn't load.

My stomach dropped. I tried another file. Same error. Another, and another.

"No." The word came out strangled. I shoved back from the table in frustration. "No, no, no!"

"The files are corrupted," Vivienne said. "Water and sand got in."

"Or someone tampered with them before Peyton buried it." My hands shook. I pressed them flat against the table. "Can they be recovered?"

Vivienne tapped a few keys on the laptop. After a moment, she shook her head. "This is beyond me. You'd need a forensic specialist. The police have—"

"NO!"

We both turned. Mia stood pressed against the counter, eyes wild.

"Why not?" I asked.

Mia's gaze dropped. She traced the counter edge with one finger and wouldn't meet my eyes.

"Mia." Vivienne's voice was gentle but firm. "If Peyton buried this camera, she was hiding something that incriminates *her*, not you. The police can—"

"They can't see it." Mia's voice cracked. "They can't."

Something cold slithered down my spine. The way she'd said it. Terrified. Guilty. "Why not, Mia?"

She wrapped her arms around herself, rocking slightly. "The pictures might show... they might..."

Vivienne stood and strode around the table, toward Mia. "Show what?"

Mia flinched away. "I can't. You'll hate me. Both of you will hate me."

"Mia..." I started.

"I did something." The words burst out of her like a wound opening. "That night. I did something, and if they see the pictures they'll know and—" Her breath hitched. Tears spilled down her cheeks. "I'm sorry."

Vivienne had gone very still, very pale. "What did you do?"

The question sat between us, sharp as glass.

I wanted to move, to go to my daughter, but my legs wouldn't work. My voice sounded far away. "What are you saying?"

Headlights swept the kitchen. A car door slammed. Close, right outside. The police lights bled through the slats of Vivienne's shutters, red-blue-red, steady as a heartbeat.

Every maternal instinct screamed at me to grab Mia and run. But there was nowhere left to go. I crossed to Mia in three strides. I gripped her shoulders. "Look at me."

She did. Tears streamed down her blotchy face, her eyes wild with anguish and fear. Mascara traced black rivulets down her cheeks. She looked haunted.

I kept my voice low, urgent. "I can't help you unless you tell me the truth. All of it. Right now."

"They'll arrest me."

"They're going to arrest you anyway. The only chance we have is the truth. Do you understand? The *truth*."

Someone knocked on the front door. Hard, authoritative. "Mr. and Mrs. Cho? This is the police. We need to speak with you."

Vivienne didn't move. Her gaze stayed locked on Mia. "What did you do to my daughter?"

Mia looked between us. Trapped. Terrified.

"Mom..." Her voice was so small. "Chloe wasn't completely lying."

The floor seemed to tilt beneath me. My brain refused to process her words. "What?"

The words tumbled out in a rush. "I was there. When it happened. When Leah fell. I was there."

Chapter Thirty-Nine

A cold draft moved over the back of my neck like a ghost. Outside, the knocking came again. Harder. The police at the door.

Vivienne blinked at Mia. "What are you saying?"

"She was saying mean things." She pressed the heel of her hands to her eyes like she could stop the memory from unwinding inside her brain. "It was an accident. I didn't mean it. Mom, I promise. I didn't. We argued. I got so mad. I—I pushed her."

I gaped at Mia. My daughter. Present when Leah fell. Every rationalization I'd built—the scratches from thorns, the DNA from the nosebleed—collapsed like a house of cards. I couldn't breathe.

Everything I'd fought for, every sleepless night investigating, every confrontation, had been built on a lie.

My daughter had pushed Leah Cho off a cliff. And I hadn't known.

My mouth tasted like copper. "You pushed Leah?"

Vivienne made a sound, a half-sob, half-growl of agony. Her hands came up to her mouth, then dropped. She stared at Mia as if seeing her for the first time, and something in her face broke. Not grief this time. Something harder. Colder. "You killed my Leah? You?"

Mia shook her head hard, strands of hair sticking to her mouth. She looked gaunt suddenly, hollowed out. Her eyes were feverish. "I didn't mean to—she grabbed me and I... she just fell."

Another knock at the front door. Harder, insistent. "Police! Open the door!"

"It was an accident!" Mia said. "I didn't want to hurt her! Please believe me!"

Vivienne moved woodenly toward the front door. She swung it open and stepped aside.

My gaze darted to the camera sitting on the kitchen table, evidence in plain sight. Without thinking, I grabbed the Nikon and shoved it into my purse.

Detective King stepped inside. His immense shadow filled the doorway. Two uniformed officers came in behind him, followed by Detective Callahan. Their attention zeroed in on Mia.

King said, "We have an eyewitness account from Chloe Westinghouse stating you pushed your friend Leah from the bluff. Mia Kincaid, you're under arrest for the murder of Leah Cho."

Instinctively, I stepped in front of my daughter, placing myself between her and the people who would take her from me.

Daniel strode down the hallway into the kitchen. His face was ashen. He took in the cuffs, the uniforms, Vivienne's shattered face. The muscles in his jaw jumped. He put his hand around his wife's arm as if to steady her or himself.

Vivienne made that raw, tortured sound again, higher this time. A wounded animal.

King strode into the kitchen. His sharp gaze never left my daughter's face. "Move aside, please, Ms. Kincaid."

Reluctantly, I did. It was the hardest thing I'd ever done.

"Mom!" Her frantic eyes were glued to mine. Huge and terrified and pleading.

But I couldn't help her. I couldn't save her. My daughter. My child. The girl who still slept with the stuffed sloth she'd had since she was four years old.

Detective Callahan went to Mia, handcuffs already in hand. The corner of her mouth twitched with satisfaction. Not quite a smile, but close. "You have the right to remain silent." She read Mia her rights. I barely heard the words over the frantic buzzing in my brain.

Mia blanched. "It wasn't like that. It's not what you think, I didn't mean it—"

"Don't," I said sharply. The word scraped my throat raw. "Do not say anything. Do you hear me? Not one word."

Detective Callahan held out the cuffs.

"Please don't do that," I begged. "You don't need to do that. She's a kid. She's not a threat."

Callahan did it anyway. "Hands."

Mia hesitated. Then she lifted her wrists. The metal cuffs clicked shut. They looked obscene on her slim wrists, too big, too heavy. Mia's shoulders curled inward as if she could make herself disappear.

Pure panic clawed at my insides. Instinctively, my hand found the ring at my throat. I clutched it so hard the chain dug into the back of my neck.

Marcus was gone. Now I was losing Mia, too.

King turned to me. His expression softened. The lines around his eyes deepened with genuine sympathy. "You can follow us to the station and have Mia's lawyer meet us there."

Mia no longer had a lawyer. What were we going to do?

As if reading my mind, King said, "We can assign a public lawyer for her."

A public lawyer. For my daughter. For murder.

"Let's go." King touched Mia's elbow. He was gentle, not rough, which made me hate him more. The uniformed officers flanked him as they passed me with Mia in tow, small and fragile and terrified. King steered Mia toward the foyer.

"Mom!" Mia twisted to find me. Her eyes were drowning. "Mommy, please! Don't let them take me away!"

The sound pierced me like a spear to the heart. My daughter calling for me to protect her when I stood powerless. My vision tunneled until all I could see was Mia's terrified face.

I took one step after her.

The nearest officer lifted a palm to stop me. "Ma'am," he warned.

I froze. My arms hung uselessly at my sides. Every cell in my body screamed to grab her, to run, to fight. But there was nothing I could do. Nothing.

"Let me tell her—" I didn't know what. That I was sorry? That I should have known? That I should have been a better mother, prevented all this somehow? I couldn't bear to lie to her with platitudes. We both knew nothing was okay. "I love you. Be strong. You are so strong. I love you so much."

Her hair fell into her face. "Please don't be mad."

Then they hustled her out the door.

Numbly, I followed into the hall, past Vivienne's framed family photos. Leah's fourth-grade picture smiled out at me with her porcupine bangs and gap-toothed grin.

I stood on the front porch and watched them take my daughter away. The lights flashed over the porch. The police cruiser pulled away from the curb. It rolled down the street, turned the corner, and was gone.

Daniel stood in the doorway behind me, his arm around his wife's shoulder, keeping her physically upright. The porch light carved shadows under Vivienne's eyes. Grief had hollowed her out. Her face was a stranger's.

"I didn't know." It sounded like pleading. Like defense. I hated how small it was. "Viv, I swear, I didn't know."

"You brought her into my house. You let her stand in my kitchen. You both lied to me." She was shaking. Her fingers clenched and unclenched at her sides. "My daughter is dead."

"I know." I could feel my heartbeat in my mouth. My pain was nothing compared to Vivienne's. Despite everything, my daughter was alive. Vivienne's was not. "Viv, please. I'm sorry, so incredibly sorry."

Daniel stiffened. His once kind face had gone cold and hard. "You need to leave." He didn't raise his voice. The quiet finality in his tone made it worse. "Now."

The grief staggered me. I could barely stand under the weight of it. Accident or not, my daughter did this. My daughter had killed someone. Ended the life of their child.

I reached out my hand. "Viv—"

"Go!" Daniel's voice boomed. He tightened his protective hold on his wife, holding her upright as she collapsed into him, disintegrating right in front of me. "You've done enough damage here."

They turned away. Daniel ushered his wife inside. The door closed in my face.

Vivienne was lost to me. Not just tonight. Forever.

I stood alone on the porch in the dark. The street was empty now, no police lights, no sirens, just the sound of the wind tearing through the trees, the distant roar of the waves, and my own ragged breathing.

I turned and stumbled from their home, down the porch steps, and into the night, expelled from the last place where anyone had offered shelter.

There was nowhere left to go.

Chapter Forty

The houses of Blackthorn Shores loomed around me like a silent tribunal, their windows dark and accusing.

Somewhere, a dog barked. A sprinkler switched on with a hiss. The mundane sounds of suburban life continued while I stood paralyzed with grief.

I pressed my fist against my mouth. The tears came, the frantic sobs.

I was shattering. Breaking down right there in the middle of the street for everyone to see. It was like falling from a great height. The blood rushed to my head, white spots danced in front of my eyes. My legs went weak. There was no longer solid ground beneath me.

My knees buckled. My body refused to hold me upright any longer as my knees hit the asphalt. Pain shot up my thighs. The rough surface scraped my palms, my kneecaps. My dress tore. My purse slipped to the pavement.

I didn't care about the pain. Nothing could compete with the hollow ache consuming my chest. Like someone had carved out my heart and left it beating raw and exposed on the ground beside me.

Around me, curtains swished. They watched from the safety

of their homes. As if anything they had or did could keep tragedy from finding them.

It couldn't. We were all exposed.

I knew that better than anyone.

The memories washed over me. The sharp sound of the gunshot. Marcus's stunned face. The way his hand reached out to me as he fell.

In an instant, he was gone, our lives shattered. And now Mia was gone, arrested for the murder of her best friend.

The asphalt bit deeper into my palms. My kneecaps throbbed. The night wind tangled my hair across my tear-streaked face.

The physical pain was almost a relief, something I could name, something with a sharp edge. Not like the formless terror of losing Mia. Not like the guilt of believing her innocent when she'd confessed with her own mouth.

Something niggled at the back of my mind, though. Something that still didn't make sense.

The bloody rock planted in Mia's room. The slashed painting. The notebook stolen from my desk. The buried camera.

If Mia was already guilty, if the DNA and scratches and witness testimony proved it, then why frame her? Why go to such elaborate lengths to terrorize us, to manufacture additional evidence?

Unless someone needed to ensure Mia took the fall.

My ragged gasps slowed, steadied. I wiped my face with the back of my hand. I sank back on my heels and forced myself to breathe.

The wind coming off the lake carried the smell of rain. The waves crashed loud and angry against the shoreline. The comforting rhythm had soothed me to sleep on my first nights here. Now they sounded like a monster at the gates, thrashing to get inside.

So many things didn't make sense about that night.

Mia's confession rang in my ears. She was guilty of something.

But deliberate murder? I couldn't believe that. I didn't. I knew my daughter.

For "accident" and "murder" were separated by a chasm of intent. Manslaughter versus premeditated murder. Juvenile detention versus first-degree murder as an adult—the two were worlds apart.

This wasn't over.

I couldn't stand by and do nothing. I had to be strong. I couldn't let her go down for murder, not even manslaughter. Not until things made sense. Until all the puzzle pieces fit into place.

I would stand by her side, every step of the way.

I rose to my feet, using a parked Lexus bumper to steady myself. My legs shook. I pulled my snarled hair into a messy bun, smoothed the torn fabric of my dress, and straightened my shoulders.

I picked up my purse, the camera still tucked inside, and slid it over my shoulder. If the detectives had searched me at Vivienne's, I'd probably be in handcuffs. But they'd had no probable cause, so they hadn't.

The camera's weight pressed against my hip. Solid, incriminating, the only piece of evidence I had left. I needed to find a way to use it.

And I needed to get Mia the best defense attorney in town. Someone who understood how these families operated, who knew their secrets, who could navigate their power structures.

I had to convince Camille to take the case back. Even if it meant confessing everything I'd hidden, every rule I'd broken, every line I'd crossed. No matter what it cost me.

Chapter Forty-One

I stood beneath the porch light in bare feet smeared with grass and dirt, facing the imposing double doors of Camille Hayward's home. The square panes reflected my drawn face, muddy dress, wind-tangled hair, and the purse digging into my shoulder.

I knocked. The door opened a crack. Camille's face hardened when she saw me. Her voice came out flat and cold. "What are you doing here, Dahlia?"

She had changed out of her dress from the memorial and wore gray pressed slacks paired with an emerald cashmere sweater, no jewelry. Even at this hour, she looked composed.

I, on the other hand, looked like I'd crawled through a war zone. "They just arrested Mia. I need you to represent her at the precinct tonight."

She opened the door wider. "I told you I can't help you."

"This isn't about me. Please, Camille. She's fourteen."

"Call the public defender. That's what they're for."

I kept my voice steady. "She deserves more than just a warm body going through the motions. She needs the best. Please. She needs you."

Her gaze flicked to my purse, where the corner of the camera peeked out. Her mouth tightened. "I'm not interested."

"Mia confessed to pushing Leah."

Camille didn't move. Behind me, the wind whipped through the trees. "She confessed?"

"She said it was an accident. She says she didn't mean..." My voice cracked. I forced the rest out. "She didn't mean for Leah to fall."

"Did she say why?"

"There wasn't time. The police showed up and arrested her."

Something in her expression shifted. A flash of controlled anger. "Your daughter admits she pushed her best friend off the bluff, and now you show up on my doorstep after interrogating my daughter and implying all kinds of sordid things about my family?" Her tone sharpened. "You made this worse, and you know it."

I flushed hot with shame. My pulse fluttered in my throat. "I never meant to implicate Zara. I was trying to track what really happened that night. I got it wrong. I'm sorry."

She let out a harsh laugh. "You're sorry."

"You're the only thing between Mia and a first-degree murder charge."

She leaned against the doorjamb and looked past me into the dark, contemplating whether to shut the door and let me drown on the porch. "You're asking for too much."

"I'm asking you to do what you've always done. Fight for the right thing."

She stared at me for a long moment, her intent gaze searching my face, her mouth pursed. Finally, she stepped back and opened the door wide. "Come inside."

I followed her inside before she could change her mind. The foyer opened into a great room with soaring ceilings framed with walls of glass. Above the fireplace, a large abstract canvas painted in cobalt-blue and burnt-orange commanded the space. Just like Camille: bold and fearless.

She led me toward the kitchen, a sleek open-concept design with mid-century lines, smooth wood cabinets without hardware, and a white quartz island with a waterfall edge.

The TV was on in the living room, tuned to ESPN. Zion and Jerome sat on the plush sofa, watching a baseball game together.

On the breakfast nook table, a slim laptop glowed blue. Zara sat in one of the linen chairs, knees drawn up under her familiar fluorescent yellow hoodie, her braids tucked over one shoulder. Earbuds dangled around her neck.

She looked up in surprise. "Hey."

"Go to bed, Zara," Camille said.

Zara didn't move. "What's going on?"

"Nothing you need to worry about."

"The police arrested Mia," I said. "She's at the precinct."

Zara's face tightened. She looked at me, then at her mother. "We literally have to do something."

Camille shot me a warning glance, then faced her daughter. She put her hands on her hips. "This is not your concern."

"It's totally my concern," Zara said. "Leah loved Mia, you know she did. She'd hate all of this. There's no way Mia would've intentionally killed her. That's insane. If there's something we can do to prove it was an accident, we should help."

"You don't decide my cases," Camille cut in, her tone clipped. "It's late. Go to your room."

Jerome wandered in from the hallway. He'd changed out of his suit and wore faded Snoopy pajama pants with a white T-Shirt. "Hey, who's hungry? And why does this house always smell like somebody's cooking even when nobody's cooking?"

He stopped when he saw us sitting at the island. The tension in our bodies, our faces. "What's all this about?"

Camille crossed to him. She put her hands on his forearms, leaned in, and kissed him firmly on the mouth. She pulled back. "I'm sorry, honey, but this is a privileged conversation."

Jerome met my gaze across the table. It was steady, intensely curious, but without judgment or reproach. That was something.

"Well, Zion and I will enjoy our Tigers game in the den with some popcorn and pizza, then. Don't be jealous." Jerome ruffled Zara's braids.

Zara ducked her head. "Dad!"

"Jerome," Camille said.

He winked at me. "I can see when I'm not wanted."

As soon as he was gone, Zara gave me an imploring look. "Is there anything? Any proof that might help Mia?"

I pulled the Nikon D780 from my purse by the yellow strap and set it on the table like an offering. "Mia's camera."

Zara let out a gasp. "Wait, you actually found it!"

A spark of interest lit in Camille's gaze. She moved closer to the table, as if drawn to the camera against her will.

"Peyton buried it at the base of the bluff. Some files are corrupted from water damage, I think. But there may be something on here. If we can pull even a frame with a time stamp, audio, anything, it could help. Peyton stole it for a reason."

Zara reached for the camera. "Can I see it?"

"Of course. Mia says you're the tech genius. Can you recover the damaged files?"

She hesitated, glancing at her mother for permission, and when Camille didn't stop her, she plugged a cable into the port with quick, sure movements. "Let me try."

"Zara," Camille warned, but she didn't make a move to thwart her daughter.

Zara rolled her eyes. "I know what I'm doing, Mom."

"That's not what I'm concerned about."

"You taught me to do what's right, not what's easy."

"Don't lecture me." Camille closed her eyes and pinched the bridge of her nose. She sighed heavily. "You're impossible."

"Thanks." Zara grinned, revealing dimples I hadn't noticed before. She bent her head, focused on the computer screen. "Okay, so the SD card's water-damaged, but the file allocation table's still intact, which means I can try to recover what's salvageable. Metadata survived on some of these. Timestamps, GPS coordinates. These are all from 12:17 a.m. to 12:39 a.m."

Camille stiffened. "Right before Leah fell."

"Wait." Zara leaned closer. She muttered something under her breath, adjusted something, and tried again. "There are several photos. And a video fragment timestamped 3:31 a.m. Mom, that's literally when I heard those noises on the bluff."

Camille's expression sharpened. Her attention narrowed as if she were about to cross-examine someone into oblivion. She moved around the island to stand behind Zara, one hand braced on the back of the chair, eyes tracking the screen. "Can you retrieve the damaged files?"

"I think so," Zara said. "The data's still physically there. But the water damage corrupted some sectors, so I'm running a deep scan to reconstruct what I can. Video files are way bigger and more fragmented. It's gonna take a second."

Fragile hope bloomed in my chest. "This could help Mia's case."

"It could also hurt her," Camille said. "Depending on what it shows."

Those files would reveal something that would change everything. I'd bet my life on it. "It won't."

Zara looked up at her mother with a pleading expression. "If I'd spoken up sooner, if I'd just said something... maybe none of this would've happened. Maybe Leah would still be alive. We can actually do something now."

Camille's shoulders dropped. She looked as tired as I felt. "Even if I wanted to, Dahlia, you and I, there's a conflict. I withdrew because you refused to follow advice, and because you interfered with witnesses and endangered your daughter's case, which made my continued representation untenable."

Pride was a luxury I couldn't afford. I would beg. I would do anything. "I won't say a word without you. I won't talk to witnesses. I won't breathe unless you tell me to."

"Too late."

"I know you're angry with me. I deserve that. But Mia—she's not a murderer. She's a kid who panicked and made a terrible mistake. Whatever you feel about me, please, don't let them eat her alive."

Camille let out a heavy sigh. "I'm not forgiving you."

"I'm not asking you to. I'm asking you to save my daughter."

"Fine. I'll represent her through the arraignment. After that, we reassess whether I stay on or refer you out. That's all I can promise."

Relief hit me so hard my vision blurred. I braced a hand on the island until the room steadied. The words were too small for what I felt, but they were all I had. "Thank you."

Camille was already moving toward the back door. "Zara, save whatever you find to an external drive. Make a copy to the cloud. Email me anything that looks exculpatory. Chain-of-custody issues are going to be a problem, but right now we need leverage."

Zara didn't glance up from her work. "I'm on it."

Camille grabbed her keys from a hook by the door to the garage and slid on her zebra-print heels, all business now. Her gaze lowered to my bare feet. "You can wear a pair of my shoes. Let's go."

Chapter Forty-Two

Mia stared down at the scarred metal table, motionless, not meeting my gaze. My heart squeezed at the sight of her, her eyes red and swollen like she'd been crying for hours.

I brought a hoodie for her to wear over her dress to keep her from being too cold. Her small frame was lost in the oversized hoodie, like a child playing dress-up in someone else's clothes. She pulled the sleeves over her hands and held her hands tight in her lap like she might break into a thousand pieces if she let go.

Detective Callahan sat beside Detective King, elbows on the table, her eyes bright like a hunter who'd just cornered her prey. King settled back into his chair and reached across the table, turning on the small black recorder. The red light blinked to life. Detective King read Mia her rights again for the recording.

"Mia, you were arrested earlier tonight based on probable cause. No formal charges have been filed yet. The district attorney will review this interview and all evidence before deciding what charges, if any, to bring. Do you understand?"

"Yes," Mia said.

"Then let's begin," King said. "Tell us what really happened that night."

"Everything was normal until after we all got ready in our

dresses. Then suddenly they started being nice to Leah and mean to me instead." Mia wiped roughly at her reddened eyes. "Peyton said my dress looked like something from a charity bin, that I was a try-hard. When I got upset, Leah said I was being extra. Then she called me needy, said I was obsessed with Chloe, and it wasn't a good look. When *she* was the one who wanted to be included so badly, who talked about them literally all the time. Leah kept saying she had, like, a plan. That something big was gonna happen."

"What did she mean?" Callahan asked.

"I don't know. Leah said she'd found something out. She wanted me to help her, like find whoever was behind this awful account that was bullying other girls, especially Leah, but I didn't want to. I was scared. I figured it was one of the other girls, and I didn't want them to treat me like they did Leah. I didn't want to help her. She was gonna tell me everything when I got there, in person, only that's not what happened. She just... it was like she got around Chloe and the rest of them, and she changed back to who she was before. She always wanted to be in their group, more than anything. Suddenly, she was one of them. They'd whisper in her ear and laugh at inside jokes, saying I wouldn't understand. I kept trying to get her alone, to talk to her, to see what was going on, but she just ignored me."

Guilt twisted in my chest. I dug my fingernails into my palms. I'd pushed her toward these girls. I'd wanted this for her so badly. I'd wanted belonging for both of us.

"We went back out for the photo shoot. At midnight. It was Chloe's idea. It was Chloe, Leah, and me. Chloe said she needed me the take good pictures. She said she couldn't trust anyone else to get the angles right. But then Chloe wanted Leah to stand near the edge, and I stopped shooting. I got scared and told her not to go so close."

King nodded encouragingly at her. "Keep going."

Mia sucked in a nervous breath. "Leah said, 'Don't be such a pick-me. You're so desperate it's embarrassing.' She said it like it was funny, like it was a joke, but it wasn't. It didn't sound like Leah. Chloe laughed and said, 'It's not like anyone wants to look at you anyway.'"

The pen in Callahan's hand was still now. Even she didn't interrupt.

Mia pressed both sleeves to her face like she hated the words coming out of her mouth. "I was so hurt, so upset. I couldn't think straight. I—I slapped Leah."

Indignation burned like a brand in my chest. My gentle, anxious, people-pleasing daughter had struck her best friend. The image wouldn't form in my mind. It didn't fit. But the shame radiating from her being told me it was true.

Camille's hand went to Mia's forearm. "Mia, stop."

But Mia kept going. "I didn't even think. My hand just... It just happened. I was so upset. Her nose started bleeding. She put her hand up, and blood went on her fingers and then on my dress because she touched me. She was trying to grab me, but I was so mad. Chloe just stood there, watching."

"What happened next?" King asked gently.

"She said something mean about my dad, about how he died."

Anger flooded through my veins. Marcus had been everything to both of us. For Leah to use our deepest wound as ammunition in a petty teenage fight made my hands curl into fists. I wanted to defend Mia, to rage at a dead girl.

"I got so mad," Mia whispered. "I was crying so hard, I couldn't even see straight. Leah kept looking at Chloe like she was a goddess or something. I told Leah she'd picked them over me, over our friendship. Leah came toward me. She grabbed my arms and I pulled away. I didn't mean it. I swear it. I just wanted space. I pushed her. Hard. In the chest."

There it was. The truth I'd been dreading and denying in equal measure. My daughter had pushed her best friend off a cliff. Accidentally, I believed that with every fiber of my being, but the fact remained: Mia's hands had sent Leah over the edge.

The weight of it pressed down on my lungs until I couldn't draw breath.

Camille cut in. "Mia, that's enough. Detectives, my client is distraught. Anything further risks—"

"No." Mia's voice was small but firm. "I need to say it. I need them to know."

Camille's jaw tightened. She gave a single, reluctant nod. "Against my advice," she said for the record.

Callahan kept her expression carefully neutral, but I caught the glint in her eyes, the smug look of a detective who'd just been handed a signed confession. King's posture shifted, his shoulders squaring as he leaned forward. They'd scented blood in the water.

"I lost my balance and fell onto my hands and knees. That's how my dress got dirty. I thought... I thought she was fine. We were both fine. I was on my knees, looking down at my dress, thinking I'd ruined it and you would kill me, Mom. Then there were these, like, crashing, thrashing, thudding noises. Leah screamed."

Guilt and remorse filled her voice. Tears streamed down her cheeks. Camille handed her a tissue, and Mia held it to her face, her breathing jagged.

"I heard her fall, Mom. I heard her. I looked up, and she just wasn't there anymore. She was standing there one second, and the next she was gone."

I tried to imagine it—the terror as your best friend vanished into the darkness, the sickening sounds that followed. Mia had been alone with that horror for days. She'd carried it, kept it hidden deep, let it eat her alive from the inside. And I hadn't known.

Mia's breath hitched. "I scrambled down the bluff to help her. I crouched beside her, but I had to hold onto a branch to keep from falling. There was blood. Her body was all twisted up. She wasn't moving. I begged Chloe to call 911. I'd left my phone back at the house. My hands were shaking so bad. I put my fingers on her neck. I couldn't find a pulse. I tried her wrist. I didn't know if I was doing it right. I said her name. Over and over. But she wasn't moving. She didn't move."

She pressed the tissue to her mouth and breathed through it, frantic, shaking, devastated. She was only fourteen. Just a child. I would have given anything to take her place, to take her pain, shame, and grief, but I couldn't do anything but watch her shatter in front of me.

"I climbed back up," Mia said. "In the dark, I almost fell a few times. I was so scared. I told Chloe to call 911, to get an ambulance, to help Leah. I begged her."

"Why didn't you make the call?" Callahan asked.

"Chloe said she was going to help me. She said she knew what to do, and I had to trust her. Leah was already gone. We couldn't help her. We could only help ourselves. I couldn't think. Leah was...she was...She was dead."

She pressed her fist to her mouth, made an agonized noise in the back of her throat. "Chloe said no one would believe that it was an accident. We had to go back to the house and leave her like that and not touch anything else. She said we should say we went to bed, and we didn't see Leah leave. That she would say the same thing as me. If we had the same story, everyone would believe us. She hugged me and said she would make it all better. She could fix it. I just had to do everything she said."

Mia looked at me with desperate, beseeching eyes. "She was helping me. She was trying to protect me. She was the only one who understood."

Cold fury filled my veins. Chloe hadn't been thinking of Mia; she'd been thinking of herself. She covered up Mia's crime not out of loyalty, but out of self-preservation.

"What did you do?" King asked.

"Chloe told me to go back to the house first. She said we should go separately to be quieter. I went back to the house. I just... I left Leah there."

Callahan leaned forward, elbows on the table. Watching Mia like a hawk tracking a mouse. "What about the camera?"

"I had it then. When I got back inside, I put it in its case beside my overnight bag, by the patio doors."

"What time was it when you returned to the basement?" King asked.

"It was almost 1 a.m. I remember seeing my phone charging beside my sleeping bag."

King underlined something in his notebook. "Then what did you do?"

"It was dark. Everyone was asleep. I mean, I thought they were. I couldn't really see. Except Alexis's sleeping bag was empty. Peyton was on my other side. She rolled over. I remember being afraid that she'd seen me. I lay down in my sleeping bag and put the pillow over my head. I... I wanted everything to go away, to erase it all, what happened."

"Did you hear or see anything else that night?" King asked.

Mia looked at her hands. "I think I heard footsteps, maybe, like someone going out into the hall and up the stairs, but I don't know. I had the pillow pressed over my ears, trying to block everything out. It could've been earlier, or later. I wasn't keeping track."

"Did you go back outside after that?"

Mia shook her head mutely.

"Why didn't you tell us this before?" King asked.

"I thought if I told the truth, you would think I was a murderer." Mia's hands curled into fists. "I didn't mean it. I swear, I didn't want her to fall."

Detective King let Mia's last sentence sit in the air. Then he leaned back. The chair creaked. He steepled his fingers and looked at Callahan. She looked back. Something passed between them.

"Here's the problem with your story, Mia," he said. "The ME found evidence of two injuries."

Mia blinked slowly. The color leeched from her face. "I don't..." She looked at Camille, then at me, then back at King in bewilderment. "What?"

My stomach dropped as if I had missed a step and kept falling. My blood roared in my ears. "What do you mean?"

King pulled a folder from beneath his notebook, one I hadn't noticed before. He opened it and scanned the top page. "The medical examiner's report came back this afternoon. Leah sustained two separate skull fractures. At two different times."

The room seemed to contract. I couldn't breathe. My brain couldn't decipher the words he was speaking. Everything went tinny and far away.

"The first wound is consistent with the fall you described. A linear fracture at the back of the skull, caused by impact against a fallen log on the bluff." He paused, letting that sink in. "The second wound is a depressed fracture on the left temporal region. The ME determined it was caused by a separate blow, a blunt object striking her head with considerable force. Based on the injury pattern, blood evidence, rigor progression, and the difference in hemorrhaging around each wound site, these injuries occurred hours apart."

"Someone returned to the scene between 3 and 4 a.m.," Callahan said. "They crushed Leah Cho's skull with a blunt object. Someone who knew exactly where Leah fell. Someone who had a motive to silence her."

The temperature dropped ten degrees in a heartbeat. Aghast, I glanced at Camille. Her eyes held a horror that matched my own. Two injuries. Hours apart. My brain tried to reject the information, to reorder it into something less terrible.

Mia made a strangled sound, raw and primitive, something between a sob and a scream. Her hands flew to her mouth. "Wait—what? No. No, that's not... Someone went back? Someone actually... I thought—I thought she died from the fall. From my... that's what I thought happened." Her chest heaved. "Someone went back down there? While she was still—while she was still alive?"

"Mia," Camille said sharply. But Mia wasn't listening.

"Who would do that?" She choked out, the words barely intelligible. "Who would go back and—and—" She couldn't say it aloud. She shoved her chair back and doubled over, arms wrapped around her stomach like she'd been gutted. "Leah was down there alone, and someone killed her? Murdered her on purpose?"

"Yes." Callahan's sharp eyes never left Mia's face. "And the evidence points to you."

Mia broke down completely. Her body shook with great wracking sobs. Her hands clawed at her hair, her face. Her breath came in ragged, panicked gasps as she curled into herself, rocking back and forth.

I couldn't bear it any longer. I leaned over and gathered her into my arms. She crumpled into me, weeping in a keening, wordless grief. I stroked her trembling back, held her as close as I could. As if I could protect her from all this, save her somehow.

Camille shot to her feet. "My client has admitted to an accidental push during an argument. She was emotionally distraught and following instructions from another minor who told her calling 911 would destroy her life. She attempted to render aid. She believed Leah was already dead. You have zero evidence placing her back on that bluff during the window for the second injury. If you want to charge her with manslaughter for the push, do it. But if you're building a murder case on speculation and intimidation, I'll rip it apart in court. This interview is over."

King nodded. "Fair enough, Counselor."

"Let me take her home. Please," I begged. My heart shattered inside the cage of my ribs. I couldn't bear the thought of leaving her here in this awful place. It felt like dying. "Please."

"I'm sorry, but not at this time." King's expression softened. "Mia, you'll be held in juvenile detention pending arraignment. That will happen within forty-eight hours. At that hearing, the DA will formally charge you based on everything we've discussed tonight."

Mia just clung to me, her fingers digging into my arms like she was drowning and I was the only solid thing left in the world. In hours, she'd be in juvenile detention, surrounded by strangers, facing charges that could destroy her entire future. The injustice of it felt like being torn in half. I wanted to fight, to scream, to tear these ugly walls down with my bare hands.

Everything inside me was shattering all at once, jagged edges pressing against the inside of my skin. My bones no longer supported me. I held her close and kissed her forehead. "I love you, I love you, I love you."

King stepped forward. I was forced to let her go.

Then I watched them take my baby away.

Chapter Forty-Three

I sat in the passenger seat as Camille eased the Mercedes out of the precinct parking lot. My hands clenched and unclenched helplessly in my lap. I'd never felt so impotent in my life.

I kept my eyes on the smear of our headlights in the darkness. If I looked at her, I might break. "What happens next?"

"They booked Mia," Camille said. "Juvenile intake. They'll hold her in detention overnight. Tomorrow, at the earliest, they'll bring her before a juvenile court judge for a detention hearing. It could take up to forty-eight hours. The DA will review the interrogation transcript, the evidence, and consult with the homicide unit. They'll file formal charges after that."

I pictured Mia spending the night in a cold alien place far from home. Stricken and devastated, curled on a thin mattress in some institutional room, lying alone, replaying Leah's scream, imagining the horrific last hours of her life, how she'd failed to save her best friend, leaving her out there to be killed. How it had started with Mia, with that one terrible push.

I couldn't be there for her. Couldn't hold her. Couldn't promise it would be okay or mop up her tears. My chest constricted with a pain so visceral it felt like a physical wound.

"With that second skull fracture, we're not talking involuntary manslaughter. They'll argue felony murder or possibly first-degree if they can show deliberation and malice, and they'll charge her as an adult. If they try to transfer, we'll fight it, but given the publicity and the nature of the homicide, we need to be prepared for a murder charge against Mia."

I saw Callahan's predatory gaze in my mind's eye. "Mia will have to face the consequences for the part she played, I know that. But I do not believe that she should be locked away for the rest of her life for this. Someone else went back down the bluff that night, someone who wanted to make dead certain that Leah never came back up."

"Yes," Camille said.

The terrible implications were still sinking in, reshaping everything I thought I'd known. During the interrogation, the shock had numbed me. I wasn't numb anymore. It felt like being flayed alive.

I pictured it. Someone creeping down the bluff in the darkness. Finding Leah broken and bleeding. Picking up that rock. Raising it. Bringing it down. The sound it would make. The deliberateness of it.

The same rock planted in Mia's room with Leah's hair stuck in dried blood.

The rock wasn't just evidence of Leah's tragic fall. It was proof of premeditated murder. Someone had gone back to that bluff, picked up a rock, crushed Leah's skull, and then carried that bloody rock into our home and placed it in Mia's room.

And I'd hidden it. Moved it. Contaminated it.

My vision tunneled. My hands shook. I pressed them flat against my thighs, trying to steady myself. If the detectives found out what I did, if they knew I'd discovered potential murder evidence and buried it in a hollow tree like some kind of criminal...

Camille's hands tightened on the wheel. The dashboard cast her tensed features in a ghastly blue wash. "We have another problem.

The camera. The chain of custody is broken. You took a piece of physical evidence from the scene of a suspicious death. You brought it to my home. Zara, a civilian minor, handled it and attempted to access it. If the prosecution learns that, they will argue tampering, contamination, and fruit of the poisonous tree. Best case, a judge excludes it. If the judge finds out I sat on this camera for even twelve hours, I could be disbarred. I'm already on the line, Dahlia."

My stomach dropped. I'd thought finding the camera was a victory. Instead, I'd contaminated the one piece of evidence that might be able to save Mia.

I was supposed to keep Mia safe. That was the only job that mattered. And I was failing.

Guilt burned beneath my ribs. I had to tell Camille everything. She would hate me, but I had to come clean. First, I told her about the sandy slippers, my worry that Mia had been lying about where she'd been that night, how she'd washed them without telling me.

"That doesn't prove anything," Camille said. "There's no evidence the girls were on the beach at any point."

Her words were meant to reassure me. They didn't. I had to keep going. I had to say everything. "There's more."

Camille winced. "Please don't say that."

I swallowed and steeled myself. "I found a strange rock in Mia's room, on her windowsill. Someone put it there when we were out of the house. A rock with blood on it. And a few black hairs. Leah's. It's the murder weapon, I'm certain of it. Whoever used it to crack Leah's skull open put it there to frame Mia."

"What did you just say?" Camille turned her head and gaped at me. Her eyes were bright with disbelief. The car drifted onto the shoulder. Camille jerked the wheel and corrected. "Where the hell is it?"

"I hid it. It's at the playground behind the community clubhouse. There's a hollow oak by the swings. That's where I put it."

Camille's brows rose. "Are you serious right now?"

"I had to." I swallowed, fear tight in my chest, my breath

coming fast and shallow. "They already suspect her. If they found the murder weapon in my daughter's room, they'd lock her away for decades. Who would believe that it was planted? That we're being framed? No one. I panicked."

For an eternal moment, Camille didn't speak as she nosed the car onto a side street by a darkened strip mall and put the car in park beneath the weak halo of a streetlight. The engine hummed. Rain ticked on the windshield.

She turned to me, her spine straight, her body stiff with barely controlled fury. "That is obstruction of justice, tampering with evidence. If the state finds out you moved that rock, they will charge you. And they will leverage that to crush Mia."

"I used gloves and a plastic bag," I said lamely. "Mia and I didn't touch it. Could it have the killer's fingerprints on it?"

"It's unlikely the oils could be picked up even after 24 hours on a rough, irregular object, but that's not the relevant point here." Her nostrils flared. Her voice dropped, becoming quieter and more precise, each word deliberate and clipped. "Do you understand what you did? Not just to your daughter's case, but to me? To Zara? My license is at risk, my reputation, my career. I'm committing professional suicide right now."

I understood her anger, I did. I hated the position I'd put her in, but I was too desperate to flinch now. "It was one of the girls, I know it. We must stop them, Camille. No one else will. Please."

For a long moment, Camille didn't say anything. Abruptly, the anger seemed to drain out of her. With a sigh, she leaned back against the headrest and closed her eyes, deflated. "Don't think I don't understand, Dahlia. Because I do. I understand more than you know. I get what this place can do, how it gets inside of you. How the people embrace you, make you think you're safe, then they tear you to shreds."

I looked at her in the shadowed darkness. I'd never heard Camille sound so uncertain or admit to anything resembling weakness, a chink in her impenetrable armor. Out of all of us, she was the confident, unshakable one. The one who always knew what to do.

"I worry about Zara, too," she said in a near whisper, as if confessing her deepest secrets. Or her deepest fears. "I worry every single day. She thinks she's invincible because society tells girls like her that they're untouchable as long as they're beautiful, as long as they smile pretty. If they fit in, say and do the right things, wear the right clothes, and believe the right things. But as soon as you don't, as soon as you fall out of line..."

Camille touched one of her gold hoop earrings. "They could've turned on Zara as easily as they did Leah or Taylor before her. And Mia. Those girls, they ruin lives for entertainment, out of boredom. They're the ultimate mean girls. And the thing is, so are their mothers. They're still mean girls, just older. They don't change. They learn to hide it better behind their charm, their beauty, their polished manners."

For the first time since this nightmare began, I didn't feel so completely alone. Camille understood what I struggled to articulate—the suffocating pressure of this place, the disquieting way it smiled while it sharpened its knives. She knew what it meant to be an outsider here, to never quite know who to trust, forced to watch your daughter navigate waters teeming with sharks in ponytails and designer clothes.

We were mothers trying to keep our girls safe in a place that ate its young.

We sat in the hum of the car for a beat. I placed my hand on Camille's arm. "They think they can get away with murder. We can't let them. They'll just do it again."

Eventually, she nodded. "Whatever you think of me, Dahlia, I do know that."

Camille's phone buzzed hard on the console. She seized the phone. "It's Zara. She's still trying to recover the corrupted files." She typed out a text: *Keep working on it.*

Camille shifted the car back into drive. We rolled out of the parking lot. Her expression had closed, all business again. "We need to build a timeline with an alternate suspect. We need to instill doubt. The person had to know Leah was down there, and they had to get back down to Leah in the dark without being seen. They had to have a reason to risk it."

Whitney's face flashed in my mind. The precise hair, the practiced empathy, the money that opened every door and disappeared every problem. And Peyton—beautiful, feral, a predator in a school uniform.

"Peyton Alistair," I said. "She broke into my house and slashed Leah's painting. She dumped the spray paint in your trash can to cover her ass. Zara saw red paint on her fingers. She also saw Peyton bury the camera. Chloe could have told Peyton what had happened with Leah when they went back inside."

I thought back to Monday after school, when I saw Peyton leaning toward Mia at the drinking fountain, her hand on Mia's arm, the way Mia's face had gone carefully blank. Not an act of comfort as I first thought, but a threat.

I'd mistaken manipulation for kindness. And so, apparently, had my daughter.

I'd been so wrong about so many things.

"What's her motive?" Camille asked.

"Leah suspected either Alexis, Chloe, or Peyton was behind the LakeshoreTea cyberbullying account. Zara said Leah was planning to find and expose them. Maybe at the slumber party, Leah discovered Peyton was the guilty one."

"According to the detectives, Leah's phone came back clean," Camille said. "No screenshots, no saved messages, no relevant deletions, nothing incriminating. It makes sense if Leah was paranoid about digital evidence after what happened with those AI-altered images. She didn't trust phones. That's why she kept her diary hidden, not in her bedroom, and why she planned to get Zara to physically clone someone's phone at the sleepover. She needed proof that couldn't be deleted or denied."

I said, "Once she got proof, Peyton would've been outed. Expelled from school, kicked off the swim team, humiliated.

Public humiliation is as good a reason as any for a girl to kill to protect herself, especially these girls. Mia said Peyton, Chloe, and Alexis were suddenly cozying up to Leah, so maybe Peyton recruited Alexis and Chloe to help her, and they had something awful planned for her all along. and Mia's accidental push accelerated the timeline. Then Peyton went down and made sure Leah would never talk again."

Camille's brow furrowed. "The camera is a problem, though. Why would there be anything on it that would incriminate Mia? Why bury it? And if there was something on it, why not smash it? Throw it in the lake? Remove the memory card and burn it? Why take the risk of leaving it where it could be found?"

"Maybe she planned to retrieve it later, and then something prevented her. She panicked and didn't know what to do with it. She may be a killer, but she's still a kid."

Camille made a noncommittal sound in the back of her throat. "Or Chloe did it herself. She was on that bluff. She told Mia to leave Leah's body there."

"But Chloe had been right there with Mia, equally panicked, or at least, she'd acted that way, according to Mia's account. Why would she go back if she believed Leah was already dead?"

Chloe's beautiful, doll-like face flashed in my mind—her devastating performance at the memorial, the way she'd coached Mia to keep quiet in the aftermath of Leah's fall. She'd told Mia she was protecting her, and perhaps in her mind, she was.

I tried to think back, to conjure the specific details from the shock and horror of that Saturday morning. Had there been a guilty tension on Chloe's face? On Peyton's? A furtive, knowing glance passed between Alexis and Peyton?

The panic of that morning cast everything in a frenetic fog. I couldn't recall clearly, couldn't know for certain whether the memory was accurate or if it had shifted, subtly altered by the knowledge I had now.

"Mia was the one who pushed Leah, not Chloe, " I said. "Chloe had everything to lose by going back out to the bluff and killing

Leah. She didn't bury the camera, either. Peyton did. She didn't enter our house with the spare key and slash Leah's painting, deface it with GUILTY in red spray paint, and then toss the can in your trash. Peyton did that, too."

"Granted, that pisses me off," Camille admitted. "That pretty little asshole." She tapped her thumb against the wheel, considering. "What about Alexis? She had access to your house. She assaulted Leah once before. She could be behind the cyberbullying as easily as Peyton."

"Leah saw Brooke hit Alexis at the Christmas party," I said slowly. I thought of Alexis's gentleness with Falcon, her tangible fear of her mother. Anger on her behalf clogged in my throat. "Alexis cut off Leah's hair as a threat to protect her family. She was terrified CPS would get involved. But that was months ago. Why wait until now to do something so drastic? And Alexis seemed genuinely confused when I asked about the camera and slippers. She didn't know what I was talking about."

"Fear makes people good liars."

"Maybe. But the evidence points more to Peyton, not Alexis or Chloe."

Camille pursed her lips. She looked like she wanted to say something, then thought better of it.

"What?" I asked.

She shrugged. "This is hearsay. Take it with a grain of salt."

"Tell me."

"At the Christmas silent auction, that humane society fundraiser Rowan hosts every year, Brooke got a little too buzzed at the open bar. She was slurring her words, stumbling a bit, definitely drunk. She leaned in and told me that everyone always judged her for drinking to deal with her son's special needs, but that Rowan and Whitney weren't as perfect as they pretended."

I waited, hardly breathing.

"She said Rowan's husband was always gone because he's been having an affair. Their marriage was on the rocks, but Rowan didn't want anyone to know." Camille glanced at me to gauge my reaction. "And Whitney and Graham were nearly sued the summer before last. They'd had to pay off the Everett family to make a scandal disappear."

My pulse quickened. "What kind of scandal?"

"Something about Taylor Everett's near drowning being suspicious. There were drugs involved. Pills. Taylor had been in competition with Peyton to make swim captain, and then after her accident, Peyton got the title." She shook her head in disgust. "That's all I know. As I said, just drunk gossip from Brooke. But..."

The lorazepam bottle prescribed to Brooke but found in Whitney's trash. It made sense now. "But it tracks," I finished.

"It tracks."

My scalp prickled with sweat. I rubbed at the tension headache forming behind my eyes. The pressure had been building for hours, a dull throb that matched my pulse.

Mia had made a terrible mistake, yes, but she wasn't a murderer. Somewhere in Blackthorn Shores, someone was walking free who had deliberately ended a young girl's life.

Chloe remained on the suspect list, and so did Alexis, but perky, blue-eyed, blond-haired Peyton Alistair fit the most pieces of the puzzle.

A fourteen-year-old girl. That's what kept snagging in my mind: not a monster, not some criminal mastermind. Just a kid. A kid who'd been taught that consequences were for other people.

The Mercedes glided to a stop by the curb opposite my cottage. Hydrangeas heavy with blooms lined my cracked walkway. The rain had thinned to a mist, but heavy clouds still obscured the moon as thunder boomed in the distance.

Camille put her hand on my forearm. "This is where you let me do the job you hired me to do. I will see Mia first thing in the morning and fight for her release pending adjudication. I will do everything I can. Just don't do anything stupid."

"I hear you." I opened the door and stepped out of the car. The night wrapped around me, close and damp and stifling. Behind me, the Mercedes idled and then pulled away. The taillights smeared red in the wet air and vanished around the curve.

What Camille said made sense. I knew I should go inside, lock the doors, and let Camille do what she did best, but good sense had stopped mattering somewhere around the moment they put handcuffs on my daughter.

I stood in my driveway, keys in hand. The front door was ten feet away. Apollo was waiting inside, alone for hours. The right thing, the sane thing, was to go in, lock the door, and trust Camille.

Every piece of evidence we had was tainted. The camera was compromised. The rock was hidden. Mia's confession was damning, and Chloe's testimony would seal Mia's fate like a tomb. Along with the DNA evidence, Mia's skin cells, and Leah's blood.

Even if Zara recovered more footage, it might not be enough.

I needed something irrefutable.

But if Peyton was the killer, she'd left evidence somewhere. Killers always did. And Whitney would do anything to protect her daughter. I knew that like I knew my own mother's heart. That's where the truth would be found.

The threat of danger had a strange effect. It steadied me. There wasn't a safe path. There wasn't even a good one. The only way forward was straight into the mouth of the dragon.

Without Mia, I had nothing left to lose.

That realization should have terrified me. Instead, it clarified everything. The police weren't going to find the answers that would free Mia. But I could. I had to.

I'd been helpless and impotent long enough. No more.

I waited until Camille had enough time to park in her garage, then I started walking north along Wyld Wood Lane. My legs felt heavy. Each step required conscious effort, like wading through Jell-O. I kept moving.

The house loomed larger with each step. Curtains framed wide panes of warm light as movement behind the glass.

The Alistairs were home.

Chapter Forty-Four

I faced Whitney's front door. Exhaustion pulled at me but desperation propelled me forward.

Mia was alone, terrified, believing I'd failed her. I had a fragment of a plan with no backup and no evidence that would hold up in court. I was just a desperate mother running on fumes and fury, about to bluff a woman who could afford lawyers that would eviscerate me.

I hit the brass knocker. A light blinked on overhead. Through the frosted glass, a tall shape moved. Whitney, her posture perfect, pace unhurried.

She opened the door an inch and started to close it again the second she saw me. "You again."

"We need to talk. Now."

The door opened slightly. She wore a blush-pink loungewear set, her hair down. Her fluffy Pomeranian Percival yapped shrilly at her ankles until she nudged him back with her foot.

She glanced warily past me to the dark yard, twisted to look behind her up to the staircase, where a soft wash of light glowed at the second-floor landing, then back to me. "It's past eleven. This is harassment."

"I found Mia's camera. The one Peyton buried on the beach, that you tried to keep me from finding."

Whitney stilled. Her grip tightened on the doorframe. "I don't know what you're talking about."

"I recovered the corrupted files. Time stamps, metadata, everything."

"You're lying."

"Am I?" I pulled out my phone and held it up. "One call to Detective King. Or I can send the footage to the Detroit Free Press first. Hell, all I have to do is exit the community gates, and there are a hundred reporters who'd love to see this. Your choice."

She glanced up the stairs again, listening for Graham probably, for witnesses. When she looked back, I saw it—the crack in her perfect façade. Her pupils too wide. Her breathing too fast. She was nervous, apprehensive, guarded.

For days, these women had looked at me with pity or contempt, their smiles sharp as scalpels. They'd whispered about Mia at the memorial, clutched their daughters closer as if poverty and trauma were infectious diseases.

An ugly satisfaction unfurled in my stomach. Whitney was afraid of me. Good. Let her know what it felt like. Let her feel a fraction of the agony I'd felt watching the police handcuff my daughter.

"Not here." She grabbed my arm and pulled me inside, her nails digging through my sleeve.

The foyer was all marble and white walls. She steered me through the hallway into the gleaming kitchen. Percival trotted after us, sniffing at my ankles.

Graham sat at the expansive island. He looked up from his phone, a craft beer sweating in one hand. "Hey, Dahlia." His tone was pleasant, distracted. His gaze dropped back to the screen.

He had no clue. Just sitting there with his beer and his phone, living his comfortable, placid, perfect life while his daughter buried evidence of murder. While his wife orchestrated cover-ups.

The obliviousness might've been funny if it weren't so obscene.

Whitney didn't slow down. "We'll be outside."

Before he could respond, she slid open the sliding glass door, ushered me through, and shut it behind us. Percival pressed his nose against the glass, his tiny breath fogging the pane as he watched us intently.

I followed Whitney onto the covered deck. Cedar beams bracketed the vaulted ceiling overhead. The deck stretched the length of the house, the glass railings framing the view of the custom pool ringed by a slate stone patio. Light rain misted the lit pool's surface, turning it a ghostly blue. Beyond the yard, the bluff dropped to away to endless black water.

Whitney straightened, her chin lifted. "What the hell do you want?"

"The truth. Peyton was on that bluff. She killed Leah."

Whitney sneered. "Your daughter pushed her best friend off a cliff. Chloe saw her. Everyone knows."

"The medical examiner knows Leah didn't die from the fall. She was alive for hours, and not only that, but someone came back and crushed her skull with a rock."

Whitney's features flickered with surprise, then rearranged into wary calculation. Not horror, not grief for Leah, just concern for how it affected her and her family. She sniffed. "That has nothing to do with us."

"Peyton buried the camera because she's in the footage. She panicked. She hid evidence."

"That's absurd." But her voice wavered.

"Here's what's going to happen. You're going to walk into the precinct tomorrow morning with Peyton and you're going to tell Detective King everything, or I send this footage to every media outlet in the country."

Whitney took a step back, closer to the deck furniture, the sleek low-slung sofa and chairs. The rain hissed against the deck. "You can't prove anything."

She was right. I couldn't. I had nothing but a massive bluff, a reckless bet for everything that mattered. If Whitney called the police right now, I'd be the one arrested.

I'd learned something from these mothers, though. Sometimes the threat of exposure was more powerful than proof. That fear was all I had left.

I kept my face carefully blank, my voice steady. This was it, the moment my bluff either worked spectacularly or collapsed around me.

I smiled at Whitney. "I don't have to, the media will do it for me. News vans at your gate. Cameras at the school. They'll arrest her in front of everyone. You know how this works, Whitney. Once the story breaks, it doesn't matter if she's guilty. The damage is done."

Whitney's tense gaze slid past me to the far end of the deck, where the stairs went down to the lawn and the bluff beyond. The glass railings had fogged. Wind lifted the string lights strung over the outdoor dining table and grill.

"Show me the footage, then." She held out her hand. "If you have it, prove it."

"Not until Peyton talks."

"Our lawyers will destroy you. You know that, right?"

"Your lawyers can't stop a media firestorm. Beautiful young Peyton Alistair, swim team captain, privileged Blackthorn Shores princess, who murdered a girl and buried the evidence. That's the headline, that's what Graham reads on his phone over breakfast. How do you think that will play?"

Whitney flinched. For the first time, real fear cracked through her composure. "If you think you can come in here and threaten us, threaten my family, you have another think coming."

The sliding glass doors opened. Peyton stepped out, barefoot in plaid pajama pants and a white tank top. Her hair hung loose and damp around her shoulders. "Mom."

"Go inside," Whitney said sharply. "This is not for you."

Peyton's eyes went hard, her jaw set. The pool lights carved shadows under her cheekbones. She'd lost weight in the last week, just like Mia. "I heard everything."

Whitney took a step toward her. "Go upstairs. Now."

Peyton didn't move. Her gaze locked on mine, unflinching. Angry. "You don't understand anything. You don't know what happened."

"Don't you say anything," Whitney said, her voice rising in restrained panic. "Not a word. We will call Mr. Avery in the morning and deal with this."

"It's not what you think," Peyton said.

"Then tell me." My voice sounded deadly calm but inside, I was shaking. My hands felt numb, fingers tingling from adrenaline. The exhaustion I'd been ignoring crashed over me in waves. I hadn't eaten in hours, hadn't slept properly in days.

I locked my knees and kept my chin up. Peyton was watching me for weakness. So was Whitney. I couldn't afford to retreat an inch or they would pounce. "From where I stand, you're a killer, Peyton."

Peyton's eyes blazed with a hot and reckless outrage, at her mother, at me, at the trap closing around her. "Fine. You want the truth? Let's do this."

Whitney stepped toward Peyton as if to attempt to physically stop her.

"No more." Peyton sidestepped her mother and moved from the doors across the deck toward the glass railings. She stopped a few feet from the edge of the deck and spun to face us. "I didn't kill Leah, and I didn't frame Mia."

"You broke into my house multiple times. You moved things around, stole the notebook from my desk, and slashed Leah's painting and defaced it with spray paint."

I could smell chlorine mixed with rain-soaked wood and Whitney's expensive perfume. A flash of lightning lit up the clouds gathered over the lake. Our shadows stretched long and twisted across the deck.

"My daughter would never do such a thing!" Whitney said.

"Shut up," I snapped at Whitney. "You had your chance. It's Peyton's turn."

Whitney gaped at me, stunned speechless for once. No one spoke to Whitney Alistair like that in her own home. But something in my eyes warned her not to push.

I turned to Peyton. "Just tell me what happened."

Peyton's shoulders were rigid, hands fisted at her sides. Her chin raised, defiant and unapologetic. "Yeah, I did it. The key was hanging on our hook by the door. It was easy."

"You made us feel afraid in our own home."

She sniffed. "It wasn't that deep."

White-hot anger seared my veins. She'd terrorized Mia. Invaded our house. Slashed a dead girl's painting. These girls, they destroyed lives and couldn't be bothered to care.

Peyton was a child, but she was also dangerous. There was nothing childlike in her eyes but cold calculation and years of entitlement. I didn't have time for pity. Child or not, she'd chosen this.

I said, "You planted a bloodied rock in Mia's room to frame her for murder."

Peyton's eyes went wide. "What? No! I didn't plant any rock!"

"Come on, Peyton. You just admitted to breaking in multiple times."

"I moved stuff, yeah. I took the notebook and wrecked the stupid painting. But I didn't plant anything bloody. Why would I?"

"You tell me. Why the hell did you break in?"

She shrugged, defensive. "It was just playing around, okay. We thought it'd be funny. I had the key, so why not?"

I moved closer, backing her toward the glass railing. "When did you plant the rock? Before or after I changed the locks?"

"I don't know anything about any rock!"

I studied her face. The shock in her eyes was too raw, too immediate. Perhaps she truly hadn't known about the rock. If that was the case, it meant my entire theory was somehow wrong, or at least, incomplete.

If Peyton hadn't planted the murder weapon, who had? Chloe? Alexis? Whitney? Someone else entirely? My certainty fractured. I'd been so sure, so desperate to be sure, that I walked into this house ready to burn it down.

Now the ground shifted beneath me again.

I kept pushing Peyton. The evidence still pointed at her. "Then someone's trying to make it look like you did."

"It wasn't me!"

"Then prove it. Who was it?"

"I don't know! The stupid painting was just supposed to remind Mia to keep her mouth shut. That's all I know, okay?"

Thunder rumbled in the distance. My pulse raced. "Keep her mouth shut about what?"

Peyton looked down at her feet. She didn't answer.

Whitney stepped forward. "That's enough! You have no right to interrogate my daughter. Leave now!"

I ignored her, focusing on Peyton. "Did Mia suspect what you did? Maybe you didn't plan it, but when you saw Mia accidentally push Leah over the edge, you realized you had an opportunity. Your secrets would be safe. All you had to do was go down the bluff and make sure Leah Cho never climbed back up."

"I wasn't even out there. I was inside, sleeping!"

"That's why you hid Mia's camera."

"I didn't—"

"Someone saw you on the beach that morning."

Peyton's mouth opened, startled. She hadn't expected that.

"You were seen, Peyton. You buried the camera because you're in the footage. You killed her."

"No! I didn't hurt Leah. I didn't do it."

"Then why did you take the camera?"

She shook her head, hard. "I—I can't."

Lightning forked across the sky, turning everything white for a heartbeat. The thunder that followed vibrated through the deck boards beneath my feet.

I changed tactics. I needed to shake her up while she was still talking, or she'd clam up, and I'd never get the truth out of her. I bluffed again. "I know about Taylor Everett."

Peyton's face paled.

Whitney's head snapped toward her daughter. "Don't you dare say anything."

"That wasn't my fault! She wasn't supposed to get hurt. Nobody was supposed to get hurt." She stopped, her mouth clamped shut.

My pulse hammered. "Did Leah find out? Is that why you killed her?"

"I didn't kill anyone! I took the camera, okay? That's it. Is that what you want to hear? I buried the camera because..." She hesitated, eyes darting to her mother.

"Because why?" I stepped closer, pressing the advantage. I stood three feet from her now. Close enough to see the whites of her eyes, the spray of pimples on her chin. "Why, Peyton?"

"Leverage," she said finally. "I needed leverage."

"Peyton, stop!" Whitney lunged forward, grabbing her daughter's arm. "Not another word. We're calling Mr. Avery right now!"

Peyton wrenched free, spinning to face her mother. Years of resentment blazed in her eyes. "I'm sick of covering for her!"

My breath caught. "Who? Who are you covering for?"

"She holds it over your head. Acts like she's helping you, like she's your friend. But it's always there—that thing you did because of her, but you'll get blamed for it. She can tell everyone whenever she wants, and she wants you to know it, every second, that she can ruin your life, that she has that power."

"Who?"

Thunder cracked overhead. Rain hammered the roof.

Peyton's gaze fixed on mine. "Chloe," she said. "It's all Chloe."

Chapter Forty-Five

"Chloe," I said.

Peyton held my gaze. "Yes. Chloe."

The name landed like a stone dropped into still water. For one beat, I couldn't process it. Then the ripples spread, reordering every assumption, every piece of evidence I assembled.

Whitney hovered a foot from her daughter, her hand rising toward Peyton's arm again, and then dropping. "Peyton, don't—"

"No." Peyton's voice was flat, final. "I'm done."

I kept my eyes locked on Peyton. "What does Chloe have to do with Taylor Everett?"

Peyton shifted, half-facing the pool. Its pristine surface rippled in the rain. Something had broken in her, some last thread of loyalty. Or fear. "Chloe came up with it. The whole thing."

Whitney made a strangled sound. "Stop. Please."

But Peyton didn't stop. The words came faster, like a dam breaking. "She said Taylor had to go, that she was in my way. My times were good, but Taylor's were better. Mom had all these plans—elite scouts coming to watch, recruitment letters, everything riding on me making captain, on being number one. Chloe said she'd help me, we could make it so Taylor didn't compete in the next meet, which meant she wouldn't be first."

"How?"

"Sedatives. Sleeping pills. I crushed them up and slipped them into her fruit punch at the pool party Mom does every year, just to make her sick enough to miss the end-of-season meet the next day. That's all it was supposed to be. To embarrass her, too, and make her look stupid in front of everyone. It was supposed to be funny. How was I supposed to know what it would do to her? Or that she'd be so out of it she'd fall in the pool and like, forget how to swim."

The air felt thinner, deprived of oxygen. I couldn't get a full breath. I glanced at the blue water shimmering in the rain. This very pool is where Taylor Everett nearly died. Where she was permanently brain-damaged from lack of oxygen.

My stomach heaved. I couldn't afford to be sick. Not here. Not now. "Where did you get the pills?"

"Alexis got them. Her mom has bottles of everything. Uppers, downers. Meds for anxiety, for sleep, for pain. Alexis sells them sometimes, at school. Her mom is so drunk most of the time that she doesn't even notice what's missing. Chloe paid her for half a bottle of lorazepam."

I thought of the prescription bottle in Whitney's trash, Brooke's name on the label. Everything connected. "What happened?"

"Taylor started acting weird. Dizzy, confused. We thought it was hilarious. She was stumbling around, slurring her words. Then she wandered toward the pool. The music was loud, and everyone was distracted. The adults were drinking like they always do, gossiping by the lounge chairs. The dads were grilling. It happened so fast that no one saw it. She fell into the deep end. She hit her head on the side of the pool and just... drifted down to the bottom. By the time Chloe saw her and screamed, she'd been under for like four minutes or something. Leah's dad pulled her out and called the ambulance. Mrs. Everett wouldn't stop screaming."

I closed my eyes. They'd laughed. While Taylor stumbled and slurred, disoriented and vulnerable, these girls had found it amusing. Entertainment at a pool party while the adults sipped wine twenty feet away.

"She was in the hospital for a week, in a coma. She's basically like a zombie now. Chloe told me that if I told anyone, we'd both go down. But it would be worse for me because I was the one who gave Taylor the drink. I had the motive. Everyone would believe it was my idea."

Whitney stood frozen, her face gray. Not shocked. Not horrified at the confession, but chagrined that I knew, not that it had happened.

Peyton sneered. "Mom paid them off and made them sign papers, an NDA, so they wouldn't sue us. They moved away, like, two weeks later."

"Peyton, please." Whitney's lips pressed into a thin bloodless line. She refused to meet my eyes, but she didn't deny it. We were past that point. "It was standard. Our lawyers recommended it," she attempted weakly, wringing her hands.

We both knew she was full of it.

Whitney had known. Maybe not the precise mechanics—who crushed the pills, whose hand tipped the cup—but she'd known enough. That her daughter had done something terrible. Instead of accountability, instead of facing it, she'd opened her checkbook and made a family disappear.

I'd envied her. Her confidence, her belonging, her effortless authority in this community. I'd wanted Mia to have what Peyton had. How could I not have seen who she truly was?

"Peyton, that's enough." Whitney's spine went rigid like she was bracing for a blow. Or preparing to give one. "You're exposing us to potential lawsuits—"

"Shut up!" Peyton's gaze was cold with fury. "You thought I did it, didn't you, Mom? You thought I was guilty this whole time!"

"No, of course not. I'm only trying to protect you. That's all I've ever done."

Peyton gave a harsh laugh. "Not me. You had to cover it up for yourself and your precious reputation. God forbid anyone in this family was less than perfect."

Whitney looked stricken. Her hand fluttered at her throat.

"It was Chloe's idea to bully Leah." Peyton turned to me with a smug, satisfied smirk. Her confession was to spite her mother. The more agitated Whitney became, the more Peyton revealed.

I could work with that. "Tell me about the bullying."

"Leah was so annoying, so clingy, so needy. She wanted to be around us all the freaking time. Chloe's mom had hired Leah to help tutor Chloe, but Chloe basically had Leah write her papers and do her math homework for her. Chloe needed her around, but she despised her. Chloe had to be nice to her face because of her mom being friends with Leah's mom, so she had this account she used to make fun of Leah anonymously."

I swallowed, fighting back the indignation, the anger, the sorrow. I had to focus. I dug my nails into my palms to keep my thoughts clear. "The LakeshoreTea handle. That was Chloe, too."

Peyton nodded. "She made the Instagram account to tear apart any girl she didn't like. Which was like, everyone but us, pretty much. It started with Taylor in sixth grade. Chloe likes manipulating people, to pick a girl and torture her. To see if she can get everyone in school to join in, too. They always do. It's a game she plays when she's bored. She's bored a lot."

"And the rest of you went along with it? Alexis and Zara, too?"

Peyton gave a dismissive shrug. "They didn't know Chloe started the Instagram account. She kept that tight because of what happened last year. Only I knew, because she knew I'd never tell after what happened to Taylor. But the rest, yeah. They knew. It wasn't, like, that bad."

"Wasn't that bad?" I said, incredulous. Fresh rage surged through me. I thought of Mia's crumpled form in her bed, her devastation when her friends turned on her, the sheer cruelty of LakeshoreTea. I could have strangled Peyton for what she'd done to hurt my child.

"It was just fun, okay? Some girls are too sensitive and get all offended." Peyton frowned, defensive again. "No one really got hurt."

I struggled to rein in my anger. "Until they did."

"That's not my fault, okay? It's all Chloe. It's always Chloe. It was Chloe's idea to do the break-ins, too. To rattle Mia. To scare her. To make sure she knew we could get to her anytime we wanted. She had me do her dirty work, though."

Things were becoming clearer. Despite Peyton's denials, she'd been eager to violate my home, to steal and mutilate our things. I could see it in her face, her whole defiant demeanor, but I had more important things to focus on now.

"What happened at the slumber party? Did Leah find out about Taylor and threaten to tell? Everyone would know. You would've been expelled from school, probably kicked off the swim team."

Peyton's expression darkened. "Leah did find out, okay? But it wasn't like that. Leah found Chloe's burner phone that she used to run the Instagram account and post stuff. That night, when the rest of us were getting ready for the photoshoot in the downstairs bathroom, Chloe went back up to her room, and Leah followed her, to find proof, I guess. She was always quiet and sneaky like that. Chloe told me later that Leah saw Chloe uploading a post on the burner phone. She had it out for us. She was going to tell people."

It was all making terrible sense. That explained why the police didn't find anything incriminating on any of the girls' phones. "I thought Leah reconciled with you guys at the slumber party."

Peyton shrugged. "Leah always wanted to be one of us. Chloe used that to get Leah to change her mind about outing us. Chloe came up with the idea to accept Leah into the group, like Leah always wanted. All she had to do was turn on Mia at the slumber party. Chloe thought it'd be hilarious to watch their friendship implode right in front of us."

My vision tunneled. For a moment, I couldn't breathe.

Mia's worst night, the night that had broken something fundamental in her soul, that had devastated her whole being, had been orchestrated. A game. A social experiment to see if Chloe could turn best friends against each other for sport.

And it had worked. Leah had chosen belonging over loyalty. She had willingly hurt Mia to earn a place at the table. And Mia had been gutted and bewildered, hurt and angry. Just like Chloe wanted.

Chloe had set the stage for what led to everything that followed. The fight. The fall. The murder. She'd wound them up like toys and watched them destroy each other.

And then she'd walked into my house with roses.

The planted rock.

It must have been Chloe.

I'd invited her into my home. She'd been in Mia's room. She must've placed the murder weapon with Leah's blood on it among the sea glass and beach stones.

My hands shook. I clenched them into fists, my nails biting into my palms. The pain helped. It grounded me. I forced myself to take steadying breaths, to keep from screaming.

Peyton recognized the indignation in my face because she backed up a step, raising her palms as if to ward me off. "Look. I didn't hurt Leah. I didn't plant any murder weapon."

"You stole the camera."

"I didn't know what else to do. I knew I should probably get rid of it, but I thought I might need it later, just in case. To protect myself. Everyone was watching. My mom. The neighbors. The cops. I just... I thought it would be safer there, out of my house, just in case."

"To protect yourself from what?"

"Chloe," Peyton said quickly, averting her gaze. "She's the one who called the Detroit Free Press, you know. She leaked Mia's name, told them about the 'violent fight.' That's what she does. She destroys you."

I noted that she hadn't answered my question, but she'd deflected, giving me something else to focus on instead. It worked.

My stomach lurched. The lurid headlines. The "source" who'd known details only someone inside could know.

Chloe had called them and fed them the intimate details, shaping the narrative for maximum damage. She'd wanted Mia publicly condemned. Wanted her branded a murderer before she ever saw a courtroom, the trial over before it began.

This was about annihilation. Chloe didn't just want to get away with murder—she wanted to make sure Mia paid for it.

I saw her then, at the memorial, her gaze focused on Mia, her devastating words like an explosion: *I saw Mia push Leah.* She'd been waiting, all this time, for the perfect moment to detonate that bomb. And boy, had she.

I needed to keep Peyton talking. The more information I had, the more I could use. I'd circle back to the camera and Chloe later. "What happened that night after the midnight photoshoot?"

Peyton closed her eyes for a moment and sucked in a sharp breath, as if trying to remember. "It was like, almost 1 a.m. when Mia came back. Mia was crying, trying to be quiet about it, but I could hear her stumbling around when she put the camera in the case by the patio doors. Leah had gone out with them, but she didn't come back. I thought maybe she walked home, but all her stuff was still in the basement."

"Wait. Mia came back inside, but not Chloe?"

"Not right away. It was like, twenty minutes later. Chloe tiptoed in, then she went to the bathroom, came back in, and laid down in her sleeping bag."

My mind raced. Mia had returned to the basement, terrified and devastated, believing her best friend was dead, while Chloe remained out on the bluff. Doing what? Did she climb back down the bluff to check the body only to realize Leah was alive? Had she already decided this was her opportunity, her perfect scapegoat, her way out?

But then, Chloe couldn't have gone back down the bluff immediately, or at least, she hadn't killed Leah right then, because hours had passed before Leah's death blow. Maybe she had climbed down the bluff later.

I needed more. Whitney watched me with growing consternation. She kept anxiously touching the diamond bracelet at her wrist, her fingers worrying the clasp.

I felt the ticking clock in my blood. It was only a matter of time before she shook herself out of her shocked stupor and physically dragged Peyton back into the house or called the police.

"What happened next?" I asked.

"I couldn't sleep. I can't sleep if I'm not in my own bed. I was worried Leah would tell someone what she'd found out about me anyway, that Chloe's ploy would backfire and just make Leah angrier, and Mia, too. I guess I finally dozed off because a while later, I heard rustling again. Someone was moving, getting out of their sleeping bag. I glanced at my phone—it was just after 3 a.m. I could see enough to know that it was Chloe." Her voice dropped. "She left the basement and went up the stairs. I waited, listening, but she didn't come back down. That's why I was still awake when I saw someone outside."

Everything went still and quiet. The storm, the rain, Whitney. Everything faded. "What?"

"I saw movement through the windows. A dark shape was walking across the yard. It was like 3:30 a.m. I was curious, a little worried. I wanted to see what was going on. I couldn't find my socks or shoes, and it was cold in the basement, and I didn't want to wake anyone else, so I grabbed Mia's fuzzy sloth slippers. They were right by the door."

I kept my face calm, but sheer relief weakened my knees. That explained one mystery, one small piece of the puzzle that vindicated my daughter. She hadn't been lying about the beach, after all. She hadn't knowingly destroyed evidence when she'd washed them.

"Who did you see?" I asked.

"I couldn't tell any details from where I was. It was too dark. I crouched by the window next to the patio doors. There was someone on the bluff. I could see her silhouetted in the moonlight."

"What were they doing?"

"I wasn't sure. Mia's camera was right there by the doors, next to her overnight bag. I used it to take some photos and video so I could zoom in on the screen to see who it was."

My pulse kicked hard in my throat. I wanted to hear her say Chloe's name, to confirm it. "Who was it?"

Even in the dark, I saw the look that flashed across her face. Naked fear. Panic in her eyes, contorting her features. She was afraid of something, or someone.

Peyton was genuinely afraid. Not of legal consequences or her mother's fury—of Chloe.

I saw it clearly now. The leverage. The control. The way Chloe had kept Peyton silent about Taylor for over a year, holding that knowledge over her head like a guillotine, weaponizing it against her. Peyton wasn't just an ally or a friend; she was also a hostage.

"Peyton, who did you see?"

"I..." Peyton's face went white. Her hands trembled. She glanced warily toward the house, then back at the dark bluff. She shot a pleading, frantic look at her mother. "I can't say. The photos are my insurance. That's why I buried it instead of destroying it."

"Just a minute." Whitney straightened, jolting back into herself. "You have the camera. Don't you already know what's on there?"

I hesitated a fraction too long. "We're working on recovering a few corrupted files. And if we can't, the police can—"

"Enough!" Whitney's face shifted. Shock hardened into something sharper. Survival. She stepped forward and grabbed Peyton. Her fingers dug into Peyton's arm, knuckles bone white. "We're done here."

This time, Peyton allowed her mother to take charge. Whitney steered her across the deck toward the French doors. As she passed me, Peyton offered an apologetic look. "I'm sorry. I can't. If I tell you, she'll..."

"She'll what? Who? Who was it?" I called after Peyton. "Tell me it was Chloe!"

Whitney paused at the doors and glared at me over her shoulder. "Leave us alone. If you set foot on this property again, or if you speak a word to my daughter, I'll have you arrested for trespassing and harassment. Go to hell, Dahlia."

Then they were inside, swallowed by the warm light.

I moved off the deck with stiff legs, taking the stairs along the side of the house to the yard. Cold rain slapped me in the face. I ducked my head and moved toward the road, toward home.

The waves roared. The wind buffeted my back. My hair was plastered to my skull, my neck, my cheeks. My clothes were instantly drenched. I hardly noticed.

My mind scrambled to catch up, replaying every interaction through this new lens. The memorial performance. The nightmares. Everything I thought I knew reordered itself around a different center of gravity. Around Chloe.

Beautiful, fragile, sweet Chloe. Her true nature hidden behind that perfect white-teeth smile, the designer clothes, the practiced charm.

She'd been right there, the whole time.

But how could I prove it to save Mia?

My phone buzzed in my soaked pocket. I fumbled it out, shielding the screen as best I could from the rain.

It was Zara.

"Um, I got your number from my mom," she said. "I got into the corrupted files. My mom is here, too. You should come take a look. Like, right now."

I was already sprinting down the street. "I'm on my way."

Chapter Forty-Six

Early morning fog hung low over the water and the street, swallowing houses whole. I stopped at the base of Rowan's driveway. An unmarked sedan sat at the curb three houses down, its windows dark. I didn't let myself look at it.

It was 8:10 a.m. on Monday, April 18th. Ten days after Leah's murder. Two hours until Mia's arraignment. Until the court charged my daughter with murder.

My breath came shallow and fast. I shivered in my jean jacket and hoodie as I climbed the porch steps. I knocked on the door before doubt could pull me back.

Rowan opened the door as if she'd been waiting for me. Her hair was smoothed into a low knot, her makeup pristine despite the early hour. Concern slid across her face like a curtain drawn into place.

"Oh, sweetheart." Her voice dropped to a crisis-management murmur, the one she used for PTA emergencies and charity-gala meltdowns. "Let's get you inside. Quickly, before anyone sees you like this."

Warm air enveloped me, thick with the scents of lemon cleaner and something floral. A bouquet was arranged on the console table, brimming with yellow marigolds, pale roses, and spiky red dahlias, my namesake.

In the mirror behind the bouquet, I caught a glimpse of my reflection: red-rimmed eyes, sallow skin, hair tangled wild from wind and sleeplessness.

I looked wrecked. Good.

Rowan's hand settled at my elbow. The door clicked shut behind me. "You poor thing. You haven't slept, have you? Of course you haven't. Let's get you warmed up. I made Rosemary and Sea Salt Focaccia last night. I'll slice you some. And tea, obviously. Sit. I'll handle everything."

"Tea would be nice," I said. Talking felt like rubbing sandpaper over my throat.

She steered me down the hallway into the sunken living room and guided me to the sofa, one hand still at my elbow. "Gregory just left for a round of golf at Harbor Shores, and Chloe's upstairs sleeping, still not well enough for the trials of school yet, so we have the place to ourselves for now."

Outside the wall of windows, white fog pressed against the glass like something trying to get in. The room was immaculate, clean, and catalog-perfect. The throw pillows sat at precise angles. Coffee table books stacked by size. The throws on the couch folded primly.

My eyes burned. I blinked away tears. "I didn't know where else to go. You're the only one who will talk to me. I don't know what to do."

"Sit," Rowan said. "I'll be right back."

I sank into the couch, still shivering. I hunched forward, arms wrapped tightly around my ribcage, making myself small. Part performance, part real. I hadn't slept, hadn't eaten. My bones were vibrating inside my skin.

Rowan returned a few minutes later with two steaming mugs with gold rims. She handed me one and set hers down on the white oak coffee table. "Jasmine Hibiscus. You'll love it."

The mug was heavy in my hands. Heat seeped into my stiff

fingers. I held it close to my chest and let the steam warm my face. "Thank you."

She disappeared into the kitchen and appeared again with a plate of warmed focaccia drizzled with honey. She set one beside me and seated herself on the linen armchair opposite me.

"You haven't slept." Not a question, an assessment. Her gaze moved over my face like she was cataloging damage. "When did you eat last?"

"I don't remember."

She made a soft sound, sympathy or disapproval, I couldn't tell. "Tea and artisanal bread, then I'll make you something else if you're still hungry. You can't think straight if you're running on empty."

I hadn't seen my daughter in over twelve agonizing hours. Sleep eluded me entirely last night as I tossed and turned in my bed, plotting and planning, my mind racing in circles like a trapped animal.

"Chloe's devastated." Rowan's fingertips traced the rim of her mug. "She hasn't been sleeping, either. Keeps replaying it in her head, wishing she'd never suggested the photoshoot, never planned the party at all." A pause, perfectly timed. "She blames herself for what happened."

I kept my eyes on the tea and let her talk.

"I can't imagine what you're going through," she continued, leaning forward slightly. "With the arraignment. With everything."

Of course, she'd already heard. Rumors traveled fast in Blackthorn Shores.

"The detectives have new information." I watched her face. "Leah didn't die right away. She was alive after the fall."

Rowan's eyebrows rose in a flicker of surprise. "What?"

"She was unconscious for hours, that's why Mia and Chloe thought she was dead, but she woke up. She tried to crawl back up the bluff."

Rowan's hand went to her throat. "How tragic. Vivienne must

be beside herself. Any mother would be. Poor Leah, suffering like that before she died."

"She didn't make it, though. Because someone got to her first."

Rowan went still. The only sound was the ticking clock and our breathing. "That's—that's terrible."

"Someone went back a few hours later. They climbed down the bluff and bashed her head in."

Rowan's fingers tightened on her mug. "Bashed—you mean—"

"The ME says the wound couldn't have happened in the fall."

The fog pressed against the windows.

"And the police believe... what, exactly? That it was intentional? Not a heat-of-the-moment mistake?"

I nodded. My eyes stung. I let the tears spill, hot and ugly. I clutched the mug to my chest with both hands. "They're going to charge her with murder, not manslaughter. Murder in the first degree."

Her face stayed composed. "I'm so sorry, Dahlia. I can't imagine."

"The thing is, Mia isn't a killer. She never meant to hurt her best friend."

She took a sip of tea. "Children make terrible mistakes sometimes. Even the sweetest ones. We never truly know what other people are capable of, do we? Not even our own daughters."

I drew a stuttering breath. "I keep thinking there's something the police missed. Something that would help Mia."

Rowan tilted her head. Compassionate, understanding. That listening posture, the one that made you want to confess everything to her. "What do you mean?"

"I couldn't sleep. I kept seeing it—the bluff, the fall. So I went out there, early this morning, with a flashlight."

Her expression didn't change. Something flickered in her eyes. "You went to my bluff? On my property?"

"I had to. I needed things to make sense." I bit my lip. "I found something."

"What did you find?"

I rubbed my palm on my jeans to steady my jangling nerves. My pulse thudded too loud in my ears. "Evidence. But I don't know what it means."

"Dahlia." She shifted, set her tea next to the plate with the untouched bread, and reached for my free hand. Her hand covered mine, warm and comforting. "You can trust me."

"I don't know what it means."

"Have you told the police?"

I shook my head.

"Why not?"

I looked at our hands, hers steady, mine trembling. "Because I don't know if it'll help Mia or make everything worse."

"What kind of evidence are we talking about? Clothing? A weapon?"

"I don't want to say until you look at it. Until you tell me what it means."

Her brows knitted together. "If you found evidence at a crime scene and moved it, that's tampering."

"I was going to call Detective King after I talked to you. I didn't want to do the wrong thing."

She studied my face. "Why didn't you call the detectives immediately? Why come to me?"

"Because you're the only person who's stood by me through all of this." I met her eyes. "I trust you."

Something crossed her face. Satisfaction, maybe. Or relief. Her shoulders dropped half an inch. She withdrew her hand, sat back, and glanced at the windows, the fog. "Is it still out there? On the bluff?"

I shook my head.

Her gaze swept over me as if trying to determine where I might be hiding something. "You have it? Here?"

I nodded. My hand moved reflexively to my hoodie pocket.

Her eyes tracked the movement as she picked up her mug and sipped her tea. "Well, I suppose we could take a look."

"Not in here." I glanced toward the windows as if afraid a nosy neighbor might materialize out of the fog. "Outside. I want to show you where I found it."

Rowan set her mug down. Her knees brushed the coffee table. The magazines shifted, the neat pile now misaligned. "Actually, yes. Let's go now."

I blinked up at her. "Now?"

She rose gracefully to her feet. "Before you call the police. Let me help you understand what it means before you do something you can't take back. I can't help you if you don't tell me everything." She paused. "No offense, but I need to make sure you're not wearing a wire or recording anything."

I stared at her. "Rowan, why would I do that?"

Her smile widened. "I want to help you, Dahlia, you know I do, but I have to make sure. Surely, you understand. This is a sensitive topic. It could easily be... misconstrued... if someone were to overhear and take it the wrong way."

I nodded dully. Obediently, I tugged my phone from my jacket pocket, showed her I wasn't recording anything, and stood stiffly, my heart jackhammering while she patted me down.

She flashed me a wry smile, like we were both in on an inside joke. "I know it's silly. Thank you for humoring me. Now we can go."

I followed her through the great room to the patio doors and stepped onto the back patio.

The fog swallowed the world. The yard, the line of ferns along the fence, the path that led toward the bluff—everything transformed into vague, smeared outlines. Sound was both muffled and amplified, the waves a rhythmic murmur, like a ghost whispering in my ear.

We crossed the flagstone patio and walked across the dew-stippled lawn toward the bluff. Rowan sauntered ahead, her shoulders squared. I followed three paces behind, one hand in my hoodie pocket, maintaining enough distance to run if I needed to.

There were no witnesses. No one would hear a scream over the waves. A dog barked somewhere, the sound flat and directionless. Then a distant scraping sound, like a window sliding open or shut. I glanced back toward the street, but the fog obscured everything.

To our left, Mrs. Atkins's house was a white blur. A row of dark pines marked the property line between the two yards, their shapes ghostly in the mist.

At the bluff, the yard ended. The water had vanished, the sky invisible. The steep drop disappeared into nothingness. Rowan didn't look in the direction of the lake but stared intently at me. "Where on the bluff did you find it?"

Inside my hoodie pocket, my fingers found the bag. Cold plastic, and beneath it, the irregular shape of the rock. I curled my fingers around the solid weight of it, the plastic crackling.

Rowan's gaze dropped to my hand inside my pocket, then back to my face. Waiting.

We were three feet from the edge. This was where Leah had stood in the moonlight, dizzy with adrenaline and panic and fear. Where she'd felt the ground disappear beneath her feet. Where hours later, she'd attempted to claw back up, broken and bleeding, to save herself.

I couldn't see the water, but I heard the relentless waves. The same sound Leah heard before she died.

I brought the bag out of my pocket. The rock sat heavy in the plastic, its weight obscene in my hand. This ordinary rock had caved in a child's skull. The dark smears showed almost black. Two fine strands caught the light—black hair, stuck in dried blood.

My stomach roiled. I wanted to drop it, hurl it into the lake, scrub my sullied hands raw. Instead, I held it between us.

Rowan stared at it in horror. "What the hell is that?"

"I found this. There's blood on it, and hair. I think someone used this to..." I couldn't finish. I didn't need to.

Rowan's pupils contracted. Her lips parted, not quite a gasp, something sharper. Her intent gaze remained on the rock.

I looked at the rock in my hand. At Rowan. Then at the water beyond the bluff, as if I might throw it in. "I need to tell you something."

Rowan watched me, waiting.

"I wasn't truthful just now."

"What are you trying to say, Dahlia?"

"I didn't find this out here on the bluff." I forced myself to meet her eyes. "It was in Mia's room."

She didn't blink. Something smoothed in her face. "The police didn't find it in their search?"

"I hid it. I was scared."

"That's understandable."

"I keep thinking, if I hadn't seen it first—if the cops had found it—Mia wouldn't have a chance. They'd charge her as an adult. They'd lock her up forever and throw away the key."

Rowan took a step toward me. Her expression softened. "We can make sure that never happens, Dahlia. I can make it disappear. Let me protect you both."

My whole body was shaking. "You'd really help us? I'm so tired of being afraid, Rowan. So tired."

"Of course I'll help. That's what friends do." Her gaze stayed on the rock, not on me. "Give it to me. I'll take care of it."

I held the rock closer to my chest. The wind tugged at my hair. "My mind keeps spinning. I can't sleep. I keep thinking I should have been a better mom. Done things differently. Then none of this would've happened. How could I not have known? My own daughter. How could she hide so much from me?"

A flash of impatience in her eyes, just a flicker, then it was gone. "I'm sure you did your best, honey. Give me the rock. Let me help you."

"I can't believe she's a killer. How could I have missed it?"

"I mean, I can see how you'd miss it," she said coolly. "Mia hiding it in plain sight like that in her beach glass collection. Besides, no mother wants to think her daughter is capable of such a thing. But she was, Dahlia. And you have to face that."

She held out her hand.

The Guilty Ones

I looked at her hand. The fog deepened, soft and heavy, stifling. "In her beach glass collection. Hiding in plain sight."

She blinked. "Exactly. Which is why you need my help."

There it was. My spine straightened. I stopped trembling. I felt Marcus's wedding ring, a solid presence against my heart. "I never said it was in her beach glass collection."

The waves rolled far below. Rowan's hand hung between us, palm held up, expectant.

Her mouth opened. Closed. Her eyes flicked to the rock in my hand, then past me—toward the street, the houses still invisible, wrapped in dense fog. "Sweetheart, you did."

"I didn't."

Her nostrils flared. "You've been awake for days. You're not thinking clearly. Remember last week when you couldn't recall if you locked the door? Or when you thought someone had broken in and moved your things? Grief does that. You're not—" She hesitated, choosing her words carefully. "You're not yourself right now. I'd forget things, too, if I were in your shoes."

"I didn't forget anything."

"It's an easy mistake to make."

"I didn't make a mistake."

She smiled that polite, indulgent smile. The kind you make when you humor a child. "Honey, everyone knows Mia collects beach glass and polished stones. You've posted pictures. It isn't a secret."

"I never told you where I found it." I held her gaze. My voice was steel. "You knew exactly where it was. Because you put it there."

Chapter Forty-Seven

My words came out calm and detached. Inside, everything had gone quiet. "You framed Mia for murder. I thought it was Alexis, then Peyton, and then Chloe, when she came over and used the bathroom, but it was you."

I imagined Rowan in my house, in Mia's room, placing the rock, tucking it among the smooth stones and colored glass like a viper coiled in a garden. Knowing the arrest warrant was coming, what the police would find.

"It must have been on Friday morning, when Mia and I left for the precinct, because the locksmith came at 11 a.m. You waited until you knew we weren't home."

I recalled how Apollo had behaved strangely, sniffing several spots inside the house, acting agitated and anxious. I thought he was responding to Mia's distress, but it was more than that. Rowan had been inside the house. Visitors always riled him up.

"You had the spare key when Brooke gave it to you before Thanksgiving. You made her think she hadn't remembered correctly when she brought it up that day, but she had. You must have made a copy before you gave it back. That was months ago. Do you make copies of all your friends' keys?"

Rowan stared at me blankly for a tense moment. Then her

expression shifted. Not in panic, not yet. Something softer, wounded. She took a small step back, one hand pressed to her chest. "Dahlia. Sweetheart. Listen to yourself. How can you say such hurtful things? Why would I do any of that?"

But I knew now, without a doubt.

"Mia didn't go back down the bluff to murder a child. And neither did Chloe." I held her gaze. "But you did."

"That's absurd. Why would I possibly want to hurt Leah?"

"To protect Chloe. And yourself."

The air between us felt sharpened, honed to a dangerous edge.

"I care about you," Rowan said. "We all do. That's why I'm trying to help. But you're not thinking clearly right now. You need rest. I hate to say it, but perhaps a clinic, a therapeutic retreat—"

"You would do anything for your daughter, wouldn't you? Even kill a teenage girl who was still alive, who could tell everyone the truth. Leah found out about Chloe. Leah uncovered who your daughter really is."

"I have no idea what you're talking about."

"You couldn't have that. You couldn't allow your perfect life to blow up. Everyone would know. You'd be the one ostracized. Whispered about. Laughed at. You'd be canceled. You couldn't allow it."

Rowan blinked rapidly. A blue vein pulsed at her temple. "I think you should leave."

"What happened?" I asked. "After Leah fell and Mia went inside crying, thinking she'd killed her best friend, did Chloe climb down the bluff and realize Leah was still alive? She went to you for help, didn't she?"

"You're projecting. Imagining things. You're clearly unwell, Dahlia."

"Peyton was awake. She saw you and took pictures. She hid the camera. I found it."

Rowan went rigid. "How dare you come here and make vile accusations against my daughter and me? How dare you!"

My throat was dry, but my voice held. "They aren't accusations. They're the truth. Each is photo is time-stamped. At 3:32 a.m., someone went down the bluff. At 3:36 a.m., the same person came back up with a rock in her hand. It was you."

"A few blurry shots at night?" she asked, shaking her head as if disappointed in me. "That could be anyone."

"The photos are clear. So is the video."

"Grief does strange things to the mind. First Marcus, now Mia's situation. Of course, you're creating stories to shift your own blame."

"Admit it," I said. "Give up the lies. You've been found out."

Something rippled across her face: a calculation, a pivot, a new mask. She leaned toward me, her voice was softer now, like velvet over sharp teeth. "It doesn't have to be this way."

I stiffened. "What way?"

"We can figure this out, you and me. Mother to mother." She smiled the dazzling gala smile, the one that used to make me want to be her. "Give me the camera. I'll destroy it. I'll have Chloe alter her statement. Leah slipped, Mia didn't push her. Chloe's testimony is the key to the prosecution's case. Memory can be faulty. It can change, clarify."

She moved a step closer. The fog wrapped around us in a thick blanket. Her voice turned intimate, conspiratorial. "We can make this go away. I'll retain Radcliffe & Simon, the best criminal defense attorneys in Michigan. Mia never sees a cell. Not for murder, not for manslaughter, not for anything."

The world narrowed to her voice. "I'll put two million in a trust for you and Mia. You will never worry about bills again. I'll have my accountant clear your debt by Friday, with a substantial college fund for Mia. You will be comfortable. Safe. One of us."

Numbers gleamed like lures. I saw tuition bills vanish, a new sea wall, the crumbling bluff shored up. I saw Mia in a sunny dorm room, laughing with girls who didn't look past her to what we lacked. I saw us not drowning. I saw us living, free and happy.

For one terrible heartbeat, I felt myself tipping toward yes. How easy it would be to capitulate. How simple.

Rowan knew exactly what she was offering. Not just money but belonging. The shining thing I'd chased my whole life.

I imagined what it might be like if I handed over the camera and the rock. If I let the fog swallow Leah's last hours as she bled and suffered, her desperate hope that someone would come to save her.

If I let Rowan make it disappear, let Mia walk free while Leah stayed buried in lies.

Vivienne's face surfaced in my mind. Her hollowed, flayed grief. And me, years from now, looking at Mia across the dinner table, knowing what I'd done, what I'd taught her about truth and consequence and the cost of loving someone.

The weight in my chest turned hard as the rock in my hand. I straightened my spine and met her eyes as I felt something settle inside me. Not peace, but certainty. Resolution. "No."

Her lip curled in disdain. In a blink, her whole face turned ugly. The speed of the transformation chilled me to the bone. "She'll go to prison. You'd do that to her? What kind of mother are you?"

The kind who tried to do the right thing. Who didn't always succeed, but who kept trying anyway. "Mia did push Leah. She did cause harm, though she didn't mean to. She'll accept the consequences, and I'll be there beside her, every step of the way. We won't hide. We won't lie."

Her mouth flattened. "How much do you want? Name your price. I'll write a check now."

"I don't want your blood money."

"You're throwing away your daughter's future. And your own."

"Chloe is going to watch you go to jail for thirty years," I said. "She's going to see you for exactly what you are. A killer."

"You think you have the high ground, Dahlia? Please. Spare me." She took a step, then another, closing the space between us. "You walk around with your nose in the air like you're better than us. You think you wouldn't do anything to protect your daughter?"

"No," I said. "I wouldn't." Almost anything, but not that.

Her smile sharpened. "You're nothing. You know that, right? I made these women accept you. I took you in, told everyone to tolerate your frumpy thrift-store clothes, your disgusting neediness, your ugly shack sliding off a cliff, as pathetic as you are."

Once, those words would have flayed me, destroyed me. Not anymore.

Rowan loomed over me, a vicious glint in her eyes. This was who she truly was.

I tried to take a step back. I realized abruptly that I couldn't. Vertigo slithered through me. Somehow, through our discussion, Rowan had shifted me nearer to the bluff. I was less than a foot from the edge.

Below, invisible in the fog, the steep drop-off lurked. The treacherous fallen logs, the lethal rocks, the spiky branches. The same perilous bluff that had broken Leah's body.

"Enough of your games." Rowan sneered. All pretext had vanished. The tendons stood out on her neck, her eyes bulging with fury. "Where's the camera, Dahlia?"

"In a safe place. You'll never touch it. It's over."

Rowan bared her teeth. "Tell me where it is or so help me—"

"What? You'll smash my skull, too?"

The fog slithered around us, between us. The houses around us might as well have been a hundred miles away. Damp tendrils of hair clung to my cheeks. "You murdered a child, Rowan."

"She was dying anyway! She would've been brain-dead. I ended her suffering." She said it like she was describing putting down a sick dog. "I did Vivienne and Daniel a favor."

There it was. Deliberate, calculated. Rowan had climbed down that bluff, found Leah broken and suffering, and decided her life wasn't worth saving. Decided it was easier, cleaner, to murder a child.

Mercy, she called it. As if she had the right.

I stared at her, sickened. "By crushing a child's skull with a rock."

"I protected my family!" Her chest heaved. "I did what any mother would do."

"Stop. Just stop with the lies. You were protecting yourself."

Her beautiful features twisted into something grotesque. The blue vein pulsed in her forehead. "Give me the camera, Dahlia."

I was done here. I'd gotten what I needed. The naked truth exposed between us, finally.

I attempted to step around her, back toward the house, toward solid ground. Away from her. "It's over, Rowan."

"No!" Rowan lunged for me. Her right hand closed around my throat. Her face inches from mine, cheeks flushed pink, eyes bright with a feverish light. "You don't decide what happens. You don't know what I've sacrificed. What I've had to do to build this life!"

Fear sliced through me. I was inches from the edge. The unstable ground shifted beneath my feet. I felt it soften and start to give.

I clawed at Rowan's wrist with my free hand. My vision tunneled. White spots danced in front of my eyes. My lungs screamed, I couldn't get air. I couldn't speak, couldn't say the words that would save me.

Panic surged in my chest. I was about to fall.

"You're nothing," Rowan snarled, her breath hot on my face. "Just like that stupid girl. She was a parasite. A waste. A nobody. She didn't get to destroy everything I've worked so hard for. Neither do you."

Her hand clenched tight around my throat. With her other hand, she snatched the rock in its plastic bag from my fingers. Then she shoved me.

The world tilted. My heels skidded in wet grass, my feet scrabbling in desperation. The edge crumbled under my shoes. Chunks of earth tumbled into nothing, the sound swallowed by fog and distance.

The same edge Leah had gone over. The same drop. The same fall.

Rowan raised the rock above my head.

I scratched at her face. My fingernails raked her cheeks. Rowan screamed. Her grip loosened. I wrenched free, twisted sideways, and fell to my knees. "Help!" I croaked.

"Stop!" A voice shouted through the fog. "Police! Hands where I can see them!"

Rowan's head snapped toward the sound. I scrambled backward to safer ground. The world wavered. My breath tore from my bruised throat, my body shaking and dizzy, like I needed to lie down or I might dissolve into a puddle of nothingness.

Fifty feet to the south, Detective King appeared from behind the line of pines that separated Rowan's property from Mrs. Atkins's. He sprinted toward us, holding a gun in both hands. "Rowan Westinghouse, don't move!"

Several more officers appeared as they sprinted toward us, all armed. Detective Callahan brought up the rear, speaking urgently into a walkie-talkie.

Alarmed, Rowan stepped back. The rock hung loose in her hand. Her eyes widened with shock, fear, and calculation: how long he'd been there, what he'd heard.

Relief hit me so hard I nearly collapsed.

Safe. I was safe. The plan had worked.

Her cold gaze fell on me. "What did you do?"

My voice rasped, my throat burning, but I could speak. "I called Detective King last night. I showed him the camera. The rock. Everything."

I confessed all of it, the things I'd done and the things I'd learned about Whitney and Peyton, Alexis and Brooke, Chloe and Rowan. And my own failures. Every single dark and dangerous thing.

Only now did I allow myself to think of the wire Callahan had placed on me early this morning, hidden so discreetly at my underwear line that only a professional would have caught it, maybe.

And Rowan, despite her considerable ego, wasn't as smart as she thought she was.

"You didn't find the wire I'm wearing. The police heard everything."

Before Rowan could react, King advanced toward us. The gun was trained on Rowan. "Move back. Step away from Ms. Kincaid. On your knees, hands behind your head. Now!"

Rowan dropped the rock as if it had branded her palm. She frantically searched for an exit, an escape, a chance. There was none. Reluctantly, she lifted her hands, palms out. "You can't be on my property! I didn't permit it!"

Callahan grinned. Those sharp eyes were focused on Rowan now. "Mrs. Atkins was more than happy to host us."

I scrambled to my feet, rubbing my raw throat as I glanced over at Mrs. Atkins's house. The fog had lifted enough to reveal a figure standing in the second-story window. Mrs. Atkins waved at me. I managed a small wave back. "Turns out not everyone adores you like you think, Rowan."

"Detectives." Rowan's signature smile came back, smooth and gracious. "You know who I am. This is all an unfortunate misunderstanding. This poor woman is hysterical. Unstable. She's been stalking me, desperate to blame anyone but her psychotic daughter for Leah's death—"

"Turn around," King repeated, ignoring her. He lowered the gun and removed a pair of handcuffs. "On your knees. I won't warn you again."

She did, carefully. "You're making a huge mistake."

King cuffed her wrists. She flinched as if he'd struck her. "Rowan Westinghouse, you're under arrest for the murder of Leah Cho."

Chapter Forty-Eight

In the distance, sirens wailed. A small voice filtered through the fog. "Mom?"

I turned. Chloe stood there, barefoot on the wet grass. Her blonde hair in disarray, her silky polka-dotted pajamas wrinkled from sleep.

Without her makeup, her bare face looked impossibly young. She was still a child. A child who had intentionally harmed other children. "What's happening?"

Part of me wanted to shield her from what was to come next. She was fourteen, barefoot, about to watch her mother dragged away in handcuffs. But another part of me remained stone cold.

Chloe had chosen cruelty again and again. She'd lied, schemed, and bullied. She'd let Mia take the fall. I couldn't forget that, not ever.

Detective King hauled Rowan to her feet. At the sight of her daughter, her face blanched. "Chloe."

"Mom?" Chloe's voice splintered in panic. "Why are the police here?"

Rowan's smile was wrong. It showed too many teeth. "Chloe, baby, I did this for you—"

"No," I said. "You did it for yourself."

Chloe flinched. She stared at her mother like she was seeing a stranger in her mother's skin. Clothes disheveled. Hair and eyes wild. Wrists pinned behind her back.

"Honey, we can fix this," Rowan shouted. "Call your father. Mrs. Davis, our lawyer. We'll call everyone. They can't do this to us!"

The sirens wailed louder. Doors slammed. Four officers rounded the corner of Rowan's house and jogged toward us across the grass. Two took positions on either side of King as one spoke into his radio. The fourth headed toward the house to secure the scene. On the bluff, seagulls cried somewhere low in the fog.

"Ma'am." One of the uniformed officers took Rowan's elbow and guided her toward the squad cars lined up in the driveway. "Let's go."

"Get your hands off me!" Rowan's voice sharpened. "You have no idea who you're dealing with. Do you know who my husband is? You touch my family, and I'll sue your whole department!"

She kept shouting at them. Threats, lawyers, a tangle of names. But the power had already drained out of her. At the corner of the house, she attempted to twist around. "Chloe, look at me!" The fog swallowed her words, then her form. "Chloe!"

Chloe didn't move, didn't react or respond. She stood with her arms at her sides, mouth slack, pupils blown wide, her eyes empty. She didn't blink, didn't cry. Just stared at the space where her mother had been, as if the fog had simply erased her.

A female officer approached Chloe, placed a jacket around her slumped shoulders, and spoke in a soft voice. The officer gently guided Chloe back toward the house, away from the bluff.

I watched until Rowan disappeared around the house. My throat throbbed where Rowan's fingers had pressed. Every swallow was glass. My vision kept pulsing black at the edges.

I'd been a heartbeat from going over the edge, a heartbeat from Leah's fate.

My knees wanted to buckle. The adrenaline that had kept me upright drained away.

I felt no triumph. There was nothing to win here. Only grief and sorrow and more loss than any of us could count.

King strode over to me. He reached out, palm up. "We'll need that, please."

I looked down at my fist. He took the rock, still in its baggie, from my hand. I didn't recall picking it up after Rowan had dropped it.

The detective passed it on to an evidence tech, who sealed the rock in a new evidence bag and took it to one of the squad cars in the driveway.

King looked over his shoulder toward the house, then back to me. "You did good."

Something in my chest loosened. Not pride, exactly. Not relief. But the acknowledgment that I'd done what I could, that I'd tried my best. After days of being dismissed, doubted, and treated like a hysterical mother inventing conspiracies, it was something.

"I had to. For Mia. For Leah." The words cracked something open inside me. I was shaking, trembling uncontrollably. Had I done it? Was it enough?

I hadn't realized I'd said the words aloud until he put a hand on my arm. "It's enough."

Hope surged so fast and fierce it felt like drowning in reverse—violent, overwhelming, almost painful. I could see Mia walking out those courthouse doors, see myself holding her, feel her weight in my arms again. Real. Solid. Mine.

King's voice gentled. "Rowan assaulted you. That's an additional crime we can charge her with. We need to get that bruising documented and take your statement. I've already called an ambulance."

It felt like gulping pure oxygen after nearly drowning. "I need to be there. I need my daughter."

I tugged my phone from my back pocket. My fingers were so clumsy, it took a second to unlock the code. I'd missed several texts from Camille. We had been in near constant communication since last night, since I revealed Peyton's confession and we saw the camera files.

With Camille at my side, I'd contacted Detective King. We made a deal: I would wear a wire and get Rowan's confession. In exchange, Mia would not be charged with attempted manslaughter or aggravated assault.

I met the detective's eyes. "I'm not going to a hospital. I'm going to the courthouse."

He gave me an appraising look. Whatever he saw in me, the fierceness, the determination, the wild reckless need of a mother desperate to see her child—he relented. "I'll have the ambulance take us to the courthouse so they can check you out on the way. I'll ride along and take your statement."

The fog was beginning to lift. The shape of the world appeared again. Somewhere in front of me, a car door slammed. Someone said my name. The minutes couldn't pass fast enough. All I could think of was Mia.

Exhaustion pulled at me, my legs shaky. I didn't care. The ambulance drove down Wyld Wood Lane and pulled into Rowan's driveway as I looked past the squad cars with their lights still spinning red and blue, through thinning fog that had finally let the morning through. Toward Mia.

I started running.

Chapter Forty-Nine

I burst through the double doors of the courtroom, sound ricocheting off the high ceiling. Moments before, the ambulance had dropped me off at the curb with King's blessing.

My shirt clung damp to my back with nervous sweat. My hands were clammy, Rowan's finger marks forming red rings on my throat, hot and tender when I swallowed.

Every head turned. For a moment, time seemed to stop.

Mia was here. That was all that mattered.

My legs threatened to give out, my knees buckling as I slid into the seat beside my daughter at the defense table. Mia hunched in her seat, her hair tugged back in a loose ponytail, purplish hollows beneath her eyes like bruises. She seemed smaller than yesterday, as if a single night in detention had hollowed her out. I had never felt this terrified of losing her.

Camille looked over and gave me a nod without breaking her low murmur to Mia.

The bailiff called the case, the judge took his seat, and the lawyers exchanged legalese that my brain could not comprehend, their words blurring into a drone of terms and citations as I waited, every muscle taut, barely breathing.

The district attorney rose. "Due to the additional evidence that has come to light, we're dropping the charge of murder in the first degree and reducing it to assault due to Mia Kincaid's youth. We are asking the court to accept the deal and set aside the charges, providing Mia and Ms. Kincaid continue to testify and cooperate against the new defendant in the murder of Leah Cho."

"Ms. Kincaid," the judge said in a deep baritone, glaring at me over his glasses. "The court has reviewed the non-prosecution agreement and the transactional immunity that goes along with it. The court is willing to accept the terms and conditions of the agreement, provided you cooperate fully with the District Attorney's office. If the charges are set aside, they will be sealed with no record. Do you understand?"

"Yes," I said.

"Yes, sir," Mia answered in a tremulous voice.

The gavel struck, sharp and final.

For a moment, nothing in the room moved. The air itself felt suspended. Camille leaned down, said something low, and gave Mia's shoulder a reassuring squeeze.

Mia turned. Her eyes found mine. They were wide, disbelieving, hardly daring to hope.

I stood before I consciously decided to move. Then Mia was on her feet, too. I hugged her to my chest as she clutched me with a ferocity that brought sudden tears to my eyes.

Her face pressed into my shoulder, her breath hot and ragged against my skin. Her ribs expanded and contracted beneath my hands. She smelled like soap and sweat and fear, and underneath it all, faintly, like herself. I held her tighter.

"It's over," I whispered into her hair. "It's over, baby."

The lie was out before I could stop it. I knew better. The ordeal was not over for those who loved Leah. It was not over for Vivienne and Daniel in their grief. It was not over for us, either.

This deal was not an eraser. It did not rewind time or unmake tragedy, nor did it absolve us of our mistakes or wrongdoings.

But it was an open door that had not been open before.

Mia pulled back enough for me to see her face. "I was so afraid."

"I know." I cupped her cheeks with both hands and rested my forehead against hers. We breathed the same air, the din of the room a haze around us.

None of it mattered. We were together.

Camille touched my shoulder. "We should go. The media are waiting."

Of course. The media were always waiting.

Outside, a dozen flashbulbs exploded in our eyes, the white afterimages burning into my vision. Reporters surged forward. Bodies and cameras and microphones jammed together to block our way.

I caught sight of Vivienne across the lawn. A mother standing alone, forlorn and straight-backed, arms at her sides. She watched us move past her. Then our eyes met.

Something passed between us. Recognition, maybe. She had lost Leah forever, while I still had Mia. That was the gulf between us. It was not forgiveness. It couldn't be, not yet, perhaps not ever.

Then she was gone, swallowed by the crowd.

The crush loosened near the curb. We moved as a unit toward the parking lot, Mia in the middle, Camille on one side, me on the other.

Mia looked up at me. In her eyes, the fear was still there, but something else had joined it, tentative and bright as a match flame. "I want to go home."

Home wasn't simply our ramshackle cottage clinging to a cliff. Home was the small castle we had built inside it, that we had constructed together with two spoons and a shared blanket, with burned toast and inside jokes, with a thousand apologies and a promise I had not always kept but had never stopped making: I will not leave you alone in the dark.

That promise had been tested. It had bent under the weight of secrets and lies, but it had not broken.

After everything, the safe place we had built remained ours. We still knew the way back to it.

I tightened my arm around her, relishing the warmth of her shoulder beneath my hand. We walked toward the car together.

"Yes," I said. "Let's go home."

Chapter Fifty

I positioned the canvas on the wall. The watercolor painting that captured Lake Michigan at sunset, the lighthouse, and the spray of wildflowers. Leah's painting.

The canvas had been slashed, defaced, but the restoration expert had worked miracles. If you looked closely, you could still see where the wound had been, faint seams like scars.

Mia stood in the doorway watching me. We hadn't discussed where to hang it. We knew it belonged here, in our living room, where we could see it every day, a reminder of Leah's life, her creativity.

"Do you think it's straight?" I asked.

Mia tilted her head. "A little higher on the left."

I nudged the corner up. "How about now?"

"Good enough for you, Mom."

I made a face at her; she rolled her eyes. The ghost of a smile touched her lips.

One month had passed since Rowan's arrest. Thirty-one days since the truth cracked open the life we'd built here and revealed the rot festering beneath. The ugliness, the secrets, the lies.

Rowan had been charged with murder in the first degree. She sat in a county jail cell, denied bail, waiting for a trial that would determine whether she'd spend the next thirty years behind bars. The confession I'd tricked from her had given the D.A.'s office everything they needed to lock her away.

When the detectives searched her home, they found a collection of copied keys hidden in her nightstand, mine included. She kept them like trophies, silent proof of the control and power she wielded over the people who trusted her. The neighbors who'd smiled at her. The mothers who'd sat beside her at fundraisers, galas, and PTA meetings, believing they were safe.

She wasn't in control anymore.

Last week, Camille met us in her office with a stack of papers and a measured smile. With Camille's help, Mia's sentence had been reduced to simple assault. The juvenile family court had sentenced her to 500 hours of community service, in which she'd participate in an anti-bullying program, sharing her story with thousands of students within our local school district.

None of it brought Leah back.

The fallout still haunted us. The unforgiving public did not absolve Mia for her role in the bullying or Leah's death. Not that they should, but the continued media persecution wasn't an easy thing to endure, but we had to.

This was our life now. Choices had consequences. So did our mistakes, however unintended.

I'd put Mia in therapy. Money was tight, it was always tight, but Mia needed this, and I would do whatever I had to do to help her. I'd also removed her social media accounts for the foreseeable future. We talked every night out on the patio, overlooking the water as the sun set fire to the horizon.

Now, the scent of cut grass drifted through the open windows, mingled with the distant thrum of a mower and children's laughter. Outside, early summer had arrived in a burst of green.

Apollo's nails clicked across the floor as he settled at Mia's feet with a contented sigh. She reached down to scratch behind his ears.

I moved into the kitchen and started the coffee maker. We

carried steaming mugs to the back patio and stood near the edge of the crumbling bluff. The concrete had cracked further in recent weeks, with another slab loosening, sloping toward the beach far below.

Like our house, we were living on the edge. Our lives a bit unstable perhaps, but also incredibly beautiful.

The lake and its endless shifting light spread below us. Sunlight on the water flashed like thrown coins. From here, the beach looked smooth, clean, pure.

"Do you ever think about that night?" Mia asked.

She still had nightmares several times a week. So did I. "All the time."

She shivered, though it wasn't cold. "I still feel like it was my fault."

I placed a hand on her shoulder. For a long moment, I couldn't speak. How do you tell your daughter whose hands pushed a girl who died that she still gets to live? That she will carry this the rest of her life, and the burden will be both unbearable and survivable?

"What Rowan did was deliberate," I said. "You made a mistake. Rowan made a choice. Intent matters."

Mia's eyes filled. I wasn't sure she believed me, but the words needed to be said. I would keep saying them until someday, she did.

Apollo nudged my leg with a cold nose, impatient for his walk. I patted his head. "Just a second, buddy."

After we finished our coffee, I headed to the mudroom to grab his leash. The familiar framed photo caught my eye on the shelf near the window. The one with the six girls on Rowan's boat last summer.

A shudder passed through me. In the photo, they looked like any group of teenage girls: sun-drunk, immortal, safe. But I could see it now, the way Chloe's arm draped possessively over Mia's shoulder, how Leah stood slightly apart, already on the outside. How Zara's smile didn't quite reach her eyes.

Or maybe I was reading into it, seeing the cracks before everything fell apart.

"You coming?" Mia yelled from the kitchen.

I turned from the photograph, clipped Apollo's leash to his collar, and took him on his walk.

The neighborhood we'd once chased like a promise had shed its sheen. At the Alistair house, Whitney unloaded groceries from her car. She and Peyton came and went with their heads down, no longer queens of the neighborhood but pariahs instead.

Whitney glanced up as we passed, then quickly looked away. The little Pomeranian yapped furiously at us, desperate for attention. Apollo ignored him. So did we.

Mrs. Atkins sat on her porch as usual, monitoring the street with sharp eyes. She nodded a greeting. I waved back. Some things never changed.

But others had. The Westinghouse mansion stood empty, a FOR SALE sign prominent on the lawn. Rowan's prized roses had withered. Her husband had accepted a job in Grand Rapids. After the LakeshoreTea account had been traced back to Chloe, the school expelled her.

Last week, Camille mentioned seeing Chloe's Instagram account online. She'd posted from her new private school, smiling in a crisp uniform, surrounded by new friends, thriving.

It was Chloe's mother, not Chloe, who'd killed Leah. And yet I couldn't help the surge of anger at Chloe for the vile acts she had committed, for her casual cruelty, her petty malice toward Leah, Mia, and the other girls she'd hurt.

Once again, she'd gotten away clean, free to torment new classmates, neighbors, and supposed friends. Justice was never fair, I'd learned. And seldom blind.

But I couldn't dwell on things beyond my control. We had to move on, or the unfairness of it could drive a person to become bitter, depressed, and miserable. I didn't want to live like that.

Down the street, we spotted Alexis walking a golden retriever puppy, her little brother Falcon watching intently as the dog frolicked around his ankles. The kids looked lighter, happier, with color in their cheeks.

Two weeks ago, Brooke had voluntarily entered rehab, announcing her secret alcohol addiction on her social media accounts. The family had started therapy, even Jason.

"Alexis apologized," Mia said. " She said she was sorry for going along with Chloe. That she realized how toxic it all was."

"That was brave of her."

Mia shrugged. "We're not friends. But we're not enemies, either."

It was something. A small step toward healing. Tomorrow, Camille and I had made plans to meet at Forté Coffee in St. Joe, just to talk. Another small step in the right direction.

We took the wooden stairs down the bluff. New warning signs were bolted to the posts. The air cooled as we descended. Sand crusted our toes.

The beach stretched empty but for a solitary figure walking along the waterline. As we drew closer, I recognized Vivienne Cho. She was wrapped in a light cardigan despite the sun, her black hair shot through with gray and twisted into a loose bun. Leah's jade pendant rested at her throat.

Vivienne saw us and stopped. For a beat, I thought she would turn away. Instead, she waited.

"Hello, Dahlia," she said. "Mia."

"Vivienne." I didn't ask how she was. There was no adequate shape for that question. "It's good to see you."

She tucked a strand of hair behind her ear. The wind tugged at her cardigan. "We're selling the house. Daniel and I can't stay. Too many memories."

"Where will you go?"

"Chicago. Near my sister in Rosemont."

Apollo bounded up to her, offering his head to Vivienne, who stroked his snout. "Leah loved this dog. She would come home smelling like wet fur."

"My old paper asked me to write about what happened here," I said. "A book. They have interest from several publishers. If you're willing, I'd like you to help me tell Leah's story right. I won't do it if you disapprove."

It was the only thing I knew how to do. I couldn't bring Leah back, I couldn't undo what happened on that bluff, but I could make sure people remembered her as more than a tragedy. As a girl who loved art, dogs, and her friends. As someone who mattered.

Her eyes found mine. "I know you'll tell the truth."

We stood together with the waves rippling behind us, the sun rising high in the cloudless sky. She looked out at the water. The lines around her eyes had deepened.

"I don't blame you, Mia," Vivienne said. "I want you to know that. What you did was a mistake with grave consequences, but Rowan took my daughter away from me, not you."

Mia made a sound like a sob in the back of her throat. "I think about her every day. I miss her every day."

"So do I." She reached out and touched Mia's arm. "I find comfort knowing Leah had a real friend. Someone who loved her."

The simple grace of it cracked something open in Mia. She bowed her head, shoulders shaking as she wept. I slipped an arm around her, felt the tremor pass through both of us.

Vivienne resumed walking. Her slight figure grew smaller against the glittering horizon as the wind kicked up, ballooning her cardigan like wings.

We watched her until the distance softened her into the shoreline, while Apollo cannoned into the shallows and barked at his reflection with bemused delight. Gulls skated the updrafts over our heads, flecks of white against the cobalt blue.

"It's still beautiful here," Mia said.

"It is." I slid my hand into hers. We stood that way, not speaking, until the sun warmed the tops of our feet.

"Ready?" I asked.

She wiped her cheeks with the back of her hand and looked toward the stairs, then at me. "Yeah."

We turned toward the bluff. The stairs creaked under us.

Halfway up, Apollo paused to look back the way we'd come, tongue lolling, ears forward, and then tugged onward, eager for home.

At the top of the staircase, the yellow caution tape flapped in the breeze. I rested my palm on the weathered railing, felt the heat of the sunbaked wood, and held on.

The Night of the Fall

Moonlight splinters across Lake Michigan, transforming the water's surface into a rippling silver tapestry. From the edge of the bluff, the 100-foot drop to the beach below vanishes into darkness.

Chloe Westinghouse inhales deeply, savoring the fresh night air, the glimmer of the moon. A perfect night for secrets.

She positions herself several calculated steps from the precipice, the distance measured with the precision of an architect. The Italian silk of her Valentino dress whispers against her calves as the lake breeze lifts her blonde hair into a pale halo.

"I can't believe you," Mia says, her voice splintering like thin ice. "I thought you were my friend, Leah. How could you do this?"

Chloe suppresses the smile twitching at her lips. She watches Mia's face contort with rage and betrayal, emotions so raw they're almost vulgar. Between them, Leah shifts her weight, her chubby body silhouetted against the glittering lake far below, her heels close to the bluff's ragged edge directly behind her, where Chloe has positioned her for the last photo.

The trap has sprung. The pieces move across Chloe's mental chessboard with satisfying inevitability. It almost seems too easy.

Chloe studies the trembling line of Leah's acne-studded shoulders, the nervous flutter of her hands, her darting, too-big eyes.

Leah Cho is so frantic to belong that she'd cut her own heart out if Chloe asked her to.

The memory of their earlier conversation crystallizes in Chloe's mind with perfect clarity. She'd cornered Leah in the upstairs bathroom, surrounded by marble countertops, gold fixtures, and gleaming tile. The other girls were downstairs, putting on heels, glitter, gauzy dresses, and finalizing their hair and makeup for the photoshoot.

"You want in, don't you?" Chloe asked as she reapplied her lip gloss. "For real this time?"

Leah nodded, her reflection in the mirror revealing eyes wide with that desperate pick-me energy that always made Chloe's skin crawl with contempt. Leah has a face like a turtle. Chloe can barely stand looking at her.

"Then prove it," she said, capping her lip gloss. "Tell Mia what you really think of her. That she's needy. Desperate. Pathetic. Tell her you've only been pretending. You actually hate her."

"But I don't—" Leah's fingers twisted together, bitten nails digging into her palms.

"But nothing." Chloe turned, allowing her expression to harden enough to make Leah shrink back against the cool tile wall. "You're either in or out. And you don't want to be on the outside. You already know what that's like, and trust me, I can make it so much worse. You can be with us. Isn't that what you want?"

Leah knew too much. She'd overheard conversations she shouldn't have, not to mention her suspicions about the sleeping pills incident at Peyton's pool party. Then Leah had snuck into Chloe's room earlier tonight, walking in on Chloe using the burner phone, the one Chloe had secretly purchased with her generous allowance, using the prepaid SIM number to create the LakeshoreTea profile.

Chloe had made a tactical error, underestimating boring dumb Leah. It wasn't a mistake she would make again. Because of their mothers' friendship, she had to let Leah hang around, plus she was useful enough to do Chloe's pre-algebra homework and write a few research papers for her. Now, AI could do all that.

Leah was a problem that needed eliminating.

Now, in the silver-drenched darkness, Chloe watches her handiwork unfold with dispassionate interest.

"I thought you were different." Mia steps closer to Leah, her voice rising to match the wind combing through the pines behind them. The whites of her eyes catch the moonlight, giving her the appearance of something wild, something feral. "But you're just like them!"

"It's not like that—I didn't want to—" Leah stammers, her hands twisting in front of her like pale birds. Her frantic gaze darts to Chloe, seeking guidance, approval, rescue, and finding only a blank stare.

Chloe watches it all, keeping her expression deliberately neutral. Inside, she catalogs each detail with meticulous precision. The betrayal on Mia's face. Her ugly thrift store dress, as ugly as she is, as ugly as the bulky camera clutched in her hands, with the ratty yellow strap.

"I'm sorry, Mia," Leah whispers, her words barely audible over the rhythmic lapping of waves against the shoreline far below. "I just... I'm tired of being targeted all the time. I just want it to stop."

"You pretended to be my friend?" Mia's voice cracks. "You laughed at me behind my back with them?"

"No, I mean, only once or twice," Leah confesses. Her gaze drops to the ground. A droplet of red leaks from her nostrils. Another one of her disgusting nosebleeds. "I didn't mean it."

"Tell her, Leah," Chloe prompts, her voice carrying just the right note of sympathetic encouragement. "She deserves to know the truth."

"Tell me what?" Mia asks.

"How Leah tells us all your dirty little secrets. Especially that one about your dad. You know, your little incontinence problem?"

Mia recoils like she's been doused in acid. "You promised. You swore you'd never tell anyone."

Chloe sees her opportunity and pounces. She tilts her head, her tone casual, almost sympathetic. "She told us everything. How you were so scared you literally pissed yourself."

The words land like a slap. Mia's face drains of color.

"We couldn't stop laughing." Chloe pitches her voice low, each word designed to cut deep. "Leah did this whole impression of you standing there with pee running down your legs while your dad was bleeding out. I mean, everyone must've smelled it when the paramedics and cops came, right? I'd just die if I were you."

The lie slips from her lips with effortless grace. Truth is irrelevant. What matters is the reaction, and Mia's transformation from hurt to fury unfolds with glorious predictability.

Chloe found Leah's journal last month, hidden under her mattress, after her mother had made her bring some fancy bread over to Mrs. Cho when Leah was at a painting class. The diary entry had been raw, anguished, pathetic. Leah, processing her own helplessness, was unsure how to support her grieving friend.

Perfect ammunition unleashed at just the right time.

"I would never—!" Leah's voice rises in panic. Blood drips from her nostrils, leaking down her chin. "Mia, I swear, I never said it like that! I didn't—"

"You told them?" Mia's voice breaks on the words. Her entire body trembles in humiliation. "That's what you said about me? About the worst night of my life?"

"Mia, please—!"

"You made fun of me." The hurt in Mia's voice shifts, hardens into something colder. "You laughed about my dad dying."

Chloe bites the inside of her cheek to keep from smiling. The raw devastation saturating each word is absolute perfection. This is going even better than planned.

Leah's expression contorts. Her whole face turns beet-red with shame. "It's not like that. I'd never say that, I swear."

But it is too late.

"You bitch!" The camera slips from Mia's shaking fingers. It hits the grass with a muffled thud as Mia slaps her friend across the cheek.

Leah's face crumples. "Mia, wait! I made a mistake. I'm so sorry—" She reaches out in desperation. Her fingers close around Mia's forearms, trying to hold on, to make her understand.

Mia jerks back. Leah's fingernails rake down Mia's arms as she tears free. A few droplets of blood from Leah's nose splatter across the front of Mia's bodice. Mia doesn't even notice through her blinding rage.

"Get off me!" Mia pushes Leah away from her.

Leah stumbles backward, her arms flung wide. For one suspended moment, she teeters on the bluff's edge, feet scrambling awkwardly for purchase in her heels. Then she regains her balance, chest heaving, eyes wide with shock.

Mia slumps to her knees. Appalled, crying hard, she stares down at her dress—once rose-gold, now mud-stained, torn, ruined. Blood wells from the scratches on her forearms.

For that critical moment, her attention is diverted. Away from the edge. Away from Leah.

Chloe recognizes her opportunity with the clarity of an apex predator. She steps forward and stands next to Mia, who's still on the ground.

Leah regains her balance. Inches from the bluff's edge, wavering but upright. Her eyes lock with Chloe's, not two feet apart now. Something shifts in her expression—a dawning comprehension, a sudden clarity. And then, pure scintillating anger.

Leah's lips part, perhaps to cry out a warning, to confess, to expose everything she knows. That cannot happen.

Chloe moves with liquid precision. Her hands connect with Leah's shoulders. She feels momentary resistance. Leah tenses in surprise, a gasp catching in her throat.

Chloe shoves Leah violently.

The sensation is oddly satisfying. The give of flesh, the sudden absence of weight. Leah's arms flail, a graceless windmill against the star-spattered sky. She screams. A startled, abbreviated cry. Her body drops away into darkness.

The silk of her dress makes a sound like tearing paper. The crack of breaking branches. The dull impact of flesh against something hard, unforgiving.

Then silence.

Mia looks up, stunned.

Chloe injects horror into her voice. "What did you do?"

Mia gapes at Chloe in alarm. She scrambles to her feet, dirt cascading from her ruined dress. "Leah?"

"You pushed her." Chloe's voice slices through the night air like a blade. "You pushed her!"

"No—I—I didn't mean to—Leah!" Mia leans over the edge, peering down into the consuming darkness. "Leah!"

"Keep your voice down." Chloe digs her fingers into Mia's arm as she yanks her back from the edge. "Do you want people to know what you did?"

Mia stares at her in terror, mouth working soundlessly. "We— we have to call 911."

"She's dead," Chloe declares with certainty she doesn't feel. But Leah certainly looks dead from her glimpse over the edge. Forty feet down, pale limbs splayed at unnatural angles against a fallen tree caught on the steep incline. All that dark wet blood.

Does she dare hope it might be true? This mess might resolve itself neatly, with Mia cast as the perfect scapegoat.

A surge of satisfaction floods Chloe's veins. She watches Mia's face crumple with horror. This is unfolding more perfectly than she could have orchestrated. Leah silenced, potentially forever. Mia implicated. All of Chloe's problems wrapped up in one tragic "accident."

She frowns as Mia begins a treacherous descent down the bluff, clinging to exposed roots as she climbs downward, tears streaming down her cheeks.

"Stop! Come back here!" Chloe commands in a harsh whisper. "What do you think you're doing?"

Mia's hands shake violently as she navigates the steep slope. The darkness swallows her small form as she disappears. Chloe creeps forward cautiously, peering over the edge. In the moonlight, she can barely make out Mia kneeling beside Leah's motionless body below.

A sound drifts up from the darkness. Mia's voice, choked and frantic. "Leah? Leah, please. Please wake up."

The sobbing that follows is low, guttural. Like an animal.

Chloe feels nothing but mild impatience, a calculation of risk. How long will Mia stay down there? Will she touch the body, contaminate the scene with her fingerprints, her DNA? Good. Better, actually.

"Mia, get back up here!"

"Call 911!" Mia cries.

"Get up here now!"

Mia moves as if underwater, shock rendering her compliant. She climbs back up the bluff, slipping twice, her hands covered in dirt and something darker that gleams wetly in the moonlight.

"I didn't—I didn't mean to," Mia stammers when she reaches the top. Her eyes are unfocused. "I thought she was fine, she just took a step back, what—what happened?"

"You pushed her, stupid," Chloe snaps, her patience thinning. "Really hard."

"No—I—"

Chloe grips Mia's shoulders, feeling the tremors running through the other girl's body. "Look at me. You were mad. You pushed her. She fell. Now she's dead." She leans closer, her breath warm against Mia's tear-streaked face. "If you call 911, what do you think happens next? The cops will throw you in jail and toss away the key. You did this."

Mia crumples. A wounded sound escapes her throat.

"I'm going to help you." Chloe softens her voice and molds her features into an expression of sympathetic concern. "We stick together, tell the same story. She came out here alone and fell. She was always clumsy, right? Literally tripping over her own feet." She gives Mia a little shake. "But you have to do exactly what I say. I'll save you, but you can't be stupid. You and me, we're a team now. Do you understand?"

"I don't—I can't—what if she's only hurt—what if—"

Chloe shakes her harder. Anger flashes behind her carefully constructed mask. Hysteria won't serve either of them. Mia has always been too sensitive, too emotional, too weak to handle the hard stuff. "Listen to me. She's gone. There's nothing you can do. Think about yourself."

"We can't just leave her—"

"Shut up!" Chloe hisses. "You can't think about her. She's gone. She's dead! You can't bring her back. You call 911 and admit what you did? You're going to prison. Forever. You'll destroy your mom. Is that what you want?"

"No, but—"

"I'm the only one who can save you. Are you with me or not?"

Slowly, dully, Mia nods.

"Good. Here's what you're going to do. Go back to the basement, change your dress in the bathroom, and get into your sleeping bag. Go to sleep. Do not get up for anything. Wipe your puffy face and stop blubbering. When you wake up tomorrow morning, you have no idea what happened. That's it. Now go."

Chloe picks up the camera from the grass, shoves it into Mia's limp hands, and pushes her toward the house. She watches as the other girl stumbles across the manicured lawn, moving sluggishly, like a sleepwalker.

Once Mia disappears inside, Chloe turns back to the bluff's edge. She activates her phone's flashlight and directs the beam downward.

The body moves. A small, pained groan floats up from the darkness.

Chloe's breath catches in her throat—not from horror, but

from the sudden recalibration required: a live witness can speak, a corpse cannot.

Her heartrate accelerates. This complicates everything. Leah can't wake up. She can't climb back to the world of the living and tell everyone what she knows, especially not now.

Chloe recalls the moment of recognition in Leah's eyes just before the push, the dawning awareness, the determination that had flared across her face like lightning. Leah was turning on Chloe. She was going to pick Mia, no matter the consequences.

Then there would be nothing to stop her from ruining Chloe's life utterly. She could testify to everything Chloe has done, including the push.

Chloe needs to do something. To silence her permanently.

Chloe studies the steep incline, glances down at her gown, and considers her options with methodical precision. Mia barely navigated the treacherous descent without falling. No way is Chloe attempting it, especially not in her current outfit.

Besides, this will get messy. She'll need to touch the body, the blood. No. It'll ruin her brand-new Valentino gown. There must be another way.

The lake breeze intensifies, carrying the scent of damp earth from last night's rain. Chloe shivers, though not from the cold.

She needs to think clearly, carefully. The way her mother taught her.

When faced with a problem, calculate every option. Choose the one with the least risk to you.

Her mother's words echo in her mind with perfect clarity. Her mother is rarely wrong.

Chloe takes one step toward the bluff edge. The soft earth sinks. Her heel catches, and she stumbles a mere foot from the drop-off. Swiftly, she steps back, heart thumping.

Chloe's hands shake. She can't go down there. She can't risk being seen. But her mother never shakes. Never doubts, never blinks.

Chloe straightens her shoulders, decision made. Her mom will know what to do. *Always clean up your messes*, her mother constantly reminds her.

Well, this mess has grown too large to handle alone.

She turns away from the bluff, her mind already crafting the narrative she'll present, the frantic tears she'll summon on command, the trembling voice with which she'll describe what happened, and how terrified she is now.

Her mother will help her, she always does.

After all, her mother helped resolve the sleeping pills incident that put annoyingly perfect Taylor Everett in the hospital and made Peyton swim captain.

It had gone sideways a bit, but Chloe hadn't minded. Standing there by the diving board, watching that girl slip under the surface of the water, so still and quiet, the water making barely a ripple. The way her hair had shimmered like a mermaid's.

Her phone screen reads 12:52 a.m. Chloe calculates quickly. Her mother took an Ambien around ten p.m., so she'll be groggy, possibly incoherent for another hour or two.

And downstairs, Mia has just gone inside. She'll be awake, moving around, and possibly some of the other girls too. Going to her mother now, with potential witnesses stirring, with her mother barely lucid, would be a mistake.

Judging by all the blood, Leah isn't going anywhere for a while.

Chloe can afford to wait.

She walks back toward the house. Her footsteps are oddly light despite the weight of what has transpired. A curious sense of relief floods through her veins, as if she's shed something cumbersome, something that's been dragging her down.

She'll slip inside, change her dress, wash her hands, then lie down quietly in the basement and wait until everyone is dead asleep. Then she'll climb the stairs to her mother's room, let the tears come, and tell her mother everything. Well, almost everything.

Her mother will save her.

That is, after all, what mothers do.

Afterword

Thank you for reading *The Guilty Ones*! I hope you enjoyed it. This was my first psychological thriller, and I found it both difficult and incredibly rewarding to write, even though at one point I was cursing myself for creating so many mother/daughter pairs for readers to suspect.

As a reader, I love psychology and thrillers, so psychological thrillers are terrific fun to sink my teeth into. Some of you may have read my post-apocalyptic survival thrillers first, particularly the *Edge of Collapse* and *Lost Light* series, both of which include survival and thriller elements even as the characters grapple with the end of the world as they know it.

While I loved putting my characters in horrible situations at the end of the world, it's also great fun to do the same thing in the "real world."

The world doesn't have to end for everyone for it to feel like it has ended for one person, for everything they know to splinter and fall to pieces.

What do they do when the solid ground they'd depended upon shifts beneath their feet? Who do they become? How do they deal with horrific, life-altering events? Do they rise above,

Afterword

becoming their best selves, or do they sink into their worst impulses?

These are the questions I love to explore in my books, no matter the genre. I hope you'll come along for the journey to uncover the answers.

Thank you so much for reading my books. I couldn't be a writer without my readers, and I appreciate each and every one of you, and I'm incredibly grateful for your support of independent authors, which is critical now more than ever.

Until next time!

-Kyla

Acknowledgments

Thank you as always to my awesome beta readers. Your thoughtful critiques and enthusiasm are invaluable. As I start a brand new genre, your support and encouragement meant everything to me. Thank you to Ana Shaefer, Samantha Montgomery, and to D.J. White for the investigative research, background, and expertise, and for always answering my every strange and crazy question. And to my parents for reading everything I write.

To Donna Lewis for her line editing skills.

A special thank you to Jenny Avery for catching those last pesky errors and for her genius with maps and geography. This woman catches everything. Any remaining errors are my fault completely.

And to my husband, who takes care of the house, the kids, and the cooking when I'm under the gun with a writing deadline. To my kids, who show me the true meaning of love every day and continually inspire me.

Thanks to God for His many blessings.

And to my loyal readers, whose support and encouragement mean everything to me. Thank you.

Also by Kyla Stone

Lost Light:

The Light We Lost

The Dark We Seek

The Hope We Keep

The World We Burn

Edge of Collapse:

Edge of Collapse

Edge of Madness

Edge of Darkness

Edge of Anarchy

Edge of Defiance

Edge of Survival

Edge of Valor

Nuclear Dawn:

Point of Impact

From the Ashes

Into the Fire

Darkest Night

Stand Alones:

Queen of Fate and Fury

Beneath the Skin

Before You Break

The Last Sanctuary

The Guilty Ones

About the Author

Kyla Stone is the *USA Today* Bestselling author of over 25 novels. With over two million copies sold worldwide, her books have been translated into several languages, and her *Edge of Collapse* series has been optioned by Sony Studios for television.

She lives in Michigan with her family and spends her days writing apocalyptic, survival, and psychological thrillers. Her favorite treats while writing include dark chocolate and coffee.

When she's not writing, she enjoys reading, hiking, playing board games, and traveling around the world. She loves adventures, including rappelling down waterfalls in Costa Rica, off-roading on the dunes of Lake Michigan in her blue Jeep, parasailing in the Dominican Republic, and scuba diving in Roatan and Belize.

She loves to hear from her readers.

Email her at Contact@KylaStone.com

www.ingramcontent.com/pod-product-compliance
Lightning Source LLC
LaVergne TN
LVHW040037080526
838202LV00045B/3369